KT-143-958

by the same author

LESS THAN KIND
NIGHT'S BLACK AGENTS

DAVID ARMSTRONG

UNTIL DAWN TOMORROW

HarperCollins*Publishers*

HarperCollins*Publishers*
77-85 Fulham Palace Road,
Hammersmith, London W6 8JB

This paperback edition 1996
1 3 5 7 9 8 6 4 2

First published in Great Britain by
HarperCollins*Publishers* 1995

ISBN 0 00 649696 2

Set in Meridien and Bodoni

Printed in Great Britain by
HarperCollinsManufacturing Glasgow

For Elizabeth Walter

1

'Good morning, Inspector. Still raining?' Dr Khaliq, entombed in his subterranean mortuary, perennially inquired of his callers what the weather was like outside. This mattered less to policemen and officials, whose business was conducted with a certain professional detachment, than to distraught relatives who, summoned by the authorities to identify a corpse, and bracing themselves for the ordeal ahead, were often discomfited to find the doctor more interested in the meteorological than the frequently charged emotional climate.

'Drizzling a bit, I think,' replied Kavanagh as he approached the body on the marble slab.

'Umm,' said Khaliq, clearly disappointed by the nebulousness of the policeman's weather report. He continued his scrubbing down and called over his shoulder, 'What do you know about him?'

'Art teacher. Worked at the local college.' Kavanagh turned back the sheet a foot and stared at the drained face. He avoided the eyes. Khaliq came to the other side of the slab, drying his hands.

The inspector was aware of the pathologist's gaze upon him. It was a challenge. Kavanagh ceded the point and looked at the dead man's eyes. He nodded his head a fraction. The doctor drew back the sheet another three feet.

Kavanagh looked at his manhood. The corpse was a painting by Lucien Freud: pallid flesh, dead pubic hair;

the penis, shrunk to the size of a woman's finger; the testicles, one larger than the other, lying to one side of the inner thighs, the dark brown scrotum of creased and folded skin.

Khaliq raised an eyebrow. Kavanagh sensed the flicker of movement on the pathologist's brow and looked up to the wounds.

They were very 'clean', surgically deep. The first through the lower ribcage and into the heart. The other, just above it, perhaps two or three inches. There was no 'tearing', and the wounds, though very close, had remained separate.

Many murderers, following the convention of countless plays and films, shot or stabbed people in the place where they *assumed* the heart to be, only to find their victims giving evidence against them ten or twelve months later. The heart was much more central in the torso than many would-be killers appeared to realize. But the person who had stabbed art teacher John Lacey to death appeared to know his basic anatomy.

'What can you tell us?' asked Kavanagh without looking up from the corpse. The doctor exhaled a long breath which blew faintly off the dead man's body and brushed Kavanagh's face. The policeman recoiled from the intimacy of the contact.

Khaliq reiterated the essence of what he had spoken into his dictaphone an hour ago: 'He has been stabbed to death with a long, sharp blade. Two wounds. The first, here,' Khaliq put his finger half an inch from the upper incision, 'this wound punctured the pulmonary artery. The second wound' – he moved his finger slightly down the chest – 'into the right atrium was redundant. The haemorrhage from the artery was massive and would have meant death in three or four minutes.'

The policeman asked neutrally, 'Was he gay?'

Khaliq, a highly educated man, whose father had come

to this country from Srinagar forty years ago, had a marked antipathy towards stereotyping. 'Not very "politically correct", is it, Inspector?' And he added peevishly, 'Just because he's an art teacher, he doesn't *have* to be gay, does he?'

'Just a thought,' said Kavanagh. 'And being "politically correct" won't get some knife-wielding maniac off the streets and into the dock. I like to start with the obvious, move on to the wacky, then get the shrinks, psychics, water diviners and mystics in . . .'

'And when all that fails?' said the doctor. Meteorologist Khaliq regarded his policemen colleagues as a necessary inconvenience: inexact, shuffling people who brought him his raw material, but always returned, usually in the middle of the weather forecast, with their bad clothes, detectable body odours, irritating habits and foolish quips.

Kavanagh ignored him. 'So, was he gay?'

The doctor glanced up at Kavanagh. 'I don't think so. His sphincter has no obvious tearing or bruising, the anal muscles aren't slack. They're about right for a mid-forties male. Do you want to have a look?'

'No thanks. I'll take your word for it,' said Kavanagh.

'It's not conclusive, of course,' added Khaliq. 'These days, lots of homosexuals, the sensible ones anyway, they don't penetrate. Is he married?'

'Yes.'

'Children?'

Kavanagh looked at the face again. 'Yes, a son.' The man's beard had continued to grow in the few hours since his murder. He had a strong, dark stubble. He had been a good-looking man, handsome really, with strong features. But there was something neanderthal about the jaw. A suggestion of something that the policeman had seen in encyclopaedias on primitive man, the sort of thing that cartoonists pick up and accentuate in a deft line that makes that one feature the essence of their subject.

* * *

Kavanagh met Sergeant Presley as he walked into the third-floor incident room of the city-centre police station. 'How d'you get on down the body shop?' asked the insouciant sergeant.

'Nothing much; no revelations. Stabbed twice. Long, sharp blade. Deep cuts, straight through the heart.' There was a pause as Kavanagh actually thought of the corpse. A man of his own age.

Presley respected the moment's silence, and then asked, more considerately, 'What do you think?'

'Fuck knows,' said the DI, exasperated. He had seen it all before; knew that he would see it all again, and again. The sorrow, the grief, the pity, the terrible waste of it all. 'It's not a straightforward though.'

Kavanagh paused and mimicked a blade in his hand. At chest height he pushed it slowly through the giving air. A constable looked up and watched, intrigued, as the inspector went through his mime in the busy room. The brief piece of ham theatre over, the girl looked back to the word-processor screen and resumed her tapping of the keys.

Presley followed his boss to the coffee machine in the corner. The senior policeman continued, thinking aloud, 'The wounding's too . . . clinical. Whoever did it *knew* what he was doing. And he got close in.'

'He?' said Presley.

'Could've been a her, but I'd guess it was a bloke.'

'What do you mean, "Knew what he was doing"?'

'I dunno,' said Kavanagh. 'It doesn't look frenzied or wild. It's like an execution. And yet, whatever the poor bugger had done to "deserve" it, pros don't stab people when they want them topped. It's not a method they use, not here in Brum, any road.'

He sauntered away from the vending machine to his crowded desk. Presley picked up the muddy drink in its plastic cup and carried it to his boss.

2

At the parish centre in the churchyard of the Birmingham suburb where John Lacey had died, the scene-of-crime officers were going about their painstaking business. The whole area had been taped off, from the incongruous glass-and-concrete building that had been built from the parishioners' donations in the early 1970s, to the van that Lacey had been loading with his students' work when he had been stabbed to death the previous evening.

There was no sign of rain but, following textbook procedure, a blue plastic tent had been erected over the Toyota van and the place where the man had collapsed, bleeding, to his terrible death.

A uniformed officer lifted the tape as Kavanagh and Presley approached. Several people were gathered at the flimsy barrier. They had witnessed this scene a hundred times on television and at the cinema, and now, courtesy of John Lacey, art teacher at the local college, just as Andy Warhol had famously promised them, *their* fifteen minutes of sordid fame had finally arrived.

There was a theatrical hush amongst the expectant little crowd but also, undeniably, and rippling just beneath the surface, there was a feeling of bonhomie: the two dozen people standing there, united by this remarkable tragedy, were also bound by the smug knowledge that no matter how deep the furrows on their brows, or how gravely concerned were the looks on their faces, they were, finally, entirely untouched by this patent horror.

It was, in reality, better than the glimpsed spectacle of a motorway car crash: that was momentary, a fleeting gawp as the censorious traffic policeman hurried you off down the road. Here, like extras on a film set, there was ample time for discussion and speculation as the crowd waited patiently for the principals to make their entrances. No one had yet brought a shooting stick or a picnic stool, but one elderly man had thoughtfully provided himself and his wife with a flask of milky tea.

Inside the awning, Kavanagh and Presley stepped into plastic galoshes and pulled on disposable overalls and surgical gloves.

At the rear of the van, chalk marks on the ground indicated the position where the man had fallen. The scene looked uncannily like the cover of a cheap sixties paperback.

The two men crouched down near the chalk outlines while a young lady from forensic brushed dust and grit, moss and hair and fibres, from the ground into numbered plastic wallets. Her colleague carefully labelled each one.

Murder, reflected Kavanagh, not for the first time, was *so* time consuming. Terrible, yes, but also so *terribly* expensive. Like a blue whale cruising the southern oceans, its mouth agape, and swallowing its life-sustaining krill by the lorry load, so the beleaguered police force ate up billions and billions of pounds each year as crime detection, in reply to ever-more ingenious criminals, had to become more efficient.

True, most burglaries were never solved, and the stolen cars that *were* recovered were no longer worth having, but only seven per cent of murders had remained unsolved during the last decade.

This, of course, had little to do with sharp-eyed coppers, or the presence on the street of the public's beloved uniformed officers, but everything to do with electron microscopes, machines that could magnify a strand of cotton to the size of a tree trunk; DNA testing that could identify the blood or saliva or semen of a suspect to within a one in seven million margin of error; image enhancement and reconstruction techniques that could identify decomposed victims from the scantiest remains.

But all of this cost money: piles and piles of it. Everything by the book, everything in triplicate, everything on tape or video or film. It cost an absolute fortune.

Before Lacey had fallen, splashes of blood had hit the ground and exploded into a series of ever-larger blots on the paving slabs. They ended in a huge, dark red stain where the man's life had finally gushed out of him.

Kavanagh got to his feet and looked into the Toyota's open door. There were several canvases stacked inside the van ready to be tied into position. The man had, apparently, just taken one to the vehicle, and was on his way back into the building when the killer had struck.

Inside the parish centre, a female churchwarden was sitting in the kitchen with a policewoman. The two women drank tea from green, Beryl china cups and Miss Nicholson, her free hand lying demurely in her lap, prayed silently for the soul of the man whose violent death had led to the solemn industry that now surrounded the holy place.

She was a slim, fair-skinned woman in her late forties. She had told her story to the policemen the previous night, but had been distraught; they needed to hear it again.

A pianist who taught the suburb's promising youngsters and gave local recitals, Miss Nicholson knew about the moment's silence that should precede any performance.

When she 'had the floor', and knew that no more throats would be cleared or cups scraped on saucers by her audience of three, she focused her attention and began her reprise.

It had been dark. As arranged, after piano practice, at about 7.30, John Lacey, whom she knew a little, had come to collect the exhibition of his students' work which the centre had had on display for the last three weeks. 'It's all part of the college's policy of going out into the wider community,' she patiently explained to the two men.

She had already taken down the paintings and was wrapping them in bubble foam for their short journey to the college. Lacey was carrying them out to the van.

She heard nothing unusual. After perhaps his third or fourth trip, he seemed to be gone rather a long time. She called to him, 'John, would you like a cup of coffee?'.

There was no answer. She assumed, embarrassed, that he might have gone to the lavatory in the foyer. She remembered singing quietly to cover the awkwardness, and began to wrap another painting.

The silence continued too long, and the quiet in the building was uncanny. She listened for any sound, of water pipes or the cistern's filling.

She called his name again, this time from just inside the doorway of the meeting room where the paintings had hung. It was so quiet she could hear the fluorescent tubes humming. Suddenly she became afraid. She felt alone in the place and irrationally but terribly afraid.

She ran through the foyer and out of the front entrance. His body was lying beside the rear door of the van. She screamed. There was blood all around him. She was afraid for herself. She screamed again and again. She knelt down by the man, but was too frightened to touch him. She thought he was dead. 'I just screamed and screamed.'

And now it was time for *her* confession. She faltered, ashamed, 'I was afraid to touch him. I didn't know what to do. His face looked dreadful. In agony. He was wearing a blue denim shirt, but it was soaked dark red. I didn't know how to help. I'm sure he was dead.'

This was her fear. That she could have helped, done something, anything. And she knew she had done nothing for him. The constable laid her hand over the pianist's long fingers and said quietly, 'It's all right. You had a terrible experience. No one could have done any more.'

Miss Nicholson began again: 'Someone came running.

It was a young couple. The boy was first, but all he said was "My God! Oh, my God!". He must have thought that *I* had killed him. It never occurred to me.' She smothered a little mirthless laugh. 'The girl ran down the road and called an ambulance. The boy stood beside me, watching. I suppose he thought that I might try and kill him, too.' She reflected for a moment, lost in her own thoughts.

'Yes?' said Kavanagh quietly.

'Yes,' she repeated. 'Eventually he seemed to understand, and he brought me back in here. He put the kettle on.' She looked at the constable whose hand still covered hers. 'He used the hot water tap.'

The men looked at one another; the constable smiled.

'I didn't say anything.' She glanced at Presley. 'You shouldn't use the hot. Not for drinking. It's not *direct*, you see.'

'No, quite,' said Kavanagh.

3

The next morning, Kavanagh and Presley waited for ten minutes in Aidan McEwan's office at the sixth form college while the Scotsman spoke to his vice-principal in the adjoining room.

On the wall, behind his half-snooker-table-size desk was something called a Mission Statement. It had nothing to do with astronauts or space research, but was seven or eight lines of non-speak that ended with the phrase: *Osborne College: in training since 1936.*

'They should be ready soon!' said Presley.

Kavanagh inspected the titles on the bookshelves on the far side of the room. Most of them were American, and every author had the mandatory initial juxtaposed between fore- and surname: James C. Coady's *Motivating Managers*; Robert M. Grant's *Organizational Behaviour; Success: The Impossible Dream?*; and the pithily titled: *Talking to People who Listen, Speaking to People who Need to Hear.*

These books were clearly little short of apocalyptic, and the last one on the shelf, a huge tome called *101 Great Mission Statements*, was a work of such erudition that it had required not one, but two, editors to bring it to the notice of a mission-statement-hungry world.

Kavanagh was a policeman whose business was criminology and detection, and who knew a bit about forensic science. But they weren't the only books on his shelves. There were also a few novels, and some poetry, and a much-loved, ten-volume collected Shakespeare.

After all, everyone needs something. For some people it's hang-gliding, others build plastic models or collect stamps; some people do the garden, even read books on it. It all adds up.

But who was Aidan McEwan? A man with a 'mission statement' behind his desk, and pictures on his wall of Michael Edwardes and Ian McGregor, Margaret Thatcher's erstwhile industrial kneecappers.

When, finally, Aidan McEwan did come through the door into his office, he walked up to Kavanagh, stood very close and, without speaking, shook him solemnly by the hand.

'Gentlemen,' he said, nodding to Presley.

The men waited, but that *was* the sentence.

'Mr McEwan,' said Kavanagh.

'Terrible news,' offered the college principal. 'Terrible.'

'Yes, sir. Dreadful,' said Presley superfluously.

'Please, sit,' said McEwan, as he arranged himself behind his desk and settled himself into his high-backed, black chair.

'Coffee?'

The policemen declined.

'Please,' said the principal. 'Do begin.'

'We need background,' said Kavanagh. 'Anything at all on John Lacey. Any enemies. Was there anything that you were aware of: jealousies; rivalries; student problems; anything at all?'

McEwan leaned back in his chair, put the tips of his fingers together and, with the triangle formed there, put it to his lips. He eventually took them away, as if about to speak, looked from Presley to Kavanagh and back again, but said nothing.

Presley wondered if he had forgotten the question, was about to restate it in a slightly amended form, when the principal began.

'Education, gentlemen. Not what it was. Changes.

Significant. Sweeping. Not *all* welcome. Disruption, there is bound to be. Problems: no. Challenges: yes.'

This verbal equivalent of using the highlighting pen was not something that either of the policemen had encountered previously, and they sat fascinated but unsure of what exactly the principal was trying to say.

Eventually, when the man paused, Kavanagh said, 'And . . . Lacey? John Lacey? Did he have . . . "problems"?' ('Challenges' hardly seemed the appropriate word for the murdered man, even allowing for the unbridled optimism of Osborne College and its porcine principal.)

'None whatsoever,' said McEwan conclusively. 'None at all.' And he passed Lacey's personal folder across the wide desk to Kavanagh who, sitting in an easy chair, was a foot below him.

'I've been through it this morning. Nothing.'

Generally speaking, people did not include in their CVs the reasons for their being murdered. Minutes of meetings never gave the cut and thrust, the real story beneath the carefully chosen and recorded words.

Notwithstanding McEwan's apparently unshakeable faith in the contents of Lacey's buff folder, the policemen continued to ask questions about the deceased art teacher for another thirty minutes or so.

The principal answered in his idiosyncratic manner. But he was a man used to setting agendas, not following those of others and, at the slightest opportunity, he relapsed into his generalized educational patois of cliché and euphemism: thus, college students had metamorphosed into 'clients'; things that were being developed were 'on-line'; suggestions were 'proactive'.

There was a tired, third-hand quality about his discourse. He was a man who spent his days 'moving the goalposts'; and looking for 'level playing fields'; for he had, apparently single-handedly, 'a lot of balls to keep in the air'.

Kavanagh grew weary. He was desperate to escape the

aural, watery clasp of this man who had taken on the management equivalent of the sign that used to hang in every two-bit, one-telephone office in the land: *You don't have to be mad to work here, but if you are it helps.*

Eventually, Kavanagh and Presley thanked the principal for his time and backed away towards the door.

But he was now in full flow, escorting them down the corridors, and out to their Granada, calling after them in the car park, 'Education. It'll never be the same again, you know,' and finally offered triumphantly, 'Our people, they deliver the curriculum on Sunday after*noons*.'

Presley drove away, throwing the back end of the car into the air as he ignored the speed humps.

So, rubicund Aidan McEwan was the sort of man into whose care the education and nurturing of the country's young had now been placed. For the first time since he had been called in to investigate the art teacher's death, Inspector Frank Kavanagh found a crumb of comfort in the tragedy.

4

It was a detached house: 1930s; four bedrooms; double garage and a big front garden with a couple of birch saplings and some ornamental fruit trees with lots of late-season pink blossom on them. Kavanagh had given up trying to make sense of it any more: there were daffodils at Christmas, and strawberries in the shops in November. No wonder the prisons were full.

Presley pulled their black Ford onto the tarmac drive and stalled it by taking his foot sharply off the clutch while keeping his other firmly on the brake.

Kavanagh looked at him disapprovingly. Why not just turn off the ignition key like everyone else? He *had* mentioned it. Often.

The garage up-and-over doors were open and there was a restored maroon Morris 1000 Traveller there, a couple of well-used mountain bikes, plus strimmers and mowers and shears and extension leads. The tins of paint and primer and creosote and motor oil were neatly stacked on wide shelves beneath a big, very solid workbench.

The only things which distinguished this garage from thousands like it were the couple of painter's easels leaning against the breeze blocks, the very many paintings which were stacked against all three walls, and the tailor's dummy, propped at a crazy angle in the corner next to the aluminium stepladders.

The front door opened before they had rung the bell.

A teenager wearing a blue baseball cap bearing the white insignia of New York held it ajar.

'Inspector Kavanagh; Sergeant Presley. Hello, son. Can we come in?'

The boy opened the door a little wider, and the two men stepped along the parquet-floored hall into the front room.

Judith Lacey was tall, five feet eight or nine, and wore soft blue leather shoes that looked handmade. She was wearing a dress made of that crinkly material Kavanagh knew but couldn't remember the name of. The skirt hugged her slight tummy and came down to above her ankles. It was dark blue with little white flowers and was buttoned from the neck to the midriff.

The room was sparsely furnished, with two big Habitat linen sofas, some expensive Linn hi-fi separates, a slimline television, lots of books on the shelves, stacks of records and CDs and tapes, and a couple of matt and stainless-steel occasional tables.

The only incongruity, blot on the glossy-magazine appearance of the room, were the three ashtrays, all big, French-café copies, the names Ricard and Pernod picked out on their distinctive yellow sides, but with several crushed cigarette ends in each.

'Mrs Lacey, I'm sorry to call again so soon. We have to ask you just a few more questions.'

She acknowledged his request with a barely perceptible inclination of her head.

She sat in the corner of the huge sofa, Kavanagh sat opposite her, forward on the chair, his hands hanging between his open knees. Presley stood at the window.

'An incident like this, we have to make our inquiries as soon as possible.' The inspector cringed at his use of the word 'incident'. The 'incident' here was the death of her husband. The man to whom she had been married for twenty years.

'I'm sorry.' It was a general apology, for his crassness,

for his use of the word, and for even being here again. 'The pathologist's examination, I understand it is completed?' The question was rhetorical; he knew that the body had been released into her keeping and was at the funeral parlour.

'Yes,' she murmured.

'And the funeral?'

'On Monday. Two-thirty, at Saint Jude's.'

'I would like to attend, if I may. And my sergeant.'

'Of course,' she said.

'We will be discreet.'

'I'm sure. Thank you.'

Her son pushed open the door and brought in a tray with cups and milk and sugar on it. His mother gave him a little smile of thanks. When he had returned with the Bodum of dark coffee and left, Kavanagh began. 'Have you thought of anything, anything at all, no matter how insignificant it might appear to you, which might give us a clue as to why anyone would want to . . . ?' His question trailed away.

'Frankly, Mrs Lacey, we're struggling. We've very little to go on. Anything you can suggest could be of enormous help.'

She lit a Silk Cut cigarette, exhaled the smoke as she began. 'The students he taught, they loved him. Lots of them kept in touch, after they'd gone off to college and things. He was very popular. People don't get killed . . . for no reason. Drugs, money, robberies. Yes, I know, the world we live in, but not this, for no reason, no reason . . .' and she broke down and began to sob.

Presley, who often spent Saturday afternoons bruising in the scrum for the Birmingham Police second fifteen, stood above her and put his hand lightly on her shoulder.

She regained some control and, embarrassed for the big policeman standing awkwardly at her side, unable to comfort her, unable to move from her side, mouthed a quiet 'Thank you'.

'This is all a nightmare. I can't believe what has happened. I don't want to "come to terms" with it. Be like those people on television who say that "life must go on". I don't *want* life to go on.

'The doctor has given me pills, but I don't want to take them. I want to feel this. This pain. My husband has gone. I don't want to not feel his loss. We went to the cinema last weekend. Last Sunday, he brought the tea up. Then made the breakfast, just like always on Sundays. Today, he's not here any more. I don't *want* to forget.'

Her words made the notion of the inspector's questions entirely redundant. Yes, he knew: she taught drama, but this was no performance, or if it was, she should be in Hollywood, not Sutton Coldfield.

Presley stepped away from her and poured the coffee.

Kavanagh knew that he had to do it, but he felt a cheat, a cheapskate. 'Your husband, John. His relationship with the teacher-training student . . . ?'

'Yes?'

'You told us yesterday that that was a difficult time for you. A very difficult time.'

'Yes. Of course.'

'How long did it go on for?'

'I don't know. Not long. She was on a placement. But it didn't start straightaway. Two, perhaps three weeks, I suppose.'

'And then you found out?'

'Yes.'

'Then what? I'm sorry, we *have* to know.'

'Then she went back to her college. It was all over.'

'You came to terms with it?'

'Eventually. It was difficult. We had been married nine or ten years. Perhaps we'd let things drift. Relationships, I think they have to be nurtured. Fed. Perhaps we had begun to take ours for granted. Are you married, Inspector?'

'No, I'm separated,' he replied.

'I see.'

Kavanagh had been forced to acknowledge that there didn't seem to be an appropriate response to the statement that you were 'separated'. It wasn't like saying your wife had died, when people might pause before saying, 'I'm so sorry.'

But he was aware that the timbre of his voice, even in uttering the apparently neutral words, failed to conceal his feelings of loss.

She began again, and said, perhaps a little too defensively, 'It wasn't a love affair. It was a brief infatuation.'

'How did you find out about it?' asked Presley gently.

She smiled. 'It's not funny. Not at all. I went to my mother's. My father hadn't been well. I often used to go there overnight. They live in the Malvern Hills, near Worcester. It's not far. I took Joe, of course.

'The next day, when we came back, I was in the bathroom. John's flannel was over the rim of the bath. There was something odd about it. I reached out and touched it. It was like cardboard. Completely dry. He hadn't been in the bathroom that morning.

'I just knew. You always do.' She glanced at Kavanagh. 'I was on my knees. Joe's watching cartoons on the TV downstairs, and I'm on my knees on the tiles on the bathroom floor, John's flannel, stiff as a board over the rim of the bath, telling me he's having an affair as clearly as if he'd left me a note on the mantelpiece.

'There were a hundred questions racing through my mind: Who was it? How long? Where? When? All the usual, grisly, horrible stuff.

'I just couldn't cope. You come up with all sorts of bizarre ideas. The truth's actually better than not knowing. I wanted to go down to college that very minute and ask him to tell me.'

'And?'

'I waited. That evening, he told me. I think he'd actually

given up on her, satisfied his little yearning, but she was still involved.'

She smiled again, this time had almost to stifle a little laugh. 'We formed an alliance against her. Me and John against *his* affair. There was a sort of grim humour about the whole thing. He didn't want any scandal at college, of course. It was just a question of getting through the next couple of weeks, and then her going back to her college.'

'And that was it?'

'Yes, that was it.'

'You were very supportive, Mrs Lacey,' said Presley. 'Not everyone would have been so.'

'Yes. But it was self-serving, really. After the shock, and the initial tears and upset, I knew that I didn't want us to break up. I knew that he didn't love her, or anything like that. So it was a sort of pragmatism.'

'And you got through?'

'What does Brecht say?'

Presley looked to Kavanagh. His look asked: 'What *does* Brecht say?'

'"Whatever doesn't kill me, makes me strong." We were stronger for it, I suppose.'

'Didn't you feel a need for revenge?' asked Kavanagh.

'Revenge?' she said.

'Perhaps an affair of your own? To "settle the score"? People do, you know,' he added, conciliatory.

'Everyone's entitled to a mistake, aren't they?' she rejoined. 'No, I didn't want revenge. I wanted us to be happy, a family, and together again. That's all. Why are you asking me about these things now?' she said.

Kavanagh saw no point in subterfuge. 'If you had seen the need . . . wanted to have a relationship . . . this could have led to . . . at the very least, there would have been motives.'

'For me to take John's life?' she said.

'Not necessarily you, Mrs Lacey,' added Presley.

'Oh, *my* jealous lover!' she said with mock scorn.

'It does happen,' said Kavanagh, defensive about the suggestion, notwithstanding his lack of belief in it. And for emphasis, 'It wouldn't be the first time.'

'Of course,' she offered politely. 'I have no lover, Inspector. I've never had one. I have no idea why someone has taken my husband's life, and ruined mine, and our son's.'

While Kavanagh went upstairs to the lavatory, Presley, who barely knew a dandelion from a radish, stood at the window and made a valiant attempt at horticultural small talk with the bereaved woman.

As he dried his hands, Kavanagh looked down at the three flannels that lay over the rim of the bath. The bottle-green one, slightly apart from the others, was bone dry.

'What do you reckon?' asked Presley as they drove away. There was an objective detachment about them now that they were away from the widow's claustrophobic grief. They might have been discussing a film they had just seen.

'There's always someone with half a reason to do someone in,' said Kavanagh, 'but usually it stops at half a reason. The moment passes. It's like on the motorway. You pass a hundred thousand drivers on the M1. Every one of them, all their brains ticking, their periods menstruating, their passions throbbing, their cats dying, their mothers ill. They all make all those split-second seventy- and eighty- and ninety-mile-an-hour decisions just right. And everyone gets home. But when just one of them makes a tiny error . . . I'm surprised there aren't *more*, not *less*.'

'Crashes?' said Presley, his eyes on the road.

'Murders,' said Kavanagh.

'So, what do you reckon?'

'God knows,' said Kavanagh.

5

The next day, on the Saturday afternoon, DI Frank Kavanagh convened a meeting of the dozen detectives who had been working nonstop on the Lacey murder inquiry.

The football results were coming in on the huge old Sony in the corner of the musty social club on the fifth floor. As they stuttered across the teleprinter, Bob Wilson, the John Major of the BBC's team of football pundits, reiterated the results with his customary lack of panache.

Manchester United had won again, beating Tottenham 2–1 at home, and had started to draw away from the following pack. There was already absurdly premature talk of them doing the double (the FA Cup had not yet even begun for the league clubs), possibly even the treble.

Kavanagh stood at the front of the room, his head slightly bowed, oblivious to the results and the background hubbub and banter. Presley reached up and turned off the set. DC Andy Reeder, originally from a bleak North Wales village, groaned as the screen went blank on the tantalizingly grim news: Brentford 2; Wrexham . . .

The inspector took a pace towards the big flip charts and began without ceremony. 'I'll state the obvious, go over what you all know. Anything you want to pick up on, stop me. John Lacey was forty-six. Taught art at the Osborne Sixth Form College. He'd been there eighteen years. Popular with the kids. The odd run-in with a student, but generally well liked. Popular in the staff room, too. Lots of friends. No particular enemies that we're aware of. No professional jealousies that we've been able to turn up.

'About ten years ago he had an affair with a student teacher who was attached to his department. It was a brief, passionate thing. His wife found out, they had a rocky time for a bit, and then the student left to go back to college and, as far as we know, they haven't seen each other since.

'The girl's been interviewed; she's married herself now, lives in York, a teacher. Her boyfriend at the time never knew about her affair, so she says. She looks above board. We're going to have to trace the boyfriend; he's emigrated to Canada, but it's probably a long shot. I think she's telling us the truth, and anyway, why's her ex-boyfriend going to come back and kill her one-time lover ten years later?

'Lacey's wife, Judith, told us about the affair. The way she tells it, she was upset at the time, but they got over it and, as far as we can find out, there was nothing going on in that area.'

Kavanagh pushed his fingers through his thick, dark hair. It was greasy, needed washing. 'Like a lot of art teachers, according to his wife, Lacey wanted to be a painter, was probably frustrated in that sense. But that doesn't seem to lead anywhere. He found time to do a bit of his own work, had an exhibition last year, which didn't set the world on fire.

'Background: working class, born here in Brum; first one of his generation to go to college; got his degree, got married (his wife teaches drama). He taught at Aldridge Road Comprehensive in north Birmingham for a couple of years, and then did a post-graduate something or other in South Wales.

'Came back up here, got the job at Osborne Tech, as it was then. A few years later they have a nipper, Joe. He works at the sixth form college for eighteen years and last Wednesday evening, October 13th, taking down an exhibition of his second-year students' work in the parish centre, someone walks up and stabs him to death. Any questions?'

Detective Sergeant Jackson raised his hand. Kavanagh nodded.

'What about his missis?'

'What about her?' said Kavanagh.

'What if she was playing away? You know, she owes him one from his number with the student all those years ago. People don't forget. Well, blokes don't anyway.'

'And so she tops him?' replied the DI disingenuously.

'Not necessarily *her*,' added Jackson gamely. 'What if she's got a bloke, and they want him out of the way?'

Kavanagh was satisfied that Judith Lacey's grief and mourning were entirely genuine. But a murder inquiry was a team game, and he knew that he had to carry his team with him for days, possibly weeks.

'Yes, all right, Jacko. I think she's on the level, but we're checking her out. Good point. Anyone else?'

There were no more questions.

'OK, Kev, carry on.' Kavanagh took Presley's seat as the sergeant came to the front of the room and tried to inject some life into the proceedings.

'Right, this is where we stand at the moment. We've done all the usual: house to house; checked anything or anyone suspicious during the last couple of weeks; done a detailed search of the surrounding area: verges, drains, gardens. Checked all the council bins, skips and bags. Drained the nearby cuts and waded the streams in the vicinity. Plenty of supermarket trolleys, more bikes than Halfords, even a bloody safe, but still no murder weapon. We know it was a knife, about five inches long, and very sharp. It was plunged in with great force, only the hilt stopped it; there's bruising around the soft tissue surrounding the stab wounds.

'We all know how important finding it is. We're going

to widen the search area. Dave's got the details and the running order. We *must* find it. Also, *somebody* must've seen him leaving the scene, probably running away. He was covered in blood, for Chrissakes!

'There weren't many people around that night. It was cold, and anyway, most people were in watching England not qualify for the World Cup.' There was some token jeering as the officers recalled the refereeing in Holland that had cost England a place in America, and Graham 'Do-I-not-like-that' Taylor his job.

'Yes, it was a bad night all round,' said the sergeant ruefully.

Presley picked up the threads of his summary: 'A woman who lives in the terraced cottages a couple of hundred yards down from the centre reckons there was a car that she hadn't seen before. It's all old folk in those houses, and they don't get many cars coming and going, but she's in her seventies and doesn't drive.

'She thinks it was a big, "square" car. We've shown her photos and taken her to the showrooms but, frankly, she hasn't got much of a clue. She said it could be a Volvo or one of the big Fords, then on the way back to the station she pointed at a bloody Maestro. She *does* know it was blue, though.

'Unfortunately, it was dry that night and the SOCO and forensic people haven't come up with anything distinctive in the way of tapings, scrapings, dustings or prints. At least, not yet. There are hundreds of smudged fingerprints on the door and jamb of the centre, and lots more on the back of the college van, but it's virtually impossible to eliminate from those, and anyway, is this maniac going to have any form, even if we could?'

Presley continued in similar vein for another five minutes, but there was nothing new. It was a pep talk. When investigations were hot, there was no time for this kind of thing. Most of them were experienced detectives, and they knew that the witnesses who didn't come forward straightaway usually didn't come forward at all.

Murder weapons were usually found quickly, or they weren't found at all. Killers always panicked. Unless they didn't. And if they didn't, they weren't the kind of killers who threw the knife over the first hedge they passed. They knew what they were doing, and if they knew what they were doing, it made them very hard to catch. The atmosphere in the room was dispiriting.

'Are we sure it's a him?' asked Rees from the back of the room.

'From the force of the wound, which is just about all we've got to go on, Khaliq and his people down at pathology think so. But it could be a strong woman, or a tough kid. We can't rule anything out. We checked out the pianist, the woman who found him. No blood on her clothes, apart from a bit on her hem where she'd leaned over him. No motive, no strength. She's well out of the frame.'

The sergeant continued for a few minutes longer and then glanced over at Kavanagh, who gave him a nod of assent. 'We're going to keep up this level of operation for a few more days. Reinterview all those we've already spoken to and widen it out to anyone with past involvement with Lacey: ex-students, ex-members of staff, and of course we're still trying to trace the boyfriend of the girl he had an affair with.

'We haven't really got elimination criteria, 'cause we haven't got a motive. Everyone's in the frame. But it'll whittle down. It just needs some good, patient cop work.'

He paused, seemed to be prevaricating. There was a sense of expectation in the room, the atmosphere had changed. Presley finally said, 'Look, if we don't get anywhere by early next week, they've got a vacant slot on *Crimewatch* . . .'

Before he could finish his sentence there was a rowdy chorus of groans and hisses from the assembled officers.

Kavanagh joined his besieged sergeant at the front of the noisy crowd and took over. 'I know, I know. Listen;

they've got six or seven minutes, just come vacant. Armed robbery in Exeter. They'd filmed a reconstruction, lined the whole thing up, got some Devon yokel DS to learn his lines and everything, and then the villain gets grassed up by some lowlifer who owes him one.

'So they've got a space that's up for grabs and the Yard have been on to us to see if we want it. I asked them to give me a week; they've given us three days, and then they'll have to film and everything. Even that's cutting it fine.'

The barely good-humoured barracking continued. Kavanagh weighed in again, this time louder, and entirely seriously. 'You tell me. If we can't get anything locally, all we know is that we're looking for someone who was out at that time, who almost certainly had bloodstained clothes to clean or dispose of, and who *should* have a motive for killing Lacey.'

Finally, curtailing the meeting at the same time as showing his own exasperation, he said quietly and calmly, 'Find the knife, that's all we've got to do; just find the knife then we can keep off the telly and solve our own murders.'

The detectives began to meander away. 'Bloody TV,' said Mick Nugent to Rees as they sauntered out of the room. 'We'll be on Noel Edmonds and have the fuckin' villains on *Blind Date* next.'

Half of them were already on the stairs when Kavanagh called out, 'And remember the car. Keep it in mind, whoever you're talking to. She *says* it was blue. Cheers.'

6

There were three short tributes from the pulpit before the priest's address to the congregation.

Lacey's brother, two years younger than the dead man, said a few halting words about his sibling, 'my best mate, as well as my brother,' and lamented what he might have achieved, given a few more years.

There was no hint of forgiveness or understanding in his emotion-choked words, just resentment and bitterness at his brother's untimely, violent death.

This was the trouble with atheists, thought the young vicar, sitting a few feet away, his eyes closed, his fingers loosely intertwined; they always filled his church to mourn the things not done, paid scant heed to the many riches bestowed upon each life.

A pretty student, in black skirt, tights, and Doctor Marten shoes, stepped up to the lectern and delivered an eloquent tribute to her teacher, a man who had been, as well as an inspirational teacher, 'a really good friend' to she and her fellow pupils.

The college principal spoke next.

McEwan heaped fulsome praise upon his departed art teacher, said that his colleagues from the college would all be here, were they not 'doing what John would have wished them to be doing: teaching students, the students whose lives he has so enriched. For life must go on, even in the midst of tragedy.

'A final word,' he said solemnly. 'As a mark of respect

to John, and his contribution to the college during the last eighteen years, I have to tell you that the chairman of the governors of the college has accepted my proposal that the new sports hall, under construction now, and due for completion in May shall, hereafter, be known as the John Lacey Sports Hall.'

Was it the tone of plangent scene-setting, the archly self-important 'my proposal', or simply his grandiose use of 'hereafter', with its connotations of eternity, which made Kavanagh feel so distinctly uncomfortable in the crowded church?

When he and Presley had visited the college, they had seen the new sports hall rising from the turves of what had been the playing field. It was a big, white, aircraft hangar of a building, with ubiquitous red bricks being herring-bone filleted into the forecourt. Kavanagh doubted that it would be here in thirty years' time, much less in the 'hereafter'.

At the cemetery, on the cold, October afternoon, there were family and college students and neighbours and well-wishers and even a few people attracted merely by the size of the crowd and the numbers of cars that had followed the cortège.

Kavanagh looked at the pretty college girls and wondered, mystified as ever by changes in fashion, was there someone who sat in a room somewhere and said, 'Now!' and suddenly the world wore Caterpillar boots?

He stood with Presley at the back of the mourners and looked for signs of . . . of what? In a movie, a former lover would drop a single flower into the open grave, or some forgotten child would scowl at the widow. At the very least a long, dark car would crawl up behind the cortège, the window would slide down and a face in the rear seat would peer towards the mourners.

Kavanagh examined the cemetery road: a Mercedes hearse; a black Austin Princess, the chief mourners' car, on a 'B' plate, ten years old and looking as if it had come out of the showroom yesterday. Probably never been in fifth, thought the inspector.

Even the weather lacked drama appropriate to the graveside scene. In films, it rained cold sleet or, for ironic effect, it might be life affirming and sunny. Here, in a north Birmingham suburb, it was just very English: cold, bright, sunless sky; pale, high, thin cloud. It was weather to make a man mad. And Kavanagh felt it.

Lacey's widow looked well: deeply, mournfully attractive. Since Rachael had left him, marriage, any marriage, could make him grieve. A couple choosing pasta or apples in the supermarket hurt him. Middle-aged parents holding hands or, worse, walking with a grandchild, was torture to his soul. Joy was sorrow; sunshine, pain.

When he drew back the bedroom curtains in the morning, he gave silent thanks if it was raining or overcast and cold.

He turned off the weather forecast if the presenter was young and amiable. He watched it through (never listening) only if it was the dour man who had failed to predict the big storm of 1987, and who appeared to have been properly resentful ever since.

She was in black, of course. It became her well. She looked even lovelier than when he had spoken to her at her home three or four days ago. She hadn't eaten for nearly a week, not eaten properly, at least. Emotional trauma was the most effective crash diet that he knew. For years he had dallied with the half-a-stone extra that he carried: semi-skimmed milk; rubbery, no-fat cheese; low-fat spreads; even white wine in the pub for a couple of weeks, but it was not until he and Rachael parted that he dropped the half-stone, and nearly another half as well, within a fortnight.

He smoked all day and half the night; drank coffee, black, a few grains of sugar, and became a flat-tummied 42-year-old in days. His routine life – dull habit, soaked through with the reassurance of custom – had gone out of the window in that moment.

Driving home, he would tell himself that if the traffic lights didn't change before he got to them, or if the cyclist in front turned left, or if the next car that he passed was a Vauxhall, or red, or driven by a woman . . . she would have written to him; she would be there when he got home.

It was about the level of not walking on the pavement cracks when he was a kid. It didn't work now either. In fact, it was a dangerous game to play, because when he had hurriedly parked the car, and checked amongst the junk mail for her spidery handwriting, and walked down the hall and could see the phone's non-blinking, no-message, red light on the machine, that was when he came closest to taking not just the half-bottle of Bell's, but the bottle of paracetamol too.

He had started to look longingly, yearningly, at the most unsuitable women. Funerals so flattered women. Grief became them. Judith Lacey was lovely in her simple, dark mourning.

Funerals, anyway, were so much easier than weddings, with their ceaseless good humour, bonhomie, and brittle, enforced intimacy between people who frequently never met again.

As a young uniformed cop, Kavanagh had attended a couple of the big, family weddings that were always held in some soulless housing-estate pub and generally degenerated into a drunken brawl by ten o'clock in the evening.

They were ugly, nasty things with the groom's red-necked family battering the bride's big-knuckled cousins or friends or brothers, but there was, at least, some feeling about them.

They weren't the weak tea, poncey linen suits, champagne and tiramisu affairs that he and Rachael attended, travelling down to rural Berkshire (her side), or across to Staffordshire (his side), where everything was so well mannered that his mouth ached for a whole day after, not from a big drunken fist in it, but from too much phoney smiling.

Compared with this, funerals were a blessing, occasions clearly focused on grief and immutable mortality: what flimsy cause for celebration was the temporary union of *any* couple compared with the rock-solid certainty of a corpse in a box beside the assembled mourners?

The sextons (were they still called that, Kavanagh wondered?) were lowering the oak coffin, the vicar saying the few last words as the straps let the wooden box unevenly down.

Green plastic matting concealed the ragged edge of the freshly dug grave. It was incongruous, like plastic flowers in a restaurant, and reminded the inspector of the pineapples and avocados on greengrocer's pavement displays.

She came to the side of the hole and stood a moment before the horrible reality of the box in this dark place: inside it, her husband's body. Him. The mole on his back, the curling hair around his ears, his changeable brown eyes.

Her tears, at first no more than shallow gasps, became deep, uncontrollable sobs.

They were waiting for her to do the next thing. When she had done it, they would lead her to the car and shovel the mound of earth that lay a few yards away, covered by a tarpaulin, onto his coffin.

She dropped a handful of the soil onto the box and the grains scattered along the dark, highly polished lid. Her son put his arm around her shoulders, and they backed away from the edge. Lacey's parents and brother came to the edge of the grave and sprinkled in their handfuls of earth.

Two officers, a man and a woman, took the names of everyone who was not already known to the police as they made their way down the little slope to the waiting cars.

Kavanagh joined the widow beside the funeral car. He was lost for words, but eventually said, 'It was a nice gesture . . .'

She looked at him bemused, as if he had spoken to her in Arabic.

'The sports hall,' he said. 'A nice gesture . . . The John Lacey Sports Hall . . .'

She turned towards the waiting car, and then looked at Kavanagh through the net of her black veil. The exhaust smoke from the Austin Princess plumed onto the damp tarmac and rolled away. 'He couldn't stand Aidan McEwan. And he loathed sport.'

7

'And now to a truly baffling crime . . .'

Kavanagh was struck by the archaic language; there was a cosy reassurance about it which belied the fearful reality of most crime.

'Baffling' had a Holmesian ring to it: Sherlock, not the Home Office Large Major Enquiry System computer, a typically arcane Whitehall acronym.

This was the media at work. The show became the issue; 'the medium the message,' in the words of another age. It changed everything it touched. It dressed it, and then consumed it. Nothing was as it seemed, and the irony was that everyone knew that this was so.

Nick Ross looked directly at the camera and assumed his customary amalgam of boyish enthusiasm and earnest concern. 'In fact, police officers in Wellington, Shropshire, are not even certain that a crime *was* committed. But they have decided to appeal to *Crimewatch* viewers to see if any of them is aware of anything which might confirm their uneasiness about the deaths of Terry Sugar and his wife, Jeanette.'

Ninety-degree turn; look to camera two; head and shoulders. 'Terry Sugar was a well-known character on the streets of Wellington. He had been a street trader there for years, and was often to be seen on the High Street selling his wares. In the summer it might be lighters, miracle cleaners or sports socks; in the winter, Sellotape, ironing-board covers, boxes of chocolates or perfume.

'Just over five weeks ago, on the morning of Thursday, September 16th, the bodies of Mr Sugar and his wife were found in the front seats of their car in their fume-filled garage. They had died from carbon monoxide poisoning.

'In itself, this kind of death is not particularly unusual these days. Exhaust fumes are lethal in an enclosed space and, as everyone knows, you should never start your car in a garage without first opening the doors.

'But in this case there were certain details which suggested to the police that this tragedy might not be an accident, and initial inquiries led them to believe that they were dealing with a double suicide.

'However, in a suicide there are usually things that one expects to find, and several of these things were not there. In most suicides, there is a clear reason for the deceased's action: illness, financial worries, unemployment, or an inability to cope because of some personal problem.

'With double suicides, which are statistically much rarer, the reasons are generally even more clear.

'In the case of Mr and Mrs Sugar, investigating officers have been unable to find *any* reason why they would have killed themselves.'

There was no filmed reconstruction, for there was little to reconstruct: the short walk from the couple's flat in Newport Road to their garage fifty yards away would not, the producer had reasoned, make riveting television.

Kavanagh sat in the hospitality suite and watched the studio monitor as Ross questioned West Mercia's Inspector Tom Bromage about the supposed suicide. He winced at his colleague's stilted delivery, the stultifying jargon that policemen seemed programmed to slip into whenever there was the sniff of a television crew or a newspaper reporter. No one 'walked' down the road; they 'proceeded'. People weren't 'stopped'; they were 'apprehended'. People didn't drive cars, but vehicles, which never had tax discs on their windscreens, but excise licences.

It was a textbook pedantry that killed. The raw energy of

any police station canteen would have served their cause better.

Kavanagh pulled at his shirt collar and loosened the knot of his tie. Bromage wasn't going to win any Oscars for his performance, but when the inspector tried to remember the replies that *he* was supposed to improvise around his script they, also, suddenly became unaccountably difficult to say: completely ordinary words sounded absurd as he tried them out in his dry mouth and heard them reverberate in his head.

Kavanagh had heard of the double 'suicide' case on the inter-force grapevine, and he already knew quite a bit more about it than the nine million Thursday-evening *Crimewatch* voyeurs were being told.

Sugar was a bit of a jack the lad. As well as selling ironing-board covers and cheap lighters and fake Swiss chocolates, he was a registered smack addict.

It was almost quaint, in these harsh, violent and unpredictable times, to find people like Terry Sugar. He used regularly, his emaciated body and the prominent blue veins in his wiry arms demanded it, but he also functioned, got onto the street and sold his goods and came home and fixed himself into a temporary oblivion. But he didn't die or kill you. He didn't even steal your money.

Tom Bromage knew Sugar hadn't fallen foul of dope dealers. His personal stash was still in the house, his bit of cash hadn't been nicked, and the Amstrad video was still on the shelf beneath the telly. It was all a bit of a mystery.

Kavanagh dabbed at his prickly palms with his handkerchief. His mind was racing. This is what they meant about the media. It was a serpent that devoured the issues it dealt with whole. He wasn't even thinking about art teacher John Lacey and his violent death. He was thinking only about not making a fool of himself, and of the boys, his colleagues and subordinates, gathered around the TV in the social club back at the division.

He played a cheap trick: forced himself to think of Lacey's distraught wife in an attempt to regain focus. It didn't work. Not making a fool of himself. That was all that mattered. An hour ago, the producer's assistant had run through the dummy questions: 'Just be yourself,' she had urged. 'You'll be fine. Be sincere, but be yourself. You need the viewers' help, and it's what *you* say that they'll be responding to.'

'"Be yourself!"' Kavanagh had no idea who he was. The alien environment: the studio lights; the gliding camera dollies; the background noise; the director on the headsets; the quietly frantic arms cuing people in; the make-up girl; the microphone men; his ex-wife out there in the night somewhere; *that* was all he knew.

And now began a new level of freneticism: the animal that had been incubated in the stifling heat threatened to get out of control and escape the straitjacket of its format as information started to pour in on the banks of telephones ranged around them.

Was she watching? Would she watch? It was all he could ever do to get her in front of a movie on TV before the opening credits rolled. They'd played the Woody Allen/Diane Keaton scene from *Annie Hall* a hundred times: he wouldn't watch the movie if they'd missed a second of it; she took spunky Keaton's 'Who gives a damn, we've seen it a dozen times anyway?' role.

He was sweating freely now. He patted his brow with his handkerchief and tried to clear his salivaless throat. He only had a few minutes. Had anyone ever declined? At the last minute, just said, 'No, I can't do it,' he wondered?

His hands would not dry. Somehow he had to rebutton his collar and tighten his tie without marking his white shirt.

And then he was being escorted to the place beside the presenter. Not listening, not seeing or hearing properly, just walking, with the production assistant at his side.

Would she watch? He'd left a message on her machine.

He'd counted the rings. Four was good. Four, and then hiss, crackle. And then her message. He was the only person he knew who actually preferred the machine: it was contact, but safe, one-way contact.

There was her voice. Everything just her. The slight, self-conscious hesitation, as if surprised at having had to record her message. And then the polite, effortlessly cultured voice with its slight bruising of the vowels and blunting of the 'h's' in her customary attempt to conceal her background.

But it was the sound of her voice. Faltering, vulnerable, kindly. It was a voice that gave to charity, saw the other point of view, remembered family birthdays, never saved Christmas wrapping paper from one year to the next.

She was the kind of person who, if she won a supermarket dash, would leave some of the expensive items, just to be fair.

And it was the voice that had said, with trembling, colourless lips, as he lay on the sofa watching the second episode of *Mr Wroe's Virgins*, 'I want to talk.'

He had heard something new; in a voice that he knew better than the sound of his own. He had heard the difference, turned round and switched off the television, swung his legs down and lit a cigarette and looked at her. It was seamless and dreamlike. Yet concrete and immediate and very brittle.

It wasn't the voice of someone who has crashed the car or flooded the bath or lost their job. He'd never heard it before, but he knew immediately what it meant, as if some atavistic gene was lying dormant, just waiting to be stirred by these very words.

And from then on his life had changed. And he heard that commonplace phrase again and again and again, and it always said, 'I want to talk,' and then, before he had had time to respond, 'I think we should part.'

And every time he heard it now, driving to work, looking at Lacey's blood on the churchyard pavement, turning at night in his bed, or as the music played over the titles to *Match of the Day*, he wanted to stop it. Stop the music and stop the action, and let that time not happen.

Early days, Presley had said to him over a drink in the Chinese, late gambling club that they sometimes used, when everything else was quiet in the city, 'I'm sorry about you and Rachael, Frank. It's like a death in the family.'

Elvis was ex-army; a big, tough guy, who'd shot at people and may have hit some of them. He and Frank were Odd Couple cops, Presley's slob Matthau to Kavanagh's constipated Jack Lemmon, but somehow, past the level of Presley's greasy chip bags in the car and cigarette ash on his trousers, they were mates, good mates, and Frank had been touched by the feeling that the ex-paratrooper had conveyed in the crass cliché.

They'd sat in the corner as the waiters from the city-centre restaurants squandered their wages and tips at the roulette wheel. Elvis became lugubrious, more maudlin than Frank, but when he said again, 'It's like a death in the family,' Frank, hunched over the low table, replied bitterly, 'It's worse, Kev. She's there, but she doesn't come back. She could, but she doesn't.'

And there was her voice on the machine, saying she was out and leave a message and she'd call back. And he listened to it as if she might be saying something to *him*.

Yes, the machine was better. She couldn't reach him, couldn't probe him, in her gentle way, which reminded him of her, and what had been his love for her, and now hurt so much that he didn't know what it was: love or jealousy or grief or just plain habit.

When they talked 'properly', without the machine between them, it was worse than this. A few times, they had hit a nerve, and there had been tears. Not anger, but sadness; comforting tears of loss. And he had felt better for hours, sometimes a day.

But it was all too tricky, far too precarious, and the

machine was better. That little contact was enough.

He wondered whether they might maintain their new relationship for ever, just through the optical fibres of the telephone system. (Or were they fibre optics?)

He eventually said, after her hesitant message, 'Hello, Rachael.' (Even saying her name was odd, strangely formal. He had rarely called her Rachael, she him Frank.) 'I'm on *Crimewatch* this evening. It starts at 9.30. I thought you might like to know . . .' He tried to sound cavalier. 'Goodbye. I'll give you a ring.'

He should hang up. He'd got away with it. She might come in, pick up the phone, talk back. She might have her key in the door now. She could be walking towards the phone, or have her hand on it.

'How's things?' he said, and then, unable to let go, 'Are you OK?'

In fact, when he heard the sirens heading for the dangerous dual carriageway these days, he always said a little prayer. And the prayer was: 'Let it be her. Let her die, and free me from this pain of wanting her.'

Nick Ross was bringing the Wellington 'suicide' to a close. 'Do *you* know anything about the movements of the Sugars that Wednesday night? Did *you* see them make the short walk to the garage near the back of their flat? Were they alone? Did you see *anything* or *anyone* at all suspicious in the area at around about that time?

'If so, do please give us a call. The number to ring is 071 497 3333, or, if you prefer, Wellington, that's 0952 3322. The lines are open until eleven o'clock this evening. And please, remember, the police know that Terry Sugar's dealings weren't all strictly legitimate. But they're not interested in that. They are interested only in the death of him and his wife. Any information you give will be treated in the strictest confidence.'

Ross's assurances of confidentiality were subjected to appropriate derision in the Birmingham police social club where Kavanagh's colleagues awaited their boss's appearance before the nation's TV audience.

Ross handed proceedings over to Sue Cook. Kavanagh slipped into the seat beside her, out of vision, while she introduced Charles Maine from the *Antiques Roadshow* who went through his 'Aladdin's Cave' of recovered stolen property.

When the moment arrived, and the director counted Cook in on her earpiece, she turned to Kavanagh, outlined the stabbing of Lacey that was 'mystifying' the West Midlands force, and the filmed reconstruction began.

When it was over, Cook asked the inspector the couple of questions they had agreed on. He faltered a little, conscious as he was of hearing his own voice, but as his mind addressed the questions, rather than tried to recall the script, he picked up, found his genuine interest in the case, and got through.

His brief ordeal over, she thanked him, and appealed again for help from the public. The inspector was smiling benignly and, before he knew it, Ross was introducing the next item.

Back in hospitality, exhausted by the release of the pent-up tension and surprised at how quickly the seven or eight minutes had passed, Kavanagh and DI Tom Bromage compared notes on their performances.

Vanity satisfied, they eventually discussed the respective cases.

Bromage filled Kavanagh in on the details of the double 'suicide'. What they hadn't revealed on air was that when he was found, Terry Sugar had been sitting in the driving seat.

'So what?' asked Kavanagh.

'He didn't drive,' replied Bromage. 'It's not conclusive, of course, but it's a bit odd.

'Also, there was no note. Everybody leaves a note.' He swilled his Scotch and dry around the tumbler before gulping it down. 'Almost everybody. Especially on a double.'

'Yes, I suppose so,' said Kavanagh.

Bromage poured himself another Scotch and wagged the bottle at Kavanagh.

'Why not?' said the inspector. He always paid his TV licence fee. 'Why not?' They had been through their trial by television and now, in the warm glow of BBC hospitality, free whisky, huge sofas and deep-pile carpets, there was no torment.

'The third point, you'll like this,' said Bromage conspiratorially. 'They left the video set. Now that *would* be a first. Setting the video to record a programme and topping yourself *before* you watch it. Come on! You might top yourself *after* you've watched some of the crap that's on these days, but not before!'

Frank had grown up with the *Wednesday Play*, when it was commonplace for everyone to be talking about it on the way to work or even at school the next day. He remained unfashionably defensive about the once-hallowed institution, and thought the first ad to appear on the BBC would probably be the beginning of the end for the venerable corporation. He eschewed the opportunity to share his view with his Wellington colleague.

'What was it?' asked Kavanagh, intrigued.

'What was what?' replied Bromage.

'That he had recorded? What had they set the video for?'

'Some *Late Show* thing on a jazz bloke. Sugar was a jazz freak. The geezer was called Rollins. Sonny Rollins, a trumpeter, a profile of him.'

Kavanagh had a couple of the saxophonist's records tucked in amongst his John Coltrane, Theolonius Monk, Charlie Mingus and Miles Davis LPs. 'So you reckon they were topped. But why? No theft? No drugs involvement that you can find?'

There was a screeching of tyres as the last reconstruction played on the hospitality-suite monitors. 'Why do blaggers always leave the scene of the crime at eighty miles an hour and drive on the pavement? Don't they realize that if they drove at thirty and stopped for children on pedestrian crossings, they'd attract no more attention than anyone else going to work or down to the shops?'

Frank smiled at Bromage's facetious observation. 'So, what about the Sugars then?'

Bromage moved a few inches closer to Kavanagh on the six-seater leather sofa. 'We're sure they were killed. At least we're dead sure it's not suicide.' He leaned forward as he spoke, put his whisky tumbler on the carpet. 'If you're a junkie and you're going to top yourself, what's the last thing you do?'

The question was rhetorical. He pushed his dark blue jacket sleeve up his arm. 'You give yourself a nice, good-bye fix. The one thing they don't advertise about smack and coke, the one thing they never mention, is that people use them 'cause they make you feel good. For a while.' He sniggered. 'If you're going to kill yourself, why not feel *very* good and inject yourself a big one? Sugar had got plenty in his drawer. But he hadn't had a hit for ages.'

Kavanagh played the devil's advocate. Also, it seemed a reasonable question: 'So why would they get into a car to get killed? They've nothing to lose if they refuse.'

Bromage grew serious. 'Do you remember Amin in the seventies?'

'Of course.'

'I've always remembered reading something really horrible. Not just heads in the fridge and firing squads and bodies in the river. They used to line up poor bastards, and the second poor fucker in line would smash the head of the guy in front of him, and then the third would smash the second, all the way back down the line.'

'Yes,' said Kavanagh, 'horrible. But so what?'

'Why did they do it? You *know* you're next.'

'Why?' asked Kavanagh.

''Cause the guy looking down on you has the gun or

the machete, and if you don't do what he says, you die, not later, but that instant.

'Another minute's life. That's what we're told. Jews hiding in the latrines in the camps, up to their necks in shit. Hanging on. Another minute, another few seconds. *Maybe* the cavalry'll come. They do in the movies. *Maybe* the Russians will break through and open the barbed-wire gates. They will do, one day. It's no good if you've given up the day before. *Maybe* the guy with the gun or machete will have a heart attack, get shot, find religion, see the light, let you off, go home.'

Kavanagh resented the allusion to the Holocaust, even to make a serious point, but his three years at a Catholic primary school had left him with not only the terror of purgatory and eternal hell, but also the notion of sweet redemption: '"Between the stirrup and the ground, he mercy sought, and mercy found,"' said Sister Agnes.

'And that's why these two are prepared to get in a car and get themselves slowly killed?' said Kavanagh, sceptical.

'It's *possible*. That's all I'm saying. It's not suicide, that's for sure.' Bromage picked up his glass and peered into the filmy ginger ale as it swirled with the whisky. 'They were topped. It was original, and it was hands off. But it *was* murder.'

He had kept his ace till last, intending to cast it down with a flourish. But Kavanagh was thoughtful, didn't challenge him.

'You got any cats, Frank?'

Bromage was two or three whiskies ahead of Kavanagh, his boozy familiarity signalled in his use of the other man's forename.

Kavanagh didn't care for cats and their hauteur. He preferred animals with a little dependency. 'No, I don't have a cat,' he said, wondering where the arcane question was leading.

'You know all those wankers with stickers in their cars

– *A dog is for life, not just for Christmas; Meat is Murder* – all that crap. Who do they think is listening?'

Bromage was more drunk than Kavanagh had realized. What was all this about car stickers?

'Do they think a sticker in the back window of a car is going to have any effect on the kind of bloke who breeds dogs for killing, or chucks them out on the motorway?

'Best one I ever saw said: *Rowing, a growing sport*. Now what the fuck's that supposed to mean! *Rowing, a growing sport*. What fucking genius dreamed that up? Does the wanker driving that around on the back of his Maestro think I'm going to read it and go out and buy a boat and start rowing? I mean, if he likes fucking rowing, that's all right, but why's he want *me* to do it?'

Kavanagh didn't fancy the idea of the press (or anyone else) getting hold of the fact that one of the country's top detectives was half-pissed in the *Crimewatch* studios and tried to get back to the point. 'What *about* the cat, Tom?'

'They hadn't fed it, mate. They'd only been in the garage overnight, but when we broke into the house the next morning, the cat was starving. Suicides always feed their animals. Always.' Ross was on his feet doing his close-down piece to camera, reassuring a formerly anxious, now terrified viewing public, who had spent the last three quarters of an hour being vicariously subjected to all sorts of horror and depravity that, in fact, the incidence of violent crime was really very low.

He had once, famously, short of time, decided to drop this little homily from the end of the show. There followed over a thousand calls to the duty officer asking why Ross had not said it, as if, in not hearing it, the public would immediately become even more vulnerable. There might be armed robbers crashing through the studio walls, or anarchists setting the aged commissionaire ablaze, but it was clear that Ross would, for evermore, be expected to deliver his comforting words.

Other officers started to drift in, then the production

people, and eventually the director with her stars, Cook and Ross. The show had gone well. The atmosphere was congenial.

Bromage and Kavanagh took their coffee and returned to the studio where the incoming calls were being sifted and recorded. The lines would remain open for another twenty-four hours, but at 11.15 that night, there would be an 'update' for viewers.

There were the usual number of cranks dialling in who wanted to confess to everything. Many of them sounded plausible, and probably led otherwise blameless lives as bus drivers and accountants and media analysts, but their credibility as murderers or robbers was seriously undermined when they were unable to say exactly what weapon had been used, or what colour dress the hapless victim was wearing on the night of her death.

There were some good leads on a rape case and hard information on an armed robbery in Dorking. But there were only scraps on the Lacey killing: a couple of calls from people who had known the teacher in the past, and who were making themselves known so that they could help if needed. It was an ego thing. The punters liked to be involved, they couldn't wait to make a phone call to *Crimewatch* and tell their neighbours about it the next day. But they were a waste of time. They had nothing to add. The people who had the info generally kept mum. They didn't phone crime shows.

There was one call from someone who had driven down the road on the night in question, and who had noticed someone walking towards the cars parked near the terraced cottages down from the church lych gate.

A senior officer took the caller's number and arranged to visit him in Kidderminster the following day. It wasn't much, but it was something. Under careful questioning, he might remember some details that he didn't even know he had logged.

Kavanagh's initial reaction as he listened in to the

recording of the caller was that he didn't like the fact that the 'suspect' had been walking. It meant one of two things. If you were walking, you either weren't guilty, or you were smart.

If Kavanagh had little, Bromage had less. A few confessor cranks, a couple of people who said they'd scored for Sugar, or from him, none of whom was prepared to give an address or a name.

One caller suggested that someone called Nicky Dolan owed Sugar one, and that the police should check him out. He declined to give his name and slammed down the phone before the trace could be effected. It was probably malice, drop some poor fucker in the shit and waste twenty hours of police time, but they'd check it out.

One loony phoned in to say that someone was parked in *his* place on the night in question. 'A fucking double murder inquiry and the guy's calling about someone parked across his drive,' said Bromage to Kavanagh as they walked down to their cars at midnight. 'He can't get his fucking Skoda in 'cause some tosser's parked his Volvo there.'

Kavanagh had had enough of Tom Bromage; he wanted to get his head down. It was only early autumn, but the night was clear and the wind blew cold around the car park. The BBC building was lit up like a big ship in the night bearing down on the traffic in Wood Lane below it.

The two men shook hands. 'What colour was it?' said Kavanagh.

'What colour was what?' said Bromage.

'The car,' said Kavanagh.

'The Skoda?' guffawed Bromage.

'No,' said Kavanagh, seriously. 'The Volvo.'

Bromage leaned against his car, laughing.

Kavanagh smiled, pulled up his collar and shivered inside his blue cashmere overcoat.

Bromage clambered into the front seat beside his driver.

Kavanagh held the door open and repeated quietly, 'What colour was it, Tom?'

Bromage had stopped laughing. He had his hand on the door pull, but Kavanagh's hand resisted the pressure. Bromage wanted to go. He was tired and half pissed. '*I* don't know, Frank. I didn't ask. Why?'

'It's nothing,' said Kavanagh. He released the door, and said brightly, trying to suggest that the antagonism had been a figment of the drunk's imagination, 'Can I give you a call tomorrow? Check it out for me, will you?'

'Sure,' said Bromage without enthusiasm, and slumped back into the seat as his driver pulled away.

Kavanagh joined his driver and left the Shepherd's Bush studio for the journey home to Birmingham. On the way up the M1 he laid his head on his folded coat in the back seat of the big Ford and watched the green dashboard display until he eventually dropped off to sleep.

Once, instead of phoning or using the post, she had dropped a note through his door in the evening. He had got up to make a drink and seen the envelope lying there. It had driven him mad. She had been that close, and he hadn't known.

Since then, whenever he passed the hall, he always looked down at the mat beneath the letter box. He tried not to do it, but he couldn't stop himself. It had become a fetish.

Back at the house in Erdington, the mat was bare. He checked out the red, unblinking eye of the answering machine, poured himself a treble Bell's, and dialled Presley.

'Hello,' said the sleeping man. 'Who is it?'

'Did you ever see *Strangers on a Train*, Elvis?'

'Fucking hell, you've been on the telly for five minutes, Frank, and now you wanna be a film star! Do you know what time it is?'

'Yes. Have you ever seen it?'

'*Strangers on a Train*? Yes. I think so. The one with the two old duffers who always want to know the test match score?'

'No,' said Kavanagh, sighing. 'That's *The Lady Vanishes. Strangers on a Train* is Hitchcock, too. But it's from a Patricia Highsmith novel. 1951.'

'What is this? The National fucking Film Theatre show or something?'

Frank liked Elvis, he had a natural way with words, knew exactly when to punctuate a sentence with an expletive.

'Bear with it, El. *Strangers* is altogether different stuff. I'll show it you. I've got it on tape. You'll see what I mean.'

'You phoned me at half past two in the morning to ask me if I've seen *Strangers on a* bloody *Train*. And you're going to lend me the video. Thanks, Frank. Thanks a lot.'

'You will, mate. You will. 'Night, 'night. See you in the morning. Sleep tight!'

8

'Bollocks!'

Presley was acting gauche. He didn't have to work too hard at it, thought Kavanagh.

'Absolute bollocks! The one guy's a tennis player . . .'

'Farley Granger . . .' said Kavanagh.

'And wants to top his old man,' continued Presley. 'The other guy's a psychopath—'

'Robert Walker,' interrupted Kavanagh.

'OK, Robert Walker,' added Presley. 'He wants his missis out of the way.'

'You've cracked it, El. I knew you'd get there eventually.'

The sergeant ignored his boss's facetiousness. 'And so they do one another's murders?'

'Right,' said Kavanagh.

'So what?' said Presley.

'It's just the standard thing. Textbook procedure. We always have to look for a motive. If the suspect has a cast-iron, genuine alibi, they're out of the frame. That was the beauty of the thing. Each of the murderers was definitely somewhere else when "his" victim was killed.'

'So they got away with it?'

'Afraid not.'

'Why not?' asked Presley, genuinely interested.

'1951.'

'1951?'

'America. The Hays Code. Came in in the thirties. The

authorities were getting worried about the crime rate, and they reckoned that the movies weren't helping, so they drew up a code of ethics: no stocking tops, no cleavage, no two people of opposite sex on a bed together, and most important of all, Jimmy Cagney and his crew had to come unstuck. From now on in, the good guys had to win.'

'So Farley Granger and Co screw it up?'

'Yes. I can't remember exactly how it goes. Something to do with a fairground, and a little studio lake and a lighter on an island. But that's not the important bit for what I'm saying.'

'What you're saying's bollocks, Frank.'

'I'm not saying that someone did someone else's murder; that's fraught with danger anyway. Both people have to be pretty bright, and yet, paradoxically, unhinged enough to be prepared to kill someone, *and* in cold blood. It's still unusual to find one like that; it's off the scale that you'll find two.'

'Except in the movies,' added Presley slyly.

Kavanagh ignored him. 'At least, I reckon it is. No, what I'm saying is, we've got our Lacey killing here, with no motive, or no apparent motive. And then West Mercia get their exhaust fumes deaths, and there's no motive there.'

'Or no apparent motive,' said Presley.

'Fair enough. No apparent motives for either of them? What's the odds against that, Elvis? They're not random killings. They're executions. Thought out, planned, deliberate. There are none of the obvious suspects: family, girlfriend, boyfriend; nor any of the usual reasons: greed, money problems, insurance scams, inheritance, all that stuff. We've looked at the beneficiaries, there's been no recent topping up on policies, no one's got any treasure maps under the bed. The Sugar couple left less than a grand. The flat was rented.

'Who benefited from Lacey's death?' continued Kavanagh. 'His missis. The endowment pays off the mortgage. Big deal. You saw her at the cemetery. Are you telling me that was a woman who killed her husband so that they wouldn't have to pay the Halifax a couple of hundred a month? No, she's genuine. They had their ups and downs, but she has no more idea why her husband died than we do. So where does that leave us?'

'Tell me, Frank. Where does it leave us?'

Kavanagh ignored the heavy sarcasm. 'I think we've got related crimes, but we just can't see the link. That's what's throwing us.'

'One by gas, the other with a knife; forty miles apart, and you think there's a connection? Come on, Frank!'

'You do better, then,' said Kavanagh. 'I've been in the force twenty years, investigated over thirty murders. I've never had so little to go on. That's fair enough. A first. There's got to be one. But then, within a couple of weeks of it, it transpires there's been another murder, and not a motive or a suspect or a clue to be found. I'm telling you, El, it's too much.'

'So, all we've got is: no connection, no motive, equals a connection? Forget it, Frank. It won't stand up.'

'Do better,' challenged Kavanagh.

'You're off the wall, Frank,' said Presley.

'They were both on Wednesdays, similar times as far as we can tell, mid-evening.'

'There's a Wednesday every seven days. Two murders on a Wednesday don't make a pattern,' said Presley.

Kavanagh ignored the cavil and continued. 'There's the blue Volvo parked in the Skoda bloke's usual place near the Sugar murders in Wellington. And the old woman down the road from the Lacey stabbing picked out a Volvo 244 as being a contender for the car she saw parked outside her cottage on the night Lacey died.'

'She's seventy-eight years old, Frank. There *were* no cars when she was born.'

'Come on, Kev, there's no need to stick it on.'

'Seriously, have you seen the thickness of her glasses? You could skate on them. Can you imagine what a defence would do with her on the witness stand? And anyway, she also picked out a Maestro and a Ford.'

'Well, at least she knows it was blue, whatever it was. Will you accept that?'

'Yes, I will, as long as you accept it doesn't mean a thing.'

'I want you to put one of the lads on Volvo import figures.'

'Going back how far?'

'As long as the 244's been on the market here.'

'Do you know how many Volvos that is, Frank?'

'No, of course I don't, but we're going to. Look on the bright side, El. It's only 244s we're interested in. The guy with the Skoda was a good witness . . .'

'Yes, I bet he was. I'd always trust the judgement of someone who buys a Skoda. So, what do you want me to do next?' asked Presley, acknowledging his superior's rank, even if unconvinced by his argument.

'We do all we can: start checking blue Volvos, then we'll find out where they are. Concurrently we log and cross-reference every single detail on the two murders. And then everything on the victims. Add anything unsolved and apparently motiveless that's come up recently. Find the link. It's there somewhere.

'We'll start with the last three months. Feed in everything: method of killing, geography, gender, age, wealth, what paper the victim read, what car they drove, everything, and we look for any connection between these apparently unconnected, motiveless murders. And when we find that connection, we'll find the motive, and then we'll nip out and pick up the killer.'

'They'll never wear it; the boys'll laugh you out.'

'They can laugh all they like. They either come up with something better, or they can start feeding in everything, and I mean *everything*: what Lacey had for breakfast; where he went on his holidays in 1983; why he watched

Coronation Street only on Mondays. Get it all in, and we'll find the link.'

'You're going for this, Frank? You really want this done?'

'Run the figures on homicide, Kev. Have a look at them for the last six months. Take out the fracas and affray and domestics; pull the drug-related and aggravated burglary; weed the sex-related ones and see what you're left with.'

'Take out all those, mate, and there *won't* be anything left.'

'That's my point. Have a look. It won't leave many.'

Presley had exhausted his arguments. He walked over to the far wall, pulled out his wallet, took a twenty-pound note and stapled it to the notice board. 'Pattern be bollocksed. Here's a score says you're up the wrong tree.'

Kavanagh joined him, and put two tens beside the mauve note. 'There's a connection, El. My "little man" says so.'

'Little man?' said Presley.

'Don't you ever watch proper films?' said Kavanagh. 'Edward G. Robinson; *Double Indemnity*. 1944. Husband apparently falls to his death. The insurance company has got to pay out, a "double indemnity". It all fits. But Edward G. just *knows* it isn't right. His "little man" nags away at him, won't let go, gets at him, right in the guts.'

'And?' said Presley.

'And eventually Fred McMurray and Barbara Stanwyck get nobbled,' said Kavanagh.

Presley was more a *Nine and a Half Weeks* and *Basic Instinct*, use-the-freeze-frame-button kind of man. 'The only little man you've got's between your legs, and you'd do better playing with him than having us count bloody Volvos.'

'Yes, you may be right, Kev,' said the inspector thoughtfully.

Presley was surprised by the conciliatory tone. Was reason going to prevail?

Kavanagh walked over to the open door. 'But look,' he said, and pointed to the sign on the door: *Detective Inspector Frank Kavanagh*. 'For the time being, if I want us to count cars, we count cars.'

9

'Just tell me, whenever we're looking for a suspect motor, why is it the most popular car on the road, in the most popular fucking colour?' said Ray Merson.

Detective Constable Michael Gilks was a literalist, a graduate psychologist from Reading University with a 2:2 Honours degree, but his three years at the Berkshire university had not included a module on rhetorical hyperbole, and he therefore failed to recognize it even when its use was clearly signalled.

'It's statistics, Ray,' Gilks began patiently. He'd once explained to his colleague the complex mathematical reason why you need only twenty-five people in a room for two of them to share the same birth date. Ray Merson, a graduate, not of university, but of Hendon Police College, had been impressed, and over supper that evening tried to explain the principle to his young wife. He quickly got bogged down and, as soon as she recognized this, she stopped listening and used the remote control to bring up the volume on *East Enders*.

Gilks continued, undaunted, as they drove up the M54 from Birmingham, 'If there are more Sierras on the road than anything else, the *probability* is that it'll be a Sierra we're looking for.' He paused, concentrated on the road ahead as he overtook a huge yellow and blue Hungarian truck and its trailer. The manoeuvre completed, Gilks said, 'Let's count ourselves lucky it's *not* a Sierra. It could be worse than this, believe me!'

Merson stole a glance at his colleague's face, but there was no suggestion of irony there.

Half an hour later they parked their unmarked car on the forecourt of the Esso station on the old A5 outside Shrewsbury, and the two young men went into the brightly lit garage that sold everything from fruit and vegetables to flowers and compact discs.

Merson showed his warrant card to the girl perched behind the high counter. 'Police, love, we phoned earlier. It's about the video recording.'

'Oh, yes, I've got it here.' She slipped off her stool, reached behind her, and passed the policeman the black plastic cartridge.

'Thanks. We'll let you have it back as soon as possible.'

They were visiting every large garage within a ten-mile radius of Wellington. Most of them had video-surveillance cameras running twenty-four hours a day, and Ray Merson and his partner had the unenviable task of collecting and then viewing these hours and hours of excruciatingly dull monochrome film in their boss's hunt for a blue Volvo 244, registration number unknown.

And all this because an old lady down the road from the parish centre where John Lacey had died thought that there had been a car parked outside her house that night that might have been a Volvo.

And, weeks after the deaths of Terry and Jeanette Sugar in Wellington, a Skoda owner had phoned *Crimewatch* to say he had left a note on the windscreen of a blue 244 asking its owner not to park in 'his' place.

Frank Kavanagh had been charmed by the notion that this quaint practice was still extant in rural counties: it was like using a carrier pigeon in an era when every roofer and truck driver had a mobile phone; or taking a rattle, amidst the racist and anti-Semitic terrace abuse, to a football match. You'd as likely get coshed or shot if you asked someone in an inner-Birmingham suburb not to park in 'your' place on a public road.

Presley was still awaiting the actual production figures from the Swedish motor giant, but you didn't have to be a car buff to know that the Two series had been on sale for ever.

Originally, ownership of the austere saloon by idiosyncratic bank managers had implied, if not exactly a penchant for naturist holidays, at least a predilection for narrow-boating on English canals, rather than the dubious charms of two weeks in Torremolinos.

Since those early days, ownership of the determinedly non-aerodynamic ton of Swedish steel had percolated down to teachers, civil servants and draughtsmen, and the car had lost a little of its Scandinavian mystique.

And indeed, for a good few years now, older models, vile, mustard paintwork rusting, but their tough Nordic chassis still intact, had found their way onto the less salubrious council estates of the country, where they changed hands for two or three hundred pounds, their new owners actually bragging about how many times around the clock the venerable beast had been.

Whatever the figure, Volvo 244s had been rolling across the cold North Sea in their thousands for nearly twenty years now. That was a lot of cars. But a couple of sightings of a blue car, possibly a Volvo, was all they had.

Needle in a haystack? Sheet of metal in a foundry? Merson and Gilks in a Shropshire garage. It was routine police work. And it was what it was all about.

Kavanagh was desperate for the inquiry to move. His motives were less than pure. It was over two weeks since Rachael had been in touch with him. His ego bruised, he wondered how she could cope without him. Not cope in the sense of go to her office and show houses to her clients and get the shopping, but really cope; be without him, completely, after all these years.

They had grown apart, lost touch with one another, but then, that fateful night, when she had said, 'I've got something to tell you. I think we should part,' he had been shaken; his being rocked to the core.

In truth, there had been a little irresistible euphoria that had accompanied the shock of her words. A danger, a raw freshness that he had not known for years. It was giddying and he, so often in control, had enjoyed the initial exhilarating sensation of free fall.

He had, after all, known that this separation was where their relationship was heading. Had known it for months and months now. But she had wrested the initiative, put the plan into action with her dozen words. My God, it was happening.

He was in shock: his reason told him that this is what he had known would happen. But now, it *was* happening. Only the tense had changed. The hypothesis, so frequently imagined, even courted, was now reality.

He felt like the man who had hung on to the rope, trying with the others on that grainy Zeppelin film, to keep the airship on the ground. Seeing the danger, they had let go, fallen a few feet to the earth. He had hung on, a sort of stubborn perversity precluding his letting go.

And now he was fifty, seventy, a hundred feet in the air and could no longer let go. It was terrifying.

His heart said: No, stop this. But his head said: Yes, this is it. This is how it feels. It's new and different, of course. But hang on. And with every moment that passed, the earth was further away and he knew he could no longer jump back.

He had lit a cigarette. Put the lighter down on the floor and heard himself saying to her, inanely, 'Five for a pound. How can they make lighters that sell for five for a pound?'

He took comfort within a week of her going. There was a systems analyst; she was a civilian, a divorcee. They'd given one another the once-over at a couple of things they'd worked on together. He had been still married; she had been 'free'. Her look and manner had said, 'Yes, if you like.' And he'd been wistful and thought, 'What if?' in the same way that he used secretly to read the contact ads in the press.

And then he *had* been free, and of course, it was very different. He knew he should take some time. See what was grief, and what was pain and what was shock and what was habit. And he did none of these things but rang her and asked her out to dinner.

He heard the hesitation in her voice. It wasn't like this before, when he was married, unhappy, or at least not happy, but safe. Then, there always seemed to be women working on inquiries, and he looked, and they looked, and it looked easy.

Between the actual words she was speaking, she was implying, 'What's up? What's happened? What's changed?'

He answered her with an affirmation he didn't feel; tried to suggest everything was OK.

They met in a city-centre pub and he drank too much. He had resolved not to get maudlin.

He told her, glossing the truth of Rachael's final, dramatic initiative in leaving, that they had agreed to part. Yes, he admitted, when it finally happened, it was a shock. (A certain amount of feeling, he judged, would appear appropriate to the situation. He didn't want to appear callous.)

He tried hard to imagine what a genuine mutually agreed parting would have been like, and adopt the appropriate demeanour. It was hard, like reading a prepared script at the same time as feeling something entirely different, the mental and verbal equivalent of performing the circular motion with your hand on your tummy while the other hand patted your head. He had never been able to do that either.

He drank more. The only thing that helped him was her appearance. In the worst scenario that he had conjured, he wouldn't even fancy her any more, she would be metamorphosed into a plain and unattractive woman.

In fact, he found her alluring. Later, they went back to her flat off Hagley Road, near Five Ways. She made coffee and he slouched on the sofa and drunkenly hummed along to Nina Simone. There was even a moment where he believed that this *was* what it was all about: a meal, drinks, a different environment, an attractive woman, a *new* woman, one whose smell and body and touch he did not yet know.

Later, in bed, her kisses were deep and hungry and were accompanied by little murmurs of passion.

With every movement of their bodies her orgasm appeared imminent, but after several minutes of this nearly state, and recognizing his own imminent, urgent need, she opened her eyelids, rolled her wild eyes headboard-wise and said firmly, 'Wait.'

He obeyed. Was afraid not to. But the effort was great and the tried and tested methods of delay were chilly water to the natural heat of his sexual arousal.

Eventually, in spite of his mandatory detachment from the proceedings, he found his natural rhythm again and uttered a gruff imperative that left her in no doubt that now was the moment.

As he finally gave in to his urgent needs, she embarked upon some very loud and impressive groans which, he felt confident, must have impressed her neighbours no end.

But alas, although the folk on the other side of the wall cannot have been anything but satisfied with the couple's performance Liz, apparently, was not.

His quiet sighs of satisfaction were in vain. His feigned light sleep and benign smile, signs of *his* sexual repletion, studiously ignored.

He was made sorrowfully aware that there was unfinished business, the completion of which he was required to play some central part in.

Ten minutes later, she squeezed his hand and murmured, 'Goodnight.' Eventually, they slept.

The next day, comforted, he felt more keenly than ever that he was in danger of falling apart. His life was like watching a film of himself. The events of the previous evening had no more actuality for him than anything else that had happened in the preceding week: alienation, detachment from reality, and an unsettling sense of *déjà vu* that went on for hours, sometimes half a day.

When would it end, he wondered? He knew one thing: he certainly shouldn't be supervising a murder inquiry; sending detectives out, using valuable resources and hugely expensive overtime man-hours; setting up lines of inquiry; commandeering computers and technical resources; pursuing a car that was in the area on the night of a killing, and may have been seen elsewhere on the night of another.

He monitored Presley's reactions to him and his handling of the case. True, Presley thought he was out on a limb on the connection between the different murders. But they'd often differed on cases in the past. There *was* disquiet on the ship, but the officers weren't yet storming the bridge. They were still some way from open mutiny. Or so he thought. But how reliable was his perception of the unfolding events, he asked himself in his frequent moments of anxiety.

He was certain that he should take some leave. But leave was like money. When you had it, you didn't know what to do with it or, like all the famously rich, immediately found that it wasn't what you wanted anyway.

The apparent heart's desire had a faulty valve and sent pop stars in search of the rainforest Indians instead of a clever riff. The Roddicks went looking for a face cream; Branson went fast in boats and planes; Bardot saved the animals; Ginger Baker rode to hounds; Daltrey farmed fish.

No, he couldn't take leave. What would he do? Sit at

home and watch daytime television? Lie horizontal on the sofa, watch Channel Four racing and think about her, how much he missed her, and how much he wanted her back?

Set up in a basement room at the station headquarters, a monitor and a VCR in front of them, Merson and Gilks ran the garage tapes through on fast forward. They had been specifically instructed not to do this, but it was *they* who were suffering the narcoleptic tedium of watching hundreds of hours of Shropshire garage forecourts on black and white, poor-definition tape.

They could tell the rush hours of the day as the traffic built up, and then slowed down again until lunch time. Business picked up again at about 4.30.

There were a few Volvo 340s and 360s: the model had picked up the dubious notoriety that had once belonged to the Austin Allegro: assume the worst from their invariably elderly drivers.

There was a white 244 and an estate car, but no blue saloon throughout the day of the Sugar murders. At 17.38.53 (would it never just be 'nearly twenty to six' again, Merson wondered) a young lad and his girlfriend drove off in their battered Escort without paying, the number plate visible as he did so.

The two young men had their eyes on the rows of pumps: leaded, unleaded, diesel, as the images flicked by. It was wearing on the eyes.

'Stop it,' said Merson suddenly, and pulled his feet down from the desk. 'Rewind it.'

Gilks put his finger on the rewind button on the remote control. It was images such as these, not long ago, that had made people laugh out loud. No one even grinned now: the notion was as jaded as polystyrene ceiling tiles.

Merson leaned towards the screen as the cars reversed up to the pumps. It was a busy time of day. The shuddering white figures in the top left-hand corner of the screen said 18.17.

Gilks watched impassively as the BMWs and Renaults and Rovers came back to the pumps as the tape was rewound. Merson took the handset from his colleague and hit the pause button.

Gilks looked at the cars at the pumps. 'So what?'

'Look behind,' said Merson, and pointed at the airline in the far corner of the picture. A man was crouched at the front wheel of a big dark Volvo. Merson moved the shaky image on, one frame at a time. The man moved to the rear tyre and checked it, then the far side of the car. As he inflated the tyres, his back was to the camera. Could he possibly be doing it on purpose? Or was he an innocent driver checking his tyres?

Merson edged the tape on, frame by frame. The driver got in, fastened his seat belt, and drew slowly away, out of camera. They waited for him to reappear, to draw up to the pumps. Other cars arrived. The figures in the top left-hand corner of the screen flicked on: 18.25; 18.30; 18.33. Nothing happened. They waited and waited.

They rewound the tape another quarter of an hour to see if they had missed the man at the pumps on their first viewing. Nothing.

'The cheeky bastard,' said Merson eventually. 'He's one of those tossers who does his tyres, and doesn't buy any bloody petrol.'

But they were both pleased. They had a little shaky something-nothing. And it just *might* be something.

10

The young men's professional sang-froid precluded their beaming openly, but there was a certain something about their demeanour as they sat together in the incident room that said they were definitely the pussies who had today's cream on their whiskers.

Kavanagh's notion of a killer or killers perpetrating apparently unrelated murders, an idea never embraced with much enthusiasm by most of the officers, had begun to wear perilously thin with his colleagues.

To lighten the tone of the log-jammed inquiry, he'd even got hold of a couple of videos of *Strangers on a Train*. A lot of jokes followed: someone pinned a mug-shot of a Farley Granger lookalike on the inspector's desk; they started following the tennis stories on the sports pages and clipping items for him.

The barracking had been good-natured, but barely disguised the feelings of many of the detectives that not only were they barking up the wrong tree, but they were probably in the wrong forest.

Now, Kavanagh stood out front, the initiative, for the time being at least, back with him. Presley leaned against the pillar by the side of the flip charts. Kavanagh began. 'OK, folks, Gilks and Merson have got something. It might not be a hill of beans, but it could be something. Over to you, Kev.'

Presley arched his back, and said, 'As part of the search for a vehicle which was definitely at the scene of the Wellington murders, and may have been' – he stole a quick glance towards his boss – 'around on the night of *our* killing, Detective Constables Gilks and Merson have been down on our colleagues' patch in West Mercia collecting garage surveillance tapes.

'Naturally, we had to clear all this with Mercia's Chief Constable. Their own DI in charge of the Wellington killings, Tom Bromage, is not absolutely convinced that there's a connection between their murders and ours, but was quite happy, as long as we were discreet and shared everything we got, for our lads to be on their turf. It was, at the worst, going to do no harm, and at best, if anything came of it, would save them lots of overtime.

'So, ploughing through this year's entries for the Garage Forecourt Oscars, this is what we've got.' He nodded to Rees at the back of the room, who flicked off the lights, and then played the video recording on the trolley-mounted video monitor.

When the couple of minutes of relevant tape had been played through he handed back to his boss. The lights came up and Kavanagh started. 'It *may* be nothing. But it's Wednesday, the 15th September, the day before they found the Sugars' bodies. The bloke's in a Volvo 244. The technical boys are doing what they can with a copy of it, trying to enhance the quality.

'They may be able to ascertain the colour of the car by repeating the filming with half a dozen different model colours and then comparing them with this, but it all takes for ever, and there are other factors involved, like the age and wear and deterioration of this tape, compared with the one they use, and the amount of wear on the tape heads when this was recorded, but they're doing what they can for us.'

Using the handset, he froze the frame of the figure kneeling at his tyres. 'It's difficult to see much of the bloke. They're doing some estimates through reconstructions using models of similar sizes to try and get his height and weight.

'He's thin and tall and wearing a jacket and jeans, quite conventionally dressed, boots rather than shoes, could be suede, no shine or reflection.

'As I say, it might be nothing, but it might be the break we're looking for. It's the right car, at the right time.

'Finally, we've got something from the SOCO people. They've isolated part of a footprint in Sugar's garage that's neither his nor his wife's. Terry Sugar was a dainty soul (pun intended), size seven. This is a size ten, right foot. It's a casual shoe, or desert boot, not a trainer, some sort of welted sole. They're working on that.

'It's recent, but it's still a long shot. Being a dope head, there may be all sorts of lowlifers coming and going scoring a bit of NHS smack or methadone. But it's something.

'Anyway, let's hear it for Merson and Gilks. The boys done good, and it *could* come to something.' There was some mock cheering and jeering as the men acknowledged their boss's plaudits.

Presley took over again. 'Any questions on that before we go on to the stuff we've been feeding in for the correlations on murders and victims?'

'What about the video cameras on the motorway? Can't we pick up the driver and his car on those?'

'Good question, Reeder. Unfortunately, they haven't got them on the M54. It's a bit primitive up there; England's rural motorway. Goes from somewhere to nowhere: no services, no petrol, no food. It's like things used to be. If it doesn't work, they can close it down and open it again as a museum. Anyway, no video cameras. Part of the government's cutbacks, I suppose.

'We've been running the stuff on the M6 that joins it near junction ten, but there's so much, it's taking for ever. But we're working on it. Anything else?'

There were no further questions. 'The other side to the inquiry is feeding in everything on the victims and the murders to try and find any correlation. Both male victims, John Lacey and Terry Sugar, were in their mid-forties. Jeanette Sugar was a couple of years younger. Methods of killing, as we know, couldn't have been more different.

'Both murders were on Wednesday evenings, around about the same time. And yes, thanks to our own Patrick Moore, stargazer Detective Constable Tim Youle, it has been pointed out that they were within a day or two of a new moon.'

Immediate barracking and whistling followed. Presley held up his hands for quiet, but smiled at the notion that the phases of the moon were likely to have any bearing on the murders in hand.

When quiet had returned he continued: 'Tim says that it's not that the guy's a werewolf or a cloven-footer or anything, it's just that there's some folk who, well, are prone to certain kinds of behaviour, tend to be more susceptible to the moon's influence. Have I got it right, Tim?'

Youle acknowledged the sergeant's attempt at summarizing his knowledge of lunar influences: an increase in civil unrest, instability in prisons and mental homes; the silent power of the ocean's tides.

Young Donna Moss, on her first major inquiry, expressing the thoughts of many of the men and women in the room said, 'The differences are more significant than the similarities, surely?'

'Go on,' said Presley.

'The one man's an art teacher: middle class, professional; the other's a smack addict, a street trader. One's stabbed; the others are forced into a car and gassed. The one guy has a grown-up child; the other couple are childless. The Sugars live in Wellington, Shropshire; Lacey in a Birmingham suburb. The one guy's got a bit in the bank; the other one's living in a rented flat, has been for years. Shall I go on?'

Kavanagh stepped forward. He knew he was in danger

of losing the initiative. He'd thought the sighting of the car might swing things back his way. They were unimpressed. He was fulfilling his own prophecy, making the 'facts' fit his hunch-based hypothesis.

'Look, I'll say what I've said before. The last year for which we've got figures, there were seven hundred and twenty-six homicides. Half of those were killed in arguments or fights. Half of the female victims were killed by the bloke they were involved with. Most of the deaths were of children aged under one year. Put it another way, the "no suspect" victim was involved in only eleven per cent of the killings; of these, most were manslaughters. You can count the "no-obvious-suspect" murders on the fingers of one hand.

'Put those figures against the *apparently* motiveless murders, committed within forty miles of one another, on the same night of the week and within just four weeks of each other. Plus, there's a better than evens possibility there's a Volvo car connection. Add all that together and there's more of a link than Donna and the rest of you are suggesting.'

There was a polite but recalcitrant silence in the room. The video recorder's green figures flicked relentlessly on and off. The inquiry was in the balance. Kavanagh only just believed in what he was doing himself.

'We're sticking with it. We'll wait on the forensic and the video enhancement. We're digging further back into the victims' backgrounds, and we've got a couple of things to follow up from the TV show: someone who reckoned he'd got something on Sugar that Mercia have checked out, but we'll have a look, too.'

'And if nothing comes up?' said DC Denny.

'Maybe there'll be another "unexplained", and maybe there'll be the other half of a size ten at the scene. I dunno,' said the inspector. 'Stick with it. For now at least.'

'Sir,' said Tim Youle.

'Youle?' said Kavanagh.

'It's a full moon next Saturday. If we're logging unexplaineds, it might be a good idea for us to watch that day or two with particular care.'

'Sure,' said Kavanagh. 'Sure.'

11

The Sugars had died intestate.

Terry and Jeanette Sugar did have surviving relatives. But her aged mother was in a nursing home in Dawley, suffering from Alzheimer's disease and on a remorseless slide into oblivion.

On her daughter's weekly visits, they would sit together, and her mother would speak her garbled sentences, and often ask Jeanette when she, her daughter who was sitting beside her, bony hand enclosed in hers, was coming.

'I'm here, Mum. I *am* Jeanette. I'm here now, with you.'

Her mother would look about her and say nothing. A few minutes later, she would say, 'Our Jean's coming today. Is she here yet?'

And so it went on. 'Second childishness . . . mere oblivion.'

The 74-year-old would certainly be unable to comprehend the death of her only daughter.

Terry Sugar had a distant cousin living in the south of the country, in East Grinstead. The two men hadn't been in touch for over thirty years.

There was a flicker of avarice when the combined wit of the police, National Insurance office and the solicitor appointed to deal with their 'estate' tracked the man down to his home in Sussex. But any pecuniary interest quickly evaporated as the macabre nature of the deceased's death and his drug-dependent lifestyle was outlined to Sugar's corpulent cousin.

Reginald Sugar made it absolutely clear that he wanted nothing whatsoever to do with this part of his family. 'I'm a businessman. You saw the vans outside; I'm in central heating. It's taken me over twenty years to get this far. I employ a dozen blokes, an accountant, a secretary and a part-time wages clerk. How do you think it'd look in the local papers if this came out? I don't want anything to do with drugs and murder. I just can't afford it.' The man had a point.

The Sugars' solicitor communicated this to the local council, who proceeded with the funeral of the couple as soon as the police and the coroner had released the bodies.

An open verdict was recorded, and the ground-floor flat in the Victorian terraced house in Newport Road was secured against vandals and squatters pending its emptying and eventual reletting.

Going through the personal effects and belongings of any deceased person was a sobering task, and one that usually fell to council employees when no next of kin or beneficiary could be found to undertake it.

However, if the deaths were being treated as suspicious, it was police officers who had the unenviable job of filling thick plastic sacks with the detritus of a lifetime: photographs, letters, books, diaries, china and linen, pyjamas and bathing costumes, socks and underwear.

DI Tom Bromage's West Mercia force had already conducted a fruitless trawl through the couple's belongings in their search for clues to the deaths.

With his Shropshire colleague's reluctant permission, Kavanagh now sent in four of his own officers to see if they could discover anything that their colleagues had failed to.

'I want them to check everything, and I mean *everything,*' Kavanagh said sternly to Presley. 'We've only got one shot at this before the flat is closed down and their stuff's disposed of. It's got to be thorough. Tell them not to ignore anything that might be of any help, anything that doesn't make sense or looks odd. Anything: all right?'

'Sure,' said Presley. He flicked his eyes up to the forty pounds pinned to the notice board and flashed his boss a quick smile. 'Anything at all, Frank.'

DC Tim Youle sat at the little oak bureau and leafed through the letters and documents in the drawers there. Terry and Jeanette Sugar had not been great correspondents: there were letters from the council about window repairs and rent arrears; council tax demands; home contents insurance pitches and book club offers.

Perched on the arm of the moquette sofa, Youle read every letter as if, at some point, out of the humdrum contents, might lurch a name or a phrase, something, anything, that might throw light on the reasons for the deaths of the former occupants of the flat.

Two hours later, the drawers were empty, their contents stuffed into the plastic bag between his legs, and Tim Youle was still in his darkness.

Terry Sugar had been one of any number of prisoners who start doing education courses inside. He was bright, had the quick wit of the street trader that he was, and which might, in other circumstances, have conferred upon him a very different life.

He had started the Open University Arts Foundation course when he was doing nine months in Stafford in the mid-eighties for handling stolen goods.

Lots of prisoners dabbled with training inside; it passed their time and bestowed privileges. And, while smuggling hacksaw blades into prisons in birthday cakes to facilitate prisoners' escapes was considered very bad form, midlife sociology lecturers becoming romantically involved with their prisoner tutees was, if not the norm, by no means unusual.

There were, it appeared, women everywhere (men too, presumably, down the road at Holloway or wherever), who found a vicarious pleasure in this rough trade, thrilled to talk of heists and blaggings across prison tables, an hors d'oeuvre to more conventional sweet nothings on conjugal pillows.

Of course, most prisoners ceased their work on these, and any other, courses, as soon as they crossed the threshold of the prison gates. But a few, most famously the Jimmy Boyles and John McVicars, premier-league gangsters with tough, Barlinnie pedigrees, were accorded the ultimate accolade, the Prix Goncourt of prison celebrity: they made a page in the tabloids as they emerged with not only a university degree, but a sociologist/philosopher wife as well.

Detective Constable Andy Reeder, halfway through his own Open University law degree, was assigned the job of ploughing through Sugar's TMAs and assignments, and the associated computer-generated correspondence that had such a wearisome familiarity about it.

Reeder often told his friends: There's no need to phone Samaritans or join book clubs or send for free offers to newspapers. If you're lonely enrol for an OU course: never a day passes without a brown envelope dropping through your letter box with course information, counselling, assignments or student magazines.

Mindful of his instructions to be thorough, while DC Youle and DC Moss went through wardrobes and dressers and cabinets, Reeder opened the buff folders and glanced at the essays there: Shakespeare; T. S. Eliot; Auden; Gombrich's *Story of Art*. He scanned the letters from Milton Keynes with their details about examinations and essays and summer school arrangements for 1985.

DC Denny sat in the front room and went through the man's dark blue address book. She stuck a leaf of paper in the 'M's': entered after his GP's name, Dr Meriden, and his telephone number, and before Movies-in, a Wellington video rental store, was the enigmatic entry MND (SC) and a Shrewsbury code and number.

Back at the station, while Kavanagh was ensconced with the chief superintendent, and putting as favourable a gloss as he could on the scant progress being made on the inquiry, Youle, Moss, Reeder and Denny briefed Presley on the blank that *they* had drawn at the Sugars' flat.

Finally, Denny showed the sergeant the peculiar entry in Sugar's address book.

The dialling tone picked up and the phone began to ring. Three; four. When she was at home, and the phone caught her in the lavatory or the shower or down the garden, Denny always counted the double rings. Three; four; the pessimistic caller was considering one's not being there. Five; impatient contacts might hang up. Six; lots of people put the phone down. Seven or eight; all but the most persistent gave up.

The phone rang on; seven; eight. *They* were police. Nine; ten. This was work. They were paid for this. She let it ring on. The men around her had lost interest.

They were like the people who start to drift away from the ground, their team beaten. Eleven . . . suddenly the receiver was picked up.

'Hello,' said Denny.

It's injury time, but a faintly promising move has begun down the wing. Of course, the cross will be too long, or the fullback's tackle sweet, or the referee's whistle will blow, but they turn anyway, and wait. Presley and Youle and Reeder sauntered back towards the desk as she spoke.

'Hello?' said Denny again.

'Hello,' said the voice at the other end.

She raised her severely plucked eyebrows at her colleagues, and repeated, 'Hello, who is this, please?'

The sound of the receiver being clunked from one hand to another. 'Hello,' said a different, louder, more confident voice. 'This is Lianne.' Laughter. Excited, childish, playful laughter.

Denny could think of nothing to say. 'What's your friend's name, Lianne?'

'Jane,' came the unembellished answer.

'Where are you?' said the DC.

The laughter became hysterical.

When it subsided, she asked again, 'Where are you speaking to me from, Lianne?'

'The Precinct.'

'The Precinct? Where's that?'

'In Shewsbury.' (The 'r' had been dropped.)

'What are you doing there, Lianne?'

'Shopping.'

'Is it a public phone? A call box?'

'Yes. It was ringing so we answered it,' she said defensively.

'It's all right. You haven't done anything wrong,' Denny reassured her. 'Thank you, Lianne. Goodbye,' and she replaced the receiver.

'What do you reckon?' asked Presley.

'Sugar spoke to MND (SC) at a public call box in Shrewsbury. Maybe the person didn't have a phone? Or maybe they wanted to speak to the caller secretly, away from their own home. Who knows?' said Denny. 'Does anybody remember when itemized bills came in?' she continued.

'Check with BT,' said Presley. 'I think it was three or four years ago. But get them to send you copies of the Sugars' bills going back as far as they can.'

'It's not much of an anagram. No vowel,' said Reeder, as he played with the letters on his pad. 'They must stand for something. It *is* vaguely familiar.'

'Give the video store a ring,' said Presley to DC Youle.

'What for?' said the DC to his boss. 'You want to see a film?'

'Ask them when Sugar joined. You have to be a member, don't you? If we see when he joined, assuming he fills in his address book like everyone else in the world, we'll at least know that he *knew* MND (SC) before that time.

'And then call Dr Meriden or whatever he's called and see how long Sugar was registered with him. It'll give us a couple of dates within which we'll at least know that he must've met the initials person. It's not great, but it might be something.'

While Denny contacted British Telecom, Youle got through to the Asian owner of the Wellington video store.

The man was suspicious. Didn't understand what it was they wanted to 'clarify a point' about, doubted that they were the police. He knew of the Sugars' violent deaths, everyone in the little Shropshire town did.

Carrying his portable phone with him, he peered hopelessly out of his front window, thought it must be a practical joke. But he was a serious man, a man with few friends, who worked long hours and didn't really *know* about practical jokes, except for the ones that he saw played in the films that ran on the video recorder all day long in his shop. The man they were asking about *had* died. It had been in the *Shropshire Star*. Maybe it *was* the police.

He tapped Sugar's name into the grubby computer on the counter. Up came his address, telephone and membership number. 'He joined in April 1987,' said the man. 'Is that all?'

'Thank you,' said DC Youle, and put down the phone.

Denny tore off the faxes as they came in. When the machine had stopped its regurgitation, she came and reported to her colleagues. 'Itemized came in in Shropshire in 1990. There's nothing to our Shrewsbury call-box number between then and the latest bill. These are their bills for the last ten years though.' And after a pause, 'Eerie, isn't it, all that information logged away, just like that.'

'Do they tell us anything?' said Presley, ignoring the youngster's naïve observation.

'They're for very similar amounts,' said the DC. 'Except for one, which is nearly twice as much as the others. It's the only bleep.'

'Any ideas?' said Presley.

'None,' said Denny, wondering if this was some sort of Socratic dialogue, the unravelling of which the wise sergeant would reveal in the course of his peripatetic questioning.

'Which quarter?' he asked.

Denny leafed through the sheaf of faxed bills.

'Autumn. Dated October 1985. It's the bill for the period July to September '85.'

'So, what did you say, Tim, he's been registered with his doctor for twelve years? He's been a member of the video rental shop since '87. So he got to know MND between '81 and '87, which at least coincides with a heavy bill in '85.'

'Five years,' scoffed Denny. 'It's not enough, nowhere near. We can't link a big bill with that person just on that basis.'

'No, of course we can't,' said Presley. 'But it's an acorn, and at the moment I'll settle for that.'

Reeder stood in the doorway at the far end of the room and said,

> 'For aught that ever I could read,
> Could ever hear by tale or history,
> The course of true love never did run smooth.'

'What the fucking hell's up with you?' said the insouciant sergeant.

Reeder ignored his boss, walked to the blackboard and printed the words: *'Midsummer Night's Dream'*.

'Are you all right?' said Presley, his patience with the constable's performance wearing thin.

Reeder picked up the blackboard eraser and deleted the letters that followed the initials of each word. All that remained on the board was 'M' . . . 'N' . . . 'D'.

'Nice one, Andy. *Midsummer Night's Dream.* Shakespeare

play. So what? What does it mean? And what about the SC on the end? Where's that gone?'

'I *knew* I knew those letters. I've done the play myself. Everyone does it on the Arts Foundation course. It's the set text. I've abbreviated it every time I've taken tutorial notes or written a draft essay on it. I knew it rang a bell.'

'So, what do you reckon, then?' said Presley.

'Sugar went to OU summer school at Keele in 1985. I reckon he met someone there, had an affair with them, and he's entered her in his address book as MND . . . *Midsummer Night's Dream.*' He paused, and added conspiratorially, 'It's *A Midsummer Night's Dream,* actually . . .'

'Maybe it was!' interrupted Presley.

'And I bet if we check it out, we'll find there was someone there at the same time, with the initials SC,' said Reeder.

'Good work, Andy. So what now?'

'I thought maybe Denny and I might go down to Milton Keynes and see how many SCs were at Keele that summer.'

12

They didn't have to wait for Saturday evening's full moon. Adam Curtiss was on his way to see his mother in Leamington Spa on the late Friday afternoon train. His body was found beside the track the following morning. He had fallen from the inter-city from London between Rugby and Coventry. It had probably been dark. The clocks had gone back only the previous weekend. British summer time was over.

British Rail launched an immediate inquiry; they had been losing too many passengers falling from trains in recent months, and questions were being asked in the House about the effects of financial cutbacks and the deleterious effect they might be having on passenger safety. There were a lot of Labour Party mutterings about cutting corners as the next big target was softened up for privatization.

The police were involved at an early stage. The man was sober and had sat near other people on the train who had noticed nothing extraordinary about his behaviour. He had left his jacket, overnight bag and book on his seat as he went, they assumed, to the buffet car or the lavatory.

He didn't return and, with customary English reserve, though each of them was aware of the gap in their silent midst, they said nothing to one another about the continued absence of their fellow passenger.

At Birmingham, with the train disembarked, it fell to

a cleaner to gather his things and deposit them at Lost Property.

His mother waited for him, assumed the train had been delayed, and turned the heat down on the tarka dahl, vegetable curry and rice, that she had made for him. By ten o'clock, two hours after he was due, she was so concerned that she telephoned Birmingham's New Street station.

The train had arrived, on time. She telephoned his little flat in Finsbury Park. There was no answer. Adam was a thoughtful and reliable man, entirely dependable. She had no idea what could have happened to him.

Very early the next morning, she telephoned the police in London. They told her not to worry, took the details about her son and sent a car to his address, just one of many, siren blaring and blue lights flashing, that split the city's morning traffic every day.

At about the same time, hurtling past the spot on her way to work, Curtiss's body was spotted by a passenger. The woman felt very diffident and rather foolish but, agitated beyond endurance, the train getting further and further from the spot, she eventually shared the shocking news with a fellow commuter.

The two women walked half the length of the train before they found the guard and told him that one of them was sure she had seen a body lying at the foot of the embankment.

As one of the 'unexplained' deaths that were being monitored with even more rigour than usual, the news soon came through to Kavanagh's team. Was it just another fall from a train, or was there more to it?

The man was travelling alone; there was no possibility of drunken joshing or horseplay. Had he committed suicide? Had the door flown open and sucked the man out as he went to the lavatory? Had it been poorly secured? Had Curtiss leaned against it, and fallen to his death?

Kavanagh dispatched pathologist Dr Khaliq to the Warwickshire mortuary where the body lay.

The same week, there was a hit-and-run in Cumbria: accident and panic? A body hauled from the Thames; a tramp kicked to death near King's Cross; a middle-aged homosexual, an accountant who built model boats, bludgeoned to death in his flat in Whitechapel.

They were all long shots, but they were 'unexplaineds', 'AWMs' as they'd come to be known on the inquiry: 'apparently without motives'. All the information was fed in, cross-referenced and screened for connections.

The tramp was ruled out: according to the unreliable meths and wino witnesses, his was a cheap life extinguished by a gang of skinhead Nazis, fired up on strong lager and a basement racist gig by a bunch of Screwdriver clones.

The gay man, according to the only neighbours who were prepared to talk to the police, had almost certainly died at the hands of one of the many rent boys who visited the man. But there was no clear evidence, and he stayed in the Kavanagh file.

The Thames body was a mystery, but the river police pulled out three dozen corpses a year, and the likelihood was that this was just another tragic soul who would probably never even be correlated with his name on the Missing Persons File.

The list ran into thousands and thousands of names, and they were only the tip of the iceberg: thousands more left homes where no one cared for their fate sufficiently to even register them as missing.

That weekend, a man fell to his death from the Severn Bridge. The video cameras mounted on the bridge established that he was alone when he climbed the unforgiving metal and plunged into the swirling brown water two hundred feet below.

The train death was interesting, but there had been a

rash of these accidents recently, and this itself cast doubt on foul play. However, they'd look closely at Mr Curtiss's demise, even as the British Rail Transport Police inquiry and its technical division got on with their investigations.

Notwithstanding the possible sightings of a Volvo near the scene of both murders, Kavanagh's theory of linked killings was looking increasingly flimsy. If there *had* to be another death, he'd been hoping that that death could be used as the glue to bring the others together. Apart from its happening a day before the full moon, Adam Curtiss's demise had almost no similarities with the other killings.

A drug-using, petty-criminal street trader; a middle class, law-abiding teacher, and now a male nurse on the wards of a London psychiatric hospital.

The only common denominator was the fact that they had all died suspicious or violent deaths recently.

'Which is exactly where we started a month ago,' said Presley.

'Yes,' replied Kavanagh, as he scrolled the masses of information before him on the computer screen. 'At least we have another death which, if it was murder, was made to look like suicide.'

'Maybe it *was* suicide,' said Presley, glancing at his twenty-pound note pinned to the notice board.

'But if it was a murder, and the Sugars, too, why not just kill them?' rejoined Kavanagh.

'I suppose it buys the "killer" some time. Mixes it up for us, at least for a bit. We wouldn't be onto him for a while. If Curtiss's death *is* murder, he might have got away with it; it wouldn't normally be looked at this closely. He doesn't know we're logging all suspicious deaths for a tie-up.'

'Curtiss may not be involved with the other two,' reasoned Kavanagh, 'I agree, but he wasn't a suicide case. He was a Buddhist, for Christ's sake. Meditation and chanting, weeks away in silent Northumbria. Buddhists don't kill themselves, El. The eightfold path and all that. Life is suffering . . .'

'Sounds like a good reason for topping yourself,' said Presley, unimpressed by his boss's apparent familiarity with Eastern theology. 'Also, he did work in a nuthouse. You know, preaching to the converted and all that. Aren't all social workers ex-dope heads or something, poachers turned gamekeepers? They're unstable people, Frank.'

'Come on, Elvis, the guy was going home to see his mother. He'd phoned her that morning from work. He had a return ticket. He didn't kill himself. Anyway, you'd have to be mad to use a train. It's horrible, and you're not certain. People who use trains are disturbed.'

'You're not kidding,' said Presley. 'The crowding's terrible, and they're never on time!'

Kavanagh managed a smile at his colleague's grim humour.

The door opened and Khaliq came in.

'Well?' said Kavanagh, eschewing formal greetings.

'Sorry?' said the doctor, abstruse.

'What's the weather forecast, doctor?' said Kavanagh.

Khaliq played him a straight bat. 'Rain in the Midlands, probably before dawn . . .'

'Khaliq, what about Curtiss, please?'

'Injuries consistent with multiple trauma as a result of falling, or being ejected from, a train travelling at high speed. It's been dry. The ground was very hard there, it's a sheltered spot, and as well as the initial impact, the fall to the bottom of the embankment, at an angle of some forty-five degrees, is a good thirty feet.' He paused.

'Was he pushed?' said Presley.

'Impossible to say. Impossible for *me* to say. Forensic might help you with the door, the handle, the glass, for prints, but the rail police are all over that, and then your Coventry colleagues will no doubt want to have a go. I doubt there'll be much for you to look at by the time our people get to see it.

'And anyway,' he added. 'If I was going to kill somebody by pushing them out of a train, I'd wear gloves. Wouldn't you?'

The inspector ignored the supercilious sarcasm. 'Booze? Drugs?' he said hopelessly.

'Nothing. Last meal, a light lunch. No drink or drugs, not even traces. He didn't drink or smoke. Last clean-living man in the Western world.'

'Anything else?' asked Kavanagh.

'Nothing material, I'm afraid,' said Khaliq. 'I'll put it all in writing, let you have it by lunch time tomorrow. OK?'

'Sure. Thanks.' Kavanagh pointed to the window and the early-evening Saturday sky, a pink tinge lying across the last of the light. '"Red sky at night, shepherd's delight," my old man always used to say,' said the inspector.

'Umm,' said Khaliq, the first few drops of rain starting to fall on the black glass. 'What was it your father did for a living, Inspector?'

The information on the screen rolled up and disappeared with neither man looking at it consciously.

They tapped in the password and keyed into the Coventry force's newly compiled file on Adam Curtiss. His birth date, schooling, career and addresses; next of kin, driving-licence number, bank accounts and credit-card limits tripped up the screen. It made unremarkable reading.

'What's that?' said Presley, leaning forward.

'What?'

'There,' said the sergeant. 'What's that about Curtiss being arrested in Cardiff?'

Kavanagh took his finger from the scroll key. The green letters shimmered there. *Adam Curtiss, arrested Cardiff, 1974. Disturbing the peace. Bound over.*

'So what?' said the inspector.

'Didn't Lacey spend some time in Cardiff? A postgraduate degree, or something?' said Presley.

Kavanagh tapped in a few letters. The computer instantly flashed up a 'No match found. Try again' message.

Both men looked at the screen. The thing about computers was that they were never wrong. They said, 'Try again,' but when you did, the message always came back the same; they were unforgiving.

Kavanagh swung his legs down from the desk. 'You're right though, El. I'm sure he did,' said the inspector. 'Judith Lacey told us.'

They keyed into the file on Lacey. The text rolled away on the screen: schooling; contacts; family; student holiday jobs; NUT membership; passport numbers; holidays, and then: *1974/5 Post Graduate Degree; MA. Caerdydd.*

'What the fuck's *Caerdydd*?' said Presley.

Kavanagh grinned. 'Bloody Cardiff in Welsh. Political correctness bilingual bollocks. But the fucking computer doesn't understand. Doesn't match Caerdydd with Cardiff, doesn't tell us that two men who are now dead . . . have died violent deaths within a few weeks of each other . . . were *both* in Cardiff in 1974. Good man, Elvis.'

'Don't get excited, Frank, it's probably nothing.'

'Yes, I'm sure you're right, but at least it's *something* nothing!' said the inspector.

13

Mrs Curtiss must have been one of the very few readers of the *Morning Star* in the village of Claverdon, a couple of miles outside Leamington Spa. In fact, she may have been its only reader in rural Warwickshire. Frank Kavanagh hadn't seen the paper for years; wasn't even sure that he knew that it was still published. Hadn't the Cold War ended? Weren't there now lots of horrible little hot wars instead?

Kavanagh and his estranged wife had worried about the Holocaust, the same as the rest of their contemporaries, but at least, until the big one went off, and they all retreated to their cellars and caught up on Salman Rushdie and Stephen Hawking (until they got too ill to read anything at all), there *was* peace in those huge, dark, foreign countries.

Nowadays, the horror stories from former Soviet satellites and ex-colonial African countries were legion as they tore one another apart with a scale and savagery that was impossible to comprehend.

So, what was the *Morning Star*'s line, he wondered? Were they still waiting for the revolution? Where did the editor stand on the changes in the Eastern bloc and the all of the Berlin Wall when for a few moments it looked, like the Band Aid concerts before them, as if people really *could* change the world?

It had now been some days since the discovery of her son's body, and Ruth Curtiss had been interviewed by both British Rail Transport Police and the local CID, as well as suffering the ordeal of formally identifying her son.

She was a very fit woman, in her late seventies, and had short, grey hair, carried no spare flesh, was wiry, upright and brisk. Family and friends had supported her through the first days of her loss, but she was an independent woman and, in truth, by only the second day, she couldn't wait for the neighbours and Party friends and, most of all, her sister from Stratford-upon-Avon, to go home.

Ruth Curtiss was not without emotion; on the contrary, she mourned her only son's death deeply. But she was wholly inadequate when it came to rehearsing those feelings to others. However, with virtually all other topics of conversation suspended, her withdrawal left awkward silences that her visitors felt obliged to fill.

Now, nearly a week after her son's death, what she actually wanted, more than anything, was to be left alone. She felt the need to establish once more her routines: solitary breakfast, walking her mongrel dog, listening to *Today* on Radio Four. It wouldn't bring Adam back; but neither would the unnatural silence in her flat, which seemed to be the only alternative to the conspiratorial talk of friends and relatives in the kitchen, from which she, the subject of that talk, was rigorously excluded.

No Mother Teresa of the British Communist Party, she was, nevertheless, a pragmatist who lived an austere, an almost spartan life. Her political beliefs were the rock upon which she had built it, and it was the bulwark against all the ordeals that she had faced in that life.

Above the mantelpiece was a little bronze bust of Lenin. Kavanagh stroked the man's head with the back of his index finger as he said, pointing to that day's *Morning Star*, 'Does it still have the appeal for funds every day?'

'Yes, every day,' she replied phlegmatically. 'I'm afraid the Party needs money more than ever. Falling membership, the recession. Things are hard at present. But they'll change. It's just a cycle. It's all there in Marx. You can't keep producing goods that people don't need. And cheaper and cheaper goods at that, so that ultimately people's standard of living is driven down and down as even more oppressed labour markets are exploited.'

Hers was an evangelic faith: there was nothing that couldn't be answered by the 'good books' that filled the shelves and crowded all the surfaces in her little sitting-room.

Kavanagh was not hostile to notions of socialist collectivism, but he had always been cynical about an economy which left the average Russian more likely to see a cosmonaut float by in the night sky than to find a banana in the shops of Leningrad. But he knew, of course, that not everyone judged society's progress according to the availability of bananas and he remained silent during Mrs Curtiss's party political broadcast.

She made tea, and the three of them sat at her dining table which overlooked the neatly planted area in front of her second-floor flat. 'My sister is staying with me at the moment, but she's gone to the shops. It's about Adam's death, of course?'

'Yes,' said Kavanagh, 'I'm afraid so.'

'It's all right. I can cope, and I can talk, but I do hope that one day you will find out what really happened.'

'We'll certainly do our best,' volunteered Kavanagh. 'We're not convinced about the door coming open. As you know, British Rail are conducting their own investigations into that. But we need to make our own inquiries, to satisfy ourselves that there was no . . .'

'Foul play?' she offered.

'Quite,' said the policeman.

'Adam didn't take his life. I know that. He had an entirely different approach to life from me. He wouldn't have said so, he was too kind, but he thought all my politics were a waste of time. He believed only in the inner, spiritual search. Hence his Buddhism.'

'I see,' said the inspector. 'And was he happy?'

'"Happy"?' she reiterated. 'In this world? He was content; resigned, perhaps, would be a better word.'

'And that's why you say he would have been unlikely to . . . have taken his own life?'

'Buddhists believe that life is founded on suffering, that there are endless rebirths until one achieves a state of grace, nirvana, when one is released from the cycle of pain and death and rebirth. It's an interesting notion.' She leaned down and stroked the dog that lay quietly at her feet. 'I don't believe it, of course. Suffering *is* part of the human condition, but the intervention required to alleviate it is not divine. All that *is* required is for employers to share the fruits of their workers' toil equally amongst them, and for worker not to turn against worker.'

She spoke in quiet tones of patient exasperation, the truth of her conviction so clear as to be blindingly obvious. She poured the two policemen more tea, offered them Co-op digestive biscuits, and went through to the kitchen to refill the pot.

'Do you know of anyone who might have wished your son any harm, Mrs Curtiss?' said Kavanagh, as she stood at the doorway waiting for the kettle to boil.

'No one. He led a very quiet life. Worked at the hospital. Went to the temple for meditation three times a week. He read a lot, mostly religious and spiritual texts, and listened to the radio. He didn't really meet many people, apart from at work. I don't think he had any enemies. He was a gentle, serious, kindly person.'

Presley was intrigued. 'How long had he been involved with the Buddhism?' he asked, the use of the definite article relegating the man's spiritual quest to the level of a hobby.

'About fifteen years.'

'And before then?' said Kavanagh, faintly suspicious of the motives of people who embraced religion, suspecting skeletons in well-concealed cupboards.

'He had always been a quiet, introspective kind of person, but before that, he did see friends, had a girlfriend or two, and did all those things that people did in the seventies.'

'What sort of things?' asked the sergeant.

'I think he experimented with drugs, that kind of thing.'

When she took her seat at the table again, Kavanagh said, 'We have four unexplained deaths on our files at the moment, Mrs Curtiss. They are "unexplained" in the sense that they are apparently motiveless, but they don't appear to be the result of random attacks. We're trying to establish whether there might be any connection between these deaths that we haven't yet discovered.

'One of the other men who died in suspicious circumstances spent some time in Cardiff. I believe your son did, too. Wasn't he arrested there in the seventies?'

'Yes, he was,' she said proudly. 'It was a march in support of the miners. Between us we brought down a whole government. Cynics say that ordinary people can't change the course of history. But do you remember those days? Do you remember Vietnam? People driving in the daylight hours with their headlights on? Burning their draft cards in Washington? Marching in their thousands on Grosvenor Square? They *did* change the world.'

Kavanagh thought that Edward Heath had lost the vital propaganda war during the coal strike: the rights and wrongs of the dispute were immaterial to the outcome; the real battle was the one fought out beneath the media's spotlight glare. And he had *no* doubt that television news pictures had played a bigger part in the Americans' withdrawal from Vietnam than any number of people chanting outside the American Embassy.

He said nothing. If Ruth Curtiss believed that it was her son's arrest, and hundreds like it, that had finally forced the politicians' hands, so be it. Driving with headlights on had a kind of folksy charm, like yellow ribbons wrapped round trees, but he doubted its power to sway the hard men of the Republican Party.

'What we'd like to do, Mrs Curtiss, is get more background on your son's life from you, all the places that he visited, as many of his friends' and colleagues' and associates' names as possible. Places of work, where he drank or who he went out with, and then we can feed all of the material into the computer and see if it throws up any cross-references with the other deaths that we're looking at. Would that be all right?'

'Of course,' she said. 'Do you want us to do it now?'

'Yes, perhaps you could make a start. Sergeant Presley here will jot things down and then if you recall things that you've missed, he'll call round or you could give us a ring.'

He liked her. She was spunky. In her seventies, nearly eighty, she was fighting the good fight, would not be denied, did not waver in her belief that there was a world out there peopled with decent folk ready to embark on honest toil with an open heart.

She was the good guys, same as the folk down at the local church. You may not want to sing hymns, clap hands, clasp neighbours to you, but these people would do you good before they did you harm. What price a little proselytizing? They wouldn't steal your bag, rob your pension, rape your sister. The rest was academic.

She reminded him of his own elderly mother. She had been distraught about the break-up of his marriage. He'd even kept it from her for a while. His mother, the one with the womb-love, the deepest, most unconditional love, that nothing can supplant.

How often had he seen people put away for the most heinous crimes: child murders, dreadful sexual attacks, barbarity of every sort, and yet he had never once seen a mother desert her son, deny the monster at her side her love.

He resented Rachael as much for hurting his mother as

for what she had done to him. And yet he knew, of course, that it was his mother who was 'responsible' for himself, her own son: nature or nurture; environment or genes; one way or another, Frank Kavanagh was Rosemary Kavanagh incarnate.

And now *he* was separated; her daughter had never married; her second son, married young, was now divorced. The Kavanagh family fallout was complete.

There was no blame, no censure: his mother had had a hard life: not hard in the sense of little to eat, or having to wear thin, cheap shoes. But in the sense of life being hard for her to live. He saw it in her face. So much anxiety: anxious to be happy, to please, to feel others' suffering. The things that made it hard for her to be happy; easily, ordinarily happy, without fear of the snatching away of that happiness.

How difficult her uncompromising love had made it for those children, now grown men and women, mortgages to pay, lives to lead, marriages and friendships to fail in, again and again.

How ashamed they were of their own fallibilities.

Kavanagh loved her with a deep, resentful, unwholesome, claustrophobic love. They had become even closer since the break-up. She had stood by him, of course, for blood is blood. And he was her murderous child; pederast, paedophile or pimp.

But he resented her love, for he knew, without needing to articulate it, that it was *this* love that had always rendered his own a failure.

From Mrs Curtiss's home in Claverdon, he drove up through Solihull, into Birmingham and towards his estranged wife's flat on Stratford Road. He knew the address, but until today had detoured rather than pass it.

He thought about her virtually every waking moment; he woke to thoughts of her each day; his sleep was a thin veneer that lay over his consciousness and into which, at what seemed like every few minutes, images of her would break.

He went to bed drunk, but still woke several times each night, the slightest sound disturbing him. He tormented himself with thoughts that she was there; called out, knew that she had been at the door or the window, and might now be walking away.

He stopped his breathing and called out to her; lay without moving or sound, called again to the blackness, got up, went to both doors, looked down the empty pavement, was bitter that she was not there, knew she was somewhere else.

His imagination was in the ascendancy, the balance tipped; he didn't believe any reality of her life could be as skewering as his recurrent imaginings.

He wanted to turn away, but couldn't, he was being drawn down the busy street. On he went, towards her flat.

Two hundred yards away, he checked his rear-view mirror, saw that there was nothing close behind him, did a big U-turn and drove away towards his own house.

14

The two officers drove down to the Open University's headquarters at Milton Keynes and got into the records office with less difficulty than you can get into a First Division football match.

All the student records' information since the institution's inauguration twenty-four years earlier was logged on computers the size of small power stations.

The girl who accessed the files didn't even wear a white coat, certainly didn't look like a scientist. (What *did* a scientist look like?)

She was matter of fact about their inquiries, and gave the impression that, while it was something readily achieved, she could just as easily have told the two officers that their request was impossible to fulfil, quoting, had she wished, procedural or confidentiality rules, the need for a magistrate's warrant, or the Charter of the European Court of Human Rights.

Given that she was, albeit a little sullenly, acceding to their request, they maintained a discreet presence and stood aside as she glided around the floor on her chair and pushed the buttons that sent the memory-packed disks on their erratic stop/start spinning way.

There were several screens in front of her and she glanced from them to the piece of paper in her hand with Terry Sugar's details on it.

Eventually, his name came up: when he had enrolled; where; which course; tutors; personal tutor; essay and assignment marks; summer school; residence arrangements. It didn't say if he jerked off in room nineteen of Lindsay Hall in the summer of 1985 at Keele University, but there wasn't much else missing.

It really was an unequal struggle; criminals shouldn't have a chance these days. And yet, whether it was the blocked drains of homosexual killer Dennis Nilsen, or the out-of-date tax disc on the car of the so-called Yorkshire Ripper, it was often this kind of aberration which led to arrests.

Sugar was straightforward. They knew him, knew what to try and ascertain about him to flesh out his picture.

But MND (SC), the person whose initials appeared in his address book, and whose contact telephone number was a public call box in Shrewsbury, was harder.

From the roll of students, hundreds of thousands of them, people's names going back two and a half decades, they had to try and isolate any SCs. If they were lucky, they might then link her to a summer school in the mid-eighties at Keele.

It could be done. Yes, said the girl in her wheeled chair, but it would take some time, the best part of a day. She had other work to do as well. She would fax them the information through as soon as she had it.

The two officers left the red-brick building in Milton Keynes and joined the M1 for the journey up to Keele University in Staffordshire.

'I don't think I've quite got this,' said Kavanagh.

'Good. It makes a change, anyway,' said Presley.

'You're telling me Adam Curtiss goes to see his old mate in Cardiff?'

'For a miners' rally. Writes to him and asks if he can stay over for a day or two.'

'And Curtiss's mate . . . Jeff?'

'Jeff.'

'Jeff's missis falls for Curtiss and they have an affair?'

'Not straightaway. Nothing happens. It's all nods and winks between Curtiss and Jeff Clarke's missis, Sarah. Curtiss goes back to London, the husband doesn't suspect anything. Well, in a way, there isn't anything to suspect. Not really.'

'And then?'

'Then, about two weeks later, Sarah Clarke ups and goes to London.'

'Just like that?'

'Apparently; so Mrs Curtiss says. Called her "the bolter",' said Presley.

'"The bolter"?' repeated Kavanagh.

'It's from a book. Nancy Mitford. Don't you know it, Frank?'

'It rings a bell. Anyway, how long have you been reading Nancy Mitford?'

'I haven't. Mrs Curtiss told me. Mitford's sister was a Communist. Big anti-fascist or something. Another sister was married to Mosley though, Oswald Mosley.'

'OK, Kev. Can we get the history and literature later? So, Sarah Clarke fucks off to London.'

'To see Adam Curtiss. The Clarkes had got a little kid. She takes her too.'

'Good mother!'

'This Jeff's doing a teacher-training course. He comes home with his pile of marking and she's gone. Note on the mantelpiece job.'

'And?'

'And she phones, and they talk, and she says she needs a few days to sort out her feelings.'

'And her old man gets on the next train to London and kills them both?'

'No, he doesn't. It's the seventies, and he says, "You've got to decide what's right for you. Sort it out, as soon as you can."'

'You're having me on.'

'I'm not. That's what he says.'

'And?'

'And in two days' time he comes to London . . .'

'And kills her?'

'And takes her back. According to old Mrs Curtiss, there's this tense scene in her son's flat, with Sarah Clarke and her husband talking in one room, and then Sarah and Curtiss talking in another room, and then Curtiss and the husband talking in the kitchen, and the upshot is that she packs her bag and the Clarkes go back to Cardiff together.

'According to Curtiss's mother, her son was being "magnanimous"; the girl didn't want to go back, but Curtiss said she should. "It's Jeff you're married to, got a nipper by, and that's where you belong," he says.'

'Maybe he didn't fancy her,' said Kavanagh.

'Maybe he thought she was nuts,' replied Presley.

'Yes, maybe. Then what?'

'It didn't work out for the Clarkes. The Curtiss romance hadn't run its course, and the girl is still pining and things are all over the place. I should think he wasn't teaching very well, either! Anyway, they're going round in circles, and it's half term, so the husband, Jeff, he says, rather than *her* go away, and take the nipper and everything, *he*'ll go away for a few days and Adam Curtiss can come and be there for them to finally sort out what it is this woman wants.'

'You're kidding,' said Kavanagh calmly. 'Jeff Clarke leaves his own house to let his mate come and be with his wife?'

'You've got it, Frank. I'm telling you just what Curtiss's mother told me. She wasn't very proud, either, but she said that's the way it happened, and maybe things were different then.'

'Did Mrs Curtiss ever meet the girl?'

'Yes, she lived in London at that time and met her on her first visit. She said she liked her. Middle class, ex-military family. She'd made up her mind not to have anything to do with her, but she said she was nice. Young, mixed up a bit, but "a sweet girl" is what she said.'

'She *sounds* sweet,' said Kavanagh. 'Go on. This is the worst story I've heard all day.'

'Well, the husband goes away, and amazingly, it works. Perhaps Jeff Clarke *did* know what he was doing. He's away for a few days, three or four, I think, and in that time, maybe the strange situation or the little girl around, whatever, the spark went out.

'When he comes back, Curtiss has gone, and Sarah Clarke and Adam Curtiss were never in contact again. At least that's what his mother says.'

Eventually Kavanagh asked, 'Did she say what happened to them, the girl and her husband?'

'She doesn't know.'

'And her son becomes a Buddhist. One day he's having it off with his mate's missis, the next he's picking up woodlice so he doesn't kill them.'

'What you on about?' said Elvis. 'What's this about woodlice?'

'Karma, mate. Instant karma. John Lennon had a song about it: "Instant karma's gonna get you . . ."' sang Kavanagh, distinctly off key.

'What's karma got to do with anything?' said Presley.

'I'm just wondering if you have to wait until your *next* lifetime to pick up the tab on your misdeeds, or whether this lifetime'll do,' said the inspector.

'Fuck knows,' said Presley. 'But the good news is that her name's Sarah Clarke; *and* there's a Cardiff connection. John Lacey spent time in Cardiff doing a degree, and we think that Sugar had an affair with someone whose initials were SC.

'We've been looking for a connection and now it looks like we've got three. I hate losing money, don't you, Frank?'

15

'It's for you, Frank.' Presley held the receiver at arm's length, a cigarette in his mouth, and continued his conversation into the other phone.

It was difficult for cops not to parody themselves these days. The police college might as well lock the recruits in the TV lounge with two hundred episodes of *The Bill*. Its writers and producers knew more about police work than Chief Constables. And they had a better clear-up rate.

The inspector took the phone from Presley's outstretched hand. 'Hello, Kavanagh speaking.'

'Hello, Inspector.'

He knew the voice, but couldn't place it. He felt a little guilt and embarrassment, as if he should know it, and had been found out. He waited for her next words.

'This is Judith Lacey.'

'Ah, Mrs Lacey, I'm sorry, it's a poor line.'

She wasn't interested in the telephone lines, just said, 'I think you'd better come round.'

'Yes, of course. Now?' He glanced up at the Smith's electric on the wall with its green figures and ceaselessly sweeping hand. It was four in the afternoon.

'Yes, as soon as you can.'

'Of course; I'll be straight round.'

Although Kevin Presley's oft-remarked observation that 'Sex is all right, but not when you can do the real thing' always made Frank smile, onanism, for Kavanagh, was the sexual equivalent of a Chinese meal: it satisfied you for a while, but very soon . . .

As he drove out to the Laceys' suburban house in leafy Sutton Coldfield, he blushed to admit to himself that the voice on the phone belonged to the woman he had made love to in his imagination on several occasions since he had spoken to her at her husband's funeral.

In fact, since that day, the widow Judith Lacey, with her subtle allure, had even supplanted his former lover, Lucy Amis, in his lascivious thoughts in those most secret, dark and solitary moments.

Lucy Amis, with whom, to his considerable chagrin at the time, he had spent an illicit night three or four years into his marriage to Rachael.

Heartbroken at their separation and, by the most subtle employment of a scrawled extra kiss, or subliminally loaded word in the birthday and Christmas cards that she always sent, Lucy indicated, as clearly as was decently possible, that she was waiting patiently in the wings, understudy to the younger Rachael, the woman for whom she had been precipitately abandoned after two years of more or less contented cohabitation.

Ever vigilant, she had driven halfway across the country when Kavanagh had disingenuously mentioned to her on the telephone that he was alone at the family home, 'an urgent, pressing case', his wife still on holiday with her parents.

Four or five hours later, as they climbed into the bed in the guest room and she suffused him with the pent passion of the intervening years, she murmured the unremarkable words, 'My lust is just returning.'

At that moment, and at every moment since, when he chose to recall those prosaic words, they unfailingly acted as a clarion call to his nascent sexuality.

'I maintained it until Northampton,' she had continued breathlessly. 'And then it disappeared all the way up the M6. But now it's returning.'

This, as she unclasped her brassiere, and he nuzzled his head into the deep cleavage of that ample bosom.

The very thought of Lucy Amis hurtling across the country towards him, his self the subject of *her* sexual arousal, was a powerful aphrodisiac and his thoughts-erotic had gathered apace as he thrilled at the prospect of losing himself once more in the red hair and soft places of this Rubensesque woman.

(Had there ever, he wondered, been a woman in the history of the entire world who had monitored her salacious thoughts en route to *Birmingham*, observing their fading and finally flickering out on the ring road of Northampton?)

But now, since the tremor that had rocked his life sex, alone or with any other, was a troubled affair and even as his blood vessels filled in a kind of independent and non-aligned sexuality, he had to struggle to ignore the nation-state of his whole being.

Perhaps, from now on, it would be easier. Perhaps it was time to try again: he'd had enough Chinese meals. Now he wanted an English three-course dinner of a tryst, not just another oriental takeaway.

She opened the door and walked back into the sitting room, leaving him to follow. Her body swayed and rocked, not with self-conscious allure, but with the lack of it that comes with drink.

The oval, pale, Kashmiri carpet at the centre of the sitting-room floor was covered with paper and envelopes. There was a space in the centre where she had been sitting, and a bottle of gin close at hand. On the hearth were several empty Schweppes tonic water bottles. (Why did she buy the prohibitively expensive tiny size? Kavanagh wondered.)

The ashtrays were full of her half-smoked Silk Cut stubs.

'Drink?' she said.

'Do you have a whisky?' he asked.

He stood in front of the sofa, looking down at the detritus as she went through to the kitchen.

She came back with an unopened bottle of Bell's and a cut-glass tumbler.

'Anything with it?'

'No, this'll be fine,' he said.

She gestured for him to sit on the settee, and knelt down in her nest of letters. She lit a cigarette and the smoke sputtered out of her mouth as she spoke. 'You were right, Inspector. How did you know?'

'Right about what?' he said.

'He *had* had another affair.'

'Really?' said Kavanagh, barely surprised, given the evidence that lay about her on the floor.

'Not now,' she continued. 'Well, at least, I don't think so. But he had done.'

He poured himself a triple and leaned back into the cushions. What he was about to hear may or may not be material to the inquiry, but Kavanagh was a man who also had recently undergone major surgery: he wanted to show *his* scars, compare *his* stitches, talk about *his* operation, but only to someone who had also felt the surgeon's knife.

He had seen this woman in shock on the night of her husband's murder; in mourning at his funeral, and now she was in a volatile state of anger and hurt. It was a heady mixture. She looked as attractive as on the other occasions that he had seen her, just different: her eyes full of hurt and intense emotion. She looked as if she might cry at any moment.

She started abruptly, 'I was going through some of his things. It has to be done, I thought. I'll make a start.

'Joe's out. Gone to a rave or something. Up to no good, I'm quite sure, but they all go. What can you do?

'The clothes, the jackets, each one something particular, special. I'd done a couple of bin bags. It was about as bad as I had imagined, a bit worse perhaps. Lots of gin and cigarettes. I tried some music, but that was all too difficult, so I turned it off.

'I didn't want to handle any more of his clothes, it was upsetting me too much. His shoes in particular, I just couldn't pick them up. They had the shape of his foot so clearly.

'I was crying quite a lot by this time, just getting lower and lower, and so I said to myself, "This is stupid. Stop it."

'Anyway, I came in here, watched the TV for a bit and then wandered over to his desk and started to go through some of his papers.' She stopped as abruptly as she had begun. 'And here we are.'

'What exactly did you find?'

She swept her arm in front of her, gin and tonic spilling on the letters. He wanted to protest: the evidence, the expensive rug, but he said nothing.

'I opened drawers at random. Bank statements; old holiday bookings; credit-card records; letters; exhibition openings; all the usual stuff.

'In the middle drawer – isn't it supposed to be the bottom drawer in the films, Inspector? – there was a manilla envelope, underneath envelopes with the water rates and the gas bills in them, all labelled, just like John, very methodical. I'm surprised he hadn't written on the envelope: *Private: Love Letters*.

'The *bastard*. How could he do this to me? I'm dying of grief for him. I haven't slept since he died. I'm in agony for him. And all the time, he's had a secret affair.'

And then she did cry. Just let her head fall into her lap and sobbed and sobbed with all of her being.

Kavanagh moved uneasily on the sofa, leaned down towards her, put out a hand, but didn't touch her. He had never been able to cope with tears. Something to do with his mother, he imagined. He just had no idea what he was supposed to do. He knew from past experience that he wasn't expected to keep his distance, observe the situation clinically. Involvement was expected. Required, even. But the tears froze him. His hand hovered uncertainly above her shoulder as she wept.

'I'm sorry,' he said. 'Can I get you anything?'

She rocked her head from side to side. The worst was over; the tears were starting to abate, the breathing getting deeper. She eventually took a big, deep, nasal breath, drew herself up. She had a nice bosom. He found her extremely attractive, even with her mascara streaked and running down her cheeks. He passed her his clean handkerchief and she dabbed at her eyes with the white cotton square.

'May I?' she said, as she unfolded it and held it to her red nose.

'Please, of course,' he said graciously.

'I'm sorry,' she offered, unnecessarily.

'Please,' he said.

'Shall I go on?' she said.

'When you're ready,' he said.

'Dear John; Darling John; John, sweetest love; Dearest John. This is my *husband*, Inspector. The man I am grieving for. The man whose shoes I have just been pressing my fingers into to feel the shape of his foot.'

'I'm sorry,' said Kavanagh.

She looked up at him. There was a flash of recognition there. He was a man, as well. 'Yes, I'm sorry, too,' she said bitterly.

He felt a tinge of resentment. He didn't want to be tarred with the brush that was daubing Lacey. It seemed unfair. He'd had an affair or two during their long marriage, but so had Rachael. It was par for the course. He didn't know anyone who hadn't. But he was in a new situation; his present role was very different. He was victim; he was the aggrieved. He was suffering. It was too unfair that he should be miscast in this living-room production.

He knew all about lonely nights and terrible yearnings. He suspected betrayal now, too. His mind had started to run rampant with suspicions of deception and cheating. He was with her on this. They were together.

'May I see?' he asked, leaning forward and reaching for one of the letters.

'Of course,' she gestured with her hand. She sipped her Gordon's, stubbed out her cigarette and immediately lit another.

He glanced at the fulsome salutation, but before reading the contents of the letter, turned the page to see the signature. It ended with the words, 'All my love to you, Sarah.' He looked at a couple of the envelopes, held them up to read the South Wales postmarks.

He smiled. She caught the flicker on his face, looked up. 'Something amusing, Inspector?'

'Frank. Would you call me Frank, please? Can I take these?' he asked.

'Why not?' she said. 'Do you think they're important? Do you think dear Sarah' – she drawled the name out with contempt – 'has gone a bit loopy and come back and killed him after all these years? A woman spurned? It's a bit of a long shot, isn't it?'

'Yes, it is a long shot. But it's getting shorter.' He paused, looked at her carefully. 'How drunk are you?'

She was surprised by the candour of the inquiry; half drunk as she certainly was, she knew that it was too familiar, like someone asking you if you wore a bra or shaved your legs.

He didn't wait for an answer. 'Will you keep this to yourself?'

'Probably,' she said playfully. 'When you tell me what it is. I'm not insensible. I almost know what I'm doing.' She glanced up at him, and this time the recognition was nothing to do with his being simply male. It was entirely to do with himself, and herself.

'I actually like it when people say, "I've got something awful to tell you." There's that moment of suspense before you hear what it is. The "awful" is balanced by the excitement, like now, don't you think?'

Her knees were tucked under her. Her skirt had ridden

up her black tights. She was a bit drunk, but not crazy. The revelation about her husband's secret affair had devastated her, but it had also liberated her from her grief. These letters were the last thing she had wanted to find in the drawer of his desk amongst old Barclaycard statements. And yet, perversely, they had ameliorated her sadness.

'It's more than my job's worth,' he began, trying to communicate the seriousness of what he was telling her. 'But I want to tell you.'

'Yes?' she said.

'One of the other murder inquiries. One that I think might be linked with your . . .' He sought the word with difficulty, it no longer seemed entirely appropriate. '. . . with your husband's death . . .'

'Yes?' she said, intrigued.

'One of those other inquiries, possibly even two of them, may be related to someone with this initial,' he held one of the letters to her.

'I see,' she said, got uncertainly to her feet and went to the kitchen.

Kavanagh glanced from one letter to another, quickly read the contents. It was all personal, loving stuff: no politics or general knowledge, no sport. They were literate and loving, but the surprising thing was, they appeared to be one-way affairs.

But a note of need, then frustration, and eventually desperation crept into them. The recipient, Lacey, was either unable, or unwilling, to respond to these love letters.

They constantly asked for contact, a reciprocation of the feeling expressed in them, which evidently was never forthcoming. It occurred to the inspector that their author was either supremely confident, extremely callow, or just plain stupid.

Nowhere was there any inkling in the writer that the recipient might have, as Kavanagh felt certain must have been the case, thought better of the relationship and was trying to withdraw from it.

Eventually the tone did change and manifest a little irritation and even irascibility as the author pleaded for a word: 'Literally one word, to show that those times mean and meant as much to you as they did to me. One word, on a card, in an envelope, anywhere, anyhow. Please.'

It was rather pathetic, thought Kavanagh.

Judith Lacey swayed back into the room, carrying a tray of coffee.

He took it from her. 'Do you know who this Sarah is?' he asked.

'Yes, I did. The absolute bitch. I'd like to pull her hair out and punch her in the face. I haven't felt like this since I was thirteen years old. I didn't know I could *have* these feelings. I'm sorry.'

'It's all right,' said Kavanagh. He knew about feelings of hatred. Even without the presence of another man to focus his resentment on, he had wished his ex-wife dead. Often. He knew all about the forces that drove those people in the papers who abducted wives, husbands, girlfriends, locked them in suburban sitting rooms and killed them all; or hired second-rate Liverpool criminals to murder them. She interrupted his downward-spiralling thoughts.

'John lodged with them in Cardiff when he did his MA there in the seventies.'

'And you met her?'

'A couple of times. I had the car up here. Sometimes, when he was coming home, I used to go down and pick him up. She was nice, or so I thought. A bit airy-fairy, younger than us, but very sweet. I had no idea just how sweet she was being to John. My God, the little bitch. I wonder if her husband knew, or even knows now. Perhaps I should get in touch with him?'

She was on a roll, unpacking her thoughts and fears in a stream-of-consciousness that Kavanagh recognized.

There was the initial shock of revelation, but soon she would be falling headlong into the chasm of grief where there would be few jokes and little comfort and much pain.

She picked up her thread of the past again. 'Her husband was older than her, they had a little girl, just a toddler. They seemed a nice couple. John liked them straightaway.'

'And you had no idea?'

'Knock me over with a feather. I'm amazed. Do you know what I don't understand? When did all this happen? You know, John was working hard for his MA; her husband was doing teacher training after his degree, and she was presumably looking after their child. When did they . . . you know . . . when did they find the time, the opportunity?'

'I think her husband went away. There was some involvement with someone else, a friend of her husband's. The husband went away for a few days so that she and this bloke could . . . "sort it out". I suppose your . . . husband and she might have . . . you know.'

'Who *is* this woman for Christ's sake? She's having an affair with someone, her husband goes away, and then she fits in a little number on the side with my husband the lodger at the same time? My God, who the hell is this woman?'

'I don't know. But I'm sure I'll be seeing her soon.'

'When you said the other inquiries might be linked, how many more are there?'

'Not a word. All right? I know all this is terrible and a shock for you, but really, I'd lose my job.' He didn't wait for her affirmation, but he knew he could trust her.

'There have been three deaths recently: your husband; the man I've just mentioned, and with whom she had an affair, and another man, whom we think she met much more recently, in the eighties, when she was at Open University summer school . . .'

'What was she doing, Greek Tragedy?'

He smiled. 'Three relationships, all the men and one of their wives now dead, and killed in violent circumstances.'

'But why would she do this? Why is she killing these men that she's had relationships with? Surely it's *me*, and the other women, who should be killing *her*, or our own husbands.'

'I've no idea. I agree it makes no sense. None at all.'

'And why now? After all this time? Why is she doing it now?'

'I really don't know. It's a mystery, but we're looking for her. We'll find her and find out, of that I'm sure.'

She sipped her coffee; there was a little self-consciousness between them. She had spent her initial salvo. It was just the two of them now.

She placed her cup on the saucer and glanced up at him. There was a look between them that said, 'Well, what do you think?'

There was fellow feeling. A common agenda. Kavanagh's wife had left him; Judith Lacey's husband had been killed, but had cheated her, taken his sordid secret to the grave and left her punching air. There was a ridiculous, gung-ho, 'Well, why not us, too?' atmosphere between them.

She was fairly drunk; he liked her. But he knew that soon she would be playing the long game, feeling deep pain, not just the almost exciting, drunken miasma of emotion that accompanied the impact of discovery. Knowing this, he knew that he should not seek to take advantage of her.

'Would you like me to stay the night?'

She looked up. Her eyes said, 'Yes,' she would do it, but also acknowledged the lack of conviction in his request.

He responded instantly to her ambivalence, decided, on this occasion at least, to play for the draw, end with a handshake and a 'well played'. 'I don't mean *with* you. I mean here, on the sofa. Just so there's someone around?'

She smiled. They were both well ahead of the game. 'It's a nice thought,' she said, 'but I'll be all right, really.'

'Are you sure?' he said, a little regretfully, not sure that he couldn't simply chip a winner into the top corner by stealth alone. It might, after all, be the right thing for them both. Who knows?

'Perhaps another time?' she said.

16

Sarah Clarke was living in north London. She had changed her name by deed poll, in 1991. Kavanagh's need to speak to her had become pressing: while he had been sitting with Judith Lacey the previous evening, the Bursar's office of the Open University in Milton Keynes had telephoned DCs Denny and Reeder with the names of female students whose initials were SC, and who had been at Keele in the summer of 1985.

There were three: Sonia Coultard; Sally Cummings and, the only one of the three to have been there during the same week as Terry Sugar, Sarah Clarke.

Presley picked up his boss at his house in Erdington and drove them into Birmingham city centre. At the traffic lights on Colmore Row, Kavanagh watched as a pretty shop girl kissed her boyfriend goodbye for the day.

As the inspector watched the youngsters, Presley glanced at his boss. The man had changed: something had left him.

'Did you ever see *The Accidental Tourist*?' said Kavanagh.

Presley tapped the accelerator for his routine grid start, even though they had half an hour before the train's departure.

'No. Don't think so,' he said, concentrating on the cars on either side of him. And then, judging that he still had a second to proffer a modicum of response, 'Why?'

'William Hurt says, "It's not how much you love someone, but what matters is who you are when you're with them." Something like that, anyway.'

The lights went to amber and Presley left the cars on either side of him standing. 'Yes?' he said.

'It's a good film,' said Kavanagh, pressed back into the passenger seat. 'You'd love it!'

Presley swung the car round the concrete pillars and tight bends of the multi-storey car park on Hill Street. Before he locked the Granada, he reached into the driver's side-door pocket, pulled out a pair of stained Y-front underpants and draped them on his seat.

'Do you *have* to do that?' said Kavanagh.

'Never fails,' said Presley, jauntily.

They took the 8.15 inter-city out of New Street. Presley would have driven. Hurtled down the M1, inviolable in their official car, the three-litre Ford passing everything in sight.

But, given the choice, Kavanagh always travelled by train. He liked them: their indomitability, their power, their huge, mechanical strength.

Off it went, fixed on its silver tracks, out past the British Small Arms factory; past the Dogs' Home with its fascia of jolly puppies; past the grey, deserted go-cart track, Birmingham City's football ground in the distance. And eventually, gathering speed, through the allotments and extensions, greenhouses, satellite dishes and back gardens of south Birmingham.

In only ten minutes, the bramble, elder and discarded mattresses of the suburbs had given way to birch and ash and pollarded willow, grubby sheep and ploughed fields.

Yes, thought Kavanagh, slumped in his seat by the window, he certainly preferred this to Presley's flying down the motorway at a hundred miles an hour.

Travel by train was, for Kavanagh, inexorably bound up with childhood: the memory of distant summer holidays to Lytham St Anne's, the rail journey as much a prerequisite of the August excursion as was the four-storey guesthouse, set one street back from the sedate promenade and its expensive hotels.

The images crowded his vision: he and his brother in a prepubescent joy of bucket and spade, sand castles, paper flags on balsa sticks, fishing nets and model boats with their beautiful, deep-varnished hulls on the pond that was a summer's evening ocean, a mere nine inches deep.

By fourteen, the unselfconscious child had metamorphosed into a surly adolescent: James Dean on Lytham's promenade, a scowling youth in jeans and black linen, zippered jerkin determinedly leaning away from the little family group as they were snapped en route to the beach.

His sister at fifteen, pirouetting on the sand, glimpses of her secrets as she changed into her swimming costume, wrapped only in a beach towel. The boys from Lancashire and Scotland, like flies around her throughout the day, swatted away by their vigilant mother.

The flat, grey sea; the unrelenting August heat; children's voices all around; face down, an intermittent erection in the sand, sweat trickling through dark eyebrows.

Cliff Richard's 'Living Doll'; long afternoons on the beach; Lyon's Maid strawberry Mivvies for the children; Wall's ice-creams for the grown-ups, his mother drawing her tongue up between the wafer biscuits, leaning forward to catch the melting stuff; his father asleep in his deck chair beneath an immaculately constructed newspaper hat.

The interminable, silent ritual of the three-course evening meal, followed, an agony of waiting later, by a walk along the dusky front beneath the softly glowing, coloured lamps.

And now, in his mid-forties, this train, *any* train, could readily evoke the piquant memory of those times.

Kavanagh observed in the reflection of the glass the couple sitting opposite him. He had become inordinately, mawkishly interested in relationships. The insipid misogyny that had crept, unnoticed, into his very being, like ink into blotting paper, had become recently a deeper-hued misanthropy. Men, in particular, were a despicable species: their oppression and bullying born of nothing but fear and weakness.

Kavanagh was full of self-loathing. The age-old conundrum, the one whose truth he had recognized since he was a twitchy adolescent, the quintessential Groucho Marx line: *I wouldn't want to belong to any club that would accept me as a member*, had become his mantra.

I covet her; she accepts me; I do not love myself; *ergo*: if she loves me, she cannot be worthy of my love. *I wouldn't want to belong to any club that would accept me as a member*. Round and round. A rodent on a wheel.

It had started with Sandra Dolan, an unimaginable prize. Fifteen, dark eyes, deep, mysterious womanhood. He had caught his own father looking at her as a man looks at a woman.

Bosomy, sexual, frightening, exciting; they had done it one half-term afternoon in the bedroom he shared with his brother, the suburban house deserted.

She had known what to do, which garments to remove, which to leave on – 'Your mother might come back' – and he had come in a flash of ecstatic, wild excitement.

He didn't call for her again. He took the long way round to the bus to avoid her house. He didn't want her. Not at all. *Any club . . .*

She took up with Alan Hammond from the council estate, a dangerous, unpredictable boy. Young Kavanagh looked longingly at her. Wrote letters and poems that were never sent, peered at her from behind the bedroom curtains as she passed.

And so it went on. Down all the years, repeatedly: the apparently unattainable, attained. And then the inexorable process of rejection. Rachael had been so loving, so long-suffering, so *good* really, that it had taken him nearly twenty years to prise her love away and force her rejection of him.

But eventually, the scouring drip of his own self-loathing had worn her spirit away. He had managed it. He had estranged her so thoroughly, so completely, that she had finally left him. He was, once more, alone and cold.

And although it hurt, especially at that darkest hour, just before dawn, he knew, even then, that this *was* his rightful place, this *was* where he belonged. *Any club* . . .

The man opposite droned on, talking figures and budgets and costs. His plain, female colleague listened intently.

Kavanagh hated this man with a ferocious contempt: his facial hair, his bad suit and ill-chosen tie; his noisy yawn when he eschewed putting his hand to his mouth. 'Look, I hate her,' said his every gesture. 'I cover her with my stomach's bad breath.'

Later, he flitted in and out of articles in the newspaper. She filled in the *Daily Telegraph* crossword.

The inspector knew that she was brighter than her colleague. He was sure that she read proper novels, listened to *From Our Own Correspondent* on Radio Four, watched current affairs on TV.

Outside Birmingham's International station, she took her jacket, and he gathered his pens and photocopied figures and newspaper into a shiny, black, FisherPrice briefcase, concealing them from the world behind an array of combination locks and brass hinges.

Presley went to the buffet car for coffee.

The train passed a siding with a dozen, summer-blue painted trucks in it, weeds growing high up their sides.

Did someone in British Rail *know* about these wagons, their flaps down, their cargo long-since disembarked? They looked as if they had been there for years.

And since when had British Rail painted its freight trucks blue? They were pretty, like you might see on a clockwork model railway. But this was a siding somewhere between Coventry and somewhere else.

Was someone in an office, somewhere, aware of these twelve blue wagons, languishing in the sun, like old pit ponies taken up out of the dark and left quietly to pasture?

The train thundered through cavernous, open-to-the-sky Rugby without stopping. Presley brought the coffee. Kavanagh wondered about the trucks. He thought about Rachael. He tried again to think about the trucks.

Two nights ago, he had finally given in. At three in the morning, well over the limit, he had driven his old Citroën DS the three or four miles to her flat on the other side of the city.

He had sat outside for an hour, smoking and watching the still room above the empty street. When his eyes adjusted to the darkness of the scene, he began to make out the shapes on the windowsill.

There was a soft light filtering through from the landing into the sitting-room. Perhaps she *was* alone, his conviction that she was with someone else no more than a figment of three a.m. paranoia.

She had always slept with the light on outside their bedroom door if she was alone.

On the windowsill was a plant, a camellia, perhaps, something late in bloom and, further along, a vase full of big overstated flowers, perhaps gladioli or African lilies.

He'd never known her buy African lilies before. Perhaps they were the gift of someone. If someone was buying her flowers, were they with her now? Were they making love, at this moment, while he sat outside, ridiculous, looking up at the window from his pale grey Citroën with its beautiful maroon roof?

The sweat of anguish poured from him. Was she holding someone in her arms, calling him into her as they made love?

Everything was soft and beautiful and quiet there. It

was so simple, so delightful. And he was outside of it.

Should he go and ring the bell? Wake her up and beg her to come back? And if there was someone there, what then? He would kill him. Of that, there was simply no doubt. At the door, half dressed; in her room, naked. In the bathroom, washing her from himself. He would kill him.

This was the woman he had learned to overlook, who had done everything for him, and whom he had reduced to nothing. She was now giving herself to someone else. He knew he had to drive away. If the figure of a man cast a shadow across the yellow lamplight as he walked to the bathroom, or went for a cigarette, he would go up there and kill him. And her, and then himself.

Fight or flight? He drove away, flew through the empty Birmingham streets in his loping Citroën, drank half a bottle of Scotch in huge glugs that would not still his thoughts or anaesthetize his brain into oblivion.

Eventually, collapsed on the sofa, haunted by thoughts of gaudy flowers on a windowsill, garish lilies, risible pink gladioli, he imagined again that he was holding her, only to wake, cold and bitter, deeply sad and entirely alone.

The next day, wretched, sleepless, hung over, while the rest of the team went to the local pub for their customary pie and two pints, he had returned.

He parked around the corner and walked down an alley to the rear of her flat, drawn inexorably to the scene of her life.

He lifted the Suffolk latch on the white, wooden gate, peered in at the little patch of garden.

He was distraught to see the results of her labour. Even now, in early November, it was lovely.

There was a flower border on either side of the gravel path with the frosted remains of self-seeded, translucent nasturtiums winding through the random terracotta pots that were dotted there.

She had bought lots of winter-flowering pansies, their

garish colours of yellow and black and blue belying their wavering frailty. And against the red-brick wall there were big clumps of montbretia, planted long ago by some former tenant, and still revealing remnants of their orange flowers. All of her favourite things.

He knew that beneath the dark loam would be tulip bulbs, streaked, papery carapaces of jaunty daffodils and, even as he stood there, shivering at his exclusion, anemone corms, shouldering themselves out of their inauspicious woody husks.

He stood at the gate of the empty, quiet garden. He was the face at the window, the spectre: unable to break free, to go on, to start afresh, to make the new life.

He'd known men like this before, but he hadn't recognized their plight. Now, to his chagrin, he realized that he'd felt nothing but a kind of resentful contempt for them, as if, without his knowing exactly why, they deserved their fate.

Were all women like this? Did they all cope so much better than men with almost everything? They had more fortitude, more resolve, more inner strength, he'd always known that. It was nothing to do with all that endlessly repeated Thatcher nonsense. Gender was patently *not* the point with Margaret Thatcher. She was as rare and strange, unique really, as any of those curiosities of history: Boadicea or Napoleon or Cleopatra.

Kavanagh meant ordinary women, everyday women. The women in the pub and on the train and in the office or playing darts. Yes, of course they couldn't arm wrestle or kick a ball so far, but the stuff that mattered, really mattered, this, life, they could certainly manage that better; infinitely better.

No wonder they loathed men. No wonder they were doing without Frank Kavanagh and his ilk.

He sat in the deep seat of the car, its leather worn and scuffed into something that was his shape and person, started the engine and pushed the column-change up into first. The car rose magically those few French inches, inches that distinguished it from every other car, and its makers from every other nation.

The shipping forecast was just beginning on Radio Four. These things: the Citroën DS that he had driven for ten years and loved; the music that introduced *Desert Island Discs*; the comfort of Bailey and Rockall, Fair Isle and Mallinhead; the words that briskly issued in another day: 'And now, the weather forecast for the United Kingdom, until dawn tomorrow'; he clung to the certainty of these things, flotsam that might yet, even in this bilious sea of change, see him safely to the shore.

It was over. That glimpse of her life through the white, wooden gate set in the red-brick wall was more eloquent than any number of words.

Until that moment, he had secretly fed his life with notions of a reconciliation.

On that Tuesday lunch time, driving through the Stratford Road traffic, the sea fog off Southeast Iceland 'gathering slowly', he knew that their life together was finally over. It granted him a kind of peace, like the amputation of a painful limb, before its final, irredeemable loss is understood.

Kavanagh and Presley wandered through the marble concourse and down to the subterranean taxi rank.

The driver of their black cab didn't acknowledge in any way Presley's instruction to take them to Brecknock Road, just pushed up the window, slotted the excess fare onto the meter, and inched forward into the relentless flow of traffic on bleak Cardington Street.

Kavanagh could drive all right, but in London the cars and cabs beavered and nosed and eased into impossible places, manoeuvred through logic-defying spaces.

Another six inches, another six inches, the oncoming drivers holding their nerve against the bull-nosed throbbing diesel until there was nowhere else for it to go but out, out into the ever-moving stream.

There was something about Londoners' savoir-faire, a resignation which amounted almost to stoicism, and which intrigued Kavanagh. He suspected that there might have been a covert infiltration of the capital's entire population, like that in the *Invasion of the Bodysnatchers* or *The Stepford Wives*. The people were, certainly, unmistakably, different.

There was a resignation, an acceptance of their city falling apart. It was there from early morning, with the young people in blankets and cardboard boxes in their doorways, one hand extended: 'Can you spare any change, please? Can you spare some change?'

And it was there in the parked cars with their smashed quarter-lights, black plastic crudely taped and flapping in the breeze; in the graffiti that adorned the boarded-up churches and every bus stop and wall; it was there in the huge fire engines, sirens blaring, as they swung heavy around corners and through the parting traffic; and it was there as no one even looked up at the beautiful, big, silver jets droning by above their heads, throttling back as they dropped through the mackerel skies down to Gatwick and Heathrow.

Has earth anything to show more fair?

Occasionally, that resignation was a quiet and charming thing, and even the battle-hardened taxi driver played a strange, forgiving part as he let a scruffy minicab or a student's battered Fiat into the traffic of Holloway Road.

More usually, though, battle *was* joined, but it was with the phut of a buried grenade, the shrapnel zing ameliorated by the sand of familiarity. These people had seen it all before, saw it every day. Every third person on the street was mad or bad or violent or drunk.

It frightened Kavanagh: in a place like this, if you fell down in Charing Cross or King's Cross, you would certainly lie there, unattended and unhelped.

Everyone feared the danger of strangers, even fallen strangers, with their hypodermics and Carlsbergs and dogs and vomit. And in this city, *everyone* was a stranger.

'Seven pounds,' said the cabbie, without turning round. Presley paid him through the half-open window.

The two policemen stood on the Brecknock Road pavement and looked up at Sarah Clarke's flat.

17

Sarah Clarke, circa 1991, had become Sarah Hardy.

She was tall, slim and attractive. Her hair was streaked with fine, long grey hairs amidst the blonde. She was forty-two, Kavanagh knew, but looked five years younger.

She led the two policemen up the stairs and into the spacious front room above the furniture shop that looked down on bustling Brecknock Road in Camden.

He'd told her on the phone that it was about an old acquaintance. Any one from three. He'd chosen Sugar because he was the most recent. A mere eight years ago. If the stories panned out, her relationships with Lacey and Curtiss went back nearly two decades.

She had been intrigued. But he had avoided giving her the whole story, and time to reflect and, possibly, clam up.

You never knew how people would react. And it was in seeing their reaction, first time, as the story came out, that you learned about them.

She made them tea and offered her packet of Benson and Hedges with a slightly shaking hand.

'Thank you, Ms . . .' said Kavanagh. 'It's Ms Hardy now, not Clarke. Is that right?'

'Yes. I changed my name a couple of years ago, after my marriage ended.'

'I see,' he said. 'As I said on the phone, it's just a few questions, about Terry Sugar.'

'Yes?' she said.

He glanced around the room. 'You said to me that you have a "friend". Does he live here too?'

'Some of the time. I rent the flat and Peter rents the shop downstairs,' she said. 'He stays over sometimes. But he has a place of his own, too.'

'What does he do?' asked Presley.

'He restores furniture; strips pine, that kind of thing,' she said; and then, apparently keen to get on, 'Why are you here?' she asked directly.

'We need to fill out the picture, about what I mentioned on the phone. I'll explain as we go along,' said Kavanagh, appearing to trade off, say something, in fact giving nothing. 'Do you work at the moment? Do you have a job?'

'I work in an old people's home. I'm a supervisor there.'

'I see. And how long have you lived here?'

'About two years. Since my marriage broke up. Look, before you ask *me* any more questions, would you tell me about Terry. Is he in trouble?'

Kavanagh looked at Presley. It was a reasonable question. But they didn't want to reveal that they knew about her likely relationship with him at Open University. It was important that they should see what she would give them, volunteer unasked.

Kavanagh said, appearing to answer her, 'Do you know his background?'

'A bit,' she said guardedly. 'I didn't know him well. We were close for a short time. How do you know that I knew him?'

'From . . . documents,' said Kavanagh evasively. 'Tell us about your relationship with him.'

'Why?' she said, this time curt. 'I'm not sure I *want* to tell you. It's personal.'

'It is important,' said Kavanagh, conciliatory.

'Why?' she insisted.

He answered her with a question: 'Do you ever see *Crimewatch*, Ms Hardy?'

'No. Why?'

'Terry Sugar was featured on the programme recently. I'm afraid he's dead.' He watched for the Polaroid reaction of the woman in front of him and continued, 'He was killed. Some weeks ago now.'

She was moved by the news, but certainly not shocked. If she knew about his heroin habit, and with both his inner arms like perished cycle tubes, and veins that stood a quarter of an inch up from the flesh, it would be difficult to avoid it, she might reasonably assume that his death was drug related.

'You don't seem very surprised, Ms Hardy?'

'I know he had some drug problems. And anyway, when a policeman from Birmingham says he's tracked you down through Inland Revenue and tells you he's coming to London to "ask you a few questions about an old friend", I suppose you know it's not a parking offence he's looking into.'

'Yes, you're right, of course. And we need very badly to fill in some of the gaps in his life; his relationships. It's where you come in.'

She nodded agreement. She was going to play.

'We met at summer school a few years ago. It was 1985, I think. I'd have to check.' (It *was* '85, Kavanagh felt like saying; July '85.) 'We . . . had an affair.' She rolled her cigarette ash around the ashtray.

'And?' said Presley, too quickly.

'And what?' she said, challenging, feeling herself being judged by two men who had nothing to do with her, and no right to be asking her about her personal life.

'Was that it?' said Kavanagh, attempting to mollify.

'Yes. More or less. We spoke on the phone. But we didn't meet again. It just fizzled out.'

'You were married at that time?'

'Yes. What is this? The Vatican Council? It's a knocking shop,' she said with fierce sarcasm. 'Everybody knows that.' She looked at Presley, dared him to contradict her, her big brown eyes facing him out.

'People go there for a good time. OK, there's a few anoraks and winceyette pyjamas, a few eager beavers going to lectures and back to their rooms to study, but mostly, for the staff *and* the students, it's just an opportunity to . . . to get together.'

Both men knew plenty of coppers who'd done OU courses, summer school, the whole bit. Yes, it helped your career to have a degree in law or psychology or sociology, and yes, they both knew guys who, one way or another, were now divorced. (One sergeant's wife had even cited the OU as the correspondent in her divorce proceedings.) But whether the kind of people who did OU stuff were susceptible to marital breakdown, or whether the Open University was *responsible* for those divorces, neither man knew.

She carried on, 'It's no secret. It's an auction. You take your pick. Men and women. Here today, gone home to the wife and kids and washing-up or washing the car tomorrow.

'Everyone's been filled up with this liberal education for twelve months, struggling with assignments and tutorials and essays and early-morning and late-night TV. All that poetry and history and politics, and then there's this. They're similar people, have the same hunger, they know what you've been through, there's lots to talk about, to share. And it's the end.'

'The end?' said Presley.

'The end of term,' she said, smiling. 'School's out.'

Kavanagh was quite moved. It might, as she had gracelessly said, be a 'knocking shop' (a crude and distasteful phrase, wholly out of character with her, he thought) but she certainly made a case, in spite of herself really, for its educational value.

But he was less interested in the educational benefits of Jennie Lee's landmark creation than in the specifics of Sarah Hardy and Terry Sugar's affair.

'Did your husband know about your . . . relationship?'

'Not at the time, no.' And then, after a pause, 'I think he suspected something. People do know, I think, don't they?' she said, looking from Kavanagh to Presley and back again.

'Yes, I think people know,' said Kavanagh.

'I did tell him. But it was much later.'

'And what happened next?' prompted Presley, taking his more conciliatory tone from his boss.

'With Terry? It was impossible: my trying to get out of the house; his phoning me at a call box . . .'

'You were living in Shrewsbury then?' said Kavanagh, ever methodical, ever keen to slot the events and places neatly where they belonged.

'Yes. Jeff was teaching at a school there. Anyway, Terry, I don't think his heart was in it. I thought I was in love. I always do.' She smiled fleetingly. 'Or maybe I just have to: convince myself I'm in love so it doesn't seem like some cheap little affair.

'I think Terry *was* fond of me. Well, I know he was, but I don't think he was ready to leave home, give up his pitch on the High Street, leave his wife, the whole business. He was settled, and he'd got his habit, which softened most of the knocks he had to take.'

There was a pause. She became reflective. The policemen were prudently silent.

'He was a nice man. He'd got some problems, of course. But he was nice. I liked him a lot. Did he get some bad stuff?'

'He was killed.'

'Yes,' she said. 'But was it bad stuff?'

'No. He was killed deliberately. In his car. He was gassed to death. And his wife.'

'My God! He was murdered?'

'Yes, I'm afraid so.'

'I just . . . I just assumed it was bad stuff, cut with something, you know. Or some nasty deal. This is awful.'

'It could have been drug related,' said Presley.

'Yes, it might have been,' continued Kavanagh. 'We've got to keep an open mind. But there are other connections, things that need to be tied up. There's a possible link, too much for coincidence . . .'

'With what?' she asked guilelessly.

'Possibly with you,' said Kavanagh.

'With me?' she said, actually pointing the long fingers of her left hand at her chest.

'Did you have other affairs?' asked the inspector.

'Why?'

'I have to ask you these things, believe me.'

'Why do you?' she said.

'Please, Ms Hardy, it's very important. People have been murdered. Other lives might be at risk.'

'I don't understand.'

'Did you have another affair? More than one?'

'No.'

'Are you sure?'

'Am I sure?' she said bitingly. 'Don't you mean: "Are you telling the truth?" I *know* whether I have affairs or not.'

'What about further back in the past?'

'What about it?'

'Did you have any . . . extramarital relationships then?'

'Yes. Did *you*?'

'Ms Hardy,' said Kavanagh with a mock weariness, 'this is serious. Very serious. We're not playing. Whoever murdered Terry Sugar and his wife may have killed other people you knew. There seems to be a link.'

She was agitated, frightened: didn't know whether to believe them or not. Was this just the way they did things, by frightening people?

'Who that I "knew" has been killed?'

'Did you have any other relationships during your marriage?'

'Why?'

He wouldn't let go. 'Please, Ms Hardy, answer my questions first. Tell us about your relationships, no matter how long ago. Then I'll tell you what I know. I promise.'

'It's all so distant, like another life really. We married young. I was barely twenty. And I was having a baby.

'He was older than me, three or four years older. It was an unequal relationship from the start. He made all the decisions. It couldn't be any other way. He was the one with the information. I think he loved me for my youth; I *was* pretty. But he always made me feel insignificant and silly. I had to survive, stay alive somehow.' She paused, sucked on her cigarette, looked from Kavanagh to Presley and back again.

'So, you had an affair?' said Kavanagh sympathetically, encouraging her to start again.

'Yes. It wasn't a conscious fighting back. But I was disappearing, and it was my only way of asserting myself, I suppose. I didn't work it out or anything.'

'Who was it?' said Presley.

'Do I have to?' she said, looking at Kavanagh.

'Please,' said the inspector gently.

'It was a friend of his. A man called Adam. Adam Curtiss.'

'Go on,' said Kavanagh.

'Jeff wasn't blameless, you know,' she said defensively. '*He* had affairs too.'

'Yes. But for now, just tell us about yourself. Please, carry on.'

'We were living in Cardiff. Jeff was finishing his course. There was someone living with us, a lodger. They were very different times. We were young, things were different in every way. We were having a bad time. I had an affair with Jeff's friend, Adam. I ran away to London to be with him. Jeff came and took me back.

'It was all awful. Then Jeff went away to let me sort things out. Left me at home with Briony, our daughter.

'Adam came to see me and stayed a couple of days. But

it didn't work out. How could it? And he went back to London.

'It was then I had a brief fling with the man who was living with us, a man called John, John Lacey. I know it sounds awful, and in a way it was, but I was lost, unhappy with Jeff, and struggling to find a way out. It was insane really, the whole thing.'

'And your husband?' said Kavanagh quietly. 'He knew about this?'

'He knew about Adam. I told him about John much later, when things were better between us, and I wanted him to know everything, so we could start fresh.'

'How did he take it?' said Presley.

'Badly.'

'How badly?'

'He was very upset. Very hurt.'

'And?'

She sighed. 'And it passed. And we got on and tried to put things back together.'

'Go on,' urged Kavanagh.

'Things were all right for a while. For several years. Not brilliant, but better. Best we'd ever been. He could still bruise me with a word. But we were older.

'I'd grown up and I'd learned how to handle him: and he'd learned to be better to me. He knew I could hurt him, too. I was working. Briony was growing up. We were getting along.'

'Yes?' said Kavanagh. There was no point in interrupting. This was her story. He let her run with it.

'Everyone else we knew had a degree, they were all "educated". My father was in the army. I had been to five schools in eleven years when I was a child.

'So I enrolled for the Open University; got up early, watched the morning BBC2 broadcasts and got to quite like the regime of tea and my notepad and books spread about me, the men in flared trousers talking about architecture and the growth of literacy.

'I met Terry at summer school. He hadn't been out of prison long, and there he was, with all these housewives and teachers, tattoos on both his forearms, short hair, and a heroin habit.

'But he was sharp. Bright but vulnerable. Worse off than me, even. I liked him; there didn't seem any point in not going with him. I didn't have enough to make me not want to. Not really.

'I gave myself to him. I think he was surprised. He didn't even have to ask.

'Afterwards, we spoke on the phone, but it just faded away, shrivelled up from lack of contact. Jeff and I slipped back into our routine. And there we stayed, another few years.

'Briony had grown up. She was twenty, she had left home, was at university in Aberystwyth.'

She sighed very deeply.

'I wanted us to have a baby. I needed Jeff to show me that he loved me. I think that's all that I had ever needed from him. That's why I had kept on hurting him.

'But he didn't want one. He put up all the practical reasons for our not having one. Good, sound, sensible reasons why we shouldn't do it. He wanted to give up his job teaching. Wanted early retirement. Was looking for less responsibility, not more. He was trying to get his book written.'

'He was writing a book?' asked Kavanagh.

'Yes, an academic book. A critical work on Gerard Manley Hopkins.'

'And did he?' said Kavanagh, intrigued. 'Did he finish it?'

'Yes, eventually, he did. He kept at it. It was his "baby". Do you see?' she said, smiling slightly, without joy. 'And I wanted mine.

'He said the only way he'd be a father again would be if his book was published. He quoted all that Cyril Connolly nonsense about creativity going out of the window as soon as there's a pram in the hall.'

'And was it?' asked Kavanagh.

'No. No, it wasn't. Not in the end. But it looked as if it was going to be.

'He finished it, and sent it out, again, and again, and again. And every time, it just kept coming back.

'At first, it was a real body blow. But after the first two or three times, he became very stoical, and just mailed it out again.

'One day, instead of his book coming back, a letter came. It was a small academic publisher who said yes.'

'They took it?' said Kavanagh, really quite excited by the story.

'Yes. They accepted it. No advance, just royalties on sales. It was the best day of his life, he said.

'I came off the pill. It was what we had said. He'd agreed: if his book was taken, we could have our baby.

'Months went by: letters, phone calls, but no book. Always some reason for the delay: the estate, copyright, the man's partner out of the country, but Jeff knew things weren't right.

'And then, one day, he telephoned the man's number, a little office somewhere in Herefordshire, and there was no reply.

'He'd gone bust. Jeff's book wasn't going to get printed.

'The same week, I found out that I was pregnant. His baby dying, mine trying to be born.

'I nurtured my secret, a warm glow of a lovely secret. Not the wrong kind of deceit that we had known all too much of during our marriage, but a secret wish that was mine and that we had agreed to.'

She stopped speaking, took shallow breaths, was very close to tears.

'Please, go on,' he said gently.

'The next morning, I took him a cup of coffee. I put the

coffee cup down on the chair beside the bed next to the radio alarm.

'He opened his eyes and said, "What's the matter?"

'I held up the little tube that had gone pink. "I'm pregnant," I said.

'"Oh, no!" he said. "Oh no!" and held me to him.

'I went to see my doctor that evening. He confirmed that I was pregnant.

'I told him that Jeff wasn't sure about us having another baby. He said that by the time he was bouncing the little baby on his knee, he wouldn't have any reservations.

'But the doctor was wrong. Jeff said that he *really* didn't want another baby. He was forty-four, he kept saying.

'"You said if your book was taken we could have a baby. You said it. You *said* it. And I held on to that belief."'

'"I know I said it, but the book *isn't* being published. They've gone out of business."'

'"But you said . . ."'

'"I know what I said. And I shouldn't have done."

'I told him that I couldn't have a termination. There was a life inside me; I couldn't do it.'

'"We had our child,"' he said. "We could have been happy then . . ."'

She looked from one policeman to the other, hopelessly, pleading. 'I was being punished for our past. I wanted us to be happy. It was so easy, couldn't he see? Just let's do this wonderful thing.

'But *I* had been to blame for the bad part of our marriage, and now he was going to punish me for it by not having a baby with me.

'My best friend took me to the hospital. I was in a ward with six other women. I dozed and cried into my pillow.

'They gave me my premed, and took me down just before eleven o'clock. That's all I remember.

'When I woke up it was about two o'clock, and all of the other ladies were lying in their beds with drips and tubes.

'I looked at them but kept my head on the pillow and then closed my eyes and went back into a sort of sleep.

'They brought me some tea and asked me how I was and helped me sit up. I kept myself inside and smiled and said thank you and drank the milky tea.

'At five, Jeff came. He had flowers and a card.

'I said I was all right, but I said I didn't want to talk about things right now.

'We drove home slowly.

'On the Monday, I went back to work, and in the evening Jeff asked me if it was all right if he went out for a drink. He said he wouldn't mind if I didn't want him to go. He would quite understand.

'I said I didn't mind.'

She started to cry.

'Both our babies died. And our hopeless marriage, too. "Why must disappointment all I endeavour end . . ."'

'Sorry?' said Kavanagh.

'It's Hopkins. Gerard Manley Hopkins. He always used to say it when his book was rejected: ". . . and not breed one work that wakes." Very appropriate,' she murmured.

'I wanted to hurt him. I wanted to hurt him as much as he had hurt me.

'I knew the one thing that *would* destroy him . . . but I couldn't do it.

'I wanted to. But I couldn't.

'I told him, instead, about my affair with Terry all those years ago, at summer school.

'He asked me things. Asked me what we had *done*. And I told him. I told him everything.

'He shouldn't have made me do that thing. It was our baby. It was wrong. And *I* have to live with that.

'I'm not really an unfaithful woman. I know it sounds silly. But I'm not. Not deep down. I just needed to be loved.'

There was a long silence, with only the rumble and whine of the constant traffic in the street below.

Eventually, Kavanagh said quietly, 'What was the thing you were going to tell him, Ms Hardy? That would have destroyed him?'

'I can't tell you. I've never told anyone. I never will.'

'Whatever it is, are you sure he hasn't found out?' asked the inspector.

'No, he doesn't know.'

'And you won't tell me, in confidence?'

'No,' she said quietly, but resolutely. 'No.'

'I see.' Kavanagh drew a deep breath. 'Where is he now, Ms Hardy? Do you know?'

'He went away. He gave up teaching; well, they gave him up really, he had a sort of breakdown. He went to live in Cheshire, and then I think he went abroad. Left me to sell the house, which I did, and Peter and I moved away, came down here.'

'And your ex-husband? Is he still in touch?'

'No. We made all the financial arrangements through our solicitors, but there was no personal contact. At first he sent a few crazy letters, almost deranged really: grief, regret, anger, jealousy. Peter said I shouldn't read them. After a while I didn't. They were too upsetting.

'And then we moved and I changed my name. I don't think he knows where I am. I hope not.'

She became reflective again, almost ignored Kavanagh and Presley's presence. 'It's funny, isn't it, the person you have everything with, the person you would do anything with and for, they eventually become the person you avoid most completely, even hide from. I've never been able to get over that.

'Briony used to write to him, but I think even that's stopped now. She's in Wales, in Machynlleth. As part of her degree course.

'I've told her not to tell him where we are. I was afraid of him, to be honest. I think he was capable of anything.'

18

An hour later, she escorted them to the top of the steep stairs. They had told her the little that she needed to know about the violent deaths of her former lovers, Adam Curtiss and John Lacey.

At the street door, Kavanagh turned and said to her, 'We'll just have a word with your friend downstairs. Is he in the shop?'

'Yes, I think so. Why?' she said.

'Just a precaution,' said Kavanagh. 'Keep an eye out for anything unusual, Ms Hardy. I'll have one of the local CID watch the place, too. And let me know if you hear anything at all from your ex-husband.

'When we've finished in London, probably tomorrow, we'll go up and see your daughter, just in case he's been in touch with her.'

'You think he might come here?' she said, concerned.

'I don't know. The deaths are too much for coincidence. And you are the link. But it doesn't make sense: all this time passed.' He paused and smiled up at her. '*You* haven't been killing people, have you?'

She smiled at his bad-taste joke. 'No, I haven't killed anyone.'

'Oh, yes, Ms Hardy, one thing . . .'

'Yes?'

'Your ex-husband?'

'Yes?'

'What size shoes did he wear?'

'Are you serious?'

'Yes. What size, please?'

'Ten; ten and a half, I think. Why?'

'It's nothing. Just a thought. Thank you. Goodbye.'

Next door, in the pine shop, they introduced themselves to the man in Levis and Timberland boots, told him they were concerned about Sarah Hardy's former husband, thought he might be able to help them with their inquiries.

Peter Burchell was Scots, but had the gormless mouth and docile jaw of a Swedish tennis star. He had neither seen nor heard of Clarke since he and Sarah had moved to London.

There was some odd male territorial chemistry between Kavanagh and Burchell immediately. It signalled about a million years of animal evolution running on the gene clock as the two men stood a few feet apart from one another in the north London shop.

With his woollen, checked shirt and 150-pound boots, legs crossed as he leaned against a four-foot dresser, Burchell felt no need to mask his indifference to the policeman, a Birmingham cop with a risible accent and a not very bright suit.

Radio Three was playing from the dusty cassette recorder that sat on the battered, roll-top desk against the far wall. There was a Bodum of Traidcraft coffee perched on a pine box next to it.

It was all very civilized; the *Guardian* with attitude. Burchell on Pine; Zen and the art of pine stripping; the Never Ending Circle . . . of dressers from Wales into basement kitchens in Highgate.

'Nice day,' insisted Kavanagh, goading the man.

'It's all weather. Sometimes it rains; sometimes it's sunny. It works out,' said Burchell.

Presley glanced at his boss, taken aback by the carpenter's homily.

'Strong stuff, I suppose,' said Kavanagh, implacable, as

he walked towards the stripping tank at the back of the shop.

Burchell's Levis had several small acid-burn holes that had frayed around the edges. 'It's got to be,' said the man.

'I do mine by hand,' said Kavanagh. 'Paint stripper and wire wool.'

He'd never stripped a door in his life.

'Oh, yes,' said the man, deeply uninterested.

Only Presley looked at his boss with some surprise, impressed by his casual lying, but even more so by the inspector knowing that you *might* use wire wool to strip paint.

'Takes forever,' said the inspector, as he ran his palm down a pair of Victorian shutters. 'No matter. If a job's worth doing . . . eh?'

Kavanagh sauntered down the corridor formed by the stacks of upright doors on either side of him, every half-dozen or so separated by a batten.

He stood at the entrance to the back room and, without turning, spoke into it. 'I had one done in one of these once.' He looked down at the galvanized bath. 'Acid warped it. Glue came out. All the joints came loose.'

'Oh, yes?' said the man.

'Yes,' said the inspector.

'It's *alkaline*, actually,' said the man.

'Sorry?' said Kavanagh, not even turning as the conversational snare dropped over the Scotsman.

'Everyone thinks it's acid. But it's not. Acid would burn the wood.'

'And this strips the stuff just the same?' said Kavanagh, binding the man up.

Burchell rolled his Samson tobacco into a loose cigarette. 'If you do it slowly. The cowboys heat it up . . . then it'll do it in an hour. But your eyes and nose and ears'll be running, and it can explode. There've been a few.'

'But not this?' said the policeman.

'All you need is a fresh mix now and again,' he said.

A few bubbles came to the surface, as if confirming the man's assertion.

They'd had their opening skirmish. An away win, Kavanagh reckoned.

'Did you want something? I've got things to do,' said Burchell tetchily.

'Sorry. You carry on,' said Kavanagh, inhaling deeply, but not moving. 'I love the smell in these places. The glue and the wood shavings, all that stuff. Don't you?'

'I can take it or leave it,' said Burchell.

'Umm. I like it. Do you like it, sergeant?' laboured Kavanagh.

'Yes, sir. I love the smell,' replied Presley dutifully.

'Perhaps we'd better let you get on,' said the inspector, but in fact peered intently at the Birmingham maker's name etched into the brass spring on an old pub door. 'If you hear anything about Mr Clarke, you know, like they say in the films, "give us a call", would you? No one ever does, of course. It's just film talk.'

The man resented the baiting, took refuge in smarting silence.

'You must've noticed,' pursued the inspector relentlessly, 'they say: "Give us a call," and they give them a card. Thing is, I've never seen anyone with a card. Well, the Commissioner, Sir Paul Condon, has a card, I'm sure. But people like me. No one at the station has ever said to me, "Would you like a card, Inspector?" Much less, "What sort would you like? Embossed? Serrated edge? A bit of colour?" Nothing. Anyway, give us a ring if anything comes up.'

Presley had his hand on the door handle. There was vandal wire over the thick glass. 'Trouble with break-ins?' said Kavanagh.

'Kids.'

'There's nothing for them here, is there?' said Kavanagh, genuinely interested.

'For kicks. They smash it for kicks. No jobs; idle hands . . .' Burchell replied superciliously.

He made the local unemployment sound as if it was Kavanagh's fault.

'I see,' said the inspector, and walked back the few paces towards the big, zinc bath. Presley released the door handle and felt the springs inside the lock return.

Kavanagh nodded towards the leather apron hung on a six-inch nail from a joist. 'You have to watch yourself, I suppose?'

'Yes. You said,' replied the man.

Kavanagh peered into the bath. There was silence between the three men. A few bubbles came to the surface as a door, perhaps a hundred years old, and made from a tree planted a hundred before that, released from some sliver of grain the air that had been trapped there one day two hundred years ago.

'May I?' he asked politely, as he picked up a broom handle made smooth by a thousand immersions.

The man shrugged. Kavanagh pushed up his jacket sleeve, undid the button on his shirt cuff, and pushed the blue cotton up as far as it would go.

He drew the handle through the liquid, watched it creep up the porous pole as he trawled it through the tub.

He traced the outline of the panelled door that lay on the bottom, zigzagged slowly through the quietly fizzing liquid. When he reached the end of the tub, he turned and smiled at Burchell.

'It's bubbling,' he said, gauche.

'It's a fresh mix,' said the man. 'That's why it's bubbling.'

Kavanagh's fanciful notion of air trapped for a century or two flew out of the window.

'Was there something else?' said the man insolently.

Kavanagh looked at him. Presley saw something in that look that was no longer playful irritation. It was loathing, hatred.

The inspector continued to look at the Scotsman, opened his fingers, and let the pole bob on the surface of the mixture. 'No, nothing else,' he said.

From the window of the first-floor flat, Sarah Hardy watched as they walked away towards the Camden Road.

She didn't know a Mercedes from a Mitsubishi, and anyway, what would an old, dark blue Volvo have meant to her, its nose just around the corner in Hargrave Place, its driver slumped down in the fabric-covered seat?

19

Kavanagh and Presley picked up a couple of faxes from their hotel in Melton Street. British Rail had completed their technical investigation of the carriage door from which Adam Curtiss had fallen to his death. It was in perfect working order.

There was news on the Volvo, too. Enhancement of the video-surveillance tape taken from the garage near to the scene of Terry Sugar's murder had isolated the last two letters and one of the digits on the number plate. It had been enough to establish, via an elimination trace and lots of expensive police-hours, the last registered ownership of the car.

A description of the driver was less helpful: he was tallish and slim, but there was no prospect of a positive identification from the shaky images on the tape.

The 'W' registered car had been traded in to a Honda dealer on the south coast two months ago. The dealer had told the police that it was in reasonable nick, but far too old to be dropped in amongst the Preludes and Accords on the forecourt. (And anyway, the Japanese franchisers were inclined to inscrutability when it came to Swedish – or any other nation's – cars sharing their forecourt tarmac.)

The following Thursday, therefore, a junior salesman had driven the blue 244 down to the local auction at Hythe.

It went through at three hundred and seventy pounds.

The car was still MOT'd and had a couple of months' tax on it. Someone had picked up a bargain. The buyer had paid cash and given a name and address in nearby Folkestone. They were false.

Kavanagh was delighted. Someone buys a car in a false name on the south coast. The car is subsequently identified on video at a garage near a double murder in Shropshire. What is almost certainly the same car has a 'Do not park here, please' message left on its windscreen by a Pooter-like resident round the corner from the murders.

A few weeks later, a similar car is identified by a pensioner a couple of hundred yards from where John Lacey is stabbed to death.

Details of the Volvo were circulated to police forces throughout Britain. Identify vehicle and report. Approach driver, who may be armed, with extreme caution.

As the two men sat in the back of their cab and drove out towards Adam Curtiss's flat in Finsbury Park, Kavanagh had a quiet sense of satisfaction: things were starting to come together, the hunches paying off; his notion of a link, based initially on no more than the apparently motiveless murders of Lacey, the Sugars, and then Curtiss, had been confirmed by Sarah Hardy's story. Now, it seemed that the perpetrator of at least two of those killings was the driver of the Volvo saloon.

The inquiry's initial, tentative flicker, originally no brighter than a Turkish match was, remarkably, still glowing.

This glow, this feeling of beginning to tie up the ends, like filling in the last clue of the crossword, or placing the last piece of the jigsaw, was one of the huge pleasures. He had all but forgotten it.

But the very thought process, the slight sense of congratulation, the hubris of acknowledging pleasant things remembered, brought surging in its wake other thoughts, thoughts and feelings of deep pain, regret and loss.

He was undone. When having an injection, think of something nice: Mediterranean beaches; peaches and cream.

When fighting back nausea, the heaving, irresistible need to vomit in a public place, think of something other than greasy food, the alcohol swilling in your belly.

Trying *not* to think of his ex-wife, he was back in the sticky web of the emotional net. But before it had ensnared him anew, he had glimpsed for a second the possibility of freedom from this loop of pain. The notion of a life without the constant, accompanying memory of the past. Seen again the possibilities of savouring the unremarkable, the humdrum, the simple joy of life.

Life was not about the 'big moments': the pools win; the foreign holiday; the cup finals of one's life. It was about the quiet satisfaction, the moments of easy content, the space around the edges, space in which to be, to watch, to listen, to moan about the football and the government and, yes, the crime rate.

His fear was that those unremarkable times were much harder to realize than any of the big set pieces. It was little snippets of evanescing nothing that haunted him, rather than the 'special' occasions of their life together: a cup of tea in a motorway café; the smile on a holiday photograph; picking blackberries; even, once, making jam together.

But maybe the glimpse was a beginning. Time is the healer. That's what they said. Everybody did. Bad backs; smoking; diet; divorce. Everybody had a point of view.

Takes between one and five years to get over the separation and divorce of a long marriage; you can fit everyone in the world on to the Isle of Wight; if you join all the buses in London end to end . . . ; on aeroplanes, the pilot and copilot always eat different meals; if everyone in China were to jump up and down at the same time; it takes between one and five years to get over a . . .

Any club that . . .

It was no good peering over the edge. You had to let go. That was the whole point. Suck it and see. It was no good just *looking* at that curious, dimpled shape: smelling might give a clue, peering hard at the heart-shaped, speckled fruit might help, but you had to taste the giving, watery flesh, release the indescribable flavour onto your salivating tongue, bite into the flesh, and it was done.

The taste was in your mouth: strawberry or Paraquat. And then it *was* too late. It was there for ever. No going back. Over the ledge, free fall, no parachute, into the abyss.

He became aware that Presley was speaking to him. His sergeant was looking at him, really looking *at* him. Was he reading his thoughts? Often, these days, Kavanagh was not sure whether he was merely thinking, or actually *saying* his thoughts.

A dispatch rider skimmed their cab as it wove through the traffic on Seven Sisters Road. Presley relieved the pressure of the moment between the two men. 'We'd better get a result on this one, 'cause there's no fucking way *we're* gonna make a living down here delivering pizzas!'

They were into Green Lanes, Greek and Turkish Green Lanes; Thessaloniki or Istanbul: plate-glass windowed 'football clubs' at which, certainly, no football was played.

There were massage parlours, and tobacconists selling lottery tickets, and travel agents, and banks with darkened windows and standing fans, uselessly cooling the chilly, London air.

Every other shop was a greengrocer's, with displays of melons and beans, pineapples and aubergines that spilled onto the pavements. Deep inside, little groups of men chatted, and the girl at the till sold bleach and plastic buckets and light bulbs and toothpaste, just as if it were a dark shop in the quiet backstreets of Athens at three in the boiling afternoon, with *their* smells of soap and cheese and beef tomatoes and apricots.

At Endymion Road the thickset, silver-haired Greek landlord was waiting for the policemen in his Mercedes. During the last few days he had become very short-tempered about the place not yet being available for reletting. It had been sealed by the police since the Buddhist's death, 'pending further inquiries', but it had been nearly two weeks now, and the landlord was threatening an official complaint.

Mr Stassios showed the policemen Curtiss's former flat. He had never met his tenant: he owned half a dozen houses dotted around the Finsbury area and had a letting agent who dealt with the plumbing and the collection of his considerable rents.

While the policemen made a quiet progress through the flat and looked for clues to the sudden, violent death of the erstwhile tenant, the owner conducted an equally careful study of the window frames, carpets and general decorative order of his property.

It was a bare and nearly empty place; not sterile, but calm and ordered. One bunch of flowers had wilted and died on the uncluttered mantelpiece. There was a little shrine in the bedroom with a heavy bronze Buddha on a white napkin, and two incense holders with several burned-down sticks in each one. There were copies of the *Bhagavadgita* and the Upanishads on the floor near the prayer mat before the altar.

Even with the big, Greek landlord puffing from room to quiet room, there was an immutable quiet about the whole place: letters were filed, socks folded one into the other in the sock drawer; shirts were on hangers, towels neatly folded and stacked in the airing cupboard.

The kitchen was tidy, with the few utensils and crockery that had last been used placed on a tea-towel on the draining board with another tea towel covering them.

On the shelves were a few travel books, numerous religious and philosophical texts, and a couple of modern novels. Maybe the man didn't hoard much; maybe the whole notion of acquisition and possessions was alien to his religious beliefs.

The policemen took a few letters and bank statements (his address book and wallet had been with him when he had died, and were already in the possession of the police). Kavanagh told the landlord that he could let the flat again as soon as Curtiss's mother had collected the rest of his things.

He bid the man kalimera, and Mr Stassios, charmed by the policeman's use of the word, shook his hand warmly and bid them farewell.

20

As well as quarrying slate and being something of a railway centre, the little Welsh town of Machynlleth had manufactured snuff and supported a printing industry in the late-nineteenth century.

It had then had a hiatus of half a century or more when it slipped from view, the itinerants moving on, to build their railways and father their illegitimate children elsewhere.

But during the last two or three decades, the nostalgia industry had arrived with a vengeance in mid-Wales, and the High Street, once a sombre, almost gloomy, place, populated only by grocers and hardware merchants, butchers and outfitters, quite suddenly sprouted half a dozen 'craft' shops. Places selling socks and bonnets, cardigans and egg cups; love spoons, and all things Welsh; a hundred things in slate, from clocks and barometers, to maps of Montgomeryshire etched on half-inch-thick stone.

These people had come to retailing late, and they approached it with an evangelical fervour, clasping to their collective bosom the new-found deity of mammon, and competing zealously for worshippers at their gift-shop shrines.

Even the Hebron chapel now displayed an orange fascia board, four feet deep and thirty feet long, that obscured the original benefactors' names and proclaimed, not the

Word of a stern God, but *Bedroom quality carpet: £2.99 a square yard.*

The dour shopkeepers took the money and barely smiled, as if any levity on their part might betray their suspicion that their new-found labours were little more than fraud.

Machynlleth's disenfranchised youngsters, meanwhile, scorned the immigrants and tourists, and refused to move aside for them on the crowded market-day pavements of their town.

Sat sourly in the Black Lion, two hundred yards down the road from the Owain Glendower Centre (home, once, to the rebel prince's fifteenth-century Assembly, now a tourist attraction for the gawping trippers from Dudley and West Bromwich), they greeted with a frosty silence any stranger from the Midlands who might, haplessly, wander into their last stronghold on the edge of town.

On the way to Dolgellau, a couple of miles up the valley, was the other reason for Machynlleth's new-found celebrity: the Centre of Alternative Technology, an experiment in 'sustainable living', had been started by a right-thinking, head-screwed-on type in the early seventies.

No woolly-headed, acid-brained hippy this: Gerard Morgan Grenville had seen the light on the road, not to Damascus, but a deeply inauspicious slate quarry on the A487.

The Centre plodded on throughout the muddled seventies, but it was during the ozone-heady days of the eighties that it had soared in popularity and become a sort of low-tech Alton Towers, attracting ninety thousand visitors each year.

Briony Clarke was a clone of her mother: an inch or two taller, a younger figure, but the same long, fair hair; the big, slightly surprised brown eyes; the straight nose. They were sisters, born twenty years apart.

She welcomed them into the little house in Heol Pentrerhedyn, Machynlleth's main street, made herb tea, and brought in a plate of biscuits.

The men were big in the cosy room with its amiable clutter of packed bookshelves, magazines and papers, tapes and CDs. There was no evidence of any other occupant; in the porch was a pair of wellington boots and a nice pair of greased walking boots, but they were both size fives, Kavanagh reckoned; maybe a six, but no bigger. Inside the boots were walking socks: thick, red, woollen ones, neatly tucked and folded.

As she poured the tea the young woman chatted in an open, friendly manner, small talk about the weather and their train journey.

'And have you been here long?' asked Presley.

'About six months,' she said. 'I'm doing a year at the Centre. I'm studying environmental science at university.'

Kavanagh was glad to be listening to someone who volunteered information. He spent his life dragging sentences out of monosyllabics, people who either didn't want to talk, for fear of incriminating themselves, or were unable to, through a lack of nurturing.

'It's about your father, Briony,' said Presley.

'Yes, my mum phoned last night and told me.'

'Have you seen him recently?' asked the sergeant.

'No,' she said. 'He hasn't been in touch for ages. The last time I saw him was just before he went abroad.'

'When was that?'

'I can't remember exactly, but it was in the spring, early spring, about the time I came up here. Mum was in London with . . .'

The girl felt uneasy speaking the name of her mother's new partner. Kavanagh approved. These days, he valued fidelity above all things.

'Burchell? Peter Burchell?' helped Kavanagh.

'Yes. Peter Burchell.'

'Don't you get on with him?' asked the inspector.

'It's not that,' she said. 'Not really. It's just difficult. Mum, Dad. You know. You can't just see your mum with someone else like that. I couldn't anyway. It didn't seem fair to Dad. It seemed . . . I don't know, it's silly I suppose, like I was being a traitor. But it isn't Mum's fault. She's entitled to . . . whatever it is she wants.'

'Yes, of course,' said Kavanagh. 'Where did he go, your dad?'

'He had a friend in Italy. A friend from years back. They'd always kept in touch. From university, I think. He wanted to get away. He didn't seem to be getting over things. As time went on, he was getting worse, not better. I think he thought it might help him.'

Kavanagh was chary of hearing about time's *not* being a healer.

'Go on,' he said, bracing himself.

'Since he and Mum split up, he just seemed to fall apart. He found it hard. He'd always seen himself as strong in the relationship, and because of that, it was a much worse thing for him than it was for her. To be honest, I think it was liberating for her.'

Kavanagh winced.

'It happens. Women are in marriages and their husband dies or whatever, and suddenly the woman finds that all this mystique that had to surround paying the electricity bill and the mortgage, or getting a new tyre for the car . . . it's just that: mystique.'

He listened, sipped his bitter raspberry tea.

'I shouldn't generalize,' she offered, conciliatory. 'Every situation's different, of course. And it wasn't Dad's fault. It was *his* upbringing and conditioning; *his* parents and all, I suppose.'

Kavanagh watched the pretty girl's lips moving. She had her long hair piled on top of her head in a way that intrigued him. There was a neat plait up the back of her neck, which then disappeared into the mass of fair hair that was bunched there.

As a teenager, he had often got on well with his girlfriends' mothers. Now, it seemed, he had reached an age where he was destined to court the mothers while actually mesmerized by their daughters.

'When they split up, Dad went to pieces, just got worse and worse.'

'In what way?' said Kavanagh.

'He'd always been a bit obsessive. About his job, about his writing. Everything had to be done, whatever it was, no matter how small, right then. Just so; there and then.

'I've never been like that,' she gestured to her cluttered room. 'His life was full of little routines and habits that he had. So tiny things seemed huge, insurmountable.

'When they broke up, all that fell apart, and he was lost.'

'And?' said Kavanagh.

'He knew, deep down, that their parting had to be. It had to be, and now, here it was. He said he didn't "own" her. He had a kind of strength. A sense of moral right. But he also knew it was against *nature.*'

She paused. 'You know about the baby?'

Kavanagh nodded.

'He knew he had wronged her, but because of that, I think he believed that he had to let her go, even though it was destroying him.'

The three of them sat quietly for a few moments.

'So, what happened next?' said Kavanagh.

'She'd got involved with Peter.'

'Yes,' said Kavanagh.

'Dad tried to be rational and contained. He moved to a flat in Chester: new life; carried on with his writing, he always did that, no matter what.'

'A new book?' asked the inspector.

'Yes, a novel. It was the material *for* a book. One day, he said, he'd write it.'

'Did he show it to you?' asked Presley.

'He never showed anybody anything he was working on,' she said.

'Why not?' asked the policeman.

'He said that if you talked about stuff before you wrote it, you had no excitement in doing it, you'd talked it out of your system and you couldn't then be bothered to write it.'

'I see,' said Kavanagh. 'Please, carry on.'

'They were selling the house. I used to go and see Dad in his flat in Chester. The place was a mess. It was terrible to see. He never used to live like that.

'Mum got more involved with . . . you know, Peter. Dad was always thinking about Mum, talking about the past, what they'd had, and what they had lost.

'But it was *him* that had lost everything, really. She was all right.

'He'd talk about their past, things and people I'd never heard of. How she'd made him unhappy. These things were always on his mind, he'd just go round and round them, over and over again. He said it was only his writing that kept him sane. He was obsessed with their past.

'She told him to stop writing letters to her. He had started to threaten her with what he thought was his love, but was really just a kind of jealousy. He was drinking heavily, and not sleeping properly.

'He wanted to put back the clock, and I told him: You can't do that. It's past. That time has gone. But he couldn't accept it.

'And he has that writer thing: I think people such as him, they save up the moments, the good times and the bad times, for use in the future.

'If he'd *lived* the moment, kissed "the joy as it flies", as Mum used to say, it might have been different.'

After a long silence, she said. 'What has he done? Mum said it was serious.'

'We don't know, Briony. But it *is* serious, and we do need to speak to him, urgently.'

'Why?'

'Did your mother not tell you any more?'

'She said it involved people from her past.'

Kavanagh looked at Presley. The herb tea was cold beside him on the floor.

Presley said, 'Several people have died recently. They were known to your mother. It could be that your father is involved.'

'I see,' she said, not suggesting for even a moment that the notion was anything but reasonable.

'So, the last time you heard from your father was when?' asked Kavanagh.

'Ages. Three months at least. Just a postcard.'

'Have you got it?'

'Yes. And a few things were sent on to me from his flat in Chester. Do you want those, too?'

'Yes, we're going over there to have a look. Anything that'll help us locate him. Do you have the address of his friend in Italy?'

'Yes, of course.'

The card had been posted in Milan, and had a picture of the Duomo on it. There were several buff envelopes, social security ones, and a dozen bits of junk mail.

They declined her offer of more tea, shook hands and left her with instructions about contacting them if her father got in touch.

21

The policemen stood on the platform beside a couple of middle-aged hikers as the Chester train, a single-carriage affair, rocked into the station.

The walkers were serious people: thigh-length Gore-Tex jackets, small rucksacks neatly attached to their backs, map pouches on nylon cord around their necks.

The Machynlleth residents, off to Chester for some early Christmas shopping, were conspicuous by their track-suit bottoms, Naf Naf tops and trainers.

As soon as they were boarded, Presley went through the social security envelopes. They were markedly short of revelations: a Giro-cheque, followed by several letters explaining the Department of Social Security's cessation of payment of benefit to Jeff Clarke.

The only signs that Clarke had ever lived at the big, rambling house on the outskirts of Chester were the bits of mail that sat on the hall stand in the once grand, now rather run down, Victorian house.

He may well have been murdering people during the last few weeks, but Clarke was being offered loans, hospital and health care insurance, extra credit cards and the opportunity to buy a time share in Scotland. He was also, according to Reader's Digest, only a few numbers away from winning a hundred thousand pounds and a new Ford Escort.

Before Kavanagh could open the only piece of personal

post, a white Conqueror envelope with a second-class stamp, but addressed to Clarke in his full name and with the appendage 'Esq.' after his surname, the girl who had moved into his former room returned from work.

She showed them the room. She and her boyfriend had painted it the first week that she had been there. It was bright and cheerful and the youngster stood awkwardly beside the two policemen as they looked down at the collection of fluffy toys that sat ranged at the top of her bed.

The former tenant had left his sheets and towels and a few books and lots of papers: 'Pages and pages of writing, some longhand, some typed, chapters from a book. It was like a diary. I didn't read much of it. I like Catherine Cookson. I've got them all.' She gestured to her shelves and the popular author's books ranged there.

'What did you do with his things?'

'I kept them all for weeks, in cardboard boxes and plastic sacks, but eventually I put them out for the dustbin men.' She felt guilty. 'There's not much room here.'

'Of course,' said Kavanagh.

He looked through the sash window into the garden. Amongst the big trees and hydrangea bushes were the remnants of an iron fence that had once divided the house from the nearby fields.

Now, on the other side of the boundary, there were a dozen 'executive' houses with double garages and smooth, tarmac drives.

The policemen thanked the girl and wandered through the house, tapping on doors and speaking to the students and office workers who lived there.

A boy of nineteen on the first floor remembered the man who had lived, briefly, at the back of the house. He'd passed him in the hall, said hello. 'And then one day he was gone. I never heard any music or anything. He had a girl come sometimes. Could have been his daughter, I guess. About the right age, anyway. He looked rough. I always thought he was having a bad time.

'There's sometimes quite a bit of noise here, at weekends, or when people come back from the pub, but he never complained. Never said a word.

'Was he alcoholic? There were always bottles clanking out to the bin, and Thresher's carrier bags around. Why? What's happened to him?'

'Thanks, son, we'll be in touch if we need you. Thanks a lot.'

It was just after opening time and they sat amongst the other, miserable, Happy Hour customers at a pub down the road from the big house.

Kavanagh opened the envelope carefully, peeling back the stuck fold with barely a tear of the woven, quality paper.

Dear Mr Clarke,

Thank you for sending us your typescript, *Words of Comfort*.

I would like to say immediately that your book is infinitely better than the vast majority of unsolicited typescripts that we receive in this office and, indeed, in other circumstances, I might well have been able to make an offer to represent you.

However, as I am sure you know, the market is, at present, in a very depressed state, and only those books that we feel one hundred per cent confident of placing can we take on.

You write well and your book has good atmosphere but, at the end of the day, the domestic nature of the story is perhaps too depressing and downbeat for today's market.

Also, I feel you should try to bear in mind that readers generally want a hero or, at the very least, someone with whom they can identify. Your book, with its vengeful protagonist, markedly lacks anyone who could be thus described.

I hope these comments are not too unhelpful, and I wish you every success in placing your book with either another agent or direct with a publisher.

There was a PS.

It is, of course, essential that the senders of unsolicited typescripts submit return postage with their work. Given the very high costs involved, GouldThomas Associates are unable to return your novel unless you forward five pounds to cover these costs.

If we do not hear from you within six weeks, we will have no alternative but to dispose of your typescript.

The letter was over two months old.

Kavanagh and Presley were waiting outside the door of the literary agency's third-floor office on Manchester's Oxford Street at nine o'clock the following morning.

Neither man felt that he looked like a writer, and it was difficult to imagine that authors travelled in twos, but Mrs Copeland, the formidable receptionist, had become adept at dealing with any number of deceptions perpetrated by those wily writers who, at all costs, would *see* the agent, as if their written words alone were not sufficient testimony to their worth.

Eventually, convinced of their story, and finding about them nothing bulkier than warrant cards, she admitted the policemen and made them coffee.

Henry Gould arrived twenty minutes later.

A man in his mid-fifties, wearing brogues and an Austin Reed three-piece suit, he showed them into his office.

He apologized for the chaos and moved books and typescripts from a couple of chairs so that the men might sit down.

His desk was covered with clients' folders, correspondence, faxes and contracts. Every other available surface, and much of the carpet, was obscured by manuscripts. Even as they spoke, the receptionist brought in that morning's mail, including another four chunky parcels.

'It's about a manuscript that was sent to you recently . . .' began Kavanagh.

'Yes?' said Gould.

'It was sent to you by someone called Clarke, Jeff Clarke.'

'The name rings a bell,' said Gould as Kavanagh passed the agent's letter across to the man.

'Oh, yes. I remember it. Good book. Well, not so much a good *book* as a good *writer*. Powerful prose. What's he done?'

'We don't know. We don't even know what's *in* the book yet. Do you still have it?'

Gould glanced down at the date on the letter and, without answering, spoke into the internal telephone on his desk. 'Mrs Copeland, could you check whether a manuscript by one Jeff Clarke has been returned, or whether we still have it, please?

'Yes, as I say,' continued Gould, unprompted, 'it was a well-written book. Claustrophobic and intensely felt, written from within. No car chases, no drugs money.' He raised his eyebrows a millimetre. 'Not at all suitable for most of today's readers, I'm afraid. Of over five hundred unsolicited books that we were offered last year, we took only two. Mr Jeff Clarke's came close to being the first this year.'

Mrs Copeland knocked and entered. 'I'm afraid he didn't send a remittance. I put out all of July to September's typescripts only last week. You did *ask* me to, Mr Gould.'

'Of course, Jane. It's perfectly all right. That's all for now, thank you.' And the woman left the room.

'Sorry,' said Gould. 'We have to be very strict.' He gestured with his hand around the room. 'If authors don't forward the postage, we just don't have the room. After six weeks . . . I know it sounds awful, but believe me, it is the only way. She simply puts them out for the paper-recycling chaps every three months.'

'I see,' said Kavanagh. 'Do you remember much about the book? The actual *story*?'

Gould read his own letter again.

'Yes, I remember it,' said the agent. 'Murders, motivated by things that had happened in the past.'

'What kind of things?' said Kavanagh.

'Infidelity. His wife had been unfaithful. And now the narrator had to erase all of that past by killing her ex-lovers.'

'I see,' said Kavanagh. 'And the wife? What of her?'

'Yes, in the end, her too,' said Gould.

'How did he kill the victims?' said Presley.

'One person was strangled, another garroted, another knifed. They were low-tech murders. No fancy machines, not even firearms. Just the brutal, messy murder that a man alone can do: a kitchen knife, a piece of wire, that sort of thing.

'The killings were not remarkable in themselves. There's worse on television every night. But they were realistic. It was real death. Real murder. It was *felt*.

'And now you're telling me he's doing these things?' continued Gould.

'We are certainly very concerned,' said the inspector, with some understatement.

'They say everybody's got a book in them!' said Presley, as the two men hurried through Manchester city centre towards the railway station.

'Yes, that's what they say,' said Kavanagh. 'He tried to

get it out of his system in the book. It didn't work. And now he's doing it. What he "needs" to do to get clear of his past.'

Kavanagh thought, yet again, of his troubled sleep the previous night in their Manchester hotel. He had woken several times to thoughts of Rachael. To call them dreams would have been to suggest a distance that simply did not exist.

Once, although the days had been difficult, often very difficult, the booze-sodden nights had offered a few hours' respite.

Now, he was like a tissue, a paper towel whose absorbency had been surfeited, and he spilled over. He approached sleep with a macabre fascination, as his subconscious presented to his defenceless mind the images that, during the daylight hours, he wilfully stifled.

'Different murders, though,' said Presley.

'Yes. Not the same methods, of course,' said Kavanagh. 'You know, Kev, he's not *mad* . . .'

Presley glanced at his boss as they weaved along the crowded pavements, but there was no sign of a smile there.

'And his missis, and her bloke?' said Presley. 'They're next?'

'Yes, them next,' said Kavanagh, with a singular lack of feeling.

22

There wasn't a train to London for half an hour. Kavanagh ordered them tea and a sandwich while Presley went down the platform and phoned London.

Suddenly the sergeant was back, leaning over the formica table. 'They've found the car. A good copper. Sharp eyes. The car was filthy, knackered, but the plates were clean, brand new. They've checked it out. It's our man's.'

'Where?' asked Kavanagh.

'Tufnell Park,' said Presley.

'Where the fuck's Tufnell Park?' said Kavanagh. 'Is it near Brecknock Road?'

'Right next door,' said Presley. 'The car's half a mile from where they're doing the stakeout on the flat.'

'What about the surveillance?' asked the inspector.

'They say there's been no movement: no lights, nothing. He's knocked, but there's no answer. He doesn't think there's anyone in. They want to know if we've got the details right, and whether they've got to continue staking it out.'

'Have they phoned?'

'Yes. No reply. They want to know whether we want them to do a forced.'

Kavanagh looked down the platform. 'Tell them we're on our way. Just keep watching the place. Don't do anything. We'll be there as soon as we can. Just keep watching.'

* * *

At Euston, they were met by a uniformed officer who sped them through the parting traffic on a blue light and sirens. The driver brought them up through Kentish Town and slowed at Raveley Street where two officers were standing beside the blue Volvo, plastic 'Police' tape stretched all around it.

As they entered the bottom end of Brecknock Road, their driver turned off his blue light and drew up behind a 'B' registered Ford, parked fifty yards down from the flat.

The sergeant charged with watching Sarah Hardy's home was hunched up in the dirty, grey, smoke-filled Sierra. Presley and Kavanagh clambered into the car with the unshaven man. If he was on undercover duty, it was working: he'd more likely get hired as a minicab driver or picked up for kerb crawling than be identified as a policeman.

'When did you get here?' asked the inspector.

'This morning; nine o'clock.'

'And what about yesterday?'

'Who knows?' he said.

'Well, who did you take over from? He must have given you an update?'

'There *was* no one yesterday. I was the first shift. They couldn't get anyone over here. We'd got more on than a domestic yesterday: fucking bombs going off in the City.

'Everyone available was called in and redrafted. I've been on shift thirty-six hours already. I only came over here as a favour.'

'Sorry, mate. Cheers,' said Kavanagh.

The cop flashed him a look through half-closed eyes, looking for the signs of irony. He was ready to tell him what to do with his surveillance job, inspector or not, but there was nothing there. Kavanagh's gratitude was genuine.

'You going in?' asked the sergeant. 'There's no one there. I've been watching: no lights, no curtain movement. Nothing at the windows. I've knocked a couple of times; phoned twice.' He gestured to the mobile in the parcel shelf. 'Nothing. What are they anyway? My gaffer said something about a jealous husband. It's not one of these holding his missis up and us having to cordon the street off is it? 'Cause I'll never get home. He'll want a bleedin' helicopter or something. They always want a fucking helicopter these days, and then we'll all be here for a week!'

Kavanagh was warming to the sergeant. The Met. were an entirely different bunch. A race apart. Stereotypes *did* apply: Brummies: lowlifers; terrible accents; car dealers. Welsh: tightfisted; anti-English, whining. Londoners: criminals; back of a lorry; sell their mother; knew the score.

The job was different down here: much more crime; so much more violence. These blokes were a law unto themselves, a force within a force, different rules, different behaviour. Men and women who were barely containing a volatile city. It was more New York than Birmingham.

'It's a bit more than a domestic,' said Kavanagh. And then, hopefully, 'Or maybe it's nothing at all. Who knows? Me and Elvis'll go and have a look. You hang on here. Why not get yourself a cup of tea or something? We'll be all right for a bit.'

'Cheers. I'll just close them for a few minutes. That's what I need. Give us a nudge when you get back.'

They passed the shop and peered through the vandal wire on the door. The place looked exactly the same: the same bits of furniture; the radio cassette on the roll-top desk. There were a couple of bits of post on the floor inside the door. The shop hadn't been opened today, at least.

They walked the few yards to the street door of the flat. It had the standard burglar-deterrent solidity about it; Presley put his shoulder against it, but there was absolutely no movement. The two Chubb deadlocks and the centre mortice saw to that. Bring back *The Sweeney*, thought Kavanagh: when John Thaw and Dennis Waterman took a run at doors, they flew off their hinges.

Presley peered into the letter box, but could see nothing. He pressed his ear to the opening, but could hear nothing above the noise of the traffic thundering by.

'What do you reckon?' said Kavanagh.

'She'd have said if she was going away. Especially with us telling her to be careful and that we'd have the place watched. We can't leave without checking it out, and her nutter ex-husband's car parked down the road.'

'Do we break it down, or what?' said Kavanagh, seeking to abdicate his responsibility, and feeling less confident than usual on this alien turf.

'Fuck knows,' said Elvis, declining his boss's offer to share the initiative.

The sergeant was sleeping in the front seat of the car, his mouth wide open. They woke him and he punched the buttons on his mobile, handing the phone to Presley when he had got through.

Presley described the type and number of the locks on the solid sapele door and the Paddington CID desk arranged to have a locksmith up to them within the hour.

The locksmith arrived in a little Honda Acty van and began his work as he delivered a monologue about his work. He broke in for the police all the time. Burglar alarms that went off while residents were away on holiday; premises having to be secured after raids or break-ins. There was nothing that the man hadn't seen.

He fiddled with half a dozen keys before opening the three separate locks. The whole thing took less than five minutes. He handed them the keys so that they could lock up again when they left, took a signature from Kavanagh on his job invoice, handed the inspector the yellow copy, and disappeared down the road.

*　　*　　*

The two men stood at the bottom of the stairs and listened. Kavanagh reckoned he could look at an opaque bottle or a paint tin and, just by looking at it, tell whether there was anything in it. Houses were the same. The very knock on the door felt different if there was someone in the house; the carpet on the floor transmitted a sense of someone's presence if another person's feet were pressed into the pile.

They climbed the steep stairs, one hand on the rail, heads peering upwards towards the low-wattage light bulb that hung there.

Kavanagh's hand touched something sticky on the banister. He lifted his hand and slowly opened the palm to examine the smudge of blood there.

He showed the thin, red, veiny sight to Presley. Neither man spoke. At the top of the stairs a coat was lying on the floor. It was one thing, a nothing, but it was everything. Both men had seen enough to know the difference between a coat dropped randomly in the hall after a late night out, and the same coat lying there after violence. A car parked badly, compared with one abandoned by joyriders at the side of the road. A body lying inert on the floor: the odd, always surprising fold of the body, the incongruity of the limbs, the awkwardness and absence of vanity that accompanied death.

The sitting-room door where they had spoken to Sarah Hardy a day earlier was ajar. Kavanagh pushed it very gently with the tips of his fingers. Fools rush in . . . The blood on his hand was sticky at the base of his fingers.

His eyes swept the scene, took in the general, ignored the particular, filed that in his brain for later, in five seconds' time.

Little disarray; same room as before; a big moon waxing through the net curtains; the glow of a streetlamp illuminating the scene. In the corner, away from the window, a man in a low chair. Knife.

The man looked back at them as they stood in the doorway. His eyes revealed nothing. Without a reaction, it was impossible to gauge the situation. Without a reaction, that *was* the situation. No blink. No emotion. No interest. But in his hand, a long knife.

No one spoke. Was he a lunger? Would they be able to get down the stairs and out of the front door before being wedged in the narrow passageway, knife thrusts raining down upon them, nothing to protect them except their outstretched, flailing arms?

The man was inert. His very stillness was frightening. How long had he been sitting here? They had blown it. They had been foolhardy, entered the premises unarmed and understrength; no backup, no weapons, no body armour. The Met. would have a laugh about the dopey Brummies on this one.

The man wasn't injured, not as far as Kavanagh could see, but there were dark marks on his jeans; the knife had no reflection on its blade. Was that, too, dulled with the stuff?

Kavanagh wanted desperately to ask: Where is your wife? Where is Peter Burchell? The overwhelming wish to know. The same thing that was making his emotional life a daily torture. The need to know: to be *informed*.

Where were the couple? They were dead, of course. In the bedroom? The kitchen? Where was that?

There were no obvious wounds on the man; perhaps a graze on his forehead, nothing else.

But blood on the carpet? A nice, plain, grey carpet that Kavanagh had tacitly admired yesterday. It was heavily stained.

'Are you all right?' said Kavanagh.

It was about as ridiculous a question as he could have asked. But they couldn't stay here, like this, in this silence, for ever, the man's eyes registering nothing, the carpet stained.

Worst of all, the inspector's hand was horribly sticky,

sticky with someone else's blood. In the midst of this drama, what Kavanagh wanted, more than anything, was to wash his hand.

23

'Are you all right?'

If the question had been redundant at the first time of its asking, it was risible now. But Kavanagh had no idea *what* to say.

In a way, his mind was working well. It was very sharp, very clear; it was entering and processing information with great speed and clarity.

He'd heard all that pseudoscientific nonsense about the human brain's capacity to deal with information; it was pub-bore stuff. Absolutely no use in dealing with the man sitting in the chair ten feet away from him with a knife in his hand and an uncanny lack of feeling in his eyes.

The man in the chair was Jeff Clarke. He bore little resemblance to his pretty daughter. She had taken her looks from her mother. This man was tall and thin, hollow cheeked, gaunt.

He'd killed several people. He didn't look well. An understatement. His wife, his ex-wife, wasn't here. Nor was her lover. Where were *they*?

That guy from Ladbrokes or William Hill who kept popping up at the Booker Prize and on election nights to give the odds: he wouldn't give a good price on Sarah Hardy and Peter Burchell still being alive.

Was this the same knife that had killed John Lacey in Birmingham? Was this the man who had coerced the Sugars into their old car and filled it with carbon monoxide until they had died a gasping, ghastly death? And was this the man who had forced Adam Curtiss from a train doing over a hundred inter-city miles an hour? He was big enough, certainly.

Kavanagh's brain threw up these and a dozen other questions, and all the time he was aware of his colleague's shallow breathing as Presley stood close behind him.

Should he talk some more? Risk another question? Wait for this unpredictable character to speak. Kavanagh didn't want to pressure him, not at all, not in any way.

He was curious, and afraid; terrified, really. But he had to stay sharp.

There was a low, ornamental table between them; perhaps he would be able to kick that in the way of him. He would use the sofa cushions to try and fend off the blows as the man lunged. There was nothing else to hand.

Perhaps Clarke would topple and the two of them would then be able to bundle him down, get that killing blade away from him.

Plans were all right; but it was like girls doing judo classes, or hoku fuku or whatever it was called these days: the bad guys who attacked you in the night didn't do a ceremonial bow and adopt a 'stance'. They grabbed you from behind, cut you, tore off your clothes, stuffed things into you. It wasn't combat by numbers; it was quick and violent, and often deadly.

Maybe Clarke'd bale out of the window: film stuff, Jimmy Cagney nonsense. But Kavanagh knew that life's reality was less spectacular, more prosaic, more ghastly. More Chabrol and Hitchcock: people who didn't die easily, men and women whose limbs refused to fold, whose blood continued inconveniently to pour and drip.

And anyway, smashed through the window, falling twenty feet to his death or a certain coma on the hard Brecknock Road below, wouldn't do; even afraid, Kavanagh didn't want this: too many unansewereds. His fear was balanced by his deep need to *know*. A few hours of question and answer. The whys; the wherefores; the hows and whens that fuelled his motor.

This Othello with the knife, though, he was out of logic. *He* was up for anything. Othello: wrong thought. Rachael: betrayal; loss. Othello: green-eyed monster; jealousy; murder; Iago; bad track.

This was the result. This is where it led; *could* lead. It was powerful stuff, he knew that. He hadn't gone this far, but he'd thought of it. Murder had seemed reasonable.

One time, he'd thought of hanging a sheet from the underpass bridge, like husbands did for their wives on their fortieth birthdays.

But his sheet said, 'Come back, Rachael. *Please* Come Back.' He hadn't done it. But he'd thought it; believed it possible. At four in the morning, it had seemed reasonable.

And he'd prayed she'd die, didn't care how. Just get the fuck dead. Out of my life. Out of my mind. No prospect of being with another, any other. Was *that* so different from this?

It wasn't. He'd thought those things. Love and murderous death. They were an inch, a millimetre, a second's thought apart.

And this was reality, not just a play. *Just* a play? What about the woman in the audience at Stratford who, unable to bear Desdemona's being killed by her husband cried out to the Moor, 'She didn't *do* it; she didn't *do* it.'

He liked that. He liked Desdemona's virtue, and he liked the gauche woman from Michigan or Ohio who was moved to cry out and defend it.

Kavanagh might die. Any second: lunge, dead. Injured: punctured lung; severed arteries; multiple stab wounds.

Two paragraphs in the nationals; a page in the *Camden Express* or whatever: 'While investigating a murder, Detective Inspector Frank Kavanagh was overcome by the suspect and subsequently died from multiple stab wounds.

'The Chief Constable of the West Midlands force, to which the officer was attached, said that Kavanagh, a policeman with nearly twenty years' service, had made an outstanding contribution to the force, and would be deeply missed.

'His estranged wife, Rachael, said that he had given his life to his work.' (She had always appreciated irony, he thought.)

Fucking hell, he could see the cellophane-wrapped floral tributes lining the pavement outside the flat. Talismans of the public's vain hope that their outrage at yet another barbarous killing would arrest the tide of violence that was now endemic throughout the land.

Would injury suffice? Would she be moved to come back? Of course she would *visit*. She would come to his bedside. She didn't hate him. Just didn't love him any more. Was indifferent. That was so much harder.

And if she came, walked into the antiseptic ward, would her man be outside? Out on the green-floored corridor? In the waiting room? In his car in the car park, awaiting her return?

'Are you all right?'

The question was still ringing around the room. The period of silence. Cod psychology. True, though. Whoever spoke first lost the advantage. He knew it. He saw it played daily. It was kids' stuff. To take the advantage. But people *were* kids. *Wanted* an advantage.

Kavanagh didn't want to pressure this man in any way. He wanted him to put down the bloody blade. He'd speak; give up any notion of trying to be in control, remove any idea of threat or advantage; try another question.

'Where are they?'

The man looked up, parted his lips a fraction. He nodded slowly, acknowledging something in the question.

'Your wife? Where is she?' ventured Kavanagh.

Clarke smiled. It wasn't nice. There was an incongruity; the motionless body, the smile.

'I've not been well,' he said. He pushed his hand through his unkempt dark hair. 'Not well.'

'No,' said Kavanagh. 'Would you like something? A drink? Some tea?'

He nodded slightly.

Negotiation. Establish rapport. That was what you had to do. He'd been on the course. Watched the movies. Except. Except, of course, where you *didn't* want to be noticed. That was another one, wasn't it? That was the hostage situation. Your crazed Lebanese or Iranian captors were negotiating with the government or whatever. You were stuck in the plane with the Palestinians or on the train with the hooded South Moluccans. Then, you went 'grey'.

The last thing you wanted was to be noticed. You got noticed and then, when they wanted to take someone out, show they meant business, up the ante a little, it was *you* that was the currency.

Your life: your mum and dad's son; somebody's hapless husband/wife/grandfather/daughter, was taken out, shot, and dropped, dead, onto the tarmac.

Don't get noticed. No eye contact. Nothing. Grey. It was *important* not to mix them up. Life endangering.

But now, this situation: rapport. That was what was called for. Rapport. Name of a dating agency. Maybe he'd meet someone one day. Someone he could love, really love, and then Rachael wouldn't matter to him any more; at least not matter to him like she did now.

Rapport. That's what they were getting. The man had said yes to a drink. Kavanagh hadn't thought it through. It meant he was going to be alone with him. Was that worse? He was more vulnerable.

He had created a situation where he was going to be alone with him. Would Presley do something daft? Anything? Would he try and get help and make Kavanagh's plight worse?

The man was waiting. There was a kind of etiquette, a curious sort of propriety. Kavanagh had asked the man if he wanted a drink. The man had said yes. Now he was waiting. It was unlikely he would say, 'Excuse me, but where is my cup of tea?' But he *was* waiting.

'Tea, then?' said Kavanagh.

He nodded.

'OK,' said Frank to his sergeant, 'let's have some tea.'

'You sure?' said Presley.

'Yes. Just easy,' said Kavanagh, quietly.

Presley backed a footstep or two into the hall.

Kavanagh wanted to sit, but was afraid to. He would have less chance of defending himself if the man went for him. He leaned more of his weight against the door pillar. 'Where is your wife?' he asked again, gently.

The suggestion of a mirthless smile came back to Clarke's lips. 'My ex-wife,' he said.

Kavanagh didn't like the ambiguity in the reply: ex-alive, or ex-married? They were dead. He knew it.

'Yes, your ex-wife,' said the inspector.

'Gone,' Clarke eventually said.

'May I go to her?' said Kavanagh. 'She may need help. Perhaps I could help her.'

The man moved his head from side to side. 'No,' he said, with finality.

No, she didn't need help? Or, no, he couldn't help her?

'Is she all right?' said Kavanagh.

There was a tiny movement as his fingers tightened on the hilt of the knife and the dull blade turned very slightly in his hand. Kavanagh backed off.

From the kitchen – remarkable – came the slight sounds of familiar domesticity: cups and saucers and teaspoons, even the insistent bubbling of the electric kettle, and then the click of its shutting off.

The inspector heard the three separate sounds of the water going onto the tea bags in the cups or mugs. Tosser. He never makes it properly, in the pot.

Presley manoeuvred past his boss in the doorway, brought in the three drinks, sugar and milk on a tray.

The sergeant gestured to the low table in front of Clarke, and the man moved his head in agreement.

When he had lowered the tray, Presley took one of the mugs of steaming tea, threw it straight at the man's head and followed it by raining down a heavy blow on his face. He moved with greater speed than Kavanagh had ever seen him display before.

It was a second before the inspector realized that it was incumbent upon him, too, to be involved. But the man was barely responding. He had no fight or resistance, the knife had fallen to the floor as he cried out from the pain of the scalding tea. He had received in answer to his cries Presley's big fist which had split his nose and broken his lips and teeth.

Kavanagh picked up the knife; he knew that he lacked the wherewithal to plunge a knife into anyone, but he wanted it well away from Clarke, a man who was not so squeamish in this regard. He ran to the top of the stairs and threw it down into the hall.

He pushed open the bathroom door, then the bedroom, and finally, the utility cupboard at the far end of the landing.

He returned to the sitting-room. Clarke was on his knees, one hand cuffed to the radiator, Presley standing over him, a handkerchief wrapped around his bloody fist.

Clarke was bleeding from the nose and groaning softly as he held his fingers to the watery, pale blisters that were his big scalds.

'Where are they?' asked Kavanagh. All friendliness had gone from his voice; he felt a cheat, a fraud, like someone who talks down a suicide and then imprisons him.

'She had my soul,' murmured Clarke through his bloodied teeth. 'I had to have it back.'

'Where *are* they?' repeated Kavanagh.

'I had to have it back,' mumbled Clarke.

Kavanagh rushed out of the door and down the stairs.

He tried the handle of the shop door again. It didn't

have the immovable feel of the door to the flat, but it wasn't going to give in to a shove. And, even if he had felt so inclined, the wire mesh on the door precluded his hurtling through the plate glass behind it.

Up the pavement, a hundred yards away, the road was under night repair. He sprinted towards the labourers, shouted, 'Police!' and took a pickaxe out of a man's hands.

The other labourers, orange plastic flashes on their donkey jackets, pursued the mad police impersonator up the road.

Kavanagh swung the axe at the door and wrenched and levered at the wire as the glass fell in. He smashed out the shards as the gathering crowd watched in disbelief from a safe distance.

The undercover sergeant had materialized and now stood behind him, punching the buttons of his phone and shouting into it for reinforcements.

Kavanagh stood alone in the silence of the shop.

Familiar smells of wood shavings and glue and polish. But something else, too. Stronger, more acrid, it caught in the throat and in the nose.

The policeman slowly approached the bath. There was a deal of bubbling, and there were pools and splashes all over the floor where the gallons of displaced liquid had washed over the side.

He took the smooth pole from the corner and touched the surface. The pole immediately made contact with something soft and giving.

24

Jeff Clarke sat opposite the inspector and smoked his cigarette. The spools of the cassette recorder whirred; the red recording light glowed.

DI Frank Kavanagh had conducted many hundreds of interviews during his twenty years in the police force. He'd charged dozens of suspects with myriad crimes.

He'd sat opposite men (and a few women) who could barely hold the stub of a pencil in their ungainly hands. And watched others who wrote with the extravagant hand that he always, now, associated with deceit.

He'd seen the repressed hand of sex offenders, forcing out each word onto the lined paper, non-writing arm crooked around their confessions, just as children at junior school protected *their* work from others' eyes.

Since the sound recording of all interviews was made mandatory, Kavanagh had sat opposite the tongue-tied and the verbose, the prolix and the mute.

He'd recorded interviews with stammerers; with fraudsters and embezzlers who had the panache of government front-bench spokesmen; and with recidivist felons who, accompanied by their stone-faced solicitors, managed only two words: 'No comment.'

He'd listened to the 'prepared statement', beloved of politicians and those who emerged from the Old Bailey, case dismissed by a diffident jury, lay-people bamboozled into confusion and doubt by wily defence counsel.

The 'prepared statement' always suggested to Kavanagh

a document compiled behind closed doors; words wrought with the due caution of the culpable.

Out they came, brazen beneath the media glare, impregnable behind the solitary sheet of flapping paper.

But say the truth a thousand times, a detail added here, one omitted there, it mattered little. Lie, and when that change *did* come, in that detail altered, the alibi began to collapse. In that first trickle the sea wall was breached.

It took time, of course; for hours, sometimes days, the waves of questioning were rebuffed by the defendant's obduracy.

But Kavanagh was a wave machine; and he knew the story of Canute.

Clarke was no charlatan. He was not sly or even evasive. No, he was none of these things.

He was slow to start because he was inhabiting his person, finding the 'voice'.

You didn't go on and play King Lear straight out of the pub, or Cymbeline fresh off the squash court. You sat alone, thought about your part.

The spools of the cassette whirred. 'I'm sorry,' he murmured.

Kavanagh spoke into the microphone: 'Questioning of Jeffrey Clarke, by Detective Inspector Francis Kavanagh, suspended at 11.20 a.m., Tuesday, the 9th November.'

The red light glowed. Kavanagh sat quietly, Presley at his side, the arresting officer in the corner.

After another ten minutes of silence, the man nodded his head and said, 'All right. Now.'

Kavanagh turned on the machine and announced the interview once more.

Clarke lifted his head slightly and began in a quiet voice.

'She left me, and it was more than I could bear. At first, I thought it would be all right. We'd talked about parting. Things weren't right any more: there had been the loss of the baby. But when she went, it was too . . . sudden.

'We had been married a long time. We had our daughter. And then she left. She told me about her affair at Open University, after all those years, when I thought it had been all right between us.

'It was like replaying the past. We had been through all that. In our past, long ago.

'What would she tell me next year? Or the year after that?

'There was no trust. There never could be. I had hurt her. Now she was hurting me back. And I knew she could go on doing it.

'She could always hurt me more. What could I believe? I pleaded with her to tell me everything, so that I could carry on, start again.

'I know there was more.

'I couldn't force her. I never have. You have to let people do what they want to do. Perhaps I shouldn't have, because it hurt me so much. And then I had to do what *I* did, to all of them.

'I have feelings. I *think* about things.

'After the news, I'm thinking about what has happened. It stays with me.'

Kavanagh wanted to ask: 'Is that why you killed six people? Because you're so sensitive?' He sat silently, said nothing, let the man talk.

'I tried to carry on. But it was going round and round in my head.

'I tried to live, but I couldn't. The whole thing became one endless agonized memory of the bad things in our life, and I knew that the only way I could make things right again would be to cut them away.'

There was a pause.

'Yes?' said Kavanagh.

He looked directly at the inspector: 'I see pain on faces. A special kind of pain. A pain that only the sufferers know. I'd seen it before, but never recognized it, never knew it for what it was.

'It's a club, Inspector: the people who have been broken by loss. But you can only get in if you're a member. It's like those handshakes the Freemasons have. There's no mistaking it.

'You know, I even watch the football managers. Watch them being interviewed after the game. I watch their eyes, and they're talking about the second goal, but *I'm* looking at their eyes. And I can *tell*. I look at people in bars, and the people in the shops. And I can tell.

'We're a club. We know each other's pain; each other's special scent. It is some comfort. A little comfort.'

The man stubbed out his cigarette and looked back at Kavanagh. 'You know what I'm talking about, Inspector?'

'Go on,' said the policeman.

Clarke breathed very deeply, lit another cigarette. 'She had my soul. I had to have it back. I could die, I was not afraid of that, it would be a relief.

'But what if I died and was left in limbo, a wraith, ". . . confin'd to fast in fires"?

'You see, Inspector, my soul. You know, I had to have it back . . .'

'But why the others?' said Kavanagh. 'So long ago; why them? And why them *first*?'

'They were all involved, Inspector. I had to square it all. But her last, because you always go to the husband first. Prime suspect. You would have come straight to me. As it was, you were looking for me as soon as you made a connection between the three of them. But I knew it would take you a long time.

'It was hard enough for *me* to find them, and I knew who they were. They'd spread out, they were from different backgrounds, and it was all a long time ago.

'So, I started with Sugar.' He paused. 'I'm sorry about his wife. But I had other people to see to, and so I couldn't just leave her to come out and tell you. I had to kill her too.'

He looked up at Kavanagh. He seemed to expect the policeman to sanction the murder.

'She'd never done anything to me. But they *were* married. They should stay together.'

He appeared to be serious.

'And then it was John Lacey. All those years ago I used to like John. I think he liked me, too. I didn't even really blame him for being with Sarah that time. It wasn't *his* fault.

'But when she told me about it, years later, it was hard for me.

'I forgave her. Again. I think a man will forgive the woman he loves a lot. And I loved her, really.'

He went on seamlessly, his monologue a further purgation. 'I had a couple of affairs. But she didn't care. A bit, maybe. But she wasn't *crucified*. You know, I'm the one who remembers things.'

'Yes, you said,' said Kavanagh.

'The *Sunday Times*: "Life in the Day". Do you know that series?'

Kavanagh nodded. He always read it straight after the football results.

'There was a man who lived in a tree . . .'

Presley raised his eyebrows.

'Out in Wales somewhere, years ago,' continued Clarke. 'And I still wonder about him. Is he still there? In that tree?

'On TV once, there was a documentary: a man with a short-term memory, and every time his wife went out of the room to make a cup of tea, when she came back in, he greeted her as if they hadn't seen one another for years.'

Clarke smiled. 'It was beautiful. His wife found it exhausting. But I thought it was wonderful.

'And a man with tinnitus, that constant noise in his ears. I think about him, too. I can't *forget* these people. I should. But I can't.

'And there's me going round and round, like a hamster on a wheel: the noise in my ears is *our* past, not just some buzzing.

'Round and round on a loop of pain and memory.

'I moved away; eventually went abroad. I tried, I *really* tried. I took all the advice.

'But, do you know, the only time I felt all right, just for a while, was when I remembered the wrong that *I* had done *her*?

'I thought about the baby; our baby and her awful loss. And then I felt sorry for her. And then, I don't know why, I felt a bit better myself.

'But I couldn't make it last. How long can you go on like that, hurting yourself with memories of the past so that you can get through each day?

'I did do it, for days at a time. I would trick myself into that state, lead myself again into that hurt where I could feel guilt and sorrow, and then feel better.

'I even asked for her forgiveness; showed her my contrition. But she didn't write back. Not a word.'

'I'm not sure she got your letters,' interrupted Kavanagh. 'I think . . . after they moved away, she stopped receiving them.'

Clarke seemed not to hear. He carried on, 'I went to church and prayed. "Forgive us our sins, as we forgive those that trespass against us . . ."

'I wanted to be like one of those people on TV, after their child is killed by a joyrider, or their family is blown up by a bomb, and they say they want to forgive the killers, and they will pray for them. I wanted to be like that.

'But I couldn't do it. I couldn't make it last; I couldn't get off the loop.

'I wrote the pain into my new book, tried to exorcize it in that way. But I knew what would happen when it was ended. I became afraid of finishing.

'The book didn't matter.' He paused and smiled. 'But I think it *was* good writing.

'What would I do with my dreams when I woke in the morning and didn't have my book to put them into?'

'And?' said Kavanagh.

'And the book was finished. I couldn't say any more. I sent it away. My time had come. *I* was going to start living in the moment. I was going to be the one who "kisses the joy as it flies . . ."

'It's what Briony had always told me to do.

'Sarah was with Burchell. They were together.

'I couldn't bear it. I didn't mind killing myself, but I was afraid that my death would be the same as my life, I had to kill my past first, recover my soul from her.

'I'd put it into the book. Now, I was going to *do* it. The pen; the sword. I don't believe that proverb.

'I felt better. I was getting free. Doing it would release me. Any price was cheap for my peace of mind. Anything to stop my pain.

'And now I *am* free. It's done, and I have peace again. I will be able to sleep at night again. I know I will.'

The inspector looked at him; he thought not of murder, or manslaughter. The word that came to his mind was no word: it was mans-*laughter*.

Kavanagh suspended the interview. He would question him in detail about the crimes later.

The policemen made to leave.

'Inspector?' said Clarke.

'Yes?' said Kavanagh.

'My daughter? Briony.'

'Yes,' said the inspector, looking into the man's eyes.

'Would it be possible for me to see her?'

The inspector continued to look at the man. But whatever it was that he looked for, he did not see.

'Yes,' said Kavanagh, 'of course.'

'Thank you,' said Clarke. 'She's all I've got now, you see.'

'Yes,' said the inspector.

The policemen walked down the corridor.

'Round the fuckin' bend,' said Presley. 'Make a space, Broadmoor, here we come.'

Kavanagh was silent.

Less Than Kind
David Armstrong

1968, and Charles Somerville, son of impoverished landowner Philip Somerville, is on the run from drug dealers in the Welsh Borders.

In nearby Llantrisillio, newcomers James and Suzie find their sylvan idyll brutally and shockingly shattered by the voyeurism of a farming neighbour . . .

Also in Border country is Birmingham policeman John Munroe, liaising with Welsh colleagues on a routine inquiry. But a mysterious death in the area draws him inexorably into an investigation which is to uncover a tangle of dangerous passions running beneath the outwardly calm rural scene.

'Excellent characterization . . . skilful plot . . . Proof positive that Armstrong's fine debut novel last year was no fluke'
Literary Review

ISBN 0 00 649009 3

A Grave Talent

Laurie R. King

Kate Martinelli, a newly promoted Homicide detective with a secret to conceal, and Alonzo Hawkin, a world-weary cop trying to make a new life in San Francisco, could not be more different, but are thrown together to solve a brutal crime – the murders of three young girls.

As Martinelli and Hawkin get nearer to a solution, they realize the crimes may not be the sexually motivated killings they had seemed, and that there is a coldly calculating and tortuous mind at work which they must outmanoeuvre if they are to prevent both further carnage and the destruction of a shining talent...

'If there is a new P.D. James...I would put my money on Laurie R. King' *Boston Globe*

ISBN 0 00 649354 8

Bryan Sykes, Professor of Human Genetics at the University of Oxford, has had a remarkable scientific career. He was the first to discover [illegible] DNA from human remains thousands of years old and he has been called in as the leading international authority to examine several high-profile cases, such as the Ice Man, Cheddar Man and the many individuals claiming to be surviving members of the Russian Royal Family. Since then he has worked extensively on the origins of peoples from all over the world, using DNA from living people as well as from archaeological remains. He proved that the origin of Polynesians lay in Asia, not America, and discovered that the ancestors of most Europeans were hunter-gatherers from before the last Ice Age. He also showed that most Europeans trace their maternal genetic ancestry back to only seven women. On the male side he was the first to show the close connection between DNA and surnames, a discovery that is revolutionizing genealogy.

Bryan Sykes is the founder and chairman of Oxford Ancestors (http://www.oxfordancestors.com), which uses DNA to help explore your own genetic roots, including the tribal affinities described in *Blood of the Isles*.

He is also the author of *The Seven Daughters of Eve* and *Adam's Curse*.

In a unique first, Bryan Sykes is simultaneously publishing the detailed genetic results that led to his conclusions on the internet at www.bloodoftheisles.net.

Also by Bryan Sykes

THE SEVEN DAUGHTERS OF EVE
ADAM'S CURSE

and published by Corgi Books

BLOOD OF THE ISLES

Exploring the genetic roots of our tribal history

Bryan Sykes

CORGI BOOKS

TRANSWORLD PUBLISHERS
61-63 Uxbridge Road, London W5 5SA
A Random House Group Company
www.rbooks.co.uk

BLOOD OF THE ISLES
A CORGI BOOK: 9780552154659

First published in Great Britain
in 2006 by Bantam Press
a division of Transworld Publishers
Corgi edition published 2007

This book is a work of non-fiction and based on the experiences and recollections of the author. The author has stated to the publishers that the contents of this book are true.

A CIP catalogue record for this book is available from the British Library

Addresses for Random House Group Ltd companies outside the UK can be found at: www.randomhouse.co.uk
The Random House Group Ltd Reg. No. 954009

The Random House Group Ltd makes every effort to ensure that the papers used in its books are made from trees that have been legally sourced from well-managed and credibly certified forests. Our paper procurement policy can be found at:
www.randomhouse.co.uk/paper.htm

Typeset in 12/14.5pt Granjon by
Falcon Oast Graphic Art Ltd.

Printed in the UK by CPI, Cox & Wyman, Reading, RG1 8EX.

4 6 8 10 9 7 5 3

To my son Richard, companion on very many journeys

CONTENTS

	Acknowledgements	9
	List of illustrations	11
	Maps	14
	Prologue	17
1	Twelve Thousand Years of Solitude	21
2	Who Do We Think We Are?	38
3	The Resurgent Celts	65
4	The Skull Snatchers	83
5	The Blood Bankers	105
6	The Silent Messengers	121
7	The Nature of the Evidence	141
8	Ireland	152
9	The DNA of Ireland	182
10	Scotland	202
11	The Picts	216
12	The DNA of Scotland	226
13	Wales	263
14	The DNA of Wales	276

15 England 287
16 Saxons, Danes, Vikings and Normans 303
17 The DNA of England 316
18 The Blood of the Isles 327

Appendix 341
Index 345

ACKNOWLEDGEMENTS

The research that led to *Blood of the Isles* was a team effort. I had a wonderful team both in the field and in the lab. Eileen Hickey, Emilce Vega, Jayne Nicholson, Catherine Irven, Zehra Mustafa, John Loughlin, Kay Chapman, Kate Smalley, Helen Chandler and Martin Richards all criss-crossed the Isles in pursuit of DNA, while Lorraine Southam, Sara Goodacre and Vincent Macaulay helped to tease out its secrets in the lab. I relied on many people's generosity in the search for our origins. The directors and staff of the Scottish Blood Transfusion Service deserve special mention for their enthusiastic backing and for their tolerance as we invaded their otherwise tranquil donor sessions. The head teachers and the staff of the very many schools we visited, particularly in Wales and Shetland, I thank for the same reasons. Talking of Shetland, I must thank Beryl Smith, who organized all our visits there in advance. But, of course, none of this would have been remotely possible without the consent and co-operation of the many thousands of volunteers who agreed to having their DNA taken and analysed.

Among professional colleagues, I am particularly grateful to Dan Bradley of Trinity College Dublin for advance access to Irish genetic data, though I should stress that I have only used published material here and also that any conclusions are my own and not necessarily Dan Bradley's. So blame me and not him. I have also benefited from the publications of Jim Wilson and Mark Thomas from University College London, who have produced very useful data from parts of Britain. Among my friends and colleagues in Oxford, William James has, as usual, been a rich source of ideas and creative conversation. I must also mention Robert Young, recently of Wadham College, who introduced me to the racial mythology of the English, a subject of which I was almost completely unaware until he sent me a reprint of his work. Norman Davies, a fellow of my own college, Wolfson, was not only a source of bountiful historical references in his magisterial *The Isles – a History* (never has a book been more thoroughly thumbed), but also helped me resolve the tricky issue of what to call my own book.

But words are not enough. Books need midwives before they see the light of day. My agent Luigi Bonomi has kept me going throughout with his irrepressible enthusiasm and I am, once again, very fortunate to have in my editors Sally Gaminara and Simon Thorogood not just consummate professionalism but great encouragement as well. Thanks too to Brenda Updegraff for her immaculate copy-editing and, as before, to Julie Sheppard who rapidly transformed my erratic handwriting into legible text.

But most of all I thank the Muse without whom nothing flows.

LIST OF ILLUSTRATIONS

First colour section
English supporter at the World Cup, 2006:
© Tony Quinn/internationalsportsimages.com/Corbis

Brutus the Trojan Sets Sail for Britain, 15th-century manuscript illumination by Master Wistace from 'The History of the Kings of Britain' by Geoffrey of Monmouth: Bibliothèque Nationale, Paris/The Bridgeman Art Library; coronation throne of Edward I: © Angelo Hornak/Corbis; Tintagel Castle, Cornwall: © English Heritage/ Heritage-Images; *Merlin before King Vortigern*, manuscript illumination from 'Prophecies of Merlin' by Geoffrey of Monmouth, *c*. 1250: © The British Library/Heritage-Images; *The Last Sleep of Arthur in Avalon* (detail) by Edward Burne-Jones, 1881–98: Museo de Arte, Ponce, Puerto Rico/ The Bridgeman Art Library; Glastonbury Abbey, Somerset, detail of the ruins: © Nigel Reed/Alamy.

Head dress found at Starr Carr, Yorkshire, *c*. 7500 BC: British Museum, London; Maiden Castle, near Dorchester, Dorset, *c*. 3000 BC: Collections/Peter Thomas; inner circle of Stonehenge, Wiltshire, *c*. 2800-1500 BC: © Royalty-Free/Corbis; air view of Richborough Castle, near Sandwich, Kent, AD 43–287 : Collections/David Bowie; sword-belt buckle from the ship burial at Sutton Hoo, early 7th century, British Museum: © 2006 The British Museum; Anglo-Saxon iron helmet from the ship burial at Sutton Hoo, early 7th century, British

Museum: © Visual Arts Library (London)/Alamy; detail from the Bayeux tapestry, *c*. 1080; © Nik Wheeler/Corbis.

Callanish standing stones, Lewis, Outer Hebrides, *c*. 3000 BC: © Adam Woolfitt/Corbis; Skara Brae, Orkney, *c*. 3000 BC: © Kevin Schafer/Corbis; burial chamber at Maes Howe, Orkney, *c*. 2750 BC: © Crown copyright reproduced by courtesy of Historic Scotland; Jarlshof, Shetland, 2400 BC: HIE/stockscotland; broch at Mousa, Shetland Islands, 1st century AD: © Peter Hulme/Corbis; Hadrian's Wall, Northumberland, AD 122: © David Ball/Corbis; Pictish stone in Aberlemno, Perth & Kinross, c. AD 750: Collections/Michael Jenner.

John Beddoe, frontispiece to his book *Memories of Eighty Years*, 1910; 'A Celtic groupe', from Robert Knox *The Races of Men*, 1869; engraved portrait of Robert Knox: Wellcome Library, London; loose leaf from one of Beddoe's albums, 1882: Royal Anthropological Institute, London.

Second colour section

Adrian Targett with the skeleton of Cheddar Man, March 1997: swn.com/Darren Fletcher; drilling Cheddar man's tooth and Professor Chris Stringer with Cheddar Man jawbone: both courtesy Bryan Sykes; DNA sequence chromatogram: © Mark Harmel/Alamy.

Lindisfarne Priory and view of the seashore, Holy Island, Northumberland: both photos courtesy Bryan Sykes; Gokstad Ship, Viking Ship Museum, Oslo, *c*. AD 850–900: © Richard T. Nowitz/Corbis; Jarl squad, Lerwick, Shetland Isles, January 2000: © Reuters/Corbis; woman on Lewis: courtesy Bryan Sykes.

Neolithic cromlech, Carreg Sampson, Pembrokeshire: Collections/Simon McBride; Roman barracks and latrines, Caerleon, Gwent, 1st century AD: Collections/Robert Estall; Offa's Dyke near Knighton, Radnor, late 8th century AD: © Homer Sykes/Corbis; obverse of silver coin of Offa, AD 757–796: Ancient Art & Architecture Collection; aerial view of Pembroke Castle, late 12th to 13th century: © Jason Hawkes/Corbis; young Welsh fan, Canberra Stadium, Rugby World Cup, 2003: Gareth Copley/PA/Empics.

Burial chamber, Newgrange, County Meath, 3200 BC: Mike Bunn/Irish Image Collection; Mizzen Head, County Cork: Collections/Brian Shuel; Mound of the Hostages, Hill of Tara, County Meath, *c*. 2000 BC: George Munday/Irish Image Collection; the Broighter ship, gold, 1st century BC, found at Broighter, County Derry: Werner Forman Archive/National Museum of Ireland; Cú Chulainn: Collections/Robert Bird; spectators at the St Patrick's Day Parade, New York, 2006: © Justin Lane/epa/Corbis.

Wales Millennium Centre, Cardiff: © Photolibrary Wales; pupils at Moy School, Lahinch, County Clare: © Stephanie Maze/Corbis.

REGIONAL BORDERS
N
Shetland
Orkney
Highland
Hebrides
Grampian
Argyll
Tayside and Fife
Strathclyde
Borders
Northumbria
Ulster
Connacht
Leinster
Munster
North England
North Wales
Mid-Wales
South Wales
Central England
East Anglia
London
South England
South-west England
0
100 km
0
100 miles
12°
10°
8°
6°
4°
2°
0°
2°
60°
58°
56°
54°
52°
50°

ARCHAEOLOGICAL SITES
N
Mousa Broch
Skara Brae
Gurness
Callanish
Skye
Dun Telve Broch
Rum
Inchtuthil
Scone Abbey
Iona
Oronsay
Cramond
Lindisfarne
Arran
Mount Sandel
Jarrow
Ceidi Fields
Starr Carr
York
Newgrange and Tara
Dublin
Anglesey
Aran Islands
Chester
Pontnewydd Cave
Wroxeter
Lincoln
Plynlimmon
Dingle
Wexford
Sutton Hoo
Strata Florida
River Kenmare
Colchester
Pembroke
Caerleon
Paviland Cave
Stonehenge
Richborough and Ebbsfleet
Cheddar Gorge
Pevensey
Exeter
Totnes
0
100 km
0
100 miles

PROLOGUE

This is the very first book to be written about the genetic history of Britain and Ireland using DNA as its main source of information. It is the culmination of an ambition, almost a dream, that I first had ten years ago. Having successfully used DNA to solve several outstanding issues about the human past on a continental scale, I wanted to push the method to its limits and dissect the intimate genetic make-up of a smaller region. And where better to do this than in my own back yard, so to speak. My own country, one that I share with 60 million others and with an even greater number whose roots are here but who now live overseas. And what a land it is, full of myth and legend, brimming with archaeological treasures and set down in a rich treasury of historical documents.

For its new, scientific content, *Blood of the Isles* relies primarily on the results of a systematic DNA survey that I and my research team in Oxford University have undertaken over the last ten years, a survey involving more than

10,000 volunteers from every part of 'the Isles'. The results, explained in the book, exceeded even my most optimistic expectations of the power of genetics to make a real contribution to our knowledge of a small region.

In *Blood of the Isles*, I approach the DNA evidence in the same way as others who write about the past using their different specialities – material artefacts, written documents, human remains and so on. The most important thing about the genetic evidence is that it is entirely independent of these other sources. It does not rely on them. However, to use genetics most effectively to fill in any picture of the past, it helps immensely to have this abundance of other evidence, and I use this resource throughout the book. Nevertheless, when you have read *Blood of the Isles* I hope you will agree that from now on genetics can take its proper place alongside history and archaeology as one of the principal lenses through which to view the past.

I have written two other books on DNA and human evolution: *The Seven Daughters of Eve* and *Adam's Curse*. You may have read them, but I certainly do not assume that you have. You don't need to in order to follow the story of *Blood of the Isles* perfectly well. However, there are some topics which are covered more extensively in the earlier books than they are here, but which to repeat here in full would be unnecessary.

I have deliberately avoided, as far as possible, putting technical data into the text. A little is absolutely essential, but too much soon disrupts the flow. For those readers who want to delve more deeply into the supporting scientific evidence I have added an Appendix (page 341) and, for real enthusiasts, I am publishing additional material on the website www.bloodoftheisles.net.

Finally, a word about the title. I use 'the Isles' rather than 'Britain' or 'UK', to avoid the pitfalls that follow from political boundaries much more recently drawn than the time depth covered by this book. Many in Ireland are not British and the Irish Republic is not part of the United Kingdom. But to leave them out would be absurd. Ours is a shared history. Throughout the book 'Ireland' includes Northern Ireland and 'Britain' embraces Scotland, Wales and England.

Some names have been changed to preserve confidentiality.

1

TWELVE THOUSAND YEARS OF SOLITUDE

Everything was ready. I selected one of the diamond-tipped bits from the sterile rack and tightened it into the jaws of the high-speed drill. Turning the dial up to 500 revolutions a second, I looked carefully to see that the spinning drill was centralized in the chuck. There must not be any mistakes, especially today. In my left hand, I picked up the jaw bone and turned it so that the outer surface of the first molar tooth was facing me. I moved the jaw under the magnifier and brought the rotating drill to within a millimetre of the enamel surface of the tooth. The tooth that had never bitten into a pizza, nor crunched a piece of celery. The tooth that I was about to drill into was 12,000 years old. The last food this tooth had touched was the flesh of a reindeer or wild horse. It was the tooth of a young man, about twenty years old when he died. This man was a hunter, one of the first people to arrive in Britain since the end of the last Ice Age.

The skeleton of the young man had been dug out of the

limestone caves of Cheddar Gorge in Somerset in 1986. Ten years later, in the autumn of 1996, I had brought his lower jaw, with the beautifully preserved teeth still embedded, to my laboratory in Oxford. I was about to attempt to recover the DNA, the genetic essence, of its original owner, trapped in the dentine beneath the hard enamel which had encased and protected it for thousands of years. As the drill made contact with the enamel surface, I steadied my left arm on the lab bench and pressed the bit into the tooth. The whining pitch of the drill came down slightly as it cut into the enamel. This was a good sign. The enamel was not too soft. That would have been a sure sign of biological decay, which would have dashed any chance of finding intact DNA. Neither was the tooth granite-hard. That would have meant that all the organic remains, including the DNA, had literally turned to stone. The Cheddar tooth was somewhere in between, neither too soft, nor too hard.

After a few seconds, the drill had cut through the enamel layer and into the dentine which lay behind. I could feel the drop in pressure as the tip of the drill moved into the softer dentine, and heard its pitch rise as the speed increased. A second or two later, I caught the scent of burning – the same unforgettable smell that instantly recalled dread visits to the dentist and the fillings of a sweet-toothed youth. It was the smell of burning teeth. This was the unmistakable scent of vaporizing protein, and the moment I caught the smell of it coming from the ancient tooth my spirits rose. From that moment on, I was sure I would find his DNA, for if the protein which was being vaporized by the drill had survived for 12,000 years, then there was every chance that his DNA would have done so too. Both are biological molecules subject to the same laws of age and decay.

As soon as I smelled the burning, I pulled across the suction line. This was a device rather like a miniature vacuum cleaner which I had rigged up for collecting the powdered dentine into a sterile test tube. With this in place, I began to drill out the dentine, carefully moving the bit up and down inside the tooth, pulling back as soon as I felt it touch the hard enamel on the other side. All the time the vacuum line was transferring the creamy white powder into the test tube and collecting it in a small pile at the bottom. Within a few minutes, I had completely excavated the inside of the tooth. In the test tube lay precisely 208 milligrams of dentine powder from the Old Stone Age.

Within two weeks, and in ways that we will cover later, I had recovered enough DNA from the Cheddar tooth to read the genetic fingerprint of its original owner – a young man whose pattern of life was so utterly different from our own that it is hard to imagine any possible connection between him and ourselves. And yet the fragment of his DNA that I had recovered from his tooth is exactly the same in every detail as that of thousands of people living in the Isles today. His descendants are with us still – and you may well be one of them.

It is now almost ten years since the day I drilled into the Cheddar tooth, but the moment is still vivid in my memory. It was not the first time I had attempted to recover DNA from ancient skeletons, but it was the most scary. This was a priceless and irreplaceable specimen. But what was I, a trained geneticist, doing drilling into the tooth in the first place? I had spent the early part of my career researching the causes of inherited diseases, mainly those affecting the skeleton – hence the location of my laboratory in Oxford's Institute of Molecular Medicine. This research had led to the discovery of the genes involved in giving strength to bones – the genes which coded for bone collagen – and to the mutations in the collagen genes which caused these often devastating diseases.

It was only a chance introduction to an archaeologist, Robert Hedges, who runs the carbon-dating lab in Oxford, that got me involved in the human past at all. Robert wanted to see if he could get more from the bone samples coming to his laboratory for carbon-dating than merely finding out how old they were. Carbon-dating relies on counting the tiny number of radioactive carbon atoms that lie in the collagen of ancient organic remains. As these atoms decay with time, the fewer there are, the older the sample. Robert got in touch, having heard about my research on the genetics of bone collagen, and we started to plan what we might be able to do with these old bones. To cut a long story short, within two years we had worked out a way of recovering DNA from human and animal bones that were hundreds or even thousands of years old.

Being the first laboratory in the world to do this, we were well placed to receive exciting samples from all over the world. Over the years we have had bits of Neanderthals; Oetzi, the famous Iceman from the Alps; various claimants to being Anastasia, the last of the Romanovs; a selection of dead poets and statesmen; not to mention the odd piece of Yeti skin. To put the DNA results from this eclectic collection into some form of context, I began a programme of collecting DNA samples from living people. For instance, although it was wonderful to be able to get DNA from the 5,000-year-old Iceman, and that became a story in itself, it only became really interesting when his DNA could be compared, and indeed matched, with someone living today. The whereabouts of his modern descendants told us something about the movement of people throughout Europe during the five millennia since his death.

Sometimes the DNA from modern people can solve long-standing riddles that had proved to be intractable by any other means. The outstanding example of this was the research on the origin of the Polynesians. These are the people who live on the far-flung islands of the Pacific. All the islands, from Hawaii in the north to Easter Island in the east and New Zealand in the far south, had been settled by Polynesians well before the time Europeans began to explore the Pacific Ocean in the early part of the sixteenth century. But where had the Polynesians come from? Was it from Asia, as the bulk of the evidence from language, domestic animals and crops suggested? Or had they arrived in the other direction from America, as the legendary Norwegian anthropologist Thor Heyerdahl believed? Like many schoolboys, I had been captivated by Heyerdahl's adventures on the balsa raft *Kon-Tiki*, on which he drifted from Peru to the Tuamotu islands, not far from Tahiti, to prove his point. So it was with a tinge of regret that, in 1995, I published the genetic data which proved conclusively that Heyerdahl was wrong. The Polynesians had come from Asia, not America. This slight regret at having disproved a boyhood hero was more than compensated by the proof that the Polynesians must have explored the Pacific intentionally, driving their canoes into wind and current eastwards across the vast ocean, rather than lazily drifting with the prevailing elements from South America. The ancestors of today's Polynesians were without doubt the greatest maritime explorers the world has ever known.

The proof of their true origins came from the DNA of modern Polynesians that I had collected from dozens of Pacific islands. From the detailed genetic fingerprints of the islanders I was able to trace the route that their resolute ancestors had taken through the island chains of South-east Asia and out into the vast Pacific Ocean. In ways that I will explain later, I could follow the genetic threads that had percolated through the generations and reconstruct the 3,000-year-old journeys of these astonishing navigators.

It was because I was attempting to reproduce this first success in the much more difficult arena of Europe that I found myself drilling into the Cheddar tooth. My colleagues and I had followed the same procedure that had yielded such compelling results in Polynesia. We had collected almost 1,000 DNA samples from all over Europe and, again in ways I will later explain, come to a conclusion about the origin of modern Europeans. That conclusion was, in a nutshell, that the ancestors of most native Europeans were hunter-gatherers and not, as was commonly believed at the time, farmers who had spread into Europe from the Middle East about 8,500 years ago. To say that our conclusion caused a stir is an understatement.

There followed several years of fierce debate between ourselves and the proponents of the agricultural-ancestry theory, and the experiment with the Cheddar tooth was one of our efforts to prove our case. The idea behind it was that, if we could show that a very old human fossil, a genuine hunter-gatherer who lived well before farming arrived, had pretty much the same DNA as people living today, that would strengthen our side of the argument.

The fact that the Cheddar tooth DNA was identical to modern Europeans' had several ramifications. This was the DNA of a man who, without any doubt, was a hunter-gatherer who had lived at least 6,000 years before farming reached the Isles. Taken with all the other genetic evidence, the result helped to swing opinion towards a predominantly hunter-gatherer ancestry for Europeans and away from the prevalent theory of a great wave of ancient farmers sweeping out from the Middle East and overwhelming the thinly spread hunters. The heat has gone out of that particular debate by now, and I think it is fair to say that most people today think that the impact of migrating farmers on the genetic make-up of Europe was far less than previously thought.

A few months after finding the DNA from the 12,000-year-old Cheddar tooth I got permission to repeat the process with a younger specimen from the same cave. This was the famous 'Cheddar Man'. His remains had been excavated in 1903 and, like the other skeleton, had been stored in the Natural History Museum in South Kensington. They had been carbon-dated to about 9,000 years ago, still well before the arrival of farming in Britain and so still relevant to the hunter/farmer debate. Sure enough, after drilling out the tooth and analysing the DNA from the dentine powder, I could see that Cheddar Man's DNA was also thoroughly modern. It was not the same, in detail, as the earlier Cheddar tooth, but it did match quite a few modern Britons', one of whom lived just down the road from the Caves. A local television company had got wind of our work on the Cheddar fossils and, between us, we had dreamed up a format whereby, in parallel to the work on Cheddar Man's teeth, we would also test the DNA of the pupils at the local school. If we could find a DNA match between Cheddar Man and a modern-day nearby resident it would be a good local-interest story as well as a neat demonstration of genetic continuity.

With all the DNA results in from the school, and from Cheddar Man himself, the producer arranged a notorious 'reveal' session. The pupils, all aged between sixteen and eighteen, and the master who had organized the event at the school, gathered in the hall, nervously waiting for the results to be announced. The camera passed across the faces of the teenagers, each one apprehensive that it might be their DNA that had been matched to Cheddar Man. The presenter spoke, the match was revealed and the cameras swivelled round to bring one face into tight close-up. It was not one of the pupils at all, but the history teacher who had made the arrangements – Mr Adrian Targett. Gasps all round, a blushing teacher and a score of ever so slightly disappointed teenagers.

The following day Adrian Targett's smiling face was on the front page of every national newspaper. He was pictured crouching next to the replica of Cheddar Man's skeleton at the spot in the cave where it had been discovered in 1903. Even the tabloids carried the story, impressively assembling a topless model in a skimpy rabbit-skin loincloth and with a hastily assembled flint axe. Adrian told me later that he had been offered a 'five-figure sum' to appear in a loincloth but had, sensibly, declined. The following day the story was picked up by newspapers abroad. It proved to be particularly popular in the US, probably because it fitted in nicely with the image of a bucolic English countryside in which it takes 9,000 years for someone's descendants to move 300 yards down the road. People still remember the story even now, and when I was lecturing in California last year I was introduced by the organizers as the man who got DNA from the Cheese Man.

The Cheddar Men, though they lived a very long time ago, were not the first human inhabitants of the Isles. There are scattered shreds of evidence that the Isles were once occupied by archaic species of humans, not directly ancestral to our own species, *Homo sapiens*. A shin bone from Boxgrove Quarry near Chichester on the Sussex coast, a tooth from Pontnewydd Cave in north Wales, both over a quarter of a million years old and both the remains, as far as can be told, of much sturdier, large-boned humans, more like Neanderthals than our own species. The recent discovery of flint tools that have been exposed in a crumbling cliff near Lowestoft on the Suffolk coast is evidence, albeit indirect, of a human presence on the Isles more than half a million years ago. Fascinating though these finds are, they are merely glimpses into the world of long-extinct humans who came and went but left no lasting impression on the Isles, small bands of roving hunters whose luck finally ran out. These were not our ancestors.

The earliest evidence of our own species, *Homo sapiens*, in the Isles comes from Paviland Cave just above the rocky shoreline of the Gower Peninsula to the west of Swansea in South Wales. In 1823 the Oxford palaeontologist William Buckland excavated the partial skeleton of a man. Misled by the presence of ivory ornaments near the body, Buckland assumed that he had found the remains of a woman and, because the bones were stained with red ochre as part of an unknown burial ritual, she soon became known as 'the Red Lady of Paviland'. However, a more thorough analysis of the bones, particularly the pelvis, showed that the Red Lady was actually a man, though he still retains the title. When Buckland found these bones they were so well preserved that he thought they could not be all that old. His theory was that they were the remains of a woman who had been living in the cave while working at a nearby Roman camp. But he was wrong again. We now know from carbon-dating that the Red Lady was much older than the time of the Roman occupation. 'She' died 26,000 years ago and 'her' pendant was not made of elephant ivory but had been carved from the tusk of a mammoth. We know, from the deliberate burial, that the Red Lady was survived by her relatives, but no trace of them remains. After the time of the Red Lady, there is a long empty gap in the fossil record of the Isles. There is nothing until the time of the 'older' of the Cheddar Men, just over 12,000 years ago. Why the break? There is one very simple answer – the Ice Age.

About 24,000 years ago the temperatures in the northern latitudes around the globe, including the Isles, began to drop as the planet entered once again into the downward phase of a glacial cycle. These regular cycles of bitter cold and comparative mildness have been going on for at least 2 million years. They are caused by the slight shifts in the way the earth rotates and moves in its orbit around the sun. The shape of the orbit changes from circular to elliptical and then back to circular about once every 96,000 years. The angle of the earth's axis changes, shifting the positions of the Arctic Circle and the Tropic of Cancer up and down by 3 degrees of latitude, and several hundred miles, once every 42,000 years. Another cycle, every 20,000 years, alters the seasons when the earth is at different parts of its orbit. As the earth runs through this cycle, the signs of the zodiac slowly move round and we enter new astrological 'ages', the latest being Aquarius. The combination of all three cycles one on top of the other means the earth's climate never stands still for long. The effect is to change the amount of sunlight which hits the higher latitudes in both hemispheres, slowly increasing and decreasing as the overlapping cycles gradually shift the planet's position with respect to the sun. We are now in a warm phase of the long-term glacial cycle, but it will not last for ever and at some as yet unpredictable time in the future we will slide inexorably into another Ice Age. How soon the next cold phase will begin and to what extent its chilling effects will be tempered by 'global warming' are all uncertainties for future generations.

For the descendants of the Red Lady and the other scattered occupants of the Isles 24,000 years ago, even though they did not know it, their tenancy of the land was coming to an end. Gradually the year-on-year temperatures began to fall. Snow that covered the mountains in winter no longer melted in the summer and gradually built up into a permanent ice cap. The sea began to recede as more and more water became locked in permanent ice sheets, not just in the Isles but also at the Poles and over the mountain ranges of Europe, Asia and America. The Isles became a peninsula as the North Sea receded. Britain and Ireland were joined. Vicious winds howled around the edges of the expanding ice cap as the weather systems shifted away from the succession of moisture-bearing Atlantic depressions towards an Arctic climate of intense, dry cold. And all the time, the ice moved south. The herds of migrating game – reindeer, bison, wild horse and mammoth – moved their ranges away from the worsening conditions, and the scattered groups of humans who depended on them for food had no choice but to follow them. By the time of the coldest phase of the Ice Age, 18,000 years ago, there were no humans left in Britain, or anywhere else in Europe north of the Alps.

The descendants of the Red Lady and their contemporaries had retreated to refuges in southern France, Italy and Spain, abandoning northern Europe to the frost and ice. Great glaciers flowed downhill from the ice domes over the mountains of northern Britain, gouging out steep-sided valleys and pulverizing the bedrock as they ground their way across the landscape, obliterating everything in their path. All evidence of human occupation in northern Britain was completely erased by the ice. Only south of a line from the English Midlands to central Ireland, which marked the edge of the ice, could any trace remain.

And then, quite suddenly, the climate began to improve as the planet moved its alignment in the heavens. The warmth of the sun returned to the northern latitudes and the ice began to melt. Our ancestors followed the herds north from their huddled refuges as the frozen land began to thaw. Carbon-dating of charcoal left by campfires has traced the advancing front and by 13,000 years ago they had reached northern France. A millennium later, the older of the Cheddar Men, or his immediate ancestors, were among the first to arrive in the Isles, by foot across the land that now lies beneath the North Sea. His are among the oldest remains to be found anywhere in post-Ice Age Britain. He arrived in a landscape scrubbed clean of human occupation by the effects of the Ice Age, even though the ice itself never reached as far south as his home in Cheddar. His camp in the gorge was perfect as an ambush site to trap the migrating herds of reindeer as they moved from their summer feeding grounds on the high Mendips to spend the winter on the Somerset Levels. Remains at the site showed he was skilled at making the variety of flint tools on which the life of the hunter depended.

When he arrived, 12,000 years or so ago, the Isles were connected to each other and to the rest of continental Europe. The sea was 100 feet lower than it is now and large tracts of land that are now under water were well above sea level. Ireland was connected to mainland Britain through a broad plain that joined it to the west coast of Scotland and took in what is now the whisky isle of Islay. The Irish Sea, which now entirely separates Ireland from the rest of the Isles, was then a narrow sea inlet between flat plains, blocked at its northern end by the isthmus that joined Scotland to the north of Ireland. The Western Isles off the north-west coast of Scotland were similarly joined to the mainland with a narrow strip of dry land. The Hebridean islands of Skye, Mull, Rum, Coll and Tiree were not islands then; neither were the Orkney Islands, now separated from the far north of the Scottish mainland by the turbulent seas of the Pentland Firth. Only the Shetland Isles, 60 miles north of Orkney, were truly islands in those far-off days.

Most important of all, there was dry land connecting Britain to continental Europe. This was no narrow causeway, but a wide rolling plain joining eastern Britain to the rest of Europe from the Tyne in the north to Beachy Head near Eastbourne in the south. The entire southern section of what is now the North Sea was dry land intersected by wide rivers. The Thames was then a tributary of the Rhine, their joined waters emptying into the sea 100 miles east of Newcastle upon Tyne. What is now Britain and Ireland, separated by shallow seas, was then a great peninsula protruding into the Atlantic Ocean. The Irish Sea was open only at its southern end and the North Sea was dry land. The sea level was rising as the global temperature climbed back up after the last Ice Age. The great ice sheets that covered the northern hemisphere were melting, as their remnants in the polar north continue to do today.

Even now, the Isles are still twisting and turning in the

aftermath of the last Ice Age. The immense weight of snow and ice across the Scottish Highlands and, to a greater extent still, over the mountains of Sweden and Norway pushed these lands further down into the semi-molten layers deep beneath the earth's solid crust. The continents are floating on molten magma and, just like a cargo ship, they move up and down depending on their loadings. Unlike a ship, when one part goes down under the weight of ice, a nearby section can be pushed up. This happened to the land that now lies beneath the North Sea and which was artificially elevated by the sinking of Scandinavia under the weight of its ice dome. As this melted, the sea level certainly rose, simply because there was much more water in the oceans. But the land that had been pushed down into the magma began to rise up again as the load of ice melted away. And as Norway and Sweden floated back up towards their pre-Ice Age levels, so Doggerland, as this now vanished land beneath the North Sea is called, sank back down, quickening its submergence beneath the rising sea and accelerating the conversion of the Isles from peninsula to the real thing.

The Isles are still slowly convulsing. The southern and eastern coasts of England are sinking at the rate of an inch a year, causing the kind of coastal erosion that has shed the flint tools half a million years old from the crumbling cliffs of Suffolk. The west and north coasts are rising at about the same rate or sometimes faster. Dunbar, on the east coast of Scotland not far from Edinburgh, for example, is rising at the rate of 2 inches a year. Ireland is still lifting itself from the ocean.

By the time the 'younger' Cheddar Man lived in the same gorge, 9,000 years ago, the climate had improved even more, but the great herds of big game had gone. What had once been open tundra was now dense woodland and, though the climate was warmer, the business of living was very much harder. His diet was opportunistic: fish and crayfish from the river that tumbled out of the rocks; birds and mammals, perhaps a squirrel or a pine marten from the woods; and, on a good day, a red deer. In the autumn there were mushrooms and nuts from the woods around the gorge. Woodland was now the dominant feature of the landscape of the Isles as the chilling effect of the Ice Age wore off. Though the types of trees varied from place to place, the land was covered in dense forests from the southern shores to the glens of the northern Highlands. Only the uplands remained free of natural tree cover due to a combination of altitude and poor soil.

Since the time of the 'older' Cheddar Man, the Isles have been almost continuously occupied. During the millennia that his remains slept in the silent limestone caves of Somerset, almost everything has changed in the Isles. The landscape has been transformed from open tundra to thick forest to cultivated fields. Where once he hunted for food, tourists throng the gorge and queue for cream teas. From a total population of a few thousand in the Stone Age, the Isles are now home to more than 60 million people. Beyond the shores, a further 150 million people from all over the world can trace their roots back to the Isles. While his bones were gradually entombed by the drip, drip, drip of limestone water in the silence of his cave, the ancestors of the ancient Celts have arrived in Wales and Ireland, the ground has trembled under the marching feet of Roman legions, the shingle beaches of Kent have yielded to the keels of Saxon warships, and the blood-curdling cries of Viking raiders have echoed from the defenceless monasteries of Northumbria and the Scottish islands. While he endured 12,000 years of solitude, the world outside pulsed with life – and death. His DNA stayed where it was, but outside the cave it had another life in the generations of descendants whose stories we can now begin to unfold.

2
WHO DO WE THINK WE ARE?

On Easter Day 1278, Edward I, King of England, accompanied by Queen Eleanor and a glittering retinue of knights and ministers, arrived at the Benedictine monastery of Glastonbury in Somerset. The reason for his visit was very specific – and very deliberate. He and his court were there to open the tomb of the legendary King Arthur. In a lavishly elaborate ceremony, two caskets containing the bones of Arthur and his queen, Guinevere, were taken from the tomb, the bones removed and carefully laid out on the altar of the monastery chapel. The following day Edward wrapped Arthur's bones in sheets of silk and solemnly placed them in a painted casket decorated with Arthur's portrait and his coat of arms. Queen Eleanor then mounted the platform and performed the same rites with the bones of Guinevere. After this the caskets were placed in front of the high altar and the royal party departed.

What was Edward up to? Why did he go to so much

trouble to travel all the way to Glastonbury? He was there for one very simple reason. He was aligning himself with the legend of King Arthur and through him laying claim to the ancient kingdom of the Britons. He was able to capitalize on the predominant myth about the origins of the British people, a myth that utterly dominated the Middle Ages. We may believe that nowadays we are beyond the grasp of hazy origin myths and treat them as the sole preserve of ignorant and primitive people clinging to absurd notions of their past. But in my research around the world I have more than once found that oral myths are closer to the genetic conclusions than the often ambiguous scientific evidence of archaeology. Hawaiki, the legendary homeland of the Polynesians, was said to be located among the islands of Indonesia, and genetics proved it. The Hazara tribe of north-west Pakistan had a strong oral myth of descent from the first Mongol emperor, Genghis Khan, and his genes are still there to this day. These are just two examples.

Only when I began my research in the Isles did I come to appreciate that we are just as entangled in our own origin myths as everybody else. They are still very powerful and, as in other parts of the world, they may contain grains of truth that we can test by genetics. I believe we are just as vulnerable to the power of myth about our own origins as the Polynesians or the Hazara or, indeed, the witnesses to the elaborate ceremony at Glastonbury over 700 years ago. The modern historian Norman Davies castigates archaeologists for their over-materialist approach to the past and their disdain for myth. I am on his side. While no one would be foolish enough to suggest that they are entirely accurate in every detail, myths have a very long memory. They are also extremely influential. To see how our own origin myths have developed, let us return to the Middle Ages.

The legend of King Arthur was brilliantly exploited by Edward I and many other of the Plantagenet kings who reigned during the Middle Ages. By linking himself to the mythical dynasty of ancient British kings he was seeking to justify his attempts to become sovereign of the whole of Britain. Twenty years after Glastonbury, he argued in the papal court in Rome that his descent from Arthur and a long line of ancient British kings gave the English crown rights over Scotland and had been ample justification for his military campaigns. His great-grandfather, Henry II, had done a similar thing when he arranged for Arthur's remains at Glastonbury to be 'discovered'. His grandson Edward III showed his enthusiasm for the myth in 1348 by instigating his own version of the Arthurian Knights of the Round Table: the Order of the Garter, a select company of twenty-four grandees that still continues today. It is no coincidence that Prince Charles, the current heir to the throne, was christened Arthur among his many names.

The origin of the myth itself was a quite brilliant work of creative imagination by a Welsh cleric, Geoffrey of Monmouth, writing in 1138. *The History of the Kings of Britain* has everything an origin myth should have. It is full of heroic deeds, terrible battles, black treachery, and is woven with just enough threads of authenticity to be taken seriously. It even had its own mysterious source – a book (never discovered) 'written in the British language which told of the lives of the ancient British Kings from Brutus, the first, to Cadwallader, the last', given to Geoffrey by a mysterious archdeacon, named Walter, in Oxford where he wrote the *History*.

It is hard for us, in retrospect and living in a world where most mythologies, or so we like to think, require at least a semblance of supporting evidence, to believe that Geoffrey's *History* should have been taken quite so literally. But what gave the *History* such an enduring influence, apart from its use for political advantage, was that woven into the improbable narrative and sheer fantasy were crumbs of credible historical fact. It was very specific about the tide of events and enjoyed huge popularity because of its enthusiastic endorsement by a succession of royal dynasties. It became, quite literally, a medieval bestseller, and as its popularity increased, so the myth it created slowly transubstantiated into objective truth. It was believed every bit as much as the Greeks were certain of their Olympian pantheon of Zeus, Apollo, Athena and Poseidon.

Geoffrey begins his *History* with a description:

> Britain, best of Islands, formerly called Albion is situated in the Western Ocean, between Gaul and Ireland. It is in length 800 miles, in breadth 200 and is inexhaustible in every production necessary to the use of man. For it has mines of all kinds, the plains are numerous and extensive, the hills high and bold and the soil well adapted to tillage, yields its fruits of every species in their season. The woods abound with a variety of animals and afford pasturage for

> cattle, and flowers of many lines, from which the eager bees collect their honey. At the bases of their mountains that tower to the skies are green meads, delightfully situated, through which the pure streams flow from their fountains in gentle soothing murmurs. Fish also live in abundance in the lakes and rivers and in the surrounding sea. It is inhabited by five different nations, Britons, Saxons, Romans, Picts and Celts. Of these the Britons formerly, and prior to the rest, possessed the country from sea to sea until divine vengeance because of their pride, they gave place to the Pictish and Saxon invaders. In what manner and whence they came will more fully appear in what follows.

According to the *History*, the very first inhabitants of Britain were a race of giants under Albion, a son of the sea-god Poseidon. Albion and the other giants were the children of a band of fifty women who arrived in the empty land having been banished for killing their husbands. There being no men, the fifty women mated with demons to conceive their giant offspring. The demise of Albion came about when he joined forces with two of his brothers to steal, from Hercules, the herd of cattle he had been sent to capture in Spain as the tenth of his twelve labours. Albion and his giants ambushed Hercules as he was passing through the south of France on his way home to Greece with the cattle. Hercules fought off Albion, aided by his father Zeus who arranged for a shower of rocks to fall from the sky at just the right moment, and slew the giants. After that defeat, though the giants continued to inhabit Britain for the next 600 years, their numbers dwindled until only a few remained.

Already this is a rich history, firmly linked for the benefit of the readership to the classical mythology of Zeus, Poseidon and Hercules. The next arrivals were no less well connected to the classical world and came to Britain as a direct result of the Trojan War. When Troy fell to the Greeks, Aeneas and a group of his followers escaped and made their way to Italy, where they established the settlement that was to become Rome. The link between Troy and Britain begins with the birth of Aeneas's grandson, Brutus. The soothsayers, indispensable contributors to all good mythologies, predict that he will cause the death of his parents. Which, of course, comes to pass. His mother dies in childbirth and he accidentally shoots his father. A deer runs between the young Brutus and his father while they are out hunting. Brutus fires the arrow, which glances off the deer's back and hits his father in the chest. After this misfortune Brutus is banished. His wanderings take him to Greece, where he precipitates a revolt by slaves descended from Trojan prisoners of war, and liberates them. Looking for a new home, they sail to a small deserted island, where Brutus finds a temple dedicated to the goddess Diana. In a dream Diana reveals to Brutus the existence of a great island past the Pillars of Hercules (the Strait of Gibraltar) and out into the ocean towards the setting sun.

> Brutus, there lies in the west, beyond the realms of Gaul, an island surrounded by the waters of the ocean, once inhabited by giants, but now deserted. Thither go thou, for it

> is fated to be a second Troy to thee and thy posterity; and from thee shall Kings descend who shall subdue the whole world to their power.

Though the island is inhabited by giants, Diana reassures Brutus that, following their defeat by Hercules, they are few in number and easily overcome. Once there, Diana promises him, Brutus will build a new Troy and found a dynasty of kings that will eventually become the most powerful on earth. You can already see how Geoffrey has cleverly sculpted his *History* to make it irresistible for any British king to claim this mantle for himself.

Now on a divine mission, Brutus sets sail for Albion with his Trojans. All ancestors, whether mythical or entirely real, must place their first foot on dry land somewhere. Brutus chose Totnes in Devon, a few miles up the River Dart from the open sea. The rock on which his foot first made contact with Albion is still there. Brutus and his men made short work of the giants and set about exploring the virgin country. Their chosen site for New Troy was on the River Thames. New Troy, or Troia Nova, became Trinovantum and, later, London. Another stone, still visible today in Cannon Street near the City's financial quarter, was the altar that Brutus built to honour Diana whose divine guidance led him to Albion. Thus it was, according to the *History*, that Brutus, grandson of Aeneas of Troy, became the first king of Britain.

Twenty years after he first stepped ashore at Totnes, Brutus died and Britain was divided into three parts, England, Scotland and Wales, each ruled by one of his three sons in that order of seniority. When the two younger sons died, the whole island reverted to the eldest, Locrinus. It was his alleged direct descent from Locrinus that Edward I used as the justification for his military campaigns against both Wales and Scotland in the late 1200s. For Edward, it was entirely legitimate to restore the whole of Britain under one crown – his, of course.

From Brutus and Locrinus, a long line of kings trickles down through the centuries, a rich vein of quasi-historical material for mythologists and authors. Shakespeare's inspiration for King Lear came from this list. Another legendary king was Lud, who rebuilt the walls of New Troy; it was through corruptions of Lud's name that it eventually became London. After Lud, the next in line was Cassivelaunus, whom we shall meet again later on. It was during his reign that Julius Caesar launched his military expeditions in Britain in 55 and 54 BC. And these were certainly not mythical. Caesar was well aware of the legend of common descent of both Romans and Britons from Aeneas and the Trojans. But this did not alter his view that the Britons, during their long centuries of isolation, had become degenerate and lost their skill in the art of war.

The full-scale Roman invasion launched by Claudius in AD 43 reduced the power of the British kings but did not extinguish it. But it is the events in the centuries after the Roman occupation ended and what the myth has to say about the Saxons that give it its greatest modern significance. Not all British kings were heroes in the *History*, and as Roman power in Britain declined in the early fifth century AD, the country became the focus of Anglo-Saxon ambitions. At this point the crown passed to the ambitious and treacherous tribal chieftain Vortigern.

After the death of the rightful king, Constantine, Vortigern arranges for the coronation of Constantine's unworldly son, Constans, in exchange for his own effective management of the country. But that is not enough for Vortigern, and he orders Constans's murder. Even then he is not crowned, but assumes the title of King of the Britons. Constans's brothers, the rightful heirs, flee to Brittany and prepare for an attack to regain the crown. To protect himself against the forthcoming war, Vortigern makes the fateful decision to recruit outside help. According to the *History*, he sights three ships in the Channel which, he discovers, are manned by Saxons under their leader Hengist. They have been sent to seek settlements of their own, their homeland being no longer able to support them – an exercise carried out, apparently, once every seven years.

Vortigern promises the Saxons land on which to settle in return for their military support in the anticipated war and they receive, first, part of Lincolnshire, then, after Hengist gives his daughter Rowena to the infatuated Vortigern, he receives the earldom of Kent. Appalled at Vortigern's gift of land to the Saxons – none more so than the dispossessed Earl of Kent – the Britons make Vortimer, Vortigern's son from his first wife, their king and expel the Saxons from the shores. But Vortimer is poisoned on Rowena's orders and Vortigern is made king once more. The Saxons return in force. Hengist convenes a great assembly of British earls and barons under Vortigern's patronage to thrash out the peaceful integration of his Saxons in Britain. In the spirit of the meeting, everyone arrives unarmed. But the treacherous Hengist orders each of his men to conceal a long knife in their clothes. On a prearranged signal, each Saxon pulls out his knife and kills the Briton standing next to him. Only one man survives to tell the tale. The Saxons banish Vortigern, no longer useful to them, to Wales and take possession of England.

The mythology surrounding the arrival of the Saxons was completely transformed in later centuries, but for Geoffrey of Monmouth it began through an act of treachery and betrayal. It is against this background that the greatest hero of the *History*, Arthur, makes his appearance. The wretched Vortigern retreats to the Welsh hills, but his attempts to build himself a fortress are frustrated by the collapse of each day's work during the following night. He is told by his court bards that only by mixing the blood of a child with no father into the mortar will this nightly collapse be avoided. His men are despatched to all parts of Wales to discover such a boy; in Carmarthen they find one and bring him, with his mother, to Vortigern. But this is no ordinary boy: it is Merlin. He challenges Vortigern's bards as to why they think it necessary to sacrifice him to build the castle. What is it, he demands, that lies beneath the site to make it unstable? They cannot answer. Using his own magic powers to see into the ground, he tells Vortigern that if he excavates the soil beneath the castle site he will discover a subterranean pool. Vortigern's men dig down and, sure enough, there is the lake. Drain the pool, Merlin prophesies, and you will find two hollow stones, each containing a sleeping dragon. The pool is drained and the dragons, one red, one white, awake and begin to fight. At first the White Dragon prevails but is eventually overcome by the Red Dragon. The White Dragon symbolizes the Saxons, the Red Dragon the Britons. The message is clear. Fight back against the treacherous Saxons and you will prevail. Even today the Red Dragon, and all it stands for, is prominent on the Welsh flag and other national emblems – a direct legacy from Geoffrey of Monmouth.

The ultimate victory of the Britons over the Saxon invaders is a recurring theme throughout the *History* and no character symbolizes this resistance more than King Arthur. But his birth is not without its own dark side. If Vortigern's infatuation with Rowena sowed the seeds of his downfall and the invasion of the Saxons, it was infatuation that led to Arthur's birth.

Merlin, who is by now living by his uncannily accurate prophecies, foretells that Uther, the younger of Constantine's two surviving sons, will become the next King of the Britons. Returning from exile in Brittany (and landing at Totnes – always a good start), Uther and his brother beat back the Saxons, killing both Vortigern and Hengist in the process. But the elder of the two is poisoned, again as prophesied, and on his death a comet appears, at the head of which is a ball of fire resembling a dragon. Merlin, conveniently on hand, interprets this as a sign that the younger brother must be crowned king. Thus Uther becomes Uther Pendragon, Uther of the Dragon's Head, and King of the Britons at the same time.

At Uther Pendragon's coronation and victory celebration in London arrive Gorlais, Earl of Cornwall, and his wife Eigr, the most beautiful woman in Britain. That is when the infatuation begins. Tired of the attention that his wife is getting from Uther, Gorlais takes her from the palace and sets out home for Cornwall and his newly built castle at Tintagel among the high sea cliffs. Uther commands that Gorlais return to London at once and when he refuses Uther follows him to Tintagel. The only entrance to the castle is over a narrow and easily defended causeway, along which only one man can pass at a time. Uther appeals to Merlin for help and Merlin transforms him into Eigr's husband, in which disguise he enters both the castle and her bed, where Arthur is conceived. That same night, Uther's soldiers capture and kill the real Gorlais.

In Arthur, Geoffrey's *History* has constructed the most enduring of British mythical heroes. With scant reliable historical material to go on – or, it must be said, to get in the way of a good story – Arthur's exploits are so familiar that they scarcely need repeating here. But it was the extravagance of Arthur's adventures that sowed the seeds of the *History*'s eventual demise.

Following his father's death (another poisoning), Arthur is crowned at the age of fifteen. Immediately after the coronation, he sets off on a spree of military conquest, first in Britain, then abroad. At first he defeats the few remaining Saxons, then pushes the encroaching Picts back to northern Scotland before invading in turn Ireland, Iceland, Norway, Denmark and the French territories of

Normandy and Aquitaine – all in the space of nine years. At the celebrations to mark his return to Britain, Arthur receives a message from the Roman Emperor demanding his submission and the payment of tribute. Incensed by this insult, he sets off for Italy at once to demand his own tribute from Rome, taking the city in the process. While he is away, he is betrayed by his treacherous nephew, Mordred, who seizes both the crown and Arthur's queen, Guinevere. Arthur returns and kills Mordred at the battle of Camlan, in Devon, but is himself wounded – though not killed.

At this point, Geoffrey's *History* becomes strangely cloudy. While he is perfectly content to detail the death of the other ninety-eight kings in his account, when it comes to Arthur himself the ending is left deliberately vague. According to Geoffrey, Arthur is taken to the idyllic Isle of Avalon to have his wounds tended. Then comes the briefest of statements: 'This is all that is said here of Arthur's death', though the year AD 542 is noted – the only date in the entire *History*. After giving over almost a third of the book to every detail of Arthur's life, an ending so abrupt and so inconclusive may come as a surprise. But this kind of ending is nowadays very familiar, especially where there is even the remotest possibility of a sequel. Could it be that Geoffrey of Monmouth found it impossible to kill off his most important creation? Like so much about Arthur, we will never know. In fact, Geoffrey did write another book on his other famous creation, *Vita Merlini – The Life of Merlin* – and in this he does elaborate a little on Arthur's arrival at Avalon accompanied by his entourage:

> After the battle of Camlan we took the wounded Arthur to Avalon. There Morgen [Morgan La Fay] placed the king on a golden bed, and with her own noble hand uncovered the wound and gazed at it long. At last she said that health could return to him if he were to stay with her for a long time and wished to make use of her healing art. Rejoicing, therefore, we committed the king to her, and returning gave our sails to the favouring winds.

As Geoffrey's book became more and more popular, the ambiguity about Arthur's uncertain fate became a problem for the Plantagenet kings who so cleverly used the *History* to link themselves to the ancient line of British kings. What if Arthur were still alive, even after 700 years? And if he were, could he return? Not long after Geoffrey's *History* appeared, King Henry II, in his campaigns to subdue the Welsh, became so concerned that the slightest possibility of Arthur's miraculous reappearance would encourage resistance that he decided to do something about it. It was Henry who arranged for the remains of Arthur and Guinevere to be 'discovered' when Glastonbury Abbey was being rebuilt after a fire. And it was Henry who, in a move to reinforce the genealogical connection to the mythical dynasty which the Plantagenets claimed, had his own grandson christened Arthur in 1187. Not only that, when the boy attained the throne he was to be known not as Arthur I but Arthur II. His uncle, King John, put an end to that when he arranged young Arthur's murder in France when he was sixteen.

A century later, Henry's great-grandson, Edward I,

played the Arthurian connection for all it was worth, letting it be known during his campaigns in Wales that he was personally fulfilling Merlin's prophecy that Arthur would be reincarnated. Annoyingly for Edward, exactly the same claim was being made by his principal adversary in Wales, Llywelyn ap Gruffydd.

The legends of Arthur and Merlin have always been particularly popular in Wales. At the end of the fifteenth century, Henry Tudor, later Henry VII, used the myth very effectively in his campaign for the crown and his defeat of Richard III. To emphasize the connection, he campaigned under the banner of the Red Dragon and christened his eldest son Arthur. But alas, like Henry II's grandson of the same name, this Arthur never made it to the throne either. He died of consumption at the age of fifteen, seven months after marrying Catherine of Aragon, who later became the first of his younger brother Henry VIII's many wives.

Eventually, through repetition and royal patronage, Geoffrey's *History* became the foundation for the myth that sustained and defined racial aspirations and ambitions for half a millennium. Even now, the division between Saxon and Briton (for which also read Welsh or Celt) that is such a feature of the *History* is still not far beneath the surface. The Britons, personified by Arthur, are the truly indigenous people of the whole of Britain and the Saxons are treacherous impostors. The reign of Henry VIII saw this mythology begin to undergo at first a subtle and then a dramatic and sinister transformation.

At first, the legacy of the *History* went from strength to strength, becoming under Henry VIII a vital argument in his struggle with the Pope to divorce his first wife, Catherine of Aragon, in order to marry his second, Anne Boleyn. Henry's ambassador to the papal court, the Duke of Norfolk, used the genealogical claims to the ancient line of kings to assert Henry's supreme jurisdiction in his own realm and to back the claim that he did not need Rome's permission for anything. Norfolk told the bemused court that the *History* recorded how a British king, Brennius, had once conquered Rome, that the Roman Emperor Constantine himself was also on the list of kings, and that Arthur had been Emperor of Britain, Gaul and Germany. These arguments made little impression in Rome, which continued to resist the divorce, but they featured strongly in the laws passed by Henry to enact the break with the Roman Catholic Church and to establish the Church of England with Henry at its head. Sovereigns today still assume that title.

But even at this moment of triumph for the myth, it was being undermined. Henry VII, eager that his new dynasty should appeal to the long-established monarchies of Europe, had commissioned an Italian scholar, Polydore Vergil, to write a new history. Henry VII died before it was finished but Henry VIII allowed work to continue and it was finally completed in 1513. As a Renaissance scholar, Polydore Vergil was trained to do what few historians had done before – look for the evidence. When he came to scrutinize Geoffrey's *History*, it was soon very clear that there was hardly any. His main source, the mysterious book that Geoffrey had been given by Walter, Archdeacon of Oxford, was never found. Even worse, there was no mention of Geoffrey's principal hero, Arthur, in any other histories.

One of these, *The Ruin of Britain*, a sixth-century polemic by the Breton monk Gildas, was always thought to be extremely shaky, but another, Bede's *History of the English Church and People*, published in AD 731, is a far more serious and reliable account – and does not mention Arthur at all. Surely, argued Polydore Vergil, it is inconceivable that a serious history such as Bede's could have failed even to mention a king who had not only regained territory from the Saxons and Picts but had also conquered Ireland, Iceland, Norway, Denmark and much of France only 200 years previously. This was, it had to be admitted, a strong and rational argument. But myth and reason do not necessarily concur. So closely was the court of Henry VIII wedded to, even dependent on, the antiquity of their dynastic claims as 'authenticated' by Geoffrey of Monmouth, that the King refused to allow Vergil's work to be published for a further twenty years. That it was published at all was a sign, not of the triumph of reason, but that the myth itself was beginning to lose its political usefulness to the King. The ancient Britons and their affinity to the Catholic Church were becoming an embarrassment.

But the popularity of Geoffrey's *History* was still sufficient for the publication of Polydore Vergil's alternative *Anglica Historica* to be greeted with outrage and the author condemned as an unscrupulous papist who had set out to undermine the new self-confidence of the English Church. Even during the reign of Henry's daughter, Elizabeth I, the *History* was still a source of inspiration to poets like Edmund

Spenser, whose *Faerie Queene* links Elizabeth and Arthur, and, of course, to Shakespeare, whose *King Lear* draws its characters straight from Geoffrey of Monmouth.

Nevertheless, the currency of the myth among scholars continued to decline, even though it enjoyed a brief revival of royal enthusiasm in 1601 when the Stuart King James VI of Scotland/I of England cast himself as the embodiment of Merlin's prophecy and the restorer of the ancient unity of England, Wales and Scotland first won by Brutus and Locrinus. Eventually, the Stuarts were overthrown and the crown passed to William of Orange. Though he, one would have thought, could not possibly claim a link to the myth, coming as he did from Protestant Holland, this did not stop the poet R. D. Blackmore from portraying William as the Christian Arthur. Even more bizarrely, he managed to twist the myth to the point where William became the champion of the true religion of the ancient Britons (Protestantism!) against the heathen Saxons (Catholic!). That shameful episode was the last bow of the myth on the political stage, though its popularity even today is witness to its continuing fascination.

The real reason for the slow decline of the myth of a united, essentially Celtic Britain with ancient foundations, as elaborated in the *History*, was that, following the Reformation, it no longer suited the English Church. After Henry VIII's acrimonious break with Rome, the newly established Protestant Church of England looked back into history to provide it with the historical legitimacy to set itself apart from Roman Catholicism. To do this, scholars seized on a remark made in the sixth century by Gildas in

The Ruin of Britain that, in what became England, the original Britons had been completely wiped out by the Saxons. The natural conclusion was that the English were the linear descendants of the Saxons, not the Britons at all. This was an undiluted and direct genealogical connection, not with the defeated Britons and the mythical Arthur, but with the victorious Saxons. In this version of events the Saxons were not the malicious and unprincipled opportunists whose foothold in Britain came about only through Vortigern's treachery. Far from it: the Saxons were strong, self-confident and adventurous pioneers who had triumphed against the weak-willed Britons through the intrinsic superiority of their moral character and their love of freedom. The English Church no longer looked west and north to the mountains of Wales and Scotland for its natural affiliations, but across the North Sea to the Teutonic Germans whose stout spirit of Protestant independence had triumphed against the corruption of the Roman Church.

To recreate the myth of an Anglo-Saxon golden age before the Norman Conquest, Protestant historians needed a hero to replace Arthur. They found one in King Alfred, and the PR campaign began: 'the great and singular qualities in this king, worthy of high renown and commendation – godly and excellent virtues, joined with a public and tender care, and a zealous study for the common peace and tranquillity ... his heroical properties jointed together in one piece', wrote John Foxe in 1563. It clearly worked: even today, Alfred is the one Saxon king that most children have heard of – even if all they remember is that he burnt the cakes. Unlike Arthur, there is no doubt that Alfred existed, but how close the glowing tributes to both his military genius and his humble and scholarly character are to reality is still an open question. He reigned from 871 to 899 and was, as we shall see later, instrumental in preventing the Danish Vikings from overrunning the whole country.

At the same time that Alfred was being resurrected in England, Protestant scholars, including Martin Luther in Germany, were creating their own origin myths for the same reason. To reinforce their independence from the Catholic Church, they drew heavily on classical writers for their justification. One of these was the Roman historian Tacitus, who wrote in AD 98, 'For myself I accept the view that the people of Germany have never been tainted by intermarriage with other peoples and stand out as a nation peculiar, pure and unique of its kind.' Luther himself even managed to concoct a genealogy for the Germans right back to Adam, who for Christians like Luther was the father of the human race.

What began as a declaration of religious independence from Rome transformed over the years into a virulent doctrine of Saxon/Teutonic racial superiority over the other inhabitants of the Isles that has had immense and far-reaching political and social consequences. The reinvention of a glorious English past gathered pace. The Magna Carta, in essence an unimportant concordat between King John and his Norman barons, was reborn as a declaration of Saxon independence every bit as important to the English as the US Bill of Rights is to Americans. The Puritans appealed to the myth in their bitter struggle with the

Crown during the English Civil War when John Hare, one of the leaders of the Parliamentarians, wrote about his side in 1640, the first year of the war:

> our progenitors that transplanted themselves from Germany hither did not commixe themselves with the ancient inhabitants of the country of the Britain's, but totally expelling them, they took the sole possession of the land to themselves, thereby preserving their blood, laws and language uncorrupted . . .

Gradually the monarchy changed allegiance to suit the new origin myth. James VI/I even switched sides during the course of his own reign. Having at first asserted his entitlement to rule over both Scotland and England, based on his claim to be Merlin's Arthur reborn, he very soon afterwards basked in the appellation of the 'chiefest Blood-Royal of our ancient English-Saxon kings', according to a dedication in the influential book *Restitution of Decayed Intelligence*, written in 1605 by Richard Verstegen.

In the context of the genetics we will come to later, Verstegen was the first author to point out the potential embarrassment that the purity of the Saxon line must surely have been 'diluted' or 'contaminated' by the later arrival of large numbers of Danes and Normans. He countered this by claiming, first, that their numerical contribution was slight and, second, that both the Danes and the Normans were themselves of Germanic origin anyway, so they could have no effect on the essential racial purity of the Teutonic English.

As the myth gained momentum, the voices raised against it became fewer and further between. The writer Daniel Defoe was one exception, parodying the whole idea of English racial purity and superiority in his poem 'The True-Born Englishman', written in 1701:

> The Romans first with Julius Caesar came
> Including all the Nations of that Name
> Gauls, Greeks and Lombards; and by Computation
> Auxiliaries or slaves of ev'ry Nation
> With Hengist, Saxons; Danes with Sueno came
> In search of Plunder, not in search of Fame
> Scots, Picts and Irish from the Hibernian shore:
> And Conquering William brought the Normans O're.
> All these their Barb'rous offspring left behind
> the dregs of Armies, they of all Mankind;
> Blended with Britons, who before were here,
> of whom the Welch ha'blest the Character.
> From the amphibious Ill-born Mob began
> That vain ill-natured thing, an Englishman.

But dissenting voices were definitely in the minority, and the myth grew and grew, finding a new outlet in the development of the African slave trade. Though European attitudes to black people and a readiness to exploit them for personal gain were nothing new, the resurgent racial pride which accompanied the growth of the Teutonic myth encouraged further victimization. While there may have been some uncertainty about the purity of the Saxon pedigree within England, there could be no cause for doubt that black

Africans had no claims whatsoever to the Teutonic bloodline with its attendant virtues of enterprise, independence and high moral character.

During the eighteenth century, the myth had grown to such prominence that it was scarcely, if ever, questioned. It attained an invincibility equal to that of the Arthurian legends of Geoffrey's *History* 500 years earlier. But now its effects were felt not just in Britain, but throughout the world. The influential French political philosopher Baron de Montesquieu wrote in 1734 that the English political system came straight from the forests of Germany, imported and elaborated by their Saxon descendants. Even the great Scottish philosopher David Hume, who constantly required evidence as the foundation for any belief, accepted without question the purity of the German race first expressed so long ago by Tacitus. Thomas Jefferson, one of the draftsmen of the Declaration of Independence, who became the third President of the United States, wrote in 1774 that it was the Saxon ancestry of the American colonists that gave them a natural right to build for themselves a free and independent state, liberated from British colonial rule.

The triumph of the Teutonic myth was almost complete as its popularity reached its peak during the nineteenth century. Indeed the superiority and self-belief with which its adherents cloaked themselves was central to the construction and administration of the British Empire. The myth gave to the Englishmen abroad the absolute conviction that their ancient Saxon pedigree imbued them with inherited qualities of honour and leadership, and the political institutions to go with it, that were far superior to any in the world. Bolstered with that ingrained sense of destiny the English did, indeed, rule the world – for a while.

But the triumph of the myth came at a price. The growing sense of racial superiority among the English set them increasingly at odds with the other inhabitants of the Isles, the Welsh and the Scots on the British mainland, and with the Irish. The simple racism of the myth collapsed all three into the same denomination, 'the Celts', and poured scorn on them.

By now, science had been harnessed to the myth in an enthusiastic attempt to build a solid frame to underpin its more extravagant assumptions. And when science and racism are mixed, the cocktail becomes increasingly volatile. At the end of his rambling book *The Races of Men*, published in 1850, Robert Knox MD, surgeon and enthusiast for the new science of comparative anatomy, concludes after 350 pages of Saxon worship and Celtic insult that, 'The Celtic Race must be forced from this soil. England's safety requires it.' This outrageous suggestion, as it appears to us now, was completely in tune with the prevailing view, if not of an actual genocide, then certainly of cultural and spiritual suppression. In a superbly argued defence of the value of Celtic literature, published in 1867, the literary critic Matthew Arnold quotes a leader from *The Times* on the subject of the Welsh language:

> The Welsh language is the curse of Wales. Its prevalence, and the ignorance of English have excluded, and even now exclude, the Welsh people from the civilisation of their

> English neighbours. An Eisteddfod [the annual Welsh literary and musical festival] is one of the most mischievous and selfish pieces of sentimentalism which could possibly be perpetrated. It is simply a foolish interference with the natural progress of civilisation and prosperity. If it is desirable that the Welsh should talk English, it is monstrous folly to encourage them in a loving fondness for their old language. Not only the energy and power, but the intelligence and music of Europe have come mainly from Teutonic sources, and this glorification of everything Celtic, if it were not pedantry would be sheer ignorance. The sooner all Welsh specialists disappear from the face of the earth, the better.

Even taking into account the often strident and provocative language of a *Times* leader, it is a chilling piece.

The decline of the myth's supremacy came as the nineteenth century drew to a close. In a parallel with the undermining of the factual basis of Arthurian legend and the ancient succession of British kings recounted in Geoffrey's *History*, the absolute belief in the Teutonic myth suffered a similar fate. There was no single scholar assassin like Polydore Vergil, but rather a series of snipers. One of these, the literary critic J. M. Robertson, concluded that, far from being the heralds of a superior race honed to perfection in the forests of Germany, the first Saxons were 'pagan, non-literate and barbaric, heroes of a northern society so disorganized that they had little concept of national, racial or political loyalties'.

But it was political developments in Germany, rather

than Britain, that finally sealed the fate of the Teutonic myth. Not surprisingly, Germans also favoured the good light the myth cast on their own racial purity and superiority with the almost genetically linked qualities of freedom and independence. Also keen to distance themselves from Rome, German scholars had worked in a parallel effort to reinforce their independence with a racially based justification. It was in the late nineteenth century that the German origin myth first became firmly attached to the concept of the Aryan.

The creator of the Aryan myth was a German linguist, Max Müller, working in Oxford as a Professor of Modern Languages. Müller did more than anyone to create this myth by falling into the trap of unquestioningly conflating language with race – a temptation which even contemporary scholars often seem quite unable to resist. As a linguist, Müller was very well aware of the similarities of the major European languages to Sanskrit and Persian. This similarity hinted at a common origin and led directly to the concept, widely accepted today, of an 'Indo-European' language family. The language family was originally known as 'Aryan', from the Sanskrit word meaning 'noble'. Müller took the natural but unjustified step of mutating this theory of language to a theory of race. He concluded that there must have been, as well as an original Aryan language, an original Aryan people. That most promiscuous and malignant of racial myths was born. As his career progressed, Müller came to doubt his invention and by 1888, to his credit, he positively rejected it. But it was too late. The genie was out of the bottle.

As we have seen throughout this chapter, the career of a myth depends far less on its factual accuracy than on its congruence with contemporary political ambition, and the fervour with which people believe it. Towards the end of the nineteenth century, Germany, through its Chancellor Bismarck and later under Kaiser Wilhelm, recruited the Aryan myth, with its closely linked connotations of German racial superiority, to justify its own campaign of imperial expansion. These ambitions soon became a direct threat to the British Empire, also fuelled by the same myth. Enthusiasm among the British for the close affiliation with Germany that was so much part of the Teutonic myth rapidly dwindled as the two countries became enemies. Not surprisingly, after the First World War it vanished completely.

The growing distaste of the British did nothing to halt the rise and rise of the Aryan myth in Germany itself. The Nazis, now seeing themselves the sole inheritors of Aryan racial superiority, exploited it ruthlessly against their 'enemies' both within and without. Nothing underlines the dreadful power and the dreadful danger of racial myth more than the smoke rising from the chimneys of Belsen and Dachau, Treblinka and Auschwitz.

3

THE RESURGENT CELTS

As I write, the 2006 World Cup Finals draw closer and one of the few remaining expressions of English patriotic nationalism is beginning to show itself. The red cross of St George on the white background of the English flag is seen hanging from first-floor windows and fluttering from the rear windows of speeding cars. Supermarkets have 'Come on England' signs hanging above the aisles. If the 2004 European Cup Finals are anything to go by, the flags will be hastily taken down as soon as England are knocked out of the competition. Even the appointment of a foreign manager to the English football team is received with only mild remonstrations. That, and the enthusiasm surrounding the victory over Australia in the Ashes test series in the 2005 cricket season, is about all you are likely to see these days. The English national day, St George's Day – 23 April – is barely celebrated. The new ethnic myth is not to be found on the Saxon streets of London, but in the Celtic west. On St Patrick's Day – 17 March – the streets of

Dublin and of New York are packed with parades and partygoers. While the Teutonic myth has submerged beneath the surface, if only for the time being, the Celtic myth grows stronger as each year passes.

Visit any of the multitude of tourist gift shops in Ireland or the west of Scotland and you are immediately confronted by what is best described as the Celtic brand. Silver brooches with naturalistic intertwining tendrils; amethysts set in the centre of 'Celtic' crosses, the arms embossed with intricate 'Celtic' knotwork; reproductions of fabulously illustrated early Christian illuminated manuscripts. Though they are often imported from China, these are a tangible part of the material expression of the Celt, one that is recruited to market this part of the Isles throughout the world. It is also a brand that is understood by local people and expressed particularly strongly in music and, in a different way, in sport. One of the largest music festivals in Scotland is called 'Celtic Connections'. Home-grown bands subscribe in many ways, even in their names. Runrig, a very successful band from Skye off the north-west coast of Scotland, is named after an old land-usage system and recalls the frugal life of peasant farmers. In sport, football teams declare their links to the myth and none more so than the world-famous Glasgow side Celtic, locked in perpetual and often bitter rivalry with Glasgow Rangers. In rugby there is a vigorous Celtic League comprising teams from Scotland, Wales and Ireland.

The brand is supported by the cultural glue of the Gaelic language, which binds the west of Scotland with Ireland and, in a slightly different form, with Wales, Cornwall and

Brittany. But perhaps the dominant feature of the Celtic brand is that it joins the west together and deliberately separates it from the rest of the Isles and the perceived domination of the English. It is important for the modern Celt to be *different*.

Even though Celtishness is today mainly expressed in language, music, sport and other cultural pursuits, there lurks beneath it an unspoken belief in some form of ancient Celtic race whose descendants live on today. Could genetics test this assumption? Is there a genetic basis for this underlying belief in a race, or races, of ancient Celts and can we show it by sifting through the genes of today's 'Celts'? Or is Celtishness a purely cultural phenomenon, at once sincerely felt and eagerly exploited but with no underlying biological framework?

If behind the paraphernalia of the Celtic brand there really does lie some grain of substance in the notion of a Celtic people, this immediately begs the question of when they arrived in the Isles and where they came from. Indeed, where does the notion that the Celts ever existed as a separate people, capable of acting together, moving together and arriving somewhere, actually stem from? The notion, oddly enough, is a surprisingly recent one. It began to take shape in the years around 1700 when Edward Lhuyd, from Oswestry on the Welsh border, became the director of the Ashmolean Museum in Oxford. Lhuyd travelled widely in Ireland, Wales and the Scottish Highlands, collecting antiquities and manuscripts for the museum and recording the folklore of the lands he visited. On his travels he noticed the similarities between Welsh,

Cornish, Breton, Irish and Scots Gaelic and the ancient languages of Gaul. In his book *Archaeologia Britannica*, published in 1707, he was the first to group these languages together and embrace them under the generic term of Celtic. He was also the first to point out that the languages belonged to two distinct sets, distinguished from each other by their pronunciation. The harsher consonants of Breton, Cornish and Welsh (as in *ap*, meaning 'son of') led Lhuyd to call these the P-Celtic languages, while the softer sounds of Irish and Scots Gaelic (as in *mac* with the same meaning) were referred to by Lhuyd as Q-Celtic. Having found a language family, it was all too easy to invent a people and Lhuyd very soon constructed a historical explanation of how this linguistic continuity may have come about. He suggested that, first of all, Irish Britons moved to the Isles, but were pushed into Scotland and northern Britain by a second wave of Gauls from France, who then occupied Wales and the south and west of England.

Implicit in all of this is the concept that there existed one or more groups of Celts who moved around from one place to another, taking their language with them as they went. This is an idea in the grand tradition of migration as the sole explanation for cultural change – a tradition which until recently dominated not only linguistics but archaeology as well. A type of pottery or a particular burial ritual found in two different places was taken as proof that people from one moved to occupy the second. This type of reasoning drove archaeology for most of the twentieth century and became the standard dogma for the spread of any cultural change, be it language, weapon design, stone tools or even agriculture. In the last twenty years or so the pendulum of academic fashion has begun to swing to the other extreme, where nobody actually moves anywhere except to pass on their ideas and scurry back home.

But back to the Celts. Edward Lhuyd, though he helped create the concept of the Celtic people, did not invent the word. It makes its first appearance as *Keltoi* in ancient Greek, where it is used as a derogatory catch-all name for strangers and foreigners, people from another place. Uncivilized, rough, uncouth, not 'one of us'. By the time Julius Caesar wrote his *Gallic Wars*, around 60 BC, the people of Gaul, according to Caesar, called themselves Celts. So while the Greeks used *Keltoi* to refer to outsiders, coming from beyond the limits of the civilized Mediterranean world, the name itself might originally have come from one or more of the tribes themselves. For the Romans, the terms Celt and Gaul were pretty much interchangeable, used to describe the inhabitants of their territories in France and northern Italy and to tell them apart from the real enemy – the Germans.

However, when we come to the people of Britain and Ireland during the Roman period, nobody called them Celts. They called them a lot of things, but not Celts. Neither is there any record of anyone from the Isles using the word Celt to describe themselves until the eighteenth century, after Edward Lhuyd had reinvented the term for his language family and then for the people who spoke it. If a Celt is someone who speaks one of the Celtic languages as defined by Lhuyd, then everyone in Britain and Ireland would have been a Celt when the Romans invaded. If a

Celt is someone whose ancestors lived in the parts of the Isles where these languages are still spoken today, then the definition becomes much narrower and more akin to what the Celtic brand now represents. So, just as to the Greeks, there is no precise definition of Celt. It is amorphous, fluid, capable of many simultaneous meanings. To some, like the archaeologist Simon James, it is a shameless invention. In his angry polemic *The Atlantic Celts: Ancient People or Modern Invention?*, James concludes that 'The ancient Celts are an essentially bogus and recent invention', an invention used most recently for political purposes in the lead-up to Scottish and Welsh devolution. C. S. Lewis expressed the ambiguity and uncertainty in softer tones when he wrote, 'anything is possible in the fabulous Celtic twilight, which is not so much a twilight of the Gods but of reason.'

When it comes to getting hold of a definition of the Celt, or Celtic, a definition to be tested by genetics, I found myself struggling, enveloped in a mist of uncertainty and enigma. For sure there was the marketable expression of Celticity, the silver brooches, the tartan ties, the kilts. But these are caricatures of something much deeper. What it means to be Celtic, to feel Celtic, is very different. As is to be expected of him, Sir Walter Scott's description of the Celtic Muse is highly sentimental. He writes in his novel *Waverley*:

> To speak in the poetical language of my country, the seat of the Celtic muse is in the mist of the secret and solitary hill,

> and her voice is the murmur of the mountain stream. He who wooes her must love the barren rock more than the fertile valley and the solitude of the desert better than the festivity of the hall.

And yet there is something in what Scott says. The emotional, almost the physical, attachment to the land is central to the poetry of the Celt. Out of term time, when I am not required to be in Oxford, I live on the Isle of Skye. My house once belonged to Sorley Maclean, widely acclaimed as the greatest Gaelic poet of the twentieth century. In fact, that is where I am writing this chapter and it is in his old filing cabinet that the manuscript will remain until I send it off to be typed. Sorley's poetry is rich in reference to the woods, the sea and the hills. In 'The Cuillin' he writes:

> Loch of loches in Coire Lagain
> Were it not for the springs of Coire Mhadaidh
> The spring above all other springs
> In the green and white Fair Corrie.

Coire Lagain is a high place in the Cuillin Hills of Skye, hemmed in by hundreds of feet of the steep rock ramparts that protect the high ridge. But this is not at all a romanticized description of the land, for the poem goes on to another familiar theme which permeates the culture of the Highlands – that of loss and unquestionable sadness.

> Multitude of springs and fewness of young men
> today, yesterday and last night keeping me awake:
> the miserable loss of our country's people
> clearing of tenants, exile, exploitation
> and the great island is seen with its winding shores
> a hoodie-crow squatting on each dun
> black soft squinting hoodie-crows
> who think themselves all eagles.

The loss which Sorley mourns in this and other poems is at once the people forced to leave their homes during the notorious Highland Clearances in the late eighteenth and early nineteenth centuries and also the language, Gaelic, which was the language of his poems. At first he wrote in Gaelic and English but in 1933, when he was twenty-two, he decided to write only in Gaelic and he destroyed those of his English works that he could lay his hands on.

Gaelic and her cousin tongues are a strong unifying force of the Celtic lands. Their fortunes, in Scotland, in Ireland, in Wales and also in Brittany, are a barometer of the self-confidence of the people who call themselves Celts. Since Celtic was a linguistic definition in the first place, this seems only appropriate.

In Skye, as in many parts of the Highlands, there is a palpable sense of a Gaelic revival, a renaissance in poetry and music and above all in the language. The steady decline in Gaelic speakers – it is spoken as a first tongue by only a few thousand people in the Hebrides, most of them in middle age or beyond – has been halted by the welcome introduction in 1986, after decades of lobbying, of

Gaelic-medium education in primary schools, where all lessons are given in that language. Most children whose parents have the choice opt for lessons in the Gaelic stream rather than the English alternative. Now Skye children can go right the way through school being taught in Gaelic and, in recent years, go on to tertiary education in Gaelic at the world's first Gaelic College at Sabhal Mor Ostaig in Sleat on the southernmost of Skye's many peninsulas. Whether this very hard-fought initiative will reverse the decline in the language in the long term remains to be seen, but I have never visited a higher education institute anywhere in the world that is so brimming with confidence and enthusiasm for its mission in life.

Sabhal Mor kindly allowed me to use their library for my research – a library with what must be the best view in the world. Sabhal Mor (pronounced Sall More and meaning simply 'Big Barn' in Gaelic) is perched on a promontory overlooking the Sound of Sleat; the view takes in the distant outline of Ardnamurchan and the sands of Morar to the south and up to the hills above Glenelg and Kyle of Lochalsh to the north. But straight ahead, across 3 miles of blue and wind-blown sea, are the mountains of Knoydart, yellow and brown in the autumn setting sun. Knoydart, between the secret lochs of Nevis and Hiourn, was once a prosperous community of twenty-seven crofting townships and 3,500 people. Now it is empty, save for a cluster of white houses I can see on the shore at Airor. The Knoydart estate was cleared of people in the 1840s by the landlord, Sir Ranald McDonnell of Glengarry, to make way for the more profitable sheep. This is an all too familiar story in the Highlands, though nowhere was as thoroughly cleansed as Knoydart, and it has been vividly recounted many times. Here is one from Neil Gunn, a Scottish novelist of the early twentieth century:

> As always the recollection is dominated by dramatic images – the ragged remnants of a once proud peasantry hounded from the hills by the factors and police were driven aboard disease-ridden ships bound for outlandish colonies, their families broken, their ministers compliant and the collective agony sounded by the pibroch and the wailing of pathetic humanity.

By and large, the English were blamed for this human translocation and spiritual genocide, not that the landlords were themselves English but came from a heavily anglicized Scottish aristocracy who spent most of their time in London. Still the Celtic identity, in Ireland, Wales and Scotland, and the language, defines itself in part at least as being 'not English'. That is not to say it is an aggressive demarcation, and as an Englishman with very little Gaelic living on Skye I have never been made to feel less than welcome.

Of course, the main emigration of the late eighteenth and early nineteenth centuries, whether by the forced hand of the landlord or for the opportunities for a better life on offer in Glasgow and the other industrial towns of the Central Belt or the colonies, meant that as people left Scotland, and Ireland too, they arrived somewhere else. Estimates vary, but one set of figures has it that there are

28 million people of Scottish and 16 million of Irish descent spread throughout the world. Even if these figures are way off the mark, and they are conservative estimates, there are now far more Celts living overseas than in the Isles. Most made their homes in the New World, mainly the USA and Canada, but emigration to Australia, New Zealand and to a lesser extent South Africa adds millions to this list. In some places, like the southern part of South Island, New Zealand, the Scots practically took over the whole country and, tellingly, the principal town Dunedin has the Gaelic name for Edinburgh.

Many emigrating Celts and their descendants did extremely well, of course, but ironically, given the circumstances of their leaving, they were also sometimes guilty of dispossessing the indigenous people of their tribal lands. As Paul Besu, a social anthropologist from University College London, writes:

> Scots pioneers in Victoria (Australia) were often land-grabbers and squatters who were notorious for their ruthlessness and the Scots, like the English, Welsh and Irish, played a full part in the harsh treatment of Aboriginal peoples. It was ironic that some of the most notoriously involved were Highlanders who themselves had suffered clearance and privation in the old country.

Paul Besu was researching what it was that drew the descendants of these emigrants to search out their roots in Scotland and he interviewed people about their reasons for making these journeys from the other side of the world.

Tens of thousands of Americans, Canadians, Australians and New Zealanders come to Scotland and Ireland every year to seek out and placate their innermost desires to see and feel the homelands of their ancestors. Of course there are comparable numbers of visitors on similar missions to England too, to reconnect, but theirs is a slightly different mission, perhaps less romantic and more matter of fact. The general causes of their emigration do not usually include being driven from the land.

I have experienced the thirst for roots first hand through the company I set up to help people trace their origins using DNA. We have thousands of customers, many from precisely those locations that once received Scots and Irish emigrants. Often a DNA test will accompany a journey to the homeland and even when it does not, a DNA test which roots a person to Scotland or Ireland makes a living link between descendant and ancestor. It is all the more powerful as this talisman is carried across the generations in every cell of the body, as it was in the bodies of ancestors, including the ones who made the journeys 'aboard disease-ridden ships bound for outlandish colonies'. It was there.

There have been, as you may have suspected, plenty of theories about what draws people to search out their roots. Behind the sociology-speak, such as

> the contemporary quest for roots is a response to the trauma of displacement associated with migration which has become a global commonplace and individuals are able to conduct meaningful, morally defensible and authentic self-narratives from the ambiguities and discontinuities of their migrant

> histories, thus recovering a sense of being 'at home' in the 'maelstrom' of modernity . . .

are much pithier and more articulate reasons, as revealed in Paul Besu's survey. An anonymous Australian from New South Wales simply said, 'I want to be able to tell my children where their ancestors came from. It gives them a sense of belonging in a world that sometimes moves too fast.'

Another Australian, improbably called Anne Roots, told Besu:

> I am a fourth-generation Australian but I know that the thread reaching back to the obscure past has never been broken. The process of evolution has failed to break the translucent thread that is mysteriously joined to the Isle of Skye. I cannot explain some of my experiences, or why I wanted to go to the Hebrides before I knew some of my forebears came from there. My only explanation is that the spirit of my ancestors kept calling me back.

Janet, from Geelong, south of Melbourne, made the fascinating comparison when she visited her ancestral home of Paabay, an island in the Sound of Harris, that 'to my mind the Celt, in a British context, is to the Anglo-Saxon what the Aboriginal, in an Australian context, is to the settler.'

The intense spirituality of the Australian Aborigine, the connection to ancestors and the homeland, is in a muted form reflected in the search for Celtic roots. Displaced by the invader and forced to the margins before being forced into exile overseas, the Celt is perceived to be the British – or even the European – aboriginal. She continues, 'to have Celtic roots is to demonstrate that one also has a rich, tribal heritage rooted deeply within a landscape that is both mystical and mythical.'

And it is the case that in 'New Age' bookshops around the world, titles on Celtic spirituality are found on the same shelves as Aboriginal and Native American material in the same genre. However, be warned that I heard the distinguished American sociologist Michael Waltzer in a recent lecture dismiss excess spirituality as 'the solace of a conquered people'.

Before we move on to more solid ground, let me just mention Frank from Boulder, Colorado. After spending twelve years with Native American teachers, Frank took part in the Sun Dance ceremony of the Lakota people, an experience which set him on the path to discovering his Celtic heritage. He now describes himself as 'a poet, ecopsychologist and visionary teacher in the Celtic spiritual tradition'. Frank leads pilgrimages to the Scottish Highlands to promote what he calls 'Highland cultural soul retrieval'.

The range of emotion covered by the Celtic umbrella is vast, from a feeling of displacement and affinity with aboriginal groups, to a successful marketing tool, to a political rallying call, to the focus for sporting identity, even fanaticism. Can genetics lift the veil and see what lies beneath? Faced with this multiplicity of meaning for Celt and Celtic, what range of possibilities should we expect genetics to reveal? Might we be able to detect the waves of a large-scale migration envisaged by Edward Lhuyd? Or might we find evidence that what we now call Celts have been here all along? Will we find any genetic similarity between the present-day Celts and the people of the rest of Britain, or will there be a sharp divide? And where should we look for origins? Though not absolutely essential for success in historical genetics, it is always best to formulate some scenarios that can be tested.

One of the most striking emblems of the Celtic brand, the intricate naturalistic knotwork that inspires the modern Celtic jeweller, had its origin not in the Atlantic communities linked by a common language, but in central Europe. The evolution of this highly distinctive art form coincided with the rise of rich settlements north of the Alps, centres which controlled the trade of goods like amber and tin, flowing south to the Mediterranean world and their exchange for luxuries, such as wine and jewellery. In all likelihood, these luxury imports were used by local chieftains as a badge of status and also distributed among their subordinates in exchange for favours and services.

The trading settlements spanned the heartland of Europe where its great navigable rivers converge in a relatively small area in eastern France and Switzerland. The Loire going westward to the Atlantic, the Rhône south to the Mediterranean, the Rhine north to the North Sea and the Danube east to the Black Sea. These were the arteries of prehistoric Europe along which flowed the life-blood of trade. Whoever controlled the heads of the rivers and the land between them controlled the trade – and grew very rich on it. At the peak, around 600 BC, there was enough wealth to stimulate and support the production of a local style of craftwork, and this is where we see the first appearance, principally in the delicate metalwork, of what we now call Celtic Art. The La Tène style, which we now most strongly associate with the Celtic brand, began not on the ocean coasts of the Atlantic, but within sight of the Alps.

But was it just the goods and the ideas that moved, or was it the people migrating *en masse* from central Europe to the far west? Although there is very good archaeological and historical evidence that people from this region did indeed move in numbers east and south to Greece, where they attacked the temple at Delphi in 273 BC, before finally settling in central Turkey, there is no evidence at all that the ancestors of today's Celts of the Isles took the opposite track and ended up in Britain. Yet, although support for the popular notion that the Celtic people of the Isles travelled across land from central Europe may be entirely lacking, we may still find the evidence for it in the genetics.

However, the most obvious of routes linking today's Celts of the Isles is not the land at all but the sea. Motorways and fast roads have inverted in our minds the comparative difficulty of moving across land and water. In ancient times, and indeed until the last two centuries, getting around by boat was a lot easier than travelling over the land. Until the rise of, first, the railway and then the car and the lorry, water was the way to travel. Was a sea route to the Isles the more likely?

At school we are taught that 'civilization' arose around the Mediterranean, in the ancient cities of Egypt, and that we trace the origins of our culture and our political processes to the countries bordering that almost landlocked sea. Our taught impression of life beyond the Strait of Gibraltar is one of barbarism and savagery, rather like the Greeks' view of the *Keltoi*. We are taught nothing of the vigorous culture and the technological achievements of the Atlantic seaboard, the coastline stretching from North Africa in the south 2,000 miles to Shetland off the north coast of Scotland and beyond to Scandinavia. But this Atlantic zone has a prehistory as ancient and as colourful as any in the Mediterranean. There were people living along this coastline 8,000 years ago and they were using boats not just for cruising close to the shore but for venturing out into deep water, judging by the types of fish whose remains litter their encampments. None of these sea-going vessels survives, which is no surprise since they would have been made of perishable wood and animal skins. By 6,000 years ago, agriculture had seeped into the region via the Mediterranean coastline, evidence once again of the maritime traffic. The first, literally, hard evidence of widespread exchanges along the coast came in the form of distinctive polished stone axes, manufactured in Brittany, which found their way all along the coast of France and Spain to the south, and north across the sea to Cornwall. But the most dramatic examples of continuity along the Atlantic zone are the great stone monuments, the megaliths, which rise from the ground from Orkney and Lewis in the north to Spain and Portugal in the south. These are a purely Atlantic phenomenon, owing nothing at all to the Mediterranean world. Could it be that it was by this route that the Celts of the Isles first arrived?

4
THE SKULL SNATCHERS

The first forays of science into the highly charged arguments about British origins came at the height of the Victorian enthusiasm for Saxon superiority. It is hard to imagine how ingrained was the sense that the people of Britain were split into two entirely different 'races' and how superior the Saxons felt about themselves. Just to remind us, I quote again from the extremely popular if eccentric author, the surgeon Robert Knox. He wrote that 'Race is everything, literature, science, art – in a word, civilisation depends on it.' And Knox left his readers in no doubt where his sympathies lay in the debate on the racial character of Celt and Saxon. The Saxon, he claims, 'cannot sit still an instant, so powerful is the desire for work, labour, excitement, muscular exertion'. The Celts, on the other hand – judging by such woodcut illustrations as 'A Celtic groupe, such as may be seen at any time in Marylebone, London', in which a group of deformed and decidedly dodgy characters glowers from the page

– are the complete opposite: irredeemable malingerers. The text is no more flattering. On the notorious Highland Clearances, he writes: 'the dreamy Celt exclaims at the parting moment from the horrid land of his birth "we'll maybe return to Lochaber no more." And why should you return, miserable and wretched man, to the dark and filthy hovel you never sought to purify?'

Knox pulls out all the stops when it comes to the Celts of Ireland: 'the source of all evil lies in the race, the Celtic race of Ireland. The race must be forced from the soil, by fair means if possible, still they must leave.' A few sentences later is an entreaty to genocide no less chilling in intent than in Bosnia or Rwanda:

> The Orange Club of Ireland [an extreme protestant group] is a Saxon confederation for the clearing of the land of all papists and jacobites; this means Celts. If left to themselves they would clear them out, as Cromwell proposed, by the sword; it would not require six weeks to accomplish this work.

By the time Knox was penning his poisonous invective, in the mid-nineteenth century, science was making itself felt in all walks of life. The appeal to rational arbitration of such issues as the racial purity, or otherwise, of Celt and Saxon had obvious attractions to those with a more liberal outlook than the likes of Robert Knox. The most articulate of these, Matthew Arnold, literary critic and a prominent champion of Celtic literature, despaired of the wedge being driven between Celt and Saxon, not just by fanatics like

Knox, but by powerful and influential members of the British Establishment. Men like Lord Lyndhurst, whose description of the Irish as 'Aliens in speech, in religion, in blood, makes the estrangement [of Celtic and Saxon] immense, incurable, fatal.' Feeling forced to react, Matthew Arnold makes an optimistic appeal: 'Fanciful as this notion may seem, I am inclined to think that the march of science will insist that there is no such original chasm between the Celt and the Saxon as we once popularly imagined.'

But what was the basis for Matthew Arnold's optimism? It was this. That even if many thousands or hundreds of thousands of Saxons arrived in the centuries following Hengist, they would, within a few generations, intermarry and blend with the Britons already here. This was anathema to racial purists – it just could not happen. Races were pure and indivisible. But how could this theory of racial purity overcome the all too apparent empirical fact – especially obvious as white imperial boundaries expanded into Africa, India and America – that there were no barriers to mating between 'races'? The answer came that the offspring of such matings were weakened hybrids, incapable of sustaining themselves over more than a few generations. How this worked in practice was explained using the Spanish 'conquest' of South America and the interbreeding which followed. According to Knox:

> When the best blood in Spain migrated to America, they killed as many of the natives as they could. But this could not go on, labourers to till the soil being required. Then

> came the admixture with the Indian blood and the Iberian blood, the produce being the mulatto.

Even the name, Spanish for 'little mule', recalls the sterile hybrid of horse and donkey. Knox continues:

> as a hybrid he [the mulatto] becomes non-productive after a time, if he intermarries only with the mulatto. Thus, year by year, the Spanish blood disappears, and with it the mulatto, and the population, retrograding towards the indigenous inhabitants, returns to that Indian population, the hereditary descendants of those whom Cortes found there.

Races, in this exposition, do not hybridize and any unnatural mixing produces only enfeebled offspring whose progeny are doomed to extinction. Though the nineteenth century was dominated by the extreme views of people like Robert Knox, who believed in the sanctity and purity of racial groups – with Saxons at the top of the rankings, of course – there were a few lone voices raised against the predominant dogma. One of these was Luke Owen Pike, a Lincoln's Inn barrister. His well-argued, and witty, riposte to the Teutomaniacs like Knox was to point out that it was extremely unlikely, even if the entire population of Jutes, Angles and Saxons arrived in Britain, that they could have exterminated *all* the Britons, with their centuries of experience of Roman military tactics. Even if they had managed to kill all the men, they would not have killed all the women.

> The women and the children, at least, are doomed to a different, if not a happier fate. And for this reason it must almost always happen that, after the conquest of any country, the blood of the original inhabitants will still preponderate. There is no reason to suppose that the result was different in the case of the Saxon conquest.

Pike not only rejected the concept of the immiscibility of races, he argued for the creation of a hybrid racial mixture in which the indigenous component would usually predominate.

Although the ranting racist diatribes of Robert Knox, the moderation of Luke Owen Pike, even the commentaries of Matthew Arnold, were the expression of strongly held opinions, none of them had a solid basis of factual evidence. While the fierce argument was raging about whether races were fixed and immiscible or could happily and successfully interbreed and blend, a few people did begin to gather systematic scientific observations to inform the debate.

The first to do so on a significant scale was John Beddoe, a doctor who spent the best part of his life travelling to every part of Britain recording the physical appearance of the natives, both alive and dead. He was a classic case of the Victorian amateur scholar, amassing a huge amount of data which, in sheer bulk alone, has never been surpassed. John Beddoe was born in 1826 in rural Worcestershire, the second of eight children. Though his family was comfortably well off, John was a sickly child and missed most of his formal education. Nevertheless he managed, through family connections, to get a place at University College London to study medicine. He eventually graduated, not in London but in Edinburgh, and after a spell in the Crimea set himself up in Bristol. Building up his medical practice in the fashionable quarter of Clifton was difficult, especially as he had to compete for patients with a resident pool of extremely competent and well-established doctors. With time on his hands, he began to indulge his passion for observing and recording people's appearance.

First, he had to devise a reliable classification for the features he decided to concentrate on – the colour of the hair and the colour of the eyes – exactly those features we use ourselves in the first description of a stranger. He also wanted to be quite sure that he was looking at permanent features, not something that would change from year to year. For this reason he rejected skin colour, perhaps an obvious one to include, because he was worried that it might be influenced by exposure to sunlight, which of course it is. He also decided against recording skin colour because there was a theory doing the rounds that daily exposure to smoke and grime made city-dwellers darker and darker as they got older, while their rural contemporaries remained fresh-faced and pale in comparison.

John Beddoe was determined to break free from the generalizations that were so commonplace, and still are, about regional differences in appearance. He disregarded the clichés of short, dark Welshmen or muscular, red-headed Highlanders and set out to replace these prejudiced impressions with real observations. He frequently discovered that what had been written about a place and its people was completely at odds with reality, even when the source of the misleading reports would normally have given no cause for doubt. For example, the Church of Scotland minister in Wick, a town at the north-east tip of Scotland not far from John O'Groats, was obliged to compile a statistical account of his parishioners, including their overall appearance. The minister described his flock as 'having for the most part dark brown or black hair, and dark complexions, remarkably few having red or yellow hair'. But when Beddoe arrived, he found the complete opposite. Among more than 300 individuals whose appearance he recorded, blonds and redheads were in the majority.

How did Beddoe make his observations? You can imagine how this might get very complicated – are those eyes green or hazel? Is that hair light brunette or dark blond? But Beddoe needed something much simpler, and easy to record – we will see why in a moment – and he spent several months refining his system. He decided to create just three categories of eye colour and five for hair. For eyes they were Class 1 light, Class 2 intermediate or neutral and Class 3 dark. In the light category, Class 1, were included all the blue eyes plus bluish grey, light grey and very light green. In Class 3 he put black and deep brown eyes. Class 2 included most shades of green and hazel, very light brown and very dark grey. It is not a particularly refined system, but it succeeds in its simplicity. I've tried it and I can almost always put someone's eye colour into one of the three categories at a glance without any difficulty.

When it comes to hair, though, it is harder. Most of my women friends over the age of forty probably colour their hair. Actually several have forgotten what their original hair colour was, even growing their hair out for a few weeks to be reminded, before going straight back to the hairdresser when they find out. This is nothing new and Beddoe was well aware of artificial hair colouring and its changing fashion, even in the nineteenth century. 'When I began work in England,' he wrote, 'dark hair was in fashion among the women, and light and reddish lines were dulled by greasy unguents. In later years, fair hair has been more in fashion, and golden shades, sometimes unknown to nature, are produced by art.'

In Beddoe's time, these artificial hair colours were far more confined to the wealthy than they are now. Beddoe was much more interested in the 'ordinary folk' than the 'upper classes', as he called them, as they were, in his opinion, 'more migratory and more often mixed in blood'. He eventually settled on five classes of hair colour: R for red and shades of auburn which were nearer red than brown; F for fair, including blond and very light brown hair, along with pale auburn; B included all the other shades of mid-brown; D was reserved for very dark brown; and N for the few cases of jet-black hair which he encountered.

Beddoe developed a routine. He arrived at a location and walked casually around looking at everyone who passed within 3 yards. In the palm of his left hand he held a small card divided by lines into columns and rows. In his right hand he concealed a pencil and, as people passed by, he put a tick in the appropriate square on the card. As one card filled up he replaced it, then at the end of each day worked out a simple numerical score for that locality. He called this score the 'Index of Nigrescence', which he calculated by adding the number of dark-brown (class D) scores to twice the number of jet-black (N) then subtracting the fair (F) and red (R). The ubiquitous mid-browns (B) were omitted from the calculation. He explains why he doubled the influence of the jet-blacks in the formula. It was to 'give the proper value to the greater tendency to melanosity shown thereby'. That sounds rather arbitrary to me, but the jet-blacks were so rare it didn't make a lot of difference. The simple equation for each place was:

Index of Nigrescence = D + 2N – F – R = Brown + (2 × Black) – Fair – Red

Beddoe was not under any illusion that colour of hair and eyes were excessively important features, but they did have two persuasive advantages from a practical point of view. Firstly there was no shortage of material – everyone had eyes and most had hair. The other crucial point was that there was no need to ask the subject's permission. As we shall see, Beddoe was also fascinated by the shape of people's heads, but these observations were not so straightforward. Although everyone had a head, so again there was no shortage of material, to get any sort of shape measurement he did need the subject's acquiescence, something that was unnecessary for recording hair and eye colour.

Beddoe's medical practice in Bristol slowly improved, and he did at last succeed in getting a hospital position, the equivalent of a modern-day consultant, at the Bristol Royal Infirmary. Even though this increased his workload considerably, he still found time for his travels, card and pencil in hand, to every part of the Isles. He did not restrict himself to mainland Britain, but went often to Ireland, recording four expeditions between 1860 and 1870. By now he was a well-connected physician and his excursions were rarely solitary. On his first visit to Ireland, for example, he was accompanied at various times by a Scottish archaeologist, an expert on Irish criminology, an Irish antiquarian and a Catholic priest who acted as interpreter when they needed one in the Gaelic-speaking west. The intrepid wanderers were entertained wherever they went. In Dublin they met the leading Irish physician Sir William Wilde, 'father of the unhappy Oscar', as Beddoe describes him, and an enthusiastic amateur anthropologist, who, like Beddoe, was much taken with the contemporary craze for phrenology. By this time, Beddoe was making measurements of skull shapes when he could. As we saw, this needed the acquiescence of the subject, something he obtained by the following trick.

> Whenever a group of eligible peasants had collected around our party, two of us would get up a dispute as to which had the larger head, and I was called in to settle the doubt with my calipers and measuring tape. The interest of Paddy [*sic*] was quickly excited. Before I had finished, several of the bystanders would be wagering on the

> respective sizes of their own heads, and begging me to settle their differences by measurement. But such people if approached directly, always broke away at once, suspecting some concealed mischief devised by the 'Government'.

This was only a mild subterfuge compared to what happened next. Such was their enthusiasm for comparative anatomy that Beddoe and his companions turned into grave-robbers. 'The acquisition of skulls also had its difficulties,' he wrote. 'These relics lay about in old and deserted burial grounds, apparently quite uncared for, but their open abstraction would have aroused bitter feeling, and perhaps active opposition.'

To conceal what he was doing on these occasions, Beddoe wore a shooting jacket and, while his companions diverted the attention of any onlookers, he stuffed the skulls into large pockets sewn into the lining. These skulls eventually found their way to the museum of the College of Surgeons in London, where they remain to this day.

A professor from Galway developed an even more extravagant method for anatomical larceny. He always went hunting for skulls accompanied by his wife, who, in the fashion of the times, wore a wide crinoline skirt. When they spotted a skull, she stood nearby while the professor knelt down and quickly transferred the contraband to specially constructed pockets beneath the folds of his wife's voluminous skirt.

However, Beddoe's tours were not mere leisurely excursions between one literary salon and another, punctuated by a bit of grave-robbing. He wanted to get everywhere, driven by his passion not to miss a single opportunity to observe, to measure or even to steal. For example, to reach the Aran Islands in Galway Bay on the west coast of Ireland they were rowed over ten miles of rough sea in a small skiff. Frightened and seasick, the party arrived at Inishmore, the largest of the islands, to find they had to sleep on beds of straw. They spent two days sketching the buildings and tabulating the remote population, and were even able to 'annex' a couple of skulls 'of great but unknown antiquity' from an old cemetery.

Though Beddoe's passion for collecting skulls drove him to subterfuge and theft, he did at least confine his enthusiasm to the long dead. Not so his companion, Barnard Davis, who often visited Beddoe in his Bristol practice on the look-out for interesting specimens among his friend's still-living patients. On one visit to the Infirmary, Davis was introduced to a Bosnian sailor who was desperately ill after nearly drowning when his ship sank in the Bristol Channel. He had developed gangrene in his lungs and, in the days before antibiotics, was not expected to survive. Davis, convinced the man was not much longer for this world, was unsympathetically matter of fact.

'Now,' he said to Beddoe, 'you know that man can't recover. Do take care to secure his head for me when he dies, for I have no cranium from that neighbourhood.'

Yet Davis was to be disappointed for, as Beddoe recalls, the man 'made a wonderful recovery, and carried his head back to the Adriatic on his own shoulders'.

Beddoe's reputation began to spread after he entered, and won, the Welsh National Eisteddfod competition in

1867 for the best essay on the origins of the British nation. As a young doctor struggling to get his practice established, he needed money and the annual prize of 100 guineas was a definite attraction. The prize had not been awarded for the previous four years because the entries had failed sufficiently to impress the judges. To encourage a better field, the money was raised to 150 guineas. As soon as Beddoe heard this he rapidly wrote and submitted his essay. When, to his delight, he heard that he had won, he rushed up to the Eisteddfod at Ruthin in North Wales to collect the money. He got the 100 guineas but the extra 50 never materialized. Even forty years later, when he wrote his autobiography, this episode evidently still rankled.

It took another two decades until his prize essay, plus the additional material he had acquired in the meantime, eventually appeared in book form. It was published as *The Races of Britain* in 1885. By then a Fellow of both the Royal Society and the Royal College of Physicians, the publication of *The Races of Britain* brought Beddoe fresh honours and fresh activity. In 1891 he retired from his Bristol medical practice and moved to the nearby town of Bradford-on-Avon. Even this move could not interrupt the flow of honours and invitations, and in 1905, now aged seventy-nine, he gave the annual Huxley Lecture for the Royal Anthropological Institute. He died six years later, the year after publishing his autobiography, *Memories of Eighty Years*. In the copy in front of me as I write, the sepia photograph of the frontispiece, protected by a thin sheet of tissue paper, shows an old man with a full white beard, dressed in a three-piece suit and standing confidently, legs slightly apart, on the broad front step of his stone house. One hand in his pocket, the other on a stout pole, his chained watch just visible in his waistcoat pocket, he peers into the distance with dark eyes. Eyes that had inspected and recorded the faces of thousands upon thousands of the people of the Isles. Underneath is his signature, in jet-black ink, not faded by the years. John Beddoe. The two 'd's are a little shaky, but the flourish at the end is not. It is strange to think that the hand that signed this copy, nearly 100 years ago, was the same that marked the cards he carried with him throughout his journeys.

The real meat of Beddoe's lifetime of observation lies in the tables and maps that make up about half of the 300 pages of *The Races of Britain*. He visited and recorded in 472 different locations throughout Britain and Ireland, making a total of 43,000 observations. The tables themselves are delightfully annotated with asides such as 'Cornwall, St Austell. Flower show. Country folk' or 'Bristol. Whit-Monday. Young people numerous. Dancing.' He also got hold of a further set of 13,800 observations from the unlikely source of the lists of army deserters whose pursuers published their physical description in the chillingly titled periodical *Hue and Cry*. Finally, he recorded his own patients as they came through his Bristol surgery – a total of 4,390 altogether. These were particularly precious because there was time to make accurate observations and to check on the birthplace of each patient.

Beddoe was very well aware of the dangers of unrepresentative sampling, and of more subtle influences on the accuracy of his record. For example, were his Bristol

A rare display of English national identity. England supporters at the 2006 World Cup in Germany.

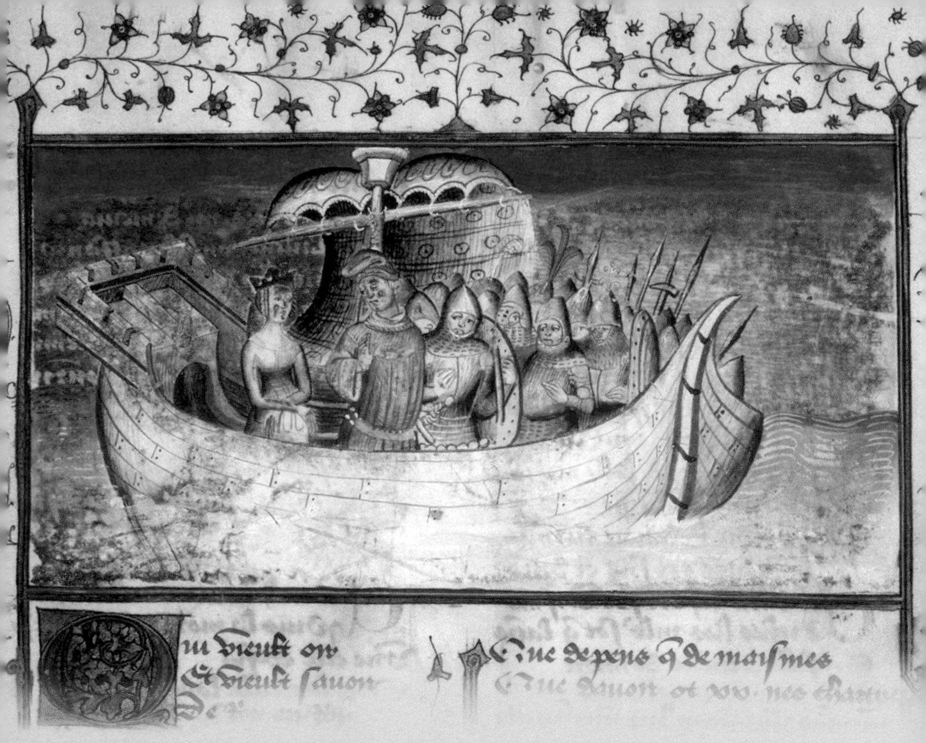

Above: Brutus the Trojan sets sail to discover Britain and become its first king – according to Geoffrey of Monmouth, at any rate.

Left: The coronation throne at Westminster Abbey with *Lia Fail*, the Stone of Destiny, before its return to Scotland.

OPPOSITE PAGE: (clockwise from top left)

Tintagel Castle on the Cornish cliffs, where Uther Pendragon deceitfully seduced Eigr and King Arthur was conceived.

Merlin before King Vortigern as he prophesies the subterranean lake containing the White and Red dragons.

King Arthur, seriously wounded at the battle of Camlan, well on the way to recovery thanks to Morgan Le Fay and her attendants on the Isle of Avalon. Or is he?

Glastonbury Abbey, scene of the ritual reburial of King Arthur's remains by Edward I on Easter Day, 1278.

Right: Mask made 9,500 years ago from the skull and antlers of a red deer, recovered from the Mesolithic site at Starr Carr, East Yorkshire.

Above: The defensive ditches of the Iron Age fort of Maiden Castle, Dorset, which fell to the II Augusta legion under Vespasian following the Roman invasion of Britain in AD43.

Below: Stonehenge, iconic religious centre of the ancient Britons. The massive stones were transported 250 miles from the Preseli mountains of West Wales, about 4,200 years ago.

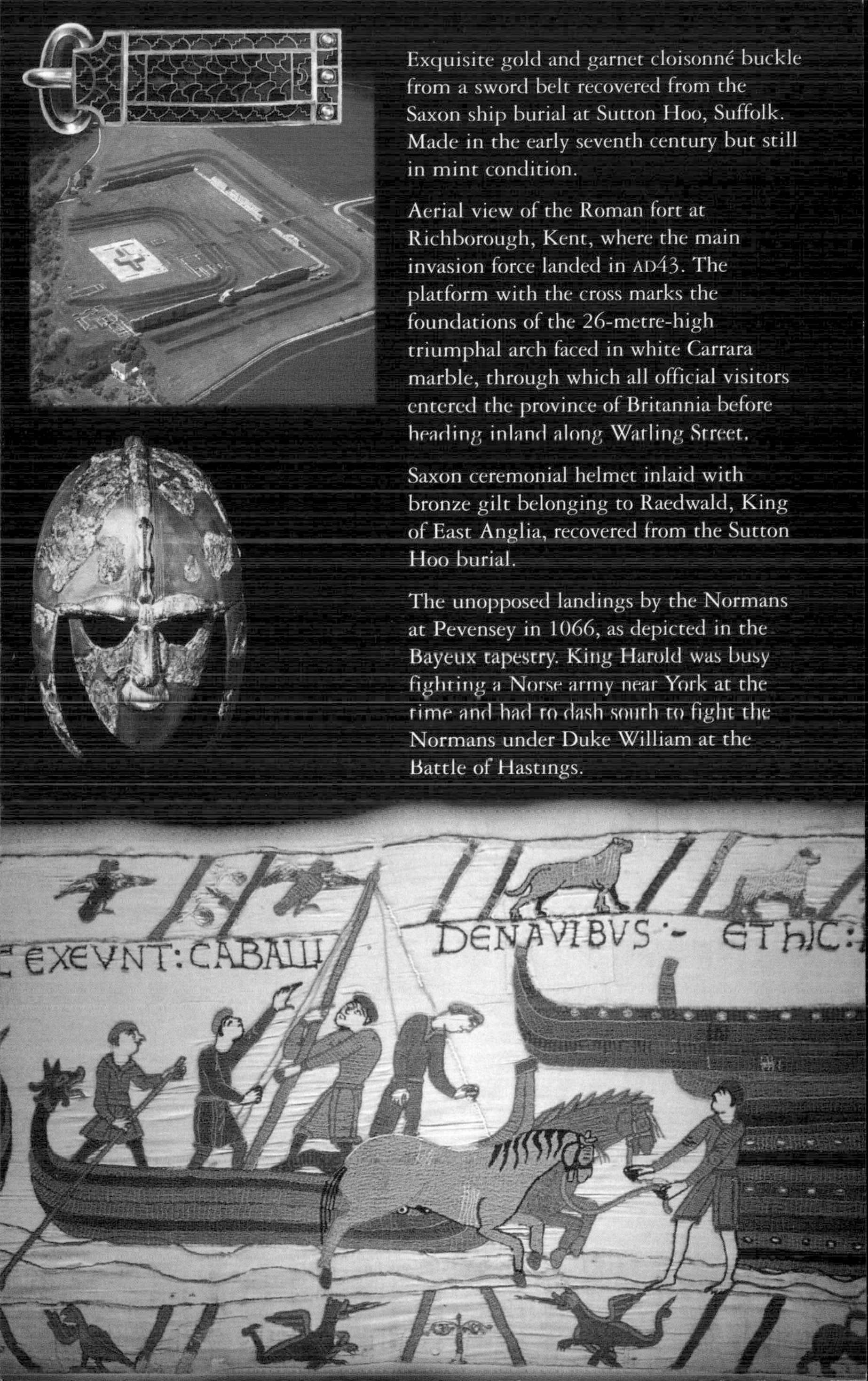

Exquisite gold and garnet cloisonné buckle from a sword belt recovered from the Saxon ship burial at Sutton Hoo, Suffolk. Made in the early seventh century but still in mint condition.

Aerial view of the Roman fort at Richborough, Kent, where the main invasion force landed in AD43. The platform with the cross marks the foundations of the 26-metre-high triumphal arch faced in white Carrara marble, through which all official visitors entered the province of Britannia before heading inland along Watling Street.

Saxon ceremonial helmet inlaid with bronze gilt belonging to Raedwald, King of East Anglia, recovered from the Sutton Hoo burial.

The unopposed landings by the Normans at Pevensey in 1066, as depicted in the Bayeux tapestry. King Harold was busy fighting a Norse army near York at the time and had to dash south to fight the Normans under Duke William at the Battle of Hastings.

Full moon over the standing stones of Callanish on the Isle of Lewis in the Outer Hebrides, one of the breathtaking megaliths constructed along the Atlantic fringe from Iberia to the Shetland Isles about 5,000 years ago.

OPPOSITE PAGE: (clockwise top left to bottom)

The exposed interior of one of the 5,000-year-old houses at Skara Brae, Orkney, complete with domestic furniture, hearth and even fishtanks to keep the lobsters fresh!

The central chamber of the passage grave at Maes Howe, Orkney, showing the vaulted roof built 5,000 years ago with the conveniently flat sandstone slabs from the locality.

Hadrian's Wall, Northumberland, built in AD122 to mark the final frontier of the Roman Empire – and to keep the belligerent Picts out.

The settlement at Jarlshof, Shetland, where the rectangular Viking longhouses have incorporated the earlier Pictish roundhouses.

The eighth-century Pictish symbol stone at Aberlemno, near Perth, depicting a battle between the Pictish King Bruide and an invading army under Ecgfrith, King of Northumbria. The Picts won. The hole in the stone was drilled to make it easier to move!

Mousa Broch in Shetland, the largest of the characteristic Pictish fortified dwellings built to a standard design between 2,100 and 1,900 years ago.

Right: Robert Knox MD, anatomist, surgeon, author – and venomous racist.

Centre: 'A Celtic groupe; such as may be seen at any time in Marylebone, London.' An engraving from Robert Knox's *The Races of Men*, in which he makes his attitude to the Celts abundantly clear.

Below: John Beddoe towards the end of a long life spent recording the physical features of the people in every corner of the Isles.

A page from Beddoe's album of photographs showing an ironworker from York of Welsh parentage coupled with a short handwritten description and a serial number. Beddoe was an avid and systematic collector.

patients representative of the general healthy population? Possibly not. They must have had a reason to be in his surgery in the first place. Indeed, he notes that the incidence of disease among American army recruits was reported to be much higher among the 'dark complexioned'. And his patients did, when averaged out, have a slightly higher Index of Nigrescence than the West Country folk that he observed in streets and marketplaces. This discrepancy he puts down to differences of moral character, allying cheerfulness and an optimistic outlook to a light complexion, while 'persons of melancholic temperament (and dark complexion) I am disposed to think, resort to hospitals more frequently than the sanguine'. Even then, blondes had more fun.

The Races of Britain was, and still is, a masterpiece of observation. The samples were not statistically controlled, his coverage of Britain and Ireland was not uniform, and he came in for criticism on these grounds – rather predictably from people who never themselves got into the field. But his work is best judged as a masterly piece of natural history and not a modern work embroidered with statistical treatments.

So what of the results themselves, and what did they tell Beddoe, and us, about the origins of the people of the Isles? Taking his measurements of hair colour and applying the formula of the Index of Nigrescence across the whole of Britain and Ireland, the values range from 0 to 80. There is a very clear difference between the far east of Britain, by which I mean East Anglia and Lincolnshire, where the Index is lowest, and Ireland and Cornwall in the west,

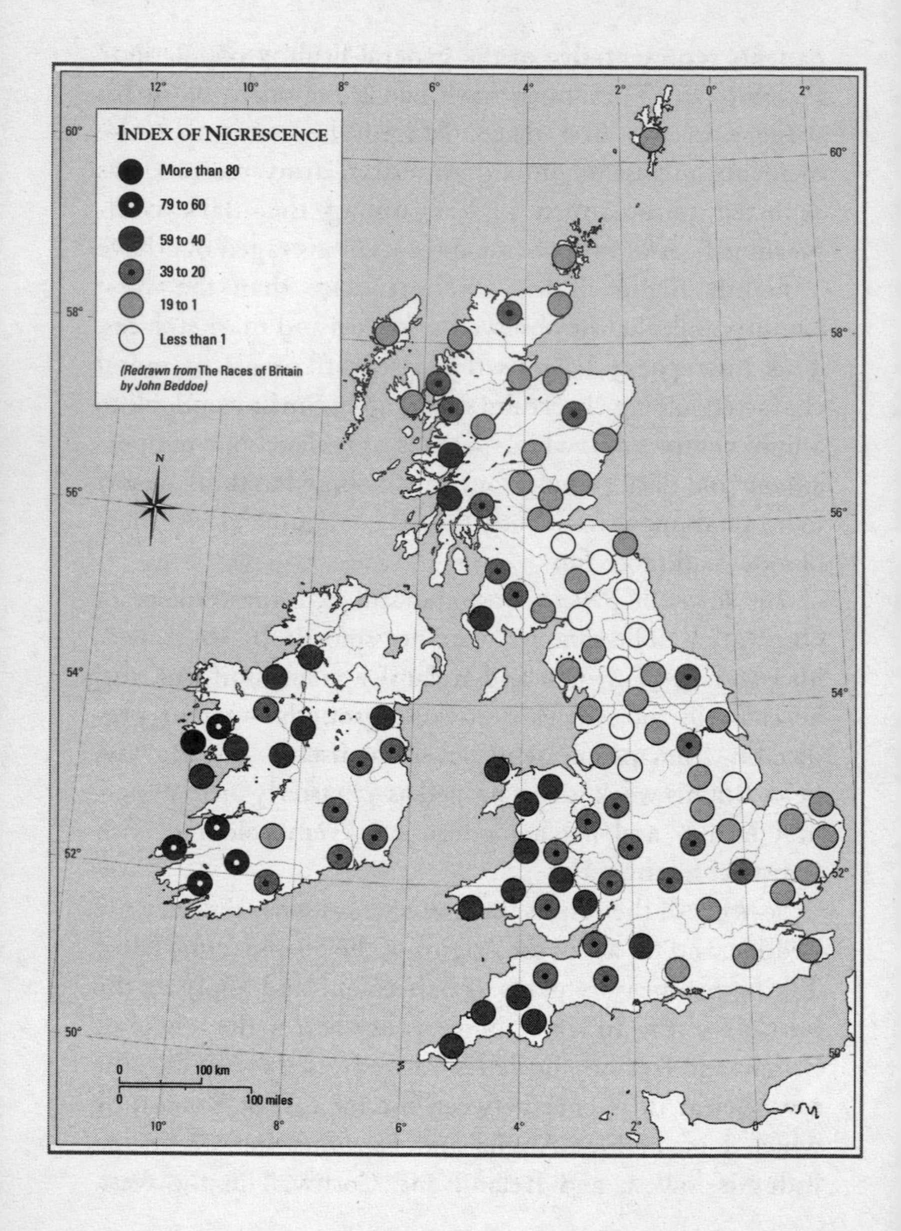

INDEX OF NIGRESCENCE
More than 80
79 to 60
59 to 40
39 to 20
19 to 1
Less than 1
(Redrawn from The Races of Britain by John Beddoe)
N
12°
10°
8°
6°
4°
2°
0°
2°
60°
58°
56°
54°
52°
50°
0
100 km
0
100 miles

where it reaches its highest value, as it also does in the west of Scotland. The low values for East Anglia are also continued across Yorkshire and Cumbria and again in the far north of Scotland and the Hebrides. In all these regions the Index is about zero, which means, in practice, that there are as many blondes and redheads as there are brunettes. In other parts of England, and in Wales, the values for the Index are intermediate between the fairer east and the darker west.

The Index is a measure of hair colour alone. When it comes to eye colour, the east–west gradient is reversed. Brown eyes are commonest in the east and south, where they exceed 40 per cent in East Anglia, but also in Cornwall. In Ireland, but also in Yorkshire and Cumbria, the same counties where red/fair hair were at their highest proportion, the number of people with blue or grey eyes rises to 75 per cent. In the far north of Scotland and the Hebrides, where fair hair was common, blue or grey eyes are even commoner than they are in Ireland. When hair and eye colour are combined to produce two basic types – what Beddoe calls 'Mixed Blond' and 'Mixed Dark' – with fair/red hair and blue/grey eyes or dark eyes and dark hair respectively – the patterns reflect the individual components to some extent. 'Mixed Blonds' outnumber their opposites in the north of Scotland, east Yorkshire and Lincolnshire, while 'Mixed Darks' predominate in Wales, Cornwall and the Scottish Highlands, along with Wiltshire and Dorset. In Ireland, especially in the west, the Mixed Blond outnumber the Mixed Dark, leading to the conclusion, when coupled with the high Index of Nigrescence, that there must be a high proportion of dark-haired people with blue or grey eyes.

Beddoe begins his conclusions in the far north. 'The Shetlanders', he says, 'are unquestionably in the main of Norwegian descent, but include other race elements also.' He draws the same conclusion for the inhabitants of Orkney and of Caithness in the far north of the Scottish mainland. He assumes the Norwegian element came with the Vikings. He also makes the strange observation that 'The excessive use of tea, the one luxury of Shetland, probably only aggravates a constitutional tendency to nervous disorders which is more prevalent among the few dark than the many fair Shetlanders.' This is the point to tell you that Beddoe describes himself as a young man 'of fair complexion, with rather bright brown wavy hair, a yellow beard and blue eyes'. Clearly it was perfectly safe for him to drink the tea.

As he works his way down Britain and across to Ireland, his observations combine preconception with perception in an extraordinarily personal record of his encounters. On Lewis, in the Western Isles, he observes the 'large, fair and comely Norse race, said to exist pure in the district of Ness at the north end of the island' and the 'short, thick-set, snub-nosed, dark-haired, often dark-eyed race, probably aboriginal and possibly Finnish whose centre seems to be in Barvas'. Barvas is 12 miles north-west of the principal town, Stornoway.

Beddoe is acutely aware of influences on the objectivity of his observations. In recording the Highlanders he says at once that 'Most travellers, on entering the habitat of a race strange to them quickly form for themselves from the first person observed some notion of the prevailing physical type.' Also he is aware that the longer he spends in a particular place, the more he can distinguish the differences between people: 'I confess that the longer I have known the Scottish Highlanders the more diversity I have seen among them.'

He also notices the presence of what he calls 'a decidedly Iberian physiognomy, which makes one think . . . that the Picts were in part at least of that stock'. We will return to that particular element of the British mix later in the book. As he crosses the border into England he finds pockets of 'a very blond race in Upper Teesdale' and, further south, 'the small, round-faced dark-haired men with almond-shaped eyes . . . in the vale of the Derwent and the level lands south of York', which he ascribes to either an Iberian or Romano-British origin. There is a growing feeling, as Beddoe moves around the country, that he is forming the view that dark-eyed and dark-haired people are the remnants of the indigenous Britons that were later supplemented, or displaced, by the Saxons and the Vikings. Even as he travels to the West Country, the connection is there: 'In the district about Dartmouth, where the Celtic language lingered for centuries, the Index of Nigrescence is at its maximum.' Onward to Cornwall, where 'The Cornish are generally dark in hair and often in eye: they are decidedly the darkest people in England.'

When Beddoe moves into Wales, he finds in the central region 'a prevalence of dark eyes beyond which I have met with in any other part of Britain'. The Snowdonians too are 'a very dark race', while around the coast eyes and hair are lighter. Across the Irish Sea, he records that 'the frequency of light eyes and of dark hair, the two often combined, is the leading characteristic'.

So much for the observations. What about the conclusions? There can be a tendency among collectors to leave interpretation of their results to others, mainly, I think, for fear of being proved wrong and thus undermining their whole legacy. This is an increasing trend, but even Beddoe was shy of absolute conclusions. None the less he ventured an explanation for the fair-haired people of England, suggesting that 'the greater part of the blond population of modern Britain ... derive their ancestry from the Anglo-Saxons and Scandinavians ... and that in the greater part of England it amounts to something like half'. So there we have it. Beddoe explains the different colouring by a very substantial settlement from Saxon, Dane and Viking. The particularly light colouring in parts of Yorkshire, which we noted previously, he attributes to the impact of the Norman Conquest. However, Normans, as we will later discover, are really no more than recycled Vikings. On Ireland and the Gaelic west generally, Beddoe thought the people to be a blend of Iberians with 'a harsh-featured, red-haired race'. The Celtic 'type', with dark hair and light eyes, he ventures to suggest, may only be an adaptation to the 'moist climate and cloudy skies' which they endure.

Beddoe concludes the account of his lifetime's work with this paragraph:

> But a truce with speculation! It has been the writer's aim rather to lay a sure foundation whereon genius may ultimately build. If these remaining questions are worthy and capable of solution, they will be solved only by much patient labour and by the co-operation of anthropologists with antiquarians and philologists; so that so much of the blurred and defaced prehistoric inscription as is left in shadow by one light may be brought into prominence and illumination by another.

It is as if John Beddoe, criss-crossing the country with card and pencil in hand, calipers and tape in his knapsack, had already anticipated the arrival of genetics. How he would have loved to be alive now.

Beddoe and his contemporaries were the first to substitute observation for deduction and prejudice in exploring the origins of the people of the Isles. But, as he himself freely admits, there was still a strong subjective element in his observations of appearance. After all, our obsession with looks is ample proof of its emotional influence. It must have been almost impossible for Beddoe not to have nurtured some preconceived ideas, which, with the best will in the world, will have influenced his conclusions.

The next stage in the scientific dissection of our origins removed this subjective element completely. It began a long way from England, just as John Beddoe was enjoying a comfortable old age and the flood of honours which acknowledged the fruits of his lifetime's passion. While he posed for the frontispiece of *The Races of Britain* on the doorstep of his comfortable mansion in the early years of the last century, a scientist in Vienna was mixing the blood of dogs.

5
THE BLOOD BANKERS

If you have ever been a blood donor, or ever needed a transfusion, then you will know your blood group. You will know whether you belong to Group A, B, O or even AB. The reason for testing is to avoid a possibly fatal reaction if you were to be transfused with unmatched blood. You cannot tell, just by looking, what blood group a person belongs to. Unlike hair and eye colour or the shape of heads, blood groups are an invisible signal of genetic difference which can be discovered only by carrying out a specific test.

Though the first blood transfusions were performed in Italy in 1628, so many people died that the procedure was banned. As a desperate measure to save women who were haemorrhaging after childbirth, there was a revival of transfusion in the mid-nineteenth century. Though some patients had no problems accepting a transfusion, a great many patients died from their reaction to the transfused blood. What caused the reaction was a mystery.

The puzzle was eventually solved in 1900 by the

Austrian physiologist Karl Landsteiner. After experimenting with mixing the blood of his laboratory dogs and observing their cross-reactions, he began his work on humans. He mixed the blood of several different individuals together and noticed that sometimes when he did this the red blood cells stuck together in a clump. This did not happen every time, but only with certain combinations of individuals. If this red-cell clumping was occurring in transfused patients, the blood would virtually solidify, which would explain the fatal reaction. It also explained why some patients tolerated a transfusion and showed no signs at all of a reaction.

Landsteiner interpreted the results of his mixing experiments by suggesting that people belonged to one of the three blood groups, A, B or O. Two years later a fourth group, AB, was discovered. This also explained the erratic pattern of transfusion complications. Giving a group A patient a transfusion of blood from a group A donor was fine; tranfuse a group A patient with blood from a group B donor and there would be trouble. But so long as the donor and patient blood groups were the same there was no problem.

It took a few years to discover the chemical basis for the different types of blood. The blood groups are the result of a simple genetic difference that occurs on the surface of red blood cells, the cells that carry oxygen and give blood its colour. On the outside of each red blood cell sits a molecule that can occur in two very slightly different forms, A or B. People in group A have, unsurprisingly, version A on the surface of their red cells while in group B, this is replaced by version B. In the rare AB group the cells have both A and B versions on their outer surface. People in group O have neither A nor B versions of the molecule. Their red cells are, in a sense, bald.

But these slight differences, which don't affect the efficiency or the working of the cells at all, are not on their own sufficient to cause trouble on transfusion. The problem arises because, after a few months outside the womb, the blood serum begins to build up antibodies to the *opposite* version of the molecule on their own cells. People in group A build up anti-B antibodies in their serum. Again, this does not interfere with normal everyday life. People never make antibodies to their own blood cells, so people in group A don't make anti-A antibodies, only anti-B. Since people with blood group AB have both versions on their red cells, they make neither anti-A nor anti-B antibodies while, for the same reason, people in group O, whose cells have neither A nor B, are free to make both anti-A and anti-B antibodies and they do.

The potentially fatal coagulation reaction occurs when the molecule meets its antibody. They stick to each other like glue and, what is worse, bind all the red cells into a sticky clump, the cause of all the trouble in mismatched transfusions. That's why no one makes antibodies against their own cells. They would coagulate their own red blood cells and die.

Under normal circumstances blood cells never encounter their own antibodies, but transfusion opens up that possibility. Transfuse a group A patient with blood from a group B donor and the antibodies will play havoc. Two things happen. The group B cells from the donor are coagulated by the anti-B in the patient's serum and the anti-A in the donor's serum clumps the patient's own cells. Group O blood is really bad news because its serum contains both anti-A *and* anti-B which will attach the cells of any other blood group. However, as good methods were developed to separate the donor's cells from the liquid serum, things got a bit easier. Group O cells, separated then rinsed free of antibody-containing serum, can be transfused into any patient, and if red cells are all you need that's fine. Group O is the universal red-cell donor, as long as you wash them thoroughly first to remove the serum antibodies. If you need serum, not cells, then a transfusion of AB serum, which is free of antibodies, will suit any patient whatever their blood group.

Once all this was understood, it was easy to see why so many transfusions failed. Without knowing in advance the blood group of donor and patient, blood transfusion was a really hit-and-miss affair. At least that was the case in Europe. Stories that the Incas of Peru had been successfully performing a form of blood transfusion without any adverse reactions were initially dismissed as nonsense. However, when it was discovered that practically all native South Americans were in blood group O, it no longer sounded so incredible. If Inca donor and Inca recipient were both in group O, as most were, then trouble-free transfusions are exactly what would be expected.

Before the First World War, blood transfusions were a personal business. Willing friends and relatives of the patient would be tested to find someone in a compatible blood group. The donor would then come to a hospital, usually the operating theatre if surgery was the reason for the transfusion, and be bled right next to the patient, who then immediately received the fresh blood. The huge increase of blood transfusions needed to treat the battlefield casualties of the First World War led directly to the setting up of blood banks and the recruitment of donors along modern lines. Under the right conditions it was found that blood could be stored for several days without losing condition and there was no need to transfuse casualties immediately with absolutely fresh blood.

Volunteer donors were bled at remote sites and the blood was despatched to the field hospitals at the Front to be matched and used as required. This soon became a large-scale activity and with it came the necessity for accurate records. Each army had its blood bank and they soon began to accumulate blood-group records from very large numbers of soldiers, each of whom was routinely tested in anticipation of being called either to give blood as a donor or to receive it as a casualty.

Hanka Herschfeld, from the Royal Serbian Army, was the medical officer in charge of the Allied blood bank on the Balkan Front. Her husband, Ludwig, had been one of the scientists who, before the war, had helped to work out the way the different blood groups were inherited. With this background it is no surprise that they became curious about the accumulating results from the blood bank. The Allies drew their troops from all over the world and the Herschfelds noticed that the frequencies of the blood groups in the soldiers of different nationalities were often quite different from one another. Certainly they were still all either A, B, AB or O, but the proportions of each were different depending on where they were from. For example, far more Indian Army soldiers belonged to blood group B than did Europeans, who were, symmetrically, higher in the proportion of group A.

The Herschfelds interpreted these differences in blood-group frequencies as having something to do with the distant origins of these different nationalities – and they were right. But in their now famous paper published in the leading medical journal the *Lancet*, just after the war, they went too far and divided the world into two separate races. Race A came from northern Europe, while Race B began in India. The varying blood-group proportions seen in the soldiers of different nationalities were explained by the mixing as people flowed outwards from these 'cradles of humanity', as the Herschfelds called them, to populate the world.

Their *Lancet* paper is a classic, and rightly so. It was the first of its kind and it opened up an entirely new field of research in anthropology. It follows on from the implicit assumption in John Beddoe's research on physical appearance that inherited features can be used to explore the origins of people. Compared to the work on hair and eye colour, skull shape and so on, blood groups come one step closer to the fundamental controller of genetic inheritance, DNA. However, no one knew about the way DNA conducted the business of inheritance at the time the Herschfelds were at their peak, nor for several decades afterwards. Blood groups, though still an indirect manifestation of the underlying DNA, were a definite improvement on the earlier, subjective parameters which were all that were available to John Beddoe and his Victorian contemporaries.

For one thing, it completely removed prejudice and human error from the equation. Blood groups are tightly defined and there is no overlap between them. No matter who does the tests, someone in group B will always be in group B. It doesn't alter with age. There is no room for doubt, at least not about the accuracy of the observation. But there is also a noticeable shift in the tone of the reports. There are no longer any barely concealed inferences of racial character, like the free-spirited, fair-haired Saxon who will not be tied to the drudgery of an urban existence but would rather make his fortune overseas, or the morose, dark-haired Shetlander driven to despair by drinking too many cups of tea. All that nonsense vanishes, as it is very hard to get worked up about the comparative personal characteristics of one blood group over another. The American physician William Boyd, who extended the Herschfelds' work around the globe, expressed this new sense when he wrote, 'In certain parts of the world an individual will be considered inferior if he has, for instance, a dark skin but in no part of the world does possession of a blood group A gene exclude him from the best society.' As a group A myself, that comes as something of a relief.

The Herschfelds' final legacy was less glorious. Their grand conclusions about the dual origins of humanity turned out to be completely wrong. It took the discovery of other blood group systems, unimportant in transfusion, and the amalgamation of results from several of them to get a more reasonable interpretation of human evolution. Slowly the searchlight illuminating the 'cradle of humanity' turned away from Europe and Asia and settled firmly on the plains of East Africa.

After the Second World War, the task of sifting through the, by then, thousands of sets of blood-group data from transfusion centres all over the world settled on the shoulders of one man, Arthur Mourant. Born in Jersey in the Channel Islands, and emotionally attached to it throughout his life, Mourant wanted at first to become a psychoanalyst and, in order to do so, he had to enrol as a medical student. He was forced to abandon his ambition after he underwent analysis himself and was judged to be 'emotionally unsuitable' to continue with his training. Despite this disappointment, he did not abandon his medical training. During the Second World War his medical school, St Bartholomew's in the City of London, was evacuated to Cambridge and he found himself working with one of the greatest geneticists of the twentieth century, R. A. Fisher.

Fisher, among many other interests, was engaged in a bitter rivalry with the American physician Alexander Wiener on the inheritance of the Rhesus blood groups. Rhesus is another type of human blood group, discovered, as its name implies, through research on Rhesus monkeys. Unlike Landsteiner's comparatively simple ABO system, the genetics of the Rhesus blood group are fiendishly complicated. There was a furious race to unravel the genetics by following the Rhesus group through families, and the young Mourant was assigned the task of finding and typing suitably large families. He quickly found the solution to the inheritance, thanks to his particularly fruitful research on a local East Anglian family. Fisher was understandably elated by this triumph and Mourant soon found himself an established member of Fisher's team with a bright career ahead of him. This career he dedicated to extending William Boyd's pre-war surveys on the geographical distribution of the ABO blood groups around the world. He also set out to enlarge on Boyd's work by including as many of the newly discovered blood groups, like Rhesus, as possible and to build up the most complete maps of blood-group distributions in every part of the globe. Mourant, like Beddoe before him, was an extremely avid collector of information.

In front of me as I write is his final masterpiece, *The Distribution of the Human Blood Groups*, published in 1976. It is an impressive tome, 6 centimetres thick and weighing 2.4 kilograms. It has 1,055 pages, 3,179 bibliographic references, 661 pages of tables and several pages of beautifully drawn maps. It has the gravitas of a life's work. To give you a taste of the scope of Mourant's encyclopaedic enterprise, there are tables of Rhesus blood-group data from the Bilwa, Sanpuka and Ulwas tribes of Nicaragua, the ABO blood groups of 13,000 blood donors from Benghazi in Libya, the MNS (another blood group) results from French and Spanish Basques and the Duffy (yet another) blood-group results from hundreds of New Guinea highlanders.

But what did it all mean? Surely there was enough information here to resolve any lingering uncertainties about the whereabouts of the 'cradle of humanity' and how our ancestors had moved from there to populate the planet. But even a cursory inspection of the maps shows the optimism is misplaced. Working along the commonsense lines that if two peoples have similar proportions of the different blood groups, then they are more likely to be related than two with very different proportions, you soon run into trouble. For example, the highest frequencies of blood group A are found in two very different parts of the world: among native Australians on the one hand and Saami reindeer-herders of northern Norway on the other. It would be preposterous to propose that these two peoples, about as far away from each other as it is possible to be, were closely related and shared a recent common ancestry. However, when you factor in the results of the other blood groups, the relationship becomes far more reasonable. The native Australians might have the same proportions of the ABO blood groups, but the composition of the other groups, like Rhesus, MNS and Duffy, are utterly different. Bit by bit, blood groups began to draw out connections between the different peoples of the world, including western Europeans and the people of the Isles.

The basic pattern which Mourant found across western Europe, the area of most relevance for *Blood of the Isles*, showed that across the whole region west of the River Elbe in Germany, group A is high and group B comparatively low. East of the Elbe the opposite is the case. There is a gradual shift from B to A, a so-called genetic cline, as we get closer to the Isles. In the Isles themselves Mourant was able to call on absolutely vast amounts of material, both from his own unit, by now incorporated as an official laboratory of the Medical Research Council, the UK's government funding agency for medical research, and from other published works. Among these were detailed records of blood-group frequencies from Ireland, Wales and the Scottish Highlands.

Mourant gave the task of collecting all the records from the 'missing' bits – that is to say England, lowland Scotland and Northern Ireland – to his long-term assistant Ada Kopec, who, with a librarian and a secretary, made up the entire staff of the Blood Group Centre. It is plain from reading the account of this mammoth piece of assimilation and statistical comparison of a grand total of 477,806 results that Ada Kopec was far more concerned with mathematical manipulation of the figures than with explanation. Indeed it is left to Mourant himself, writing in the Foreword, almost to excuse his assistant from any genetic or anthropological interpretation, which, he writes, 'will have to be made by others'. Fortunately, there were 'others' prepared to stick their necks out.

The conclusions of Mourant and Kopec's gigantic enterprise can be summarized very concisely. In Ireland there are very high levels of blood group O, the highest in Europe. The further west you go, the higher the group O proportions. And, as elsewhere in Europe, where O is high, A is low and vice versa, so in the eastern counties of Ireland, where O is lower than in the west, A is higher. The differences in different parts of Ireland are not dramatic, but because the number of individuals taking part is so high, the figures can be relied upon to be statistically reliable. So whereas in County Clare, in the far west of Ireland, 80 per cent of people are in group O, this drops to 73 per cent in County Wexford in the south-east, with a mirror-image result for blood group A. Turning to blood group B, there is a slight reversal of the trend across the rest of north-west Europe. Instead of following the rule of the further west, the lower the proportion of B, there is a distinct and statistically significant rise in the far west of Ireland compared to the east. It goes from 6.6 per cent in Wexford to 8 per cent in Kerry.

Now comes the explanation. According to Professor Geoffrey Dawson from Trinity College Dublin, the high levels of A in south-east Ireland are a direct result of successive waves of immigration into Ireland from England. In the first of many papers on the blood groups of Ireland, written in the 1950s, Dawson kicks off with a summary history of Ireland. He explains the blood-group changes from east to west by the Anglo-Norman invasion in the twelfth century, which we will revisit in a later chapter, and by attempts to settle English immigrants under Queens Mary and Elizabeth in the late 1500s.

I much prefer it when authors do advance a theory to explain their results, rather than leave it to others. But how can Dawson possibly know this is the reason for the blood-group differences? Why could they not be equally well explained by other movements of people in prehistoric times? Or by a mixture of both? The whole thrust of the explanation is based on historical events that we already know about. If we had not had a reasonable explanation to hand, would the blood-group evidence be strong enough to come up with one on its own? I really doubt that. Instead of proposing something completely original, the genetic data is rationalized and fitted in to what we already suspect from other sources.

The rationalizations reach their peak in relation to Iceland. Iceland was unoccupied until the late 800s when the systematic settlement from Scandinavia began. The language, the culture, even the written histories recorded in the Icelandic sagas, including the *Histories of Settlement*, leave no one in any doubt that the great majority of settlers were Norse. And yet, the blood-group proportions in Iceland are very different from those of modern-day Norway and almost identical to those of Ireland, as the table shows.

	A	B	O
Iceland	19	7	74
Norway	31	6	62
Ireland	18	7	75

By any token, the only conclusion from the blood-group composition is that Iceland was not settled from Norway at all. Far more likely, from the blood-group results, is a wholesale settlement from Ireland or somewhere else with similar blood-group proportions, like parts of Scotland. As we will see in a later chapter, there is at least a partial explanation for this discrepancy, but that is not the main message I want to get across here.

Faced with this disagreement in the blood results, instead of having the confidence to overturn the theory of Norse settlement, Mourant tries to rationalize by finding

Scandinavian 'homelands' that might heal the discrepancy. He cites parts of western Norway around Trondelag that have a blood-group composition a little more like Iceland than the rest of the country, then reports an isolated population in northern Sweden in the province of Vasterbotten with an even more Icelandic composition. Northern Sweden isn't even close to the Atlantic and no traditions link it to the settlement of Iceland. Mourant then highlights an old settlement at Settesdal in southern Norway with 'Icelandic' blood-group compositions. Finally, to resolve this awkward disagreement, he suggests that the modern-day Scandinavians are the descendants of people moving in from the south and east who displaced the Vikings and drove them to settle in Iceland.

All of these attempts to resolve the disparity between, on the one hand, mountains of cultural and historical evidence on the Scandinavian origin of the Icelanders, and the blood-group results on the other, highlight a fundamental weakness in the value of using blood groups to infer origins. If the results from the labs agree with what you already believe about the origins or make-up of people, then there is a cosy feeling that the genetics, archaeology and history are all in agreement with each other. But when they do not there is a temptation to fabricate an agreement with increasingly unlikely scenarios, as with Iceland.

I suspect the same has been done in the south-west corner of Wales. The southern part of Pembrokeshire surrounding the deep-water inlet of Milford Haven delights in the sobriquet of 'Little England beyond Wales', a reference to the anglicized place-names and the long use of the English as opposed to the Welsh language. The levels of group A in this small region of Wales are 5–10 per cent higher than in the surrounding areas. It is known that Henry I forcibly transferred a colony of Flemish refugees fleeing political repression in Holland and Belgium to the area in the early twelfth century. The high levels of blood group A have been attributed to this historical influx and are often quoted in popular accounts as a classic success of blood grouping confirming history. This is despite the levels of blood group A in the Low Countries not being particularly high. However, a very different explanation was favoured by the Welsh scientist Morgan Watkin, the man who originally noticed the high proportion of group A in parts of Pembrokeshire. He put it down to a substantial Viking settlement in the region, despite the fact that there is very little in the way of archaeology or place-names to support it. But the fact remains that, even after thousands of blood samples from Wales and hundreds of thousands from all over Britain and Ireland, it is still impossible to decide whether the unusual blood-group composition of this part of Wales was caused by rampaging Vikings or by a few cartloads of Belgians.

The root of the problem is that, despite there being vast amounts of very reliable data, blood groups just do not have the power to distinguish these two theories, nor the power to propose new ones that might fly in the face of historical or archaeological evidence. Blood groups, despite the advantage of objectivity, are a very blunt instrument indeed with which to dissect the genetic history of a relatively small region like the Isles. Fortunately, we can sharpen our genetic scalpel. Now we can do something that William Boyd, Arthur Mourant and the others could not. We can move to the next stage and take the last step towards the final arbiter of inheritance. We can move to the DNA itself.

6
THE SILENT MESSENGERS

Whatever their shortcomings as a guide to the past, the fact that blood groups are 100 per cent genetic makes it self-evident that they are inherited from ancestors. They are not DNA, but they are the expression of DNA. You may like to compare the relationship between DNA and blood groups like this. When you listen to a piece of music you are not hearing the written notes themselves, but the expression of the notes as interpreted by the musicians. Our inherited features, both those we notice, like hair and eye colour, and those, like blood groups, that we need tests to reveal, are the music we hear. The DNA is the equivalent of the notes on the sheet, which the musicians are reading to produce the music.

Arthur Mourant and his fellow blood-groupers were too early to see the sheet music on which the blood-group notes were written, but they knew from the way it was inherited in families that it must be very simple. The four different blood groups A, B, AB and O are the expression of three versions of a single gene, a single piece of DNA. Once it became possible to read the notes behind the music, the true cause of the blood groups was revealed to be very slight changes in the DNA of the blood-group gene itself. DNA is a coded message in the form of a sequence of four slightly different chemicals attached to each other. If you think of it as a very long string of beads, where each bead is one of these DNA chemicals, then that will give you an idea of what a strand of DNA looks like. Now imagine that there are four different colours of bead on the string, each one representing one of the four DNA chemical bases, as they are called. You can see how the string of beads might become a code purely by virtue of the sequence in which the different coloured beads are arranged. The DNA of the blood-group gene is about 1,000 beads, or bases, long.

Though it calls the shots, DNA doesn't actually do the work in the body, just as the notes on a sheet of music need musicians to be heard. DNA is the code that tells cells, all of which contain DNA, what to do. Just as notes on a musical score tell the orchestra what to play, DNA tells cells which proteins to make. And it is proteins that build and run the body. Proteins are made up of amino-acids arranged in a specific linear sequence and it is this sequence of amino-acids that gives the protein its particular properties. No two proteins are the same. The protein collagen, for example, has a very strong and rigid structure which it needs to do its job in strengthening bones and teeth. That strength is a direct result of the way the amino-acids are arranged, just as the oxygen-carrying capacity of haemoglobin comes about by the particular sequence of its own amino-acids. The same goes for the blood-group protein that sits in the membrane of red blood cells. It is all down to the sequence of amino-acids.

The DNA instructs the cell how to make proteins through the coded instructions held in the sequence of the coloured beads on the string. Cells know how to interpret this code and how to translate the DNA sequence into the amino-acid sequence of a protein. The differences between alternative versions of the same gene, which are what produce the three different blood groups, are caused by mutations. This is when, very rarely, there is an error in copying the DNA. A bead suddenly changes colour and the DNA sequence changes slightly. Cells read the new sequence like the mindless automata they are. They don't realize that they are now producing a slightly different version of the protein, which may have different properties. They just do as they are told.

Most mutations happen when DNA is being copied. Since every cell contains a full set of DNA, it has to be copied every time a cell divides. We all start off as a single cell, a fertilized egg, and grow from that by cell division to an adult with 10 million billion cells, so there is an enormous amount of DNA copying going on and plenty of opportunity for DNA mutation. However, the fidelity of copying DNA is absolutely fantastic, and of course it needs to be. If it were as poor as the average photocopier, by the time the fertilized egg had divided and divided to produce at first an embryo, then a foetus, then a baby, the DNA instructions would become so fuzzy that every child would be born with every genetic disease under the sun – if he or she ever got born at all. To prevent this happening, there are proofreading and editing mechanisms which scan the newly copied DNA to make sure it matches the original sequence. All of this is to reduce the chance of mutation. And in this we are very successful. On average, a DNA base mutates only once in every thousand million times it is copied. Even so, this minuscule error rate is enough to produce all the genetic variation in our own species and in every other living creature that we see in the world around us. Mutation is the life-blood of evolution.

Without mutation, there simply is no evolution. Most of the time mutation, even when it occurs, has absolutely no effect. Very occasionally, though, mutations do drastically affect the working of whatever protein the gene is in charge of – and that is how devastating inherited diseases can begin their life. In my earlier career as a medical geneticist, working as I did with inherited bone diseases, I saw many patients whose bones would fracture at the slightest knock. They were badly deformed and often unable to walk – but often astonishingly cheerful and optimistic. Their disease, called osteogenesis imperfecta, a very serious form of brittle-bone disease, was caused by one of these random mutations in a bone collagen gene. But instead of making a harmless change to the DNA sequence, in these patients the mutation had hit a crucial DNA base in the collagen gene. The mutations in these patients, even though they change just a single DNA base, completely alter the structure of the collagen, turning it from an extremely strong protein into the biological equivalent of putty.

Mutations can be good, bad or indifferent. Most are

indifferent, like the mutations which produce the different blood groups. A few are bad, as in the brittle-bone patients. Vanishingly few are good, in the sense that they improve the way the protein works. On the whole the bad mutations are eliminated pretty swiftly as people with inherited diseases die or have fewer children. Good mutations can find themselves increasing from one generation to the next if they aid the survival of the people that carry them or help them have more children. Indifferent mutations, and they are in the majority, have no influence one way or the other on survival or success in breeding. They just get passed from one generation to the next, their fate entirely out of their hands. They risk elimination if they end up in someone who has no children or can do well if they find themselves in a large family. They might lead less dramatic lives than the mutations that bring success or devastation. But it is these, the silent passengers of evolution, that are its most articulate chroniclers. This is precisely because they cause no ripples, they are unseen by natural selection and are neither promoted nor destroyed by its attentions. But nowadays, thanks to the breakthroughs of the last twenty years, we can see them in the read-out from the DNA analyser. And we can use them to trace our ancestry.

While Arthur Mourant did what he could with the very limited number of blood groups, there is almost no limit to the amount of different DNA sequences that we are now able to detect. It is this massive increase in our ability to distinguish one person's DNA from another which has made all the difference in our ability to trace our ancestry and discover our genetic origins. But with all this choice, which were going to be the best genes to concentrate on, and why?

During my work on ancient bones I wanted to give myself the best chance of recovering DNA so I chose to focus on a rather unusual piece of DNA. Most of our DNA is contained within the cell nucleus, attached to tiny thread-like structures called chromosomes. This is where the collagen genes, the haemoglobin genes and the blood-group genes reside. For all of them, as for most of our 'nuclear' genes, we have only two copies in each cell, one from each of our parents. However, outside the cell nucleus, though still inside the cell membrane, there is a different source of DNA altogether. In the liquid cytoplasm surrounding the nucleus are tiny particles called mitochondria. These particles control many of the steps in aerobic metabolism and they have an interesting evolutionary history, having once been free-living bacteria. From our point of view at the time, where this DNA had come from and what it did was unimportant. What counted was that there was far more of it in the average cell, maybe a thousand times more, than the DNA of any of the nuclear genes. If only a few cells survived in the ancient bones, targeting mitochondrial DNA would maximize our chances. It turned out to be the right decision, and we found mitochondrial DNA in the first batch of bones we tried. It is still extremely hard to recover nuclear genes from ancient specimens, while getting out the mitochondrial DNA is now almost routine.

As well as its abundance in each cell, mitochondrial DNA (or mDNA for short) has two other outstanding properties to recommend it as a window into the human past. Firstly, it mutates about twenty times faster than regular nuclear DNA. The error-checking mechanisms in mDNA are much less vigilant than they are in the nucleus. Our species has been around for about 150,000 years and, although this seems to us like a very long time, the nuclear DNA mutation rate is so low that the vast majority of it is completely unchanged since that time. In a typical stretch of nuclear DNA 1,000 bases long, nineteen out of twenty people will have exactly the same sequence. Within the same sized stretch of mDNA, almost everyone is different.

The second excellent feature of mDNA is its very unusual inheritance pattern. As we have seen, most of the nuclear genes are inherited equally from both parents. You have received one copy of each nuclear gene from your mother's egg and one from your father's fertilizing sperm. But you got *all* of your mDNA only from your mother, and for one very simple reason. Compared to sperm, eggs are huge cells, bulging with cytoplasm, which is crammed with a quarter of a million mitochondria. Sperm do have a few mitochondria, about a hundred, in what is called the mid-piece, which connects the sperm head, containing all the nuclear DNA, to the tail. The thrashing tail needs the aerobic energy output of the mitochondria in the mid-piece to fuel its progress towards the egg.

But once the successful sperm penetrates the egg to deliver its precious load of nuclear DNA, its mitochondria are not only vastly outnumbered but are deliberately destroyed. This is why, although the fertilized egg contains nuclear DNA from both father and mother, all the mitochondria, and so all the mitochondrial DNA, is from the mother.

The process is repeated generation after generation after generation. Nuclear DNA comes from the father and mother, mDNA only from the mother. Consider your own mDNA for a moment. It is powering your aerobic metabolism in every cell – from the cells in your retina which collect the focused image from the page, to the muscles in your arm that turn the pages, to the cells that are burning fuel to keep you warm. All these functions are controlled by your mDNA which, because of its unusual inheritance, you have got only from your mother. Who got it from her mother. Who got it from her mother and so on. At any time in the past, be it 100, 1,000, even 10,000 years ago, there was only one woman alive at the time from whom you have inherited your mDNA. Even though I have known this for years it still amazes me to think about it.

The combination of plenty of genetic variation with its matrilineal inheritance makes mDNA the perfect guide to the human past. But it needs to be complemented, because it can tell only one side of the story. Mitochondrial DNA can only tell the history of women. Very fortunately, there is a piece of DNA which can do the same for men. This companion guide to our genetic history could not be more different. This is the piece of DNA that is entirely male. It is the Y-chromosome.

Inside the nucleus of every human cell are a total of forty-six chromosomes. Forty-four out of the forty-six carry on them the great majority of the 10,000 genes that build and run our bodies. They include the blood-group, collagen and haemoglobin genes we have already met and many, many more. They direct almost everything, from aspects of our physical appearance like eye and hair colour, to our immune systems, to our innate psychological and emotional make-up. In everybody, male and female, these forty-four chromosomes come in pairs and are inherited from both parents, twenty-two from one, twenty-two from the other.

The other two chromosomes, called X and Y, are different in that they are not always inherited from both parents. And not everybody has both of them. Females have two X-chromosomes and men have one X-chromosome and one Y-chromosome. In the official notation of genetics, women are XX and men are XY. However, despite what I have come to appreciate that most people believe, the X-chromosome has nothing directly to do with sex. Women are not women because they possess two X chromosomes – the truth is far more interesting. Women are female because they don't have a Y-chromosome. How can that be?

Looked at under the microscope, the X and Y chromosomes look quite different. Both are the same shape, like tiny threads, but the X-chromosome is about five times as long. The differences between X and Y don't stop there. Thanks to the output from the Human Genome Project we now have the DNA sequence for both chromosomes. The larger X-chromosome is very like the other forty-four chromosomes. It carries about 1,000 genes which control a range of different cellular activities. The Y-chromosome, on the other hand, is a genetic wreck with only twenty-seven genes that appear to be working properly. The rest of the chromosome is made up of long stretches of so-called 'junk' DNA. This is DNA that, unlike genes that do things, has no known function. It is just there. The evolutionary implications for this tremendous difference between X- and Y-chromosomes are fascinating, but not especially relevant here. What does matter is that just one of the twenty-seven active genes on the Y-chromosome, the sex gene, is what makes males.

For the first six weeks of life, there is no visible difference between male and female embryos. At about that time, the sex gene on the Y-chromosome switches on. This sends a signal to a whole series of other genes situated on other chromosomes, which, between them, actively divert embryonic development away from female and towards male. Embryos that don't have a Y-chromosome just carry on along the normal female development pathway and are born girls. The X-chromosome has nothing to do with it. Men truly are genetically modified women.

This mechanism for deciding sex which humans have inherited from their distant mammalian ancestors creates the second of our guides to our genetic origins. Men carry both an X- and a Y-chromosome in all of their cells – except mature sperm. Sperm occur in two different genetic forms, indistinguishable under the microscope and in their swimming capabilities. Stem cells in the male testis are dividing furiously to keep up the supply of sperm and like the other cells in the body have the XY combination of sex chromosomes. At the final division, the cell divides one last time but the resulting sperm only get one of the sex chromosomes, not both. Half the sperm receive an

X-chromosome from this division while the other half get a Y-chromosome. The sex of the child entirely depends on which sort of sperm wins the race to the egg. If it's got an X-chromosome then the egg, which already has one X-chromosome, becomes XX after fertilization, develops as a female embryo and is born a girl. If, on the other hand, the winning sperm contains a Y-chromosome, the fertilized egg becomes XY and develops into a boy. The simple conclusion is this: Y-chromosomes get passed down the male line from father to son.

Looking backwards, if you are a man, you got your Y-chromosome from your father, who got it from his father. Who got it from his father. Sounds familiar? It is the mirror image of the inheritance pattern for mitochondrial DNA. The Y-chromosome is the perfect complement to mDNA, telling the history of men. But does it have enough genetic variability to be practically useful? It took a very long time to find any mutations at all on the Y-chromosome. For those scientists involved, and thankfully I wasn't one of them, it was a frustrating few years. In one of the first studies looking for diversity among human Y-chromosomes, 14,000 bases were sequenced from twelve men from widely scattered geographical localities. Only a single mutation was discovered. Another lab sequenced the same 700-base segment from the Y-chromosomes of thirty-eight different men and didn't find a single mutation in any of them. At long last, and helped by an ingenious technique for finding the elusive mutations, the Y-chromosome began to show its genetic jewels. Slowly, slowly, mutations that had changed one DNA base to another were teased out of the otherwise barren desert of uniformity.

With these two pieces of DNA we have the perfect companions for our exploration of the genetic past. One follows the female line, the other tracks the male genealogy. What could be better? They had been my guides in Polynesia and in Europe and I knew them well. Among their many qualities is that they both group people into clans. When my colleagues and I had been trying to make sense of the mDNA results from Europe in the early 1990s, we noticed that the 800 or so samples from volunteers from all over Europe fell into seven quite distinct groups based on their mDNA sequences.

Unlike the chromosomes in the cell nucleus, which are straightforward linear strings of DNA, mitochondrial DNA is formed into a circle, which is a hangover from when the mitochondria themselves were free-living bacteria. The human mitochondrial DNA circle is exactly 16,589 DNA bases in length, but fortunately it is unnecessary to read the entire sequence. Most of the mitochondrial DNA circle is taken up with genes that code for the enzymes involved in aerobic metabolism, which is the prime function of mitochondria in the cell. Because these enzymes have a very particular structure, decided by their amino-acid sequence, mutations in the genes which alter the amino-acid sequence almost always diminish or destroy the enzyme activity. The individuals who are unfortunate enough to experience these mutations in their mDNA usually die. Aerobic metabolism is such a vital part of life that we cannot tolerate even the slightest malfunction. The genetic result is that because these individuals rarely live long enough to have any children, the mutations are not passed on to future generations. If all mDNA mutations behaved like this, we would never find any genetic differences between individuals and it would be quite useless as a guide to the past because everybody's mDNA would be the same. However, fortunately for our purposes, not all mDNA does code for these vital metabolic enzymes.

Approximately 1,000 of the 16,589 DNA bases in the mDNA circle have a different function altogether, one that does not depend on the precise sequence. This stretch of DNA is called the 'control region' because it controls the way mDNA copies itself during cell division. Fortunately for us, part of this control region comprises a stretch of 400 bases whose precise sequence is unimportant. It is really just a piece of genetic padding. It must be there and it must be 400 bases long for the control region to work properly, but it doesn't seem to matter what these 400 bases actually are. This is the complete opposite to the parts of mDNA that code for the metabolic enzymes, which, as we have seen, need to have a very particular sequence. The vital consequence for us of this tolerance in the DNA sequence of the control region is that when a mutation happens it doesn't affect the performance of the mitochondria at all. Instead of killing the individual who carries it, the control-region mutations just carry on unnoticed through the generations, and we can find them.

During our work in Europe it was the mDNA sequences that we found in the control region that showed us that there were seven principal groups. Within each group, everybody shared a particular set of control-region mutations. The notation that we used to describe these mutations was as simple as we could make it. We chose one particular sequence as our 'reference sequence'. If we use the metaphor of DNA as a word, then the reference sequence is its standard spelling. The sequence we chose as the standard was the one we most frequently encountered in Europe. If a particular mDNA sequence differed from the reference at the 126th base of the 400 in the control region, then it was denoted simply as 126. If there was another mutation at the 294th position, then the notation became 126, 294. We found a lot of people who shared this particular combination of mutations and they formed one of our seven groups. In other groups there were different sets of 'signature' mutations. However, within the groups like the one defined by mutations at 126 and 294, there were plenty of other mutations as well. While about a third of people within the group had just the bare minimum of 126, 294, the rest had one, two, three or even more additional mutations.

By looking for the signature mutations it was fairly easy to place any individual DNA into one of the seven groups. Occasionally we would find individuals where one of the signature mutations had changed back to the original reference, but on the whole it was quite straightforward. But what did these groups actually signify? It had to mean that everyone within the same group must be related to one another through their matrilineal ancestors, which was the line we were following with mDNA. If two people in the same group had been able to follow their maternal ancestry back in time through their mothers and their mother's mothers and so on, at some point they would converge. There would have been a woman living in the past who was the common ancestor of both of them. It then struck me, after what now feels like an embarrassingly long time, that if this worked for two people in the same clan it must, by an inevitable logic, also work for the entire clan. If one were to trace back *all* the maternal lines of everybody within each clan, they would end up with just one woman. There was no alternative. Amazing as it sounds, this has to be true.

I realized at once that these clan mothers, as I called them, were not some kind of theoretical ancestors, but real living, breathing women. No, not just women, they were mothers as well. Mothers who had survived and whose children, or at least whose daughters, had survived and who in turn had survived and had daughters and so on, right down to the present day. Though men have mDNA, they do not pass it on to their children, but they do inherit it from their mothers. Originally to emphasize to myself that these clan mothers were real individuals, I gave them names, each of which began with the letter by which the seven different groups were by then known among scientists. So the clan mother of Group H became Helena, T became Tara, J became Jasmine, X became Xenia, V became Velda, K became Katrine and U became Ursula. Over 95 per cent of native Europeans are in one of the seven maternal clans, and so it followed that these seven women were the maternal ancestors of almost all Europeans. As soon as I had given them names, they came alive and I had to know more about them. I became quite desperate to build up a picture of their lives. I wanted to know all there was to know about these seven women, the women who soon came to be known as the Seven Daughters of Eve.

The first thing I wanted to know was how long ago these seven women had lived. Were we talking about hundreds, or thousands, or tens of thousands of years ago? The answer came by looking at the extra mutations within the clan. Taking the clan defined by the signature mutations at 126 and 294, which is the clan of Tara and the one to which I belong, everyone within the clan shares these two mutations, for the simple reason that Tara herself had these mutations and everyone in the clan is one of her direct matrilineal descendants. These two mutations have come down through the generations unchanged from the clan mother herself. But how many generations? How long ago did Tara live? That is where the additional mutations come in. Although roughly a third of people in Tara's clan have only these two mutations, the rest have additional changes. I have one extra mutation, at position 292, which makes my mDNA sequence 126, 292, 294. Other members of the clan have experienced more mutations. All these additional mutations *must* have occurred since Tara's time. Fortunately we know the mutation rate for the mDNA control region. It is approximately one change every 20,000 years. Since mutations happen completely randomly, not every line of descent from Tara will experience the same number of mutations. Some may be spared altogether and retain just the signature mutations at 126 and 294. Some maternal lines, like mine, will have been hit once since Tara's time, others more than once, some not at all. By working out the *average* number of additional mutations within the clan, we can then estimate how old the clan is, or, to put it another way, how long ago Tara herself lived. For her clan, the average number of additional mutations within the clan is almost exactly 0.85. With a mutation rate of 1 change per 20,000 years, the conclusion is that Tara lived 17,000 years ago.

Repeating the same calculations for the other six clans, we arrive at estimates for the ages of the other clan mothers. The clan with the greatest number of additional mutations on top of the clan mother's signature sequence is Ursula's. Hers is therefore the oldest of the seven clans. The average number of extra mutations in the clan is 2.75, and factoring in the mutation rate, this means that Ursula herself lived 45,000 years ago. Xenia is the next oldest at 25,000 years, Helena next at 20,000 years, then Velda and Tara both at 17,000 years, Katrine slightly younger at 15,000 years and finally Jasmine at 10,000 years ago.

Working out how long ago these women lived was a big step to discovering what their lives were like. Now I knew when they lived, could I discover where? I used three tests to find out. First, knowing the current whereabouts of the clan throughout Europe, I discovered where the clan was concentrated, reasoning that even after so many thousands of years, this might still be close to its origin. However, more important was to plot where the clan had accumulated the most additional mutations. The reasoning here was that the clan would have had longest to 'age' close to its origin, where the clan mother herself lived. To give you an example, the clan of Velda reaches its highest frequency in two places – northern Spain and among the Saami of northern Scandinavia. But it is far more varied, in the sense that it has accumulated far more extra mutations, in Spain than in Lapland. So I placed Velda herself in northern Spain, rather than in the far north of Norway and Sweden. Which brings me on to the third test. The location of the clan mother has to have been habitable at the time. In Velda's case, we know from the archaeological records that people were living in northern Spain 17,000 years ago, the date estimated from the additional mutations in the clan, but they were certainly not living in northern Scandinavia, which was under several kilometres of ice. By the same process, the other clan mothers were located to Greece (Ursula), the Caucasus mountains (Xenia), southern France (Helena), northern Italy (Katrine and Tara) and finally Syria in the Middle East (Jasmine).

With information from climate records and the archaeological evidence, I was able to find out what conditions must have been like for these women living at these locations at those times in the past. I discovered what their landscape was like, what sort of diet they had, what age they reached and, armed with this information, I wrote imagined lives for them.

Since they were published, the response has been both surprising and intriguing. My laboratory was overwhelmed by requests from all over the world from people who wanted to know from which of these women they were themselves descended. We had already repeated the process worldwide and found a total of thirty-six equivalent clans, so we could deal with requests from anywhere. We could not possibly handle this demand in the lab, if only because we were prevented from carrying on any commercial activities by the rules of our principal sponsors, the Wellcome Trust. So the University rapidly formed a spin-off company, Oxford Ancestors, to perform this service. But that is of only passing interest compared to the quite extraordinary underlying emotion that the concept clearly aroused. It proved to me that to many people, of which I am one, the idea that within each of our body cells we carry a tangible fragment from an ancestor from thousands of years ago is both astonishing and profound. That these pieces of DNA have travelled over thousands of miles and thousands of years to get to us, virtually unchanged, from our remote ancestors still fills me with awe, and I am not alone. One unexpected effect is that when two people discover that they are both in the same clan, they really do feel like close relatives, like cousins or siblings. I have seen this happen time and again, and indeed on the Oxford Ancestors website one of the most popular activities is discovering genetic relatives and then swapping personal information and often finding uncanny similarities of personality and circumstance. Even if this is all retrospective wisdom, after the test rather than before, the strength of feeling is very strong. There are even Jasmine parties organized by members of the clan.

I recently tested the DNA of our Vice-Chancellor, the executive head of Oxford University – I rarely travel anywhere without a DNA sampling brush – and discovered that he and I are not only in the same clan of Tara, but have exactly the same mDNA sequence 126, 292, 294. This means that as well as a common ancestor 17,000 years ago in Tara herself, we must share a much more recent maternal ancestor. I don't know who that is, but the point of the story is that, for better or worse, I feel now very differently about the Vice-Chancellor. So much so that, were we to have a severe disagreement, it would be hard for me to take it quite so seriously. It would be like arguing with my cousin.

A few years later, the same treatment became possible for the Y-chromosome. The details of the genetic changes were slightly different, and we will see how in a later chapter, but the principle remains the same. Whereas there are seven maternal clans which predominate in western Europe, there are only five principal paternal clans defined by the Y-chromosome. Each of these began with just one man, but for reasons that will become clear, it is much harder to know when and where they might have lived.

7

THE NATURE OF THE EVIDENCE

The collection phase of the Isles research project began ten years ago, in 1996, under the title of the Oxford Genetic Atlas Project. I obtained ethical permission to collect DNA samples from volunteers with the specific objective of discovering more about our genetic history. Over the next few years, my research team and I worked our way all over the Isles. We collected over 10,000 DNA samples and travelled over 80,000 miles by train, plane, boat, car and bus. Eventually I had to draw a line under the collection phase and concentrate on distilling some meaning from the thousands of DNA samples that now lay crowded in the lab freezers. We had been putting them through the analytical procedures more or less as they were being collected, converting the drab white threads of DNA into the sequences which would, or so we dearly hoped, hold the secrets of the ancient people of the Isles. Displayed on a computer screen they looked detached, dead – nothing like the talismans of ancient histories that I hoped they would become.

It took a lot of mental effort constantly to remind myself that every single one of these strings of letters and numbers represented the journey of an ancestor. A journey that at one stage almost certainly involved a sea crossing in a fragile craft to landfall on the Isles and an uncertain future. Fantastic though it sounds, it had to be true that each one of the thousands upon thousands of read-outs that flashed from the analyser to the computer in a fraction of a second had been carried across the sea in the cells of an ancestor. How could I get these mute listings to tell me their stories? How could I get them to sing? If only, I thought one day, I could read in the letters of the genetic code the language of the bearer. How wonderful that would be – and how much easier than the task that lay ahead. If, just by looking, I could recognize a Gaelic word or a Saxon spelling somewhere in the sequence of DNA letters. But the genes were stubbornly silent, oblivious to the tongues of their bearers.

Mathematicians have devised a whole array of statistical tests to sieve through DNA results, mechanically and without feeling. Indeed, most scientific papers on this kind of genetics spend at least half the time agonizing over what is the correct statistical treatment. It is necessary, if only to get results published, to know how to do this and fortunately we had in the lab several people skilled in the art. They, in particular Eileen, Jayne and Sara, put the accumulating genetic data through their paces. They ran Hudson tests, Mantel tests, distance-based clustering analyses, drew genetic matrices based on Fst and Nei's D, performed spatial auto-correlation tests and many more. Here are some of the results that came screaming out of the computer. It is a set of genetic comparisons from mitochondrial DNA between the four regions of the Isles.

Ireland/Wales	0.0726741243702487
Ireland/Scotland	0.0625191372016303
Ireland/England	0.1170327104307371
Wales/Scotland	0.0662071306520113
Wales/England	0.0980420127467032
Scotland/England	0.1023741618921030

You do not need to know what these mean, and I hope you do not want to. Even as I write them down, I can feel I am being drawn away from the real lives of these genes into some grey underworld where everything becomes a number. The genes are submitting to this cruel procedure, but they will never sing again. Now they are processed into numbers, with so many decimal places that they assume an importance way above their true worth. It feels as though I have handed them on to a windowless world which has severed any contact with the sea and the wind. Once a number is produced, something, perhaps everything, of value has been lost. Like so many tabulations, the numbers disguise individual stories of heroism and betrayal, triumph and defeat, and force them into bleak summaries. This is no way to treat our ancestors and you will be glad that I shall not insult them, or you, in this way again.

Since every ancestor was an individual, I was determined to treat the DNA sequences as individuals. Each one had, at some time, set off from some distant land and stepped ashore on the Isles, soaked with salt spray and red-faced from the cold. I decided that, if I possibly could, I would not treat these as anything but individual journeys undertaken with deliberate purpose and not to be grouped together in clumsy approximations. I covered the walls around my desk with photographs of the coast and the sea, of the Isles from the savage Atlantic to the smooth sands of Kent. Whenever I was tempted to revert to orthodox analysis I would glance upwards and remember to tread more carefully.

Finally, I had nearly 6,000 different pieces of genetic information from volunteers all over the Isles, each one linked to a geographical origin. By the time I came to write *Blood of the Isles*, I could add in another 25,000 genetic messages from among the customers of Oxford Ancestors. I contacted colleagues whom I knew had similar genetic information from the Isles and from other parts of Europe. I trawled all the relevant publications for material. When I finally settled down to listen to the music of the genes I had over 50,000 DNA sequences to work with.

For two solid weeks over Christmas I sat down to get to know these details. Fortunately, the weather was awful. It was raining constantly and was very, very windy. I live close to a sea loch in Skye and, when the wind is strong and in the south-west, blowing straight in from the North Atlantic, it descends in howling gusts from the Cuillin Hills. These winds tumble off the main ridge of the mountains and roll down the loch, pulling the top layer of water into the air in spiral twists of spray. The oddest thing about these winds is their intermittence. The air is calm, windless and then you hear an approaching roar and it is upon you and so strong it is almost impossible to stand upright. Then, after five minutes' battering, it is gone. After another few minutes the sequence begins all over again. The alternating spells of chaos and calm can go on for hours. Hours well suited to going through thousands of sequences one by one, giving each one a different name and a different number. The coal fire burns well and the smoke is only very rarely forced back down the chimney.

This is how I got to know the data. Thanks to a mapping program written by a colleague, I could quickly place any selection of DNA sequences on a map of the Isles. As I did this I soon noticed that some DNA sequences were found in all parts of the Isles, while others were very localized. For instance, I had found one particular mDNA sequence in the clan of Tara four times in Skye, once in Lewis in the Western Isles and once in Glasgow – and nowhere else in the world. When I looked up in my records where on Skye the four people lived, I saw they came from different parts of the island. But all traced their maternal ancestry back to the Isle of Rona.

Drive to the north end of Skye past the eroded cliffs and pinnacles of Trotternish, high above the sea, and Rona is the low rocky island on your right, lying 5 miles offshore. It looks as if it is connected to the longer, higher island of Raasay to the south, but it is not. A hidden sea channel separates the two islands. Rona is deserted now, but once held a few crofting families who fished in the dark blue seas. Their houses have been abandoned and only the lighthouse, white against the rocks, is visible from Skye.

What must have happened on Rona to account for the unusual DNA I had found on Skye was a mutation, a slight change in the DNA of one of the ancestors. Silent, unnoticed and with no effect at all on the woman in whom this event had occurred, just one DNA base, one bead on the chain, had changed. The new sequence was unique, never seen before in the history of the world. If this woman had been childless or had only sons, it would have died with her. No one would ever know it had been created. But she must have had children, and at least one of her children must have been a girl for her mDNA to be passed on. Through this girl, or her descendants, this new sequence left the island of Rona and found a home on nearby Skye, where it still remains. From there, perhaps one of the daughters in the next generation went to live on Lewis while another travelled down to Glasgow. I cannot tell exactly when this happened, but the journeys have been recorded by the genes of the descendants. I have not found this particular sequence of DNA letters anywhere else. Nor has anyone as far as I am aware. That doesn't mean it isn't there in other parts of Scotland, or Ireland, or Wales, or England. Just that we haven't found it. That is always the way, and always will be. We will never know everything there is to know about this new gene and what happened to it. We can only piece together something of its journey from the scraps of information that have both survived to the present day and that we have found in the cells of people we have tested.

This is a little story of one particular gene, a new version that has changed very slightly. If we ever do come across it again in the future, we will know it has travelled from Rona. It is a fragment, like a piece of pottery or a flint tool, and just as reliant on the twin necessities of survival and discovery as any archaeological remains. This is how I would build the genetic history of the Isles, by sifting through the thousands of fragments, trying to make sense of them. I would treat them as if they were the scattered shards of broken pottery and do what I could to understand what they meant. This was the point at which I decided to become a genetic archaeologist. I would work with fragments of DNA, perfectly preserved in the bodies of descendants, to reconstruct the travels of their ancestors with the same discipline that an archaeologist would use when excavating a site. Collect, examine, record, compare, interpret. In my mind's eye, even though they were in reality stored on my computer, I began to think of them as, literally, a pile of fragments, pottery perhaps or maybe coins. Yes, coins would be an even better metaphor. Through Chris Howgego, a friend and colleague from Oxford, I had been allowed to examine the Ashmolean Museum's collection of ancient gold coins from Britain. Many are over 2,000 years old but still fresh and lustrous, stamped with the image of an ancient tribal king or the stylized outline of a horse, a chariot wheel or an ear of wheat. I would set out to use the genes to interpret the past, just as Chris Howgego used his coins.

Of course they would tell very different stories. Coins and genes are not the same, but neither are they so very different. Both have to obey the rules of survival and discovery and, in the case of gold coins at least, both had been preserved virtually intact. Both bore inscriptions, either the name of a king or the sequence of a piece of DNA. A coin from a distant land discovered in Britain is a witness to a journey made, just as much as a fragment of mDNA must have made its way to the Isles at some time in the past in the cells of an ancestor. Coins have one thing that is conspicuously lacking in DNA and that is a date. Though the Iron Age coins in the Ashmolean Museum do not have a calendar date impressed on them, their date of manufacture can be worked out from the tribal chief whose image or inscription is on the coin. For example, several are inscribed with the letters CVNO, denoting that they were minted during the reign of Cunobelinus, King of the Catuvellauni some time between 60 and 41 BC.

With DNA we are not quite so fortunate. It does not bear a date stamp, but there is information on time depth to be had along the same lines that we have already used when working out how long ago the clan mothers lived. We can get an idea, though only an approximate one, of how long a group of mDNA or Y-chromosome 'gene-coins' has been in a location by seeing how they differ from one another. But it can be tricky, as we will find out.

I decided to excavate my first pile of 'gene-coins' from the results of the Genetic Atlas Project and I would begin with the mDNA, those fragments of history that have been passed down in the bodies of women. To begin with I did what anybody would do with a pile of gene-coins. I counted them. I had a total of 3,686. I imagined a large outline map of the Isles spread out in front of me ready for me to place each gene-coin in its correct location. But before distributing them, I sorted the large pile out into smaller groups of different types, depending on their clan. Once I decided on that course, the way forward became a little bit easier to imagine. I could now abandon the manacles of conventional statistical analysis and approach my reconstruction of past events as a genetic archaeologist. That meant, for one thing, that I could give up trying to know everything, and also stop pretending that giving answers to sixteen decimal places means anything at all.

Historians and archaeologists realized this a long time ago and make do with what they have, while being on the lookout for new material. Geneticists do not naturally think like that. They are not natural storytellers. If a geneticist does not get a watertight answer after an experiment or a survey of some kind, he or she will go back to the drawing board rather than risk saying anything that might be shown later to be wrong. If it is a survey and 1,000 samples have failed to produce a statistically significant result, our training tells us to say nothing and increase the number to 10,000, and if that doesn't work to 100,000. Having reinvented myself as a genetic archaeologist, I was free to do my best to tell the story of the Isles in my own way with what data are available. The account will never be complete, even if I were to double or quadruple the number of DNA samples. Also, even though I knew perfectly well that I would have to do the actual operations on my computer, the vision of the gene-coins as tangible objects which could be picked up and examined and then moved into position on a map was unexpectedly reassuring. I had rescued the project from the number-crunchers.

What did the pile of gene-coins look like? It was easy to decide on how to create the different piles. I would arrange them according to their maternal clan. I can tell the maternal clan of one mDNA sequence from the combination of mutations that it has. If I see the combination 126, 294 I know I am dealing with a member of Tara's clan. If the sequence contains 256, 270 this is the mDNA of an Ursulan, and so on. These mutations became the inscriptions on the gene-coins and the portraits changed from tribal chieftains to the rough profiles of the seven matriarchs, Ursula, Xenia, Helena, Velda, Tara, Katrine or Jasmine.

In my mind the action moved to a baize-covered table. I soon sorted the large pile into smaller ones, one for each maternal clan. In the largest of these clan piles I had 1,799 gene-coins with the profile of Helena. The next biggest was the 434 in Jasmine's pile, followed in sequence by 384 Tarans, 284 Katrines, 264 Xenias, 207 Ursulans and lastly 116 Veldans.

But there were still a lot of gene-coins that remained in the unattributed pile. I looked at the portraits and the inscriptions. These were of other matriarchs, not the Seven Daughters of Eve, but ones I still recognized. The most common were the gene-coins belonging to the matriarch Ulrike. There were 101 in all, only a few short of the Veldans. I had not included Ulrike as one of the what would then have been Eight Daughters of Eve because, in the research in Europe, the clan of Ulrike was considerably less frequent than the other seven in the regions we had surveyed, which were mainly the southern and western parts. As more information came in from Scandinavia and eastern Europe, we saw more and more members of Ulrike's clan. I've wondered since whether Ulrike should be promoted, as it were, into the select group of clan mothers.

But even with the Ulrikans now separated from the rest, there were still quite a few gene-coins in the pile. They were an exotic collection, from matriarchs all over the world. I stacked them together for now. There were ninety-seven in all. These, then, were the fragments with which to build the genetic history as told by women.

On the male side I had 2,414 Y-chromosome gene-coins from the Genetic Atlas Project and began to sort these into different piles according to their clans. Though the genetic details were displayed in a different form, the principle was the same. Each clan, of which there were five major ones in the Isles, traced a direct patrilineal line of descent right back to a common ancestor, the man who had founded the clan. In the Isles, these were the clans of Oisin (pronounced Osheen), Wodan, Sigurd, Eshu and Re.

Even though I knew full well that the gene-coins did not exist in reality, the concept gave me a lot of confidence. I began to relish the prospect of trying my best to interpret them and what they told of the past, rather than despairing as I had been up to then. Now, at last, I was mentally ready to launch into the final stages of the project. It was now as an archaeologist that I settled down to explore the Blood of the Isles.

8
IRELAND

The Irish landscape has often been compared to a bowl. A broad central limestone plain dotted by lakes and peat bogs and drained by sluggish rivers is surrounded by coastal ranges of hills and mountains. This upland barrier is only breached to any significant extent around the capital, Dublin. The total land area is 32,000 square miles (26,600 in the Republic and 5,400 in Ulster). The highest peaks, Lugnaquillia (926 metres) in the Wicklow Mountains south of the capital and Carrantuohill (1,041 metres) in Kerry, are on a par with the tallest mountains in Wales and England but well below many of the highest peaks in Scotland. In the west, the mountains thrust out long fingers into the Atlantic Ocean, creating a series of deep bays between, many of them now flooded river valleys. In the far south-west these rocky fingers are formed by parallel folds of sedimentary old red sandstone, like parts of northern Scotland, but further north in Galway, Mayo and Donegal, as well as in the Wicklow Mountains to the east, the rock is granite, the weathered remnants of once-molten magma forced to the surface by ancient movements of the earth's crust. On the eastern coast, facing Britain, the coastline is more orderly, without the drama or the dangers of the stormbound west.

As in the rest of the Isles, the landscape has been sculpted by ice. During the last glaciations, the ice covered only the northern half, extending as far as a line between Limerick in the west and Dublin in the east, but earlier Ice Ages enveloped the entire land in their frozen grip. The scouring of the central lowland plateau created the bedrock upon which the great peat bogs later grew and which, later still, provided the main supply of fuel for generations of rural households. The ice also ground the limestone base into a powder which formed the most important element of Irish soil. Without the glacial limestone powder to enrich it, the soil, made up of the weathering from older rocks like quartzite, granite and shale, would be infertile and unproductive like so much of the Scottish Highlands. But limestone gives it life, and thanks to this essential enrichment, and to the high rainfall, Ireland has thrived on its green pastures. Without the limestone, Ireland would not be the Emerald Isle, but the Brown.

On the 'Irish History' shelves of any high-street bookshop, the titles on display are dominated by the political struggles of the last hundred years. Books abound on the Easter Rising of 1916, alongside biographies of Michael Collins, Eamon de Valera and other heroes in the struggle for independence from Britain. A struggle which continues to this day, as Republicans strive to unite Ireland into the single nation it once was. As I write, in 2007, the intensity of the cycle of violence and recrimination has all but disappeared. Earlier this year, in a political accord no one thought possible even six months before, the leaders of Sinn Fein and the Democratic Unionist Party, the two most polarised political opposites in Northern Ireland, agreed to share power in a devolved assembly. Peace, for the time being at least, has been restored. The roots of this struggle go back a very long way and, though *Blood of the Isles* is certainly not a political history, it is as well to be aware of events which may have had some influence on the genetic patterns we are setting out to interpret.

The current struggles for Irish political unity and independence are but the latest stages in a chain of events that began over 800 years ago when, in the autumn of 1171, Henry II, the Anglo-Norman king of England, landed in Ireland to make sure that it did not become a rival Norman state to his own. Five years earlier, the ambitious Richard de Clare, Earl of Pembroke, himself an Anglo-Norman, had responded to an invitation by one of the numerous Irish kings, Dermot MacMurrough, whose lands in the Leinster had been seized by the High King, Rory O'Connor. This was a classic situation, seen many times before and since, where an invitation by a dispossessed or threatened king is used as a cover for invasion. De Clare, whose sobriquet 'Strongbow' adequately describes his attitude to conquest, seized the chance and established a secure foothold in Wexford and the south-east part of Ireland which faced his base in Pembroke, only 40 miles by sea. His military campaigns were extremely effective, thanks largely to the superior weapons he brought across. Heavily armoured knights, especially when mounted on horseback, easily overcome the local opposition armed only with light bows and spears.

Anxious that de Clare's success did not lead to the establishment of a rival kingdom, Henry arrived to impose his authority. This he did by granting Leinster to de Clare and County Meath to one of his own commanders, Hugh de Lacy, while at the same time forcing the remaining Irish kings into various forms of submission, including the obligation of giving forty days' military service and requiring Henry's permission to marry. From then until 6 December 1921, when three of the four provinces broke away from British rule to become the Irish Free State, Ireland's history and its fortunes were tied to England's. The name changed to Eire in 1937 and, finally, became the fully independent Republic of Ireland in 1948.

The occupation of Ireland by the English between these dates was never entirely convincing and oscillated between periods of calm indifference and others of turmoil and ruthless exploitation. The exclusion of Ulster from the Irish Free State was the visible residue of the Protestant Ascendancy which followed the defeat by William of Orange of James II at the battle of the Boyne in 1690. This well-remembered and, in Ulster, celebrated victory was the culmination of centuries of rebellions and uprisings within Ireland against the influence of England. In Ireland, not only the Gaelic lords but also the descendants of the Anglo-Normans frequently found their lands confiscated as, from the time of Elizabeth I, they were granted as plantations to favourites and adventurers. The policy was continued by Elizabeth's successor James I of England (James VI of Scotland), who encouraged the large-scale settlement of Ulster by lowland Scots. From the genetic point of view, what distinguishes this episode from what had gone before is that, instead of estates merely changing hands from one member of the aristocracy to another with little effect on the majority of the population, the plantation of Ulster imported tenant farmers and labourers from Scotland to work the land. The earlier Anglo-Normans had not as a rule imported their labour force, so we would not expect any genetic influence to be felt especially strongly. However, in Ulster we need to be aware of the possible effects of the plantations on the genetic patterns.

Before we leave the turbulent centuries of Irish history, there is one more episode that we must not forget. So far we have only mentioned immigration into Ireland, by Anglo-Normans at first and then through the plantations. But these are numerically dwarfed by the departures. Religious intolerance and persecution from the sixteenth century onwards, closely coupled to land seizure, drove many Catholic landowners abroad, mainly to France and Spain. Though doubtless traumatic for them, these exiles did not really affect ordinary Irish agricultural workers, for whom life continued much as before, though the land was under new ownership. However, in the nineteenth century, Irish emigration on a large scale began in earnest.

In the first decades of the century, agricultural prices fell, estate rentals declined, investment in the land was reduced to a trickle, and the rural population grew. Whatever the ultimate causes of this cycle of economic decline, the effects on the rural poor were catastrophic. Reduced to almost complete dependence on the potato as the staple crop, the countryside was decimated when the crop was infested with the potato blight and rotted in the ground. During the Great Famine of the mid 1840s, thousands died of starvation or of the infectious diseases which swept through the malnourished population. Though many thousands died, thousands also made their escape. Ireland's mid-nineteenth-century population of 8 million began a steady decline that has only very recently stabilized at 4.1 million in the Republic and 1.7 million in Ulster. The desparate diaspora of the Irish saw massive immigration both to Britain and to the New World, especially the United States. Today, there are far more 'Irish' genes abroad than there are in Ireland itself.

Though Ireland is not yet united into a single political state, the poverty and suffering which suffuse all accounts of the history of the last centuries cannot be equated with Ireland today. The economy is transformed. The bars and cafés of Dublin are as lively and as sophisticated as anywhere in Europe. There is a tangible feeling of optimism in the air wherever you go. Though we will have to wait to see how much of the turmoil of past centuries is remembered by the genes, I suspect the main effect will be of emigration and the dispersal of Irish genes around the globe. Now that the future of Ireland as an independent country is looking so good, this is the time to move the sad centuries to one side and examine Ireland before the day when Henry II arrived to begin the English occupation. That is where we must seek to interpret the patterns of the genes. What do we know of these earlier times?

The appeal that Dermot MacMurrough made to Richard de Clare to come to his aid, the appeal de Clare used as an excuse to invade, is a clear indication of the state of affairs in medieval Ireland – the struggle for dominance of one minor king against another. It is so very typical of the middle stage of evolution of any modern society and one that is only too visible in other parts of the world. Except that in those places, like Afghanistan or unstable African countries, these men are not dignified with the title 'king' but denigrated as 'warlords'. In Ireland during the first millennium AD there was a constant struggle for dominance between different minor kings. According to one source, there may have been 150 of them at any one time, lending some credibility to the common Irish boast that they are all descended from lines of Irish kings. This may be something we can test as it could be visible in the Y-chromosome gene pool by what has come to be known as the 'Genghis Khan effect'.

A few years ago, researchers from Oxford found a Y-chromosome that was very widespread throughout Asia, more or less within the geographical limits of the Mongol Empire. Finding a particular Y-chromosome with a specific fingerprint across such a wide area is highly unusual. Y-chromosomes are generally much more localized. The explanation, which I think is the correct one, is that this is the Y-chromosome of the first Mongol emperor, Genghis Khan, who lived in the first half of the thirteenth century. Not only is the Y-chromosome fingerprint geographically dispersed, it is also very common. In Mongolia, for example, 8 per cent of men have inherited the Genghis chromosome. If you compute the number of men who carry this Y-chromosome throughout Asia, and occasionally on other continents, then it comes to a staggering 16 million. Even a cursory glance at Genghis Khan's methods in warfare is enough to understand the genetic mechanism. On conquering an enemy's territory he would kill all the men, then systematically inseminate all the good-looking women – he left his commanders strict instructions on that point. When he died, the custom of patrilineal inheritance ensured that his empire was distributed among his sons, and their sons. Thus his Y-chromosome increased with each generation of male descendants, who inherited not only a portion of his wealth but also, presumably, his attitude to women. Though we have no historical records of men with quite such sexual predominance in the Isles, the confusion of minor kings is just the sort of condition where one might expect to discover the Genghis effect.

It was not all chaos in Ireland. Some kings managed to exert sufficient authority to stake a claim to the title of High King and to be installed at the sacred site of Tara, about 20 miles north of Dublin. Though none of the High Kings ever managed complete dominance over the whole island, some had a very good try and this may well be reflected in an Irish Genghis Khan effect. While such behaviour may rearrange the genes of Ireland, or anywhere else in the Isles for that matter, it is however only a rearrangement. While the Genghis effect will mean that one, or a few, Y-chromosomes may prosper at the expense of others, no amount of Khan-like behaviour can actually create new Y-chromosomes. And it has no effect whatsoever on the maternal lineages, traced by mitochondrial DNA. These will persist whatever the kings get up to.

Peering further back into the Irish past, what can we see that needs to be taken into account? Though it was Ireland's misfortune to be occupied by the English for so long, it entirely avoided being conquered by the Romans, which large swathes of Britain did not. Ireland was very lucky to escape. The Roman historian Tacitus, in his account of the campaigns of his father-in-law Agricola, tells how the great general seriously contemplated an invasion. In his fifth year of campaigning in Britain, in AD 88, Agricola brought his army and his ships to Galloway in south-east Scotland, only 20 miles across the sea from Ireland. Such were the inaccuracies in the geography of the day that Agricola believed that Ireland was midway between Britain and the Roman province of Spain. So he could see the tactical advantages of including Ireland within the Empire. He had received favourable reports about the character and way of life of the inhabitants and of the soil and climate. To a Roman they did not differ much from the British, whom he had successfully subdued during the previous five years. Tacitus wrote that he often heard Agricola say that Ireland could be conquered, and held, with a single legion supported by a modest force of auxiliaries. Agricola even took the precaution of befriending a minor Irish king who had been exiled in case the opportunity to use him should arise. In the end he decided against an invasion. Tacitus does not say why and we can only guess. But that he had serious intent is certain.

One negative consequence of this lucky escape was that there are no written histories of Ireland from the Roman period. Not until the arrival of early Christians in the fifth century AD, and of St Patrick in particular, did written accounts, however unreliable, begin to appear. St Patrick himself is credited with the authorship of the earliest documents in Irish history, written in Latin: the *Confessions*, which defines and defends his mission, and one other, a short letter excommunicating the soldiers of a British chieftain who had murdered some of Patrick's converts. Neither account throws much light on life in Ireland at the time – nor was that the intention. None the less, the beatification of St Patrick and his emergence as the supreme cult figure, which in many ways he remains to this day, did lead to further accounts of his life and his Christian mission by later authors. The early ninth-century *Book of Armagh* is the culmination of these and it established the primacy of the See of Armagh in the Irish Church.

The three centuries following St Patrick's death in AD 493 are rightly regarded as a golden age in which Ireland became one of the most important religious centres in the whole of Europe. It was from Ireland that missionaries set out to convert the pagan tribes of northern Britain, establishing Columba's monastery on Iona in AD 563 as a stepping stone. From Iona the monastery of Lindisfarne, off the Northumbrian coast, continued the mission to the eastern side of Britain. Irish missions to continental Europe were equally successful and St Columban, not to be confused with Columba, founded monasteries at Luxeuil in the Vosges mountains of eastern France and at Bobbio in the hills of the northern Apennines in Italy in the late 600s. Other Irish monks sought the opposite – a life of austere contemplation – and their search for solitude took them to increasingly remote destinations. They found what they were looking for on rocky islands off the west coast of Ireland, in the Western Isles of Scotland and even as far north as Iceland. Their journeys across the wild seas are all the more remarkable for having been undertaken not in well-constructed galleys but in curraghs – light boats with only shallow drafts and made from wooden spars covered in tarred animal hide.

But still, despite the intensity of religious devotion and scholarship, the written accounts are more or less completely bare of historical content. Even so, it is fairly clear that the reputation of these early saints was linked to the fortunes of the political dynasties to which they became attached. An association with the cult figure of St Patrick himself was the ultimate claim to authority and influence, and the opportunity was not overlooked by the first of the invading Anglo-Normans. In 1185 one of these barons, John de Courcey, arranged for the 'discovery' of St Patrick's remains at Downpatrick and their removal to Armagh. This is very reminiscent of the fabricated discovery and ceremonial reburial of King Arthur's bones by Edward I at Glastonbury a century later. Clearly, in the medieval period, any association with long-dead cult figures could be used as a claim for historical legitimacy.

Rather as in England, with the loosely based fiction of Geoffrey of Monmouth, history was written for a purpose. The Irish equivalent of Geoffrey's *History* was the *Leabhar Gabhála*, the *Book of Invasions*, compiled from earlier writing in the late eleventh century. Even though, just like Geoffrey's *History*, it is a clear attempt to link Irish history to the familiar events of the classical world, it managed to create a compelling narrative for the origins of Ireland and of the Gaels which became extremely influential as an origin myth for the Irish. And it still is. However accurate or inaccurate it may be as a record of Irish origins, we must still bear it in mind when we sift the record of the genes. Deeply held origin myths, however richly embroidered, have a habit of being right.

Although the *Leabhar Gabhála* was doubtless compiled by Christian monastic scribes, in common with the written versions of other rich mythologies in Ireland, there was no conflict or contradiction in recording the pagan myths of their native or adopted land. The phenomenal success of Irish Christianity owed a great deal to the sympathy it showed to ancient traditions and rituals and to their preservation in written form. The Irish Christian monks became the conduit of ancient knowledge, the *filidh*, and their success lay in their ability to create a seamless continuity between the rich mythical traditions of pagan Ireland and full-blown Christianity.

From our point of view, the *Leabhar Gabhála* chronicles four mythical phases of immigration. As you can imagine, all four involve great battles and heroic struggles as each wave of new arrivals ousts the former occupants. The last of these phases was the invasion of Ireland by the Gaels, bringers of the language and the alleged ancestors of today's Celtic population. Indeed the principal purpose of the *Leabhar Gabhála* is to explain the presence of the Gaels in Ireland.

According to the *Leabhar*, the Gaels were descended from the sons of Mil, also variously known as Milesius and later by the, perhaps significant, epithet of Míle Easpain, or the 'Soldier of Spain'. Mil was killed on an expedition to avenge the death of a nephew who had been killed by the Tuatha Dé Danaan, the previous occupiers and masters of Ireland. It was left to Mil's three sons, Eber, Eremon and Amairgen, to defeat the Tuatha and conquer Ireland. When the brothers could not agree on the division of the island between them, Eber was killed by Eremon, who became the first High King to reign at Tara. Mil's wife, Scota, was also killed in the expedition and the Gaels of Ireland, considering her to be their ancestral mother, called themselves Scots for that reason. Certainly the Romans referred to them as *Scotti* as well as the more familiar *Hibernii*.

According to legend, the ultimate ancestor was one Fennius Farsa, a Scythian king who lost his throne and fled to Egypt. Ancient Scythia was located north of the Black Sea in what is now the eastern Ukraine, between the two great rivers, the Don and the Dnieper. Once in Egypt his son, Nial, married the pharaoh's daughter, and she had a son, Goidel. The whole family was banished from Egypt for refusing to join in the persecution of the children of Israel and wandered throughout northern Africa, finally crossing the Pillars of Hercules to settle in Spain, where they prospered.

Many years later, from a watchtower on a cliff top, one of Goidel's descendants, Ith, saw a land far off across the seas that he had not noticed before. 'It is on winter evenings, when the air is pure, that man's eyesight reaches farthest,' explains the account of the vision in the *Leabhar Gabhála*. Although it is quite impossible ever to see Ireland from Spain, Ith wasn't to know this and he set sail with ninety warriors to explore the newly sighted country. He arrived at the mouth of the River Kenmare, one of the deep indentations in the coast at the extreme south-west of Ireland. From there, Ith tracked northwards until, at last, he encountered the Tuatha Dé Danaan, the race who inhabited Ireland. The meeting went well at first until the Tuatha began to doubt Ith's motives for sailing to Ireland and, from his fulsome descriptions of the climate and the fertility of land and sea, suspected that he intended to invade. They killed Ith, but spared his companions, who then returned to Spain with their leader's body. Ith's uncle Mil vowed to avenge his nephew's murder and set sail with his eight sons and their wives, accompanied by thirty-six chieftains, each with a ship full of warriors. With his sons at his side he defeated the Tuatha. Mil was himself killed in the battle, but his sons survived. The defeated Tuatha Dé Danaan also chose their name from their own ancestral mother, Dana. The Tuatha were a race of gods, each with their own special attributes and each as colourful as any gods of the classical Greeks. After their defeat by the Milesians, the Tuatha Dé Danaan fled to the Underworld and established a kingdom beneath the ground – a kingdom from where they were still able to harass their conquerors by depriving them of corn and milk, eventually forcing an agreement which divided Ireland into upper and lower parts and in which the Tuatha Dé Danaan are to this day the guardians of the Underworld.

In their own conquest of Ireland, the Tuatha Dé Danaan had ousted two groups of earlier occupants – the Fir Bholg and the Fomorians. After their defeat the Fir Bholg, a race of pre-Celtic humans, were banished to the Aran Islands in Galway Bay. Unfortunately, the *Leabhar Gabhála* does not say where the Fir Bholg had come from. The implication is that they had been there all the time. In this respect, the Fir Bholg resemble myths in other parts of the Isles about a race of aboriginal inhabitants, usually described as being short and dark, who were subsumed by later 'waves' of Celtic arrivals.

The Fomorians, being divine like the Tuatha Dé Danaan, were altogether more difficult to defeat. Led by the terrifying Balor of the Baleful Eye, whose gaze alone caused instant death, the Fomorians were a race of demons. Balor's one weakness was the prophecy that one day he would be slain by his own grandson. Despite hiding himself away on Tory Island off the Donegal coast and keeping his daughter away from men, she nonetheless became pregnant and bore triplets. Balor threw all three of his grandchildren into the sea, but one, called Lugh, survived. He grew up to lead the Tuatha Dé Danaan against the Fomorians and, in fulfilment of the prophecy, killed his grandfather Balor with a slingshot through his one, baleful, eye.

Lugh went on to feature in the best-known myths of the Ulster Cycle, which records the continual struggles of the *Ulaid*, the Ulstermen, against the neighbouring province of Connacht. He becomes one of the many suitors of the notoriously promiscuous Queen Medb. No man could rule in Tara without first mating with Queen Medb. Fiercely competitive, as well as promiscuous, Medb's rivalry with one of her many consorts, the King of Connacht, leads into the most famous of all Irish myths, the *Taín Bó Cúalnge*, the *Cattle Raid of Cooley*. At first sight, cattle raiding might appear to be too prosaic a topic for a major myth, but remember that cattle were as much a badge of prestige as gold or jewels. Cattle raiding was an endemic occupation in Ireland as elsewhere in the Isles – and it was a failed cattle raid which led indirectly to the defeat of the giant Albion by Hercules.

The *Taín Bó Cúalnge* begins as Medb and the King of Connacht, in bed one night, decide to compare their material assets to resolve which of them is the richer. One matches the other until only a single item separates them. Ailill, King of Connacht, is the owner of a magnificent white-horned bull Findbennach, something that Medb does not possess. In vain she searches her own lands for a beast of comparable magnificence. Then she hears of a great brown bull, Donn, and arranges to borrow it from its owner. Things start to go wrong when her soldiers brag that they could have seized the bull with or without the consent of the owner, who, overhearing their boasting, cancels the arrangement and hides the bull. Queen Medb decides on a disproportionate response and invades Ulster, precipitating a lengthy war between Connacht and Ulster. To escape the fighting, the great bull Donn is sent to Connacht for safety but, unwisely, bellows loudly as he arrives in his new home. His bellows disturb Findbennach, and he challenges Donn to a duel to the death. Their fight takes them all over Ireland until Donn eventually manages to impale his rival on his horns. Though he wins the contest, Donn does not survive to enjoy his victory and dies from exhaustion.

Forgive me for relating the *Taín Bó Cúalnge* at such length. It portrays the intense feuding and futile rivalry between the rulers of the different parts of Ireland more vividly than any purely historical account. And these are rivalries that might just have a genetic effect. The *Taín* also involves another super-hero of Irish myth, Cú Chulainn. The son of Lugh, slayer of Balor of the Baleful Eye, he is fostered as a child by two other heroes with somewhat exaggerated attributes. The first, Ferghus mac Roich, has the strength of 700 men and a prodigious appetite. He can consume seven pigs, seven deer, seven cows and seven barrels of liquor at one sitting – and he requires seven women at once to satisfy him. When Ferghus is killed, while bathing with Queen Medb and thus temporarily distracted, another hero, Conall Cernach, takes over as Cú Chulainn's foster-father.

Conall is the great champion of Ulster, who boasts that he never sleeps without the head of a Connachtman (severed presumably) resting beneath his knee. After foster-parenting like this, no wonder the boy grows up to be a super-hero. Naturally he is brave, beautiful, strong and invincible, and his chariot, helpfully, possesses an invisibility blanket to be used in the heat of battle. His weapons too are magical. His barbed spear, *Gae Bulga*, never wounds, only kills. In the war between Ulster and Connacht precipitated by Queen Medb's cattle raid, he kills vast numbers of her soldiers single-handed. His technique in battle is to transform himself into a berserk demon. His body spins round within his skin, his hair stands on end and one eye disappears into his head while the other bulges enormously. Small wonder his enemies are driven mad with terror.

Cú Chulainn is destined for a short though glorious life. By accidentally eating dog flesh one day, he breaks a vow that he made when a young man. His power drains away at the height of battle, his weapons fall at his feet and the Morrigan, a coven of divine destroyers, perch on his shoulder in raven form. Realizing he is no longer invincible, the Connachtmen pluck up the courage to approach and cut off his head.

As well as powerfully portraying the intense rivalries in early Ireland, the myths and heroes of the Ulster Cycle still exert their effect today. It is no coincidence that a bronze statue of Cú Chulainn, cast in 1916, the year of the Easter Rising, stands today in the hall of Dublin's main Post Office, which was itself the principal battleground of the Rising and the place where the Republicans held out for longest against the British. Myths are powerful things. And they often contain more than a grain of truth. But as well as these rich origin myths, there is an abundance of solid, archaeological evidence of Ireland's past.

The first signs of human occupation in Ireland are at Mount Sandel, situated on a bluff overlooking the River Bann in County Antrim. The site at Mount Sandel has all the signs of containing a substantial dwelling, with large numbers of round holes dug into the ground. Though these holes were filled by debris long ago, their outlines are clear. These are post-holes and they were dug to hold in place the wall timbers of a house. The wood itself has long since rotted, but the holes remain and, from their arrangement, the outline shape of the building can be made out. The house was round and, from the angle of the post-holes, the timbers were inclined inwards, suggesting a structure resembling a large tent 5.5 metres in diameter. Unsurprisingly, nothing remains of the roof, but plenty of later structures are known where the space between the roof timbers was covered by skins, twigs and reeds and there is no reason to think Mount Sandel was any different. Within the house there is a large square hole, probably a central hearth, and outside there are further pits, probably used for storage.

The large numbers and the variety of food remains found at Mount Sandel certainly suggest that it was used as a base camp throughout the year. There are hundreds of salmon bones, which show that the site was occupied in the summer when the salmon, fresh from the sea, pushed upstream to their spawning grounds. Huge numbers of hazelnuts and the seeds of water lilies, wild pear and crab apple show that the site was used during the autumn harvest of wild forest food. The remains of young pigs, which are born in the late autumn, are the sure sign of winter occupation. Overall, it looks as though this was an almost permanent base from where the occupants ranged over a 10-kilometre radius to cover the river, the estuary and the coast. Everything they needed was within a two-hour walk.

Carbon-dating of animal and fish bones found at the site reveals that Mount Sandel was occupied about 9,000 years ago, making the dwellings the oldest houses in the whole of the Isles. There are plenty of flint tools at the site and they are dominated by the small sharp flakes known as *microliths*. These were struck off a central core of flint and then fashioned for a number of different uses. Some were square in shape, with one or two edges finished sharply for use as cutters and scrapers. They were used for slicing animal skins and then stripping away the subcutaneous fat ready for drying and making up into clothing. Others were shaped to a sharp point for making holes in skins in preparation for sewing with sinews removed from the hind legs of deer. There are also hundreds of small flakes, some no more than a centimetre long, deliberately sharpened along one or two edges for use in composite tools such as arrows and spears. Like the roof timbers of the houses, the wooden shafts of these implements have rotted away so that only the stone remains.

The date of 9,000 years ago and the style of the material remains place Mount Sandel squarely in what is referred to as the Mesolithic period, otherwise known as the Middle Stone Age. The occupants may even have been exact contemporaries of the 'younger' of the Cheddar Men. Archaeologists divide the Stone Age into three phases. The oldest – the Palaeolithic or 'Old Stone Age' – covers the period from when the very first stone tools were discovered in Africa, at least 2 million years ago. They were not made by our own species, but by other types of archaic humans long since extinct. Our own species, *Homo sapiens*, does not make its appearance until about 150,000 years ago and the arrival of our ancestors in Europe about 45,000 years ago marks the beginning of the final phase of the Old Stone Age – the Upper Palaeolithic.

This phase lasted until the end of the last Ice Age, 13,000 years ago. The period between the end of the last Ice Age and the adoption of agriculture is known as the Mesolithic. Each phase is linked to a particular fashion of stone tool, and the microlith is the typical style of the Mesolithic. It is very much smaller and more refined than the larger flints of the preceding Upper Palaeolithic. Even so, the boundaries between the different phases are very fluid. For example, the scrapers of the Mesolithic are very similar to the scrapers of the Upper Palaeolithic.

At the time when people were living at Mount Sandel, the whole of the Isles was still connected to continental Europe. This does not mean the inhabitants of Mount Sandel did arrive overland, only that it was possible to do so at the time. The ice had begun to retreat 4,000 years before the main occupation of Mount Sandel, and the colonization of the Isles by the earlier Cheddar Man and his contemporaries had begun at least 3,000 years before. However, the earth wobbled once again in its orbit and there was a sudden and severe 'cold snap' between 11,000 and 10,000 years ago, which may have forced the human occupants back down south and cleared the Isles once more. The boundary of the ice, which had retreated to more or less its present latitudes, began to spread south again. The sea was frozen right down to northern Spain and the plains of northern Europe reduced once again to barren and inhospitable tundra. But, very fortunately, this cold phase – known as the Younger Dryas – lasted only for about 1,000 years. At the end of the cold snap the earth began to warm up very suddenly and humans could once again resume the occupation of northern Europe, this time for good – or at least until the present day. At first the landscape was bare of trees, rather like parts of northern Scandinavia today. Large herds of reindeer and wild horse roamed across the open plains once more. By the time Mount Sandel was occupied, the landscape was filling with trees as the temperatures rose. This warming was not a gradual process: the temperature literally shot up from bitter cold to very mild within less than a century. Around 9,500 years ago the average temperature was as high as, or even higher than, it is today.

The sea ice retreated way beyond the Shetland Isles and the sea level rose again as the ice melted. First Ireland was separated from the rest of the Isles at around 8,500 years ago. That put a stop to the colonization of Ireland by some land animals and explains why there are no moles, lizards or snakes in Ireland. That is, of course, unless you prefer to believe, in the case of snakes, that it was St Patrick himself who banished them. These animals, though, did have time to establish themselves in Britain before it was eventually cut off from the European mainland by the rising water levels in the North Sea 500 years later, about 8,000 years ago.

By now the Irish landscape had changed from tundra to an open forest of birch trees. As the temperature continued to rise, this open woodland slowly changed to a thicker cover of hazel and, by about the time the Isles became completely severed from the rest of Europe, they were covered in a mature forest of elm, lime and oak. The herds of large mammals moved north if they could, but in Ireland their way was barred by the sea. Many, including the magnificent Irish elk, with antlers some 3 metres across, became extinct. They were replaced in the now dense forests by wild pig, red and roe deer and the aurochs, the ancestor of modern domestic cattle, and by a host of smaller mammals like squirrel and pine marten. From the remains at Mount Sandel and other Mesolithic sites, it seems that anything that moved risked being roasted on the campfire. The ideal places to live were near rivers, such as at Mount Sandel on the River Bann, or by the sea. Here you could have the best of both worlds. Fish and shellfish from the sea and rivers, hazelnuts, pork and venison from the forest. Not a bad life at all. All the best shoreline sites accumulated huge mounds, or *middens*, of discarded shells built up often several metres high.

From the overall size of individual Mesolithic sites, archaeologists estimate that the number of people occupying them was quite low, possibly just single nuclear families. There was not the same need to join together in hunting bands of twenty or so as there had been in the colder, tundra phases. Then the main prey had been the herds of large and dangerous animals like bison, which called for organized ambushes and teamwork among the hunters. Neither was there any need to move over large distances to keep up with the herds as they migrated from summer to winter feeding grounds. Though many Mesolithic sites that have been found were obviously temporary, used for just a few days, others, like Mount Sandel, were occupied for long enough to make it worthwhile building the timber-framed houses.

Though the inhabitants of Mount Sandel were certainly hunter-gatherers, they were not above manipulating the environment to make life easier. They deliberately created open glades within the forest to encourage hazel trees to grow. They did not need to fell the mature elms and oaks to do this, but merely to ring-bark them and wait for them to die and be blown over. By stripping away a continuous band of bark from around the trunk, the capillaries that carry water to the leaves are disrupted and the tree begins to die. The next winter storm may blow it to the ground. The unremarkable life of the Mesolithic hunter-gatherers continued at Mount Sandel and elsewhere in Ireland for thousands of years, leaving little trace on the landscape and few permanent signs, shell middens apart, for archaeologists to follow.

Meanwhile on continental Europe radical changes were under way. From modest beginnings in the Middle East, farming was beginning its unstoppable march towards the Isles. Ten thousand years ago in the Fertile Crescent, in that part of what is now Syria and northern Iraq that is drained by the Tigris and Euphrates rivers, people had learned how to cultivate wild grasses and how to replace hunting with domestication. Farming ushered in the New Stone Age – or Neolithic, to distinguish it from the hunter-gatherer Mesolithic – with a whole range of new stone implements for farming. They also made pottery. The invention of agriculture seems such a small change in the tactics of subsistence, yet it has led to the complete reshaping of the world into its modern form. Whole books have been written about this, and I will resist the temptation to go off at a tangent, restricting myself instead to the implications for our remote ancestors, and for the gene patterns that await our scrutiny.

Carbon-dates from farming sites and the comparison of different pottery styles show that agriculture spread through continental Europe by two principal routes. The split probably came as the first farmers reached the Balkans and the lower Danube from Turkey around 8,500 years ago, about the time that Ireland finally separated from Britain and the residents of Mount Sandel were tucking into yet another bowl of limpet soup. One group of farmers headed north to reach the great Hungarian plains, then, after a thousand-year pause, moved rapidly north and west along the major river valleys of the Oder and the Elbe towards the Baltic and the North Sea. They needed to clear thick forest to make enough space for cultivation. This they did by ring-barking and burning the dead trees and undergrowth, thereby fertilizing the soil with ash. By 7,000 years ago they had reached northern France, southern Belgium and the Netherlands.

Meanwhile the other group moved along the Mediterranean coast of Italy, southern France and Iberia. By 7,500 years ago they had reached the Atlantic coast of France. At each point along the way, in the forest and on the seashore, each group of farming pioneers encountered the earlier Mesolithic inhabitants, but there is no archaeological evidence that their interactions were anything but peaceful. Just as in Ireland, the highest density of Mesolithic hunter-gatherers was around the coast, rather than in the dense inland forests. In several places, particularly around the coast near Lisbon in Portugal, Neolithic farming communities lived fairly close to Mesolithic settlements and carbon-dating shows that both were occupied at much the same time. However, the newcomers chose sites a little way away from the estuaries favoured by the hunter-gatherers, instead setting up camp inland on higher ground between the main river valleys. As they were not competing for the same living space, this reduced the potential for conflict.

In Ireland the same process of peaceful co-existence seems to have accompanied the arrival of farming communities. There were thriving Mesolithic settlements all around the coast, some of which, like Sutton in County Dublin, had been occupied for long enough to accumulate enormous middens of discarded shells over 100 metres long. They certainly would not have thrown in the towel as soon as the first farmer paddled round the coast. At Ferriter's Cove on the Dingle peninsula in County Kerry, the presence of polished stone axes – which, like pottery, are a reliable signal of the Neolithic – among the otherwise Mesolithic remains at this shoreline site, shows that the hunter-gatherers were in contact with farmers. Cattle bones at the site also show this interaction. So, in Ireland, just as elsewhere in Atlantic Europe, the transition to farming from hunter-gathering was gradual and piecemeal and did not necessarily involve sharp changes in the make-up of the Irish population.

These signals of the arrival of the Neolithic in Ireland are small and subtle, noticed only by the professional archaeologist. How different, then, from the gigantic stone structures that also appeared in Ireland 1,000 years later. These are the jewels of Irish archaeology, drawing tens of thousands of visitors each year to stand in awe and reflect on the grandeur, the construction and the purpose of these magnificent structures. The Oxford archaeologist Barry Cunliffe has studied megalithic structures in the Isles and also in Brittany and along the Atlantic coast of France and Iberia. Rather than a phenomenon solely linked to the Neolithic and the spread of farming, Cunliffe traces their origin to the shell middens of Mesolithic Portugal. Within the piles of shells accumulated over centuries on the banks of the River Sado, excavations have found human remains that have all the appearance of being deliberate ritual burials. The middens are enormous, some over 100 metres in diameter and several metres high, and within some of them over 100 burials have been discovered. Further north, on the southern coast of Brittany, later dated midden graves have been found lined with stone. In others, bodies were buried with personal ornaments such as drilled sea shells and stone pendants. Traces of red ochre show that, like the Red Lady of Paviland, the bodies were covered in this pigment, the purpose of which may perhaps have been to restore the flush of health to a lifeless corpse.

Barry Cunliffe sees a natural progression from these shell-midden graves to the two earliest styles of Neolithic monumental architecture: the long barrow, where soil has taken the place of shells, and the passage graves. And it is the passage graves of the Boyne valley in Ireland that visitors flock to see. Although there are over 230 passage graves in Ireland, it is the tombs at Knowth, Dowth and Newgrange that, deservedly, command the most attention. All three are roughly the same size, 85 metres in diameter and 11 metres high. These dimensions may be similar to the shell middens which provided the archetypal design, but the effort put into their construction was phenomenal. The stone-lined passage and the tomb that lies at its end involved the quarrying, transportation and setting in place of over fifty giant stone slabs, some weighing more than 5 tons. Once the tomb was in place, the whole structure was covered in the gigantic mound, which is made up of more than 200,000 tons of rocks and earth.

At Newgrange, the narrow passage which leads to the tomb itself is 25 metres long. It was aligned in such a way that the light of the rising sun at the midwinter solstice shone directly along the passage on to an intricately carved triple spiral motif on the opposite wall of the central tomb. The Knowth mound, about a kilometre to the north-west, contains not one but two passage graves, as does the Dowth mound to the east of Newgrange. Around these massive tombs are other smaller tombs and numerous standing stones. Carbon-dates of organic remains found buried within the mound date the construction of Newgrange at about 5,000 years ago, well after the dates for Ireland's first unambiguously Neolithic site at Ballynagilly in Ulster.

It is only natural to imagine that these gigantic structures, and the complex and mysterious social rituals which their presence suggests, must have been brought about by a wave of new arrivals to Ireland. Yet the clear link to similar, even if not identical, structures along the entire Atlantic coastline, coupled with the early genesis of these structures in the middens of the Mesolithic, could equally well mean that these impressive megaliths are actually one step along the path of a continuous development of monumental architecture along the entire Atlantic fringe from Iberia to the Isles. That is definitely something to bear in mind when we contemplate the living archaeology of the genes.

Before we do that, let us pause to examine the archaeological evidence in Ireland of what nearly every popular account refers to as the arrival of the Celts. We have looked at the linguistic evidence elsewhere, but what is there to see among the material remains exposed by the trowels of the excavator? Even supposedly authoritative popular world histories describe 'the Celts' as loose mobile units of warriors, on the move and destroying all in their path. The main archaeological evidence comes from the beautifully fashioned and distinctive metalwork associated with, first, the Hallstadt and then the La Tène cultures of central Europe. Certainly these have been found in many parts of Europe, including Ireland. But to take this as proof of a large-scale movement of people into Ireland is surely, in the absence of other compelling evidence, even more of a risky assumption than that the spread of agriculture can only have been accomplished by wave after wave of Middle Eastern farmers.

The 'Celtic' artefacts that have passed the test of survival and discovery are, almost without exception, high-value goods that, like a Rolex watch or a Cartier necklace today, are at least as likely to be given as a gift as to be worn by the original owner. To find a La Tène brooch in an Irish bog is no proof that a central European put it there. And, like a fake Rolex, just because a piece of jewellery looks like the original, it doesn't stop it being a copy. In fact, artefacts in the La Tène style are rare in Ireland. Many of them have been examined by the Irish archaeologist Barry Raftery, who is convinced that, far from being made in central Europe, they were actually manufactured in Ireland itself. We continually underestimate the skill and capabilities of our ancestors. Why should it come as a surprise that an Irish goldsmith could learn a new, fashionable continental style? It seems to me that the constant tendency to interpret past events in terms of movements is completely the wrong assumption. Surely the correct starting point is to assume that our ancestors were sufficiently resourceful and skilful to pick up virtually any skill. But to find out we need to look at the DNA.

9
THE DNA OF IRELAND

A good reason for choosing Ireland as the starting point of our genetic tour of the Isles is that, unlike in Britain, a concerted research programme into Irish cultural and genetic history has already been running for some years, organized through the auspices of the Royal Irish Academy based in Dublin. In Britain an even more ambitious millennium initiative came to nothing, which was one of the reasons why my research team and I decided to complete the survey of the entire Isles ourselves. You might be surprised, as I was when I first heard of the Academy, that it still retains the Royal prefix, but it is one of the institutions that has survived the 1921 partition of Ireland. It was founded in 1785 and soon became the premier learned society for the study of Irish civilization. It is in many respects the Irish equivalent of the elite academic societies in the rest of Britain, like the Royal Society and the British Academy in London and the Royal Society of Edinburgh and, also in Edinburgh, the Royal Scottish

Academy. One of the enjoyable aspects of visiting these places is that they are almost always housed in grand Georgian terraces. It is always a treat for the eyes to attend meetings in such sumptuous surroundings, with the olympians of academe, Newton, Darwin and co., peering down from their portraits high up on the walls.

Unlike its British counterparts, the Irish Academy is not restricted to particular fields of endeavour. While in England, for example, the Royal Society deals with the sciences and the British Academy covers the humanities: literature, history, philosophy and so on, the Royal Irish Academy does not restrict itself, embracing both the sciences and the arts under one roof. This breadth made the Academy the natural home of a comprehensive survey of Ireland which would integrate all the diverse strands of science, history, language and archaeology. This irresistible combination, together with some fundraising, led to a substantial amount of money being made available to the Academy from the National Millennium Committee of Ireland. Invitations to bid for money from the fund went out to all the Irish universities and I found myself on a plane to Dublin to help to judge the applications.

In the elegant surroundings of the Academy's headquarters in Dawson Street, the hopefuls presented their proposals in the form of short talks. Naturally enough, when a new pot of money unexpectedly becomes available, people build their bids around their existing expertise. The aim is to persuade the judges that what they are already doing will, with a bit more money, produce an essential and indispensable contribution to the project. Our job, as judges, was to weigh up these diverse claims and to recommend where we thought the money would best be spent. You'll not be surprised to hear that I didn't need much persuading that a survey of mitochondrial and Y-chromosome DNA would be not only relevant but completely essential.

Fortunately, all the other judges felt the same way. Which is how Dan Bradley and his team from Trinity College Dublin got the green light – and the funds – to take charge of that central aspect of the project. Dan had pioneered the use of DNA to find out how and when farm animals, in particular cattle, had been domesticated. We had worked together a little on this when Jill Bailey, one of the research students in my team, had been working on retrieving DNA from the bones of the extinct ancestor of domesticated cattle, the fearsome aurochs. After getting her degree at Oxford, Jill had spent a year in Dan's lab in Dublin and I had been over a couple of times to give talks and be an examiner for Dan's graduate students. All of which is entirely irrelevant, except that it meant that a highly experienced and competent geneticist, whom I knew and liked, would be covering the same genetic ground in Ireland as I was already starting to do in the rest of the Isles. Which in turn meant that I could concentrate on Scotland, Wales and England, knowing that Dan's lab would produce compatible genetic data from Ireland that could be integrated with the results of our Irish customers at Oxford Ancestors and, eventually, all the data from the rest of the Isles. Which is precisely what did happen and it is from this grand coalition of data that we begin our tour.

On my imaginary map, I moved all the Irish gene-coins across the Irish Sea and began to distribute them according to their geographic origins. Each one of these was the end point of a journey – the journey of a line of ancestors stretching through maternal and paternal threads way back into the deep past. We know, from the archaeological records, that every one of these ancestral journeys must have ended in Ireland within the last 9,000 years when the first Irish built their timber-framed houses on the banks of the River Bann at Mount Sandel. Before that, as we know, Ireland had been uninhabited since the Ice Age. Could it be that some of these DNA fragments from today's Irish men and women have actually been there all that time? How would we know?

I began with the maternal DNA. I knew, from the identity of their clan mothers, when and where all these journeys had begun. And from the locations on the map of Ireland, I also knew where these journeys had ended. Well, not ended, because many of these genes will go on travelling the world for millennia to come. To be more accurate, I knew where these immortal time travellers had reached by the late twentieth century.

The longest journeys, in both time and distance, had been travelled by Ursula's descendants. Ursula herself had lived in Greece about 45,000 years ago, at the start of the Upper Palaeolithic, and had shared the land with the far more ancient Neanderthals. We knew this date from counting up all the mutational changes that had happened among her descendants and dividing this figure by the mutation rate. As we have seen, among the seven principal clans in Europe there were far more changes in the descendants of Ursula than in any of the others. That simple fact meant the clan of Ursula was the oldest of the seven. We arrived at the age of the clan, and thus the time in the past when Ursula herself lived, by factoring in a mutation rate of one change in every 20,000 years. From thousands of DNA samples from all over Europe we knew that, on average, Ursulans have 2.25 mutations in their mitochondrial DNA compared to the DNA of Ursula herself. That puts the age of the clan at 2.25 × 20,000 = 45,000 years.

We arrived at Ursula's own location in Greece by looking to see where the clan today is both the most frequent and at its most diverse. So long as there was good archaeological or climatic evidence that the location was inhabited, or at least habitable, at the time, then that was where we placed the matriarch. I realize from many letters that it is a frequent and understandable misunderstanding (if there can be such a thing) that we have located the skeleton of Ursula and the other matriarchs and then worked out how long ago they lived from carbon-dating. But this is not so; it is all accomplished by reconstructions.

From the DNA fragments now displayed on the map of Ireland, I could see that almost exactly 10 per cent of Irish men and women are the direct maternal descendants of Ursula, each carrying her DNA modified by the occasional mutation. Converting that proportion of 10 per cent to actual numbers of people means that of a total population of 5.7 million there are roughly 570,000 Ursulans in all of Ireland. Altogether, counting Dan's published data, we have the mDNA sequences of 91 Ursulans from a total of 921 Irish samples. However, because the clan is so old and there has been such a long time for mutations to accumulate, we found only three people who have Ursula's sequence unmodified by genetic change. As all three are customers of Oxford Ancestors, I can trace their present whereabouts and none of them lives in Ireland! One lives in Hampshire in southern England, another in London and the third in New York. It is their grandmothers and great-grandmothers who lived in Ireland and who then joined the stream of emigrants in the nineteenth and early twentieth century. But their DNA did pause in Ireland before it resumed its journey around the globe.

I shall refer to these three as 'pure' Ursulans, while, I hope, avoiding the implication that mutations in the others have somehow sullied the pristine genetic heritage of Ursula herself. I hope I am not accused of implying that their DNA is, in contrast, somehow impure, which is complete nonsense of course. But it has been modified. Of the other Irish Ursulans, some have one change on the 'pure' Ursulan background – and I call them first-generation Ursulans. There are 22 of them. By the same token, there are 23 second-generation, 26 third-generation, 10 fourth-generation, 5 fifth-generation, one sixth-generation and one seventh-generation Ursulan. The third-generation Ursulans, with three mutations compared to Ursula herself, are the most frequent, closely followed by Ursulans of the second 'mutational' generation with two changes compared to the original. The numbers in higher generations tail off slowly until we reach the Irish Ursulan record-holder, a doctor now living in Chichester, in Sussex, with seven changes since Ursula. I had better stress once again that the 'pure' Ursulans and all the others up to and including the record-holder are separated from Ursula by the same 45,000 years and, roughly, the same number of actual maternal generations. It is chance alone that has left the three 'pure' lines untouched by mutations while the good doctor's has been hit seven times.

We are in the most technical part of the book and I beg for your indulgence to explain a very important point. From the numbers of 'pure' and first-, second- and higher-generation Ursulans, we can work out the average number of mutations over all the Irish Ursulans. It comes to fractionally over 2.5. If we now multiply this by the mutation rate of one change in every 20,000 years, it comes to just over 50,000 years, which is older than Ursula!

Actually, this is not that far from the 45,000-year date for Ursula herself and well within the mathematical error of the estimate. But it is an awful lot longer than the 9,000 years we know that people have been in Ireland. How can we explain this apparent discrepancy? We have 50,000 years' worth of accumulated mutation in an island which we know has only been inhabited for 9,000 years. It has to mean that most of the mutations in the Irish Ursulans must have already occurred *before* and not *after* they arrived in Ireland. We cannot just use the 50,000-year genetic date and say that is when Ireland was first inhabited.

My colleague Martin Richards and I got into a lot of trouble when we first used a superficially similar argument to back up our controversial proposition that the ancestors of most Europeans were Palaeolithic hunter-gatherers who had arrived a long time before the Neolithic farmers. We said that there was far too much accumulated mutation in all the major European clans, save Jasmine, to have developed in the 10,000 years or so since farming had been invented in the Middle East, and therefore these clans were Palaeolithic in origin. The counter-argument was vigorously expressed in terms of a Martian metaphor. Suppose a representative selection of Europeans had been transported to Mars and then, a few years later, had their DNA sampled and analysed – presumably by Venusians who didn't know about the landing. They had then done the calculations and showed that, according to the amount of accumulated genetic differences, the Martians had been there for tens of thousands of years, whereas we know they had arrived only a few years earlier. The flaw in the Venusians' argument – and by implication in ours – was that they had assumed that all the mutations had accumulated *after* the earthlings arrived on Mars, when, in fact, they had all occurred *before* they set off from Earth.

Although Martin and I, for a number of reasons, did not think this was a good analogy for what we had actually done, we none the less set out to try to prove that the mutations in Europeans (we are back on Earth now) had accumulated in Europe and had not been imported from the Middle East by Neolithic farmers. Martin particularly, helped by our new recruit, theoretical physicist and mathematician Vincent Macaulay, spent three long years doing this.

To cut a very long story short, they scoured the Middle

East for as many DNA samples as they could find, then searched these for matches to the DNA from Europe. The point was to find out how many of the mutations in Europe were genuinely European and how many had already happened in the Middle East. Basically, if a match was found, and if we could be certain that it had actually originated in the Middle East, rather than being carried back there from Europe by some sort of reverse migration, we subtracted it from our tally of 'European' mutations and did the time calculations once again. It was an exhaustive, and exhausting, analysis which in the end gave us a set of dates for the settlement of Europe that we could all rely on. Fortunately, they were not so very different from our original ones and did not reverse our conclusion that most Europeans had hunter-gatherer ancestors.

Turning back once more to the Irish Ursulans, could I do the same sort of thing to work out which mutations were Irish 'originals' and which were imported? If I could, then the genetic dates would mean something. This I did by checking each of the Irish Ursulans' DNA sequences against every other sequence that I knew about from all over, first Europe, and then the world. I was looking to see how many of them had also been seen outside Ireland. Although my computer helped a great deal in sorting all the results so that identical sequences appeared on consecutive lines on the screen, I also checked the list of Irish Ursulans one by one. One Irish Ursulan, a lady from Donegal, for example, had only one matching sequence and that was a man from the Czech Republic. It is very unlikely we will ever know the precise tracks that trace the wanderings of the ancestors of these two genetic relatives back to the woman whose DNA they both share. But it is in just these tracks, like footprints in the sands of time, that we can read the signals from the past.

I found, at the end, that out of the 91 Irish Ursulans, 68 had matching sequences elsewhere. Only 23 were unique to Ireland. In many cases I could find their immediate predecessors, in a genetic sense, within Ireland. So a fourth-generation Ursulan sequence, for example, would usually have a third-generation sequence nearby. In these cases I thought it was reasonable to regard that fourth mutation as having happened in Ireland. Counting up these home-grown mutations and factoring in the mutation rate as usual gave me a corrected date for the clan in Ireland of a little over 7,000 years – 7,300 to be precise. This was much more reasonable than the 50,000 years which counted all the Ursulan mutations as if they had all happened in Ireland.

Genetic dates, like the 7,300 years for the Irish Ursulans, are not very accurate. They are estimates. We find this concept particularly difficult to grasp because we are accustomed to dates being very precise. The 7,300-year date for the arrival of the Irish Ursulans is an estimate. The date could vary a thousand years either way and still fall within the scope of the estimate. Forgetting the inaccuracies for the moment, what does this date mean? It is an estimate for the length of time it would have taken for all the Ursulan mutations to have accumulated within Ireland. If the ancestors of all 91 Irish Ursulans had arrived at the same time and their mDNA mutations had accumulated since then, the genetic estimate for their arrival would have been 7,300 years ago. Of course, it is very unlikely indeed that they all arrived at once. Some would have come more recently, but in that case, to achieve the average figure, others must have arrived *more than* 7,300 years ago to balance out the more recent arrivals.

I went through the same procedure with all the other Irish maternal clans, checking to see in each one how many looked as though they had mutated to their final form in Ireland and not elsewhere. From there I calculated the clan arrival times in the same way as I had for the Ursulans. All of them came out between 7,500 and 4,500 years ago. Ursula was still the oldest clan in Ireland and, in common with the rest of Europe, Jasmine was the youngest. It was Jasmine's clan that Martin Richards and I had linked to the arrival of Neolithic farmers in Europe from the Middle East. The others clustered around the 5,000–6,000-year average. Even bearing in mind the approximate nature of these genetic dates for the settlement of Ireland by the various maternal clans, they are all way before the time, around 200 BC, when the Iron Age Celts were supposed to have arrived. It was beginning to look as if the ancestors of today's Irish had been there for a lot longer than anybody thought.

But within Ireland, when I looked at the maternal clans in the different provinces of Ulster, Leinster, Munster and Connacht, there was very little noticeable difference between any of them, though the numbers in each were too low to be sure of statistical significance.

If women had been in Ireland for a very long time, what

about the men? Just as mitochondrial DNA traces our maternal ancestry, so the Y-chromosome follows paternal genealogies. Like mitochondrial DNA, Y-chromosomes also experience random mutations over the course of time. The precise nature of the mutations might be different between mDNA and Y-chromosomes, as we shall see, but the principles are the same. The accumulation of mutations along paternal genealogies over a very long time means that there are now tens of thousands of slightly different Y-chromosomes which can be distinguished by genetic tests. If two men have the same Y-chromosome fingerprint, then they have usually inherited it from a common patrilineal ancestor. That's exactly the same principle as saying that if two people have the same mitochondrial DNA sequence they have inherited it from a common maternal ancestor. Although Y-chromosomes are quite different from mitochondrial DNA in the way they change genetically, that doesn't matter so much when it comes to interpreting the signals they are bringing us from the past.

Just as each of us belongs to one of a small number of maternal clans, so men can be assigned to a paternal clan by the genetic characteristics of their Y-chromosome. From research done throughout the world over the past decade, Y-chromosomes can now be separated into twenty-one paternal clans, eight of which occur in Europe. Of these eight clans only five occur in the Isles to any appreciable extent. Following the tradition of the maternal clans, I have given them names. They are the clans of Oisin, Wodan, Sigurd, Eshu and Re. Like the maternal clans, each founded by a matriarch, the paternal clans must, by the same logical inevitability, also have been started by a single man – the clan father or patriarch. Every man within a clan is a direct paternal descendant of the clan father and has inherited the patriarch's Y-chromosome, modified by mutations over the intervening millennia.

The different paternal clans are told apart by single DNA changes, just like the mutations in mitochondrial DNA. However, these Y-chromosome sequence changes occur far more slowly than they do in mDNA. There is usually only a single DNA sequence mutation between the Y-chromosomes of one clan and another, even though they have been separated for tens of thousands of years. Luckily for us, the Y-chromosome also experiences a second, much swifter, type of mutation that can split a paternal clan into hundreds, if not thousands of separate paternal lineages. These fast mutations happen, like all DNA changes, when cells divide and there is an error in the usually immaculate copying mechanism.

Along the Y-chromosome are patches of DNA sequence that, when looked at closely, consist of reiterated blocks of short sequences. Treating DNA sequences like a word, these are the genetic equivalent of a bad stammer. It is as if an otherwise smooth read-through just gets stuck. Take the four DNA letters TAGA, an outwardly unremarkable sequence. For some reason, TAGA tends to trip up the DNA copying mechanisms on parts of the Y-chromosome where it is repeated a number of times. Cells can handle a few repeats. The double reiteration TAGATAGA causes no difficulties. Even ten repeats, one after the other, is manageable. But after that the stammering begins. After twelve repeats cells find the blocks of TAGA very difficult to copy accurately and make mistakes much more often than they normally would with regular sequences. What they do wrong is to add an extra TAGA, or forget to copy one. So a Y-chromosome with, let's say, fourteen TAGA repeats mutates into one with fifteen repeats. Because the cell has such trouble with copying this type of stammering sequence accurately, the rate at which these mutations occur is hundreds of times faster than the regular type of spelling-change mutation, where, for example, a C changes to a T. It is an even faster rate than mDNA, with its comparatively lax error-checking mechanisms.

There are dozens of places along the Y-chromosome where these tricky stammering segments are to be found and they can be used in combination to define tens of thousands of different Y-chromosomes. Because Y-chromosomes, alone among the nuclear chromosomes, are not shuffled at each generation, the combinations can persist for a very long time, changing only when another mutation occurs at one of them. In this respect, the Y-chromosomes can be interpreted just like the mDNA with first-, second- and third-generation mutations changing the Y-chromosome fingerprint of the 'pure' patriarch. And, just like mDNA, the number of mutations can be added up to get an idea, again only approximate, of time passing. In reality, because these mutations happen so quickly, in relative terms, it is hard to know what the clan patriarch's Y-chromosome fingerprint actually was. But as we shall see, this is not really a problem when we look in detail at the Y-chromosome of Ireland.

In my mind's eye, I collect up the maternal gene-coins from the imaginary map of Ireland, move them to one side and begin to distribute the paternal Y-chromosome equivalents in their place. As soon as I look at the Irish pile, one thing stands out. The vast majority of Irish Y-chromosomes are members of just one clan, the clan of Oisin. It is precisely because of its predominance in Ireland that I gave the clan this name. Oisin was the son of the hero of another of the Irish mythical cycles, Finn mac Cumhaill, sometimes transcribed as Finn mac Cool. Finn is the leader of the Fianna, a band of warriors chosen only after an appropriately gruelling selection process. His son Oisin, meaning Little Deer, is bewitched by Niav of the Golden Hair, the daughter of the Underworld king who reigns over Tir na n'Og, the World of the Forever Young. Oisin goes to this other world to be with Niav and spends his life writing poetry and songs. Eventually he becomes homesick and is eager to visit his own world once more. Niav warns against this, but Oisin is adamant and sets out, though he promises to heed her warning not to set foot on Irish soil. He plans to avoid disobeying Niav's instructions by riding everywhere on a horse and so not touching the soil. In an extreme version of *Back to the Future*, Oisin realizes when he returns to Ireland that 300 years have passed while he was relaxing in Tir na n'Og. The shock of this discovery makes him fall from his horse and, as soon as he touches the ground, he instantly ages 300 years and crumbles into dust.

The Y-chromosome might be decaying fast, and well on its way to sharing Oisin's fate, but for the moment his clan's Y-chromosome is doing extremely well in Ireland. Almost

80 per cent of Irish Y-chromosomes belong to the clan of Oisin. Within Ireland there was very little difference to be seen in the geographical distribution of the maternal clans in different parts of the island. However, with Y-chromosomes there certainly is. Dividing Ireland into the four ancient provinces, each roughly occupying a quadrant of the Irish rectangle, the differences between them are very striking indeed. In the south-east quadrant of Leinster, 73 per cent of Y-chromosomes are in the clan of Oisin. In Ulster, in the north-east, this rises to 81 per cent. The clan reaches an even higher frequency in the province of Munster, in the south-west, where 95 per cent of men are in the clan. However, in Connacht, occupying the north-west quadrant, the proportion of Y-chromosomes in the clan of Oisin reaches an astonishing 98 per cent. This was one of the first results from Dan Bradley's genetic survey of Ireland, which he undertook in this instance with graduate student Emmeline Hill. But, rather than just leaving it at that, Dan took their analysis one stage further to look for an explanation. Recalling the twelfth-century Anglo-Norman invasion of Ireland, it occurred to them that one reason for the difference in Oisin Y-chromosome frequency between the provinces might have something to do with this invasion and the subsequent occupation. The invasion began in Leinster, in the south-east, and that was where the Oisin clan was in its lowest proportion.

The vehicle for testing this idea was to use surnames which, like Y-chromosomes, are also passed down the paternal line. There have been inherited surnames in Ireland for as long as anywhere in Europe. They were first adopted in about AD 950, a good 200 years earlier than in England. The Gaelic origin of many Irish surnames is evident from the prefix 'Mc' or 'O', meaning 'son of', as in McCarthy or O'Neill, but there are plenty more whose Gaelic origins required a little research. Fortunately, the enormous interest in genealogy over the last hundred years has led to the compilation of comprehensive surname dictionaries where the origin of almost any name can be found. Sure enough, when Y-chromosomes were compared to surname origins, Gaelic or Anglo-Norman, the correspondence was clear. Even in Leinster, the proportion of Oisin clan members was higher among the men with Gaelic names than among the men whose surname could be traced to Anglo-Norman origins. You will recall that, in his survey of blood groups, Professor Dawson explains the higher frequency of blood group A in Leinster by the Anglo-Norman invasion.

The comparison with the mitochondrial results is striking. All of the seven major maternal European clans, and most of the minor ones, were to be found in Ireland and there was not much difference in their proportions in the four provinces. Very obviously, in Ireland anyway, the version of history told by men and women was not the same. To explore this further, I want to look in more detail at the Irish Y-chromosomes, in particular the detail among the members of the clan of Oisin. A Y-chromosome fingerprint, or signature, consists of a set of ten numbers. Each of these is the number of stammering DNA repeats at the ten places on the Y-chromosome that we test. If there are 10 repeats at the first marker and 22 at the second one, the fingerprint starts off as 10–22. If there are 13 repeats at the third marker, the fingerprint continues as 10–22–13 and so on. When I am checking through 10 marker signatures from the DNA analyser, if there are Irish men among the batch it isn't long before I find this particular signature: 11–24–13–13–12–14–12–12–10–16. It is very familiar indeed. This is the quintessential Oisin Y-chromosome and huge numbers of Irish men carry it. I am not the only person to have noticed this particular Y-chromosome combination. Dan Bradley certainly knows about it, and it has also been spotted by Jim Wilson, who worked for a time at University College London. Jim is a native of the Orkney Islands, just off the north coast of Scotland, and he had noticed this same combination among his fellow Orcadians. It also cropped up, interestingly, in surveys of Y-chromosomes among the Basques of north-eastern Spain and among the people of Galicia in the north-west of Spain. Its oceanic affinities led it to be christened, not Poseidon or Neptune, but the far more prosaic Atlantic Modal Haplotype, or AMH for short. I prefer to call it the 'Atlantis' chromosome. In the Isles it is by far the commonest Y-chromosome signature within the clan of Oisin, or any other for that matter.

Among the Oisin clan in Ireland, it certainly isn't the only Y-chromosome fingerprint, but most of the others can be linked to it by one or two mutations. This gives us an opportunity to get an Irish date for the Oisin clan, rather as we did with the Ursulans and other maternal clans. The mutation rate of these Y-chromosome fingerprints is roughly one change per 1,500 years, much faster than the mDNA rate of one for every 20,000 years. By following exactly the same procedure for the Oisin clan as we did for the first Irish Ursulan calculation, we get a date of 4,200 years. This lies well within the time frame of human settlement in Ireland and, since it is still prey to the wide approximations of genetic dates, and thus quite close to the 5–6,000-year estimate for mDNA, it would be tempting to imagine we have solved the origins of the Irish.

However, we have done nothing of the sort, because we have overlooked the Martian factor. Remember that the original Irish Ursulan date was 50,000 years ago – older than Ursula herself and far too early to be a plausible date for the settlement of Ireland – assuming that all the mutations among Irish Ursulans had happened after the first ones reached Ireland. To get round this we had to decide which of the mutations happened on Irish soil, and which had already occurred before the clan reached Ireland. When we did this it made a huge difference to the date, bringing it forward to the much more plausible 7,300 years ago. Applying the same correction to the Irish Y-chromosome data brought the date forward to just 1,200 years in the past. This is far too recent to be plausible, even given the approximations involved. Something else must be going on. And it was, but it took me a while to realize the explanation. And it didn't happen until I had done a lot more work. Not in Ireland, but in Scotland. Only then was I able to make sense of the strange behaviour of the Irish Y-chromosomes.

Nevertheless, we have made a good start. In Ireland, the maternal lineages are diverse and very old, while the

Y-chromosomes are unexpectedly homogeneous, and at first glance look comparatively young. We have seen a difference between different regions of the island, a difference that may be an echo of the Anglo-Norman invasion of Ireland beginning in the twelfth century. We have seen some evidence of a genetic link between Ireland and Spain along the Atlantic fringe of Europe, which archaeologists are now beginning to realize was a much busier seaway than was once thought. What we don't yet know is how the Irish results will fit with the rest of the Isles, and to begin to do that we shall travel across the shallow sea to Scotland.

10
SCOTLAND

It is barely 12 miles across the sea from Fair Head on the north-western tip of Ulster to the cliffs of the Mull of Kintyre, rising above the waves of the North Channel. Scotland is bounded on three sides by the sea: by the wild Atlantic to the west and north and by the temperamental North Sea beyond the eastern coastline. Across its historically fluctuating southern land boundary lies England, at different times enemy and friend, but never indifferent neighbour. The western sea boundary is fringed with several large, inhabited islands and hundreds of small ones deprived of inhabitants. Off the north coast lie the Orkney Islands, and 60 miles further to the north-east and halfway to Norway are the Shetlands. The total land area, including the islands, is just over 30,400 square miles, only slightly smaller than Ireland. Mountains dominate the mainland, with the rugged Scottish Highlands reaching to over 1,300 metres. Ben Macdui (1,309 metres), highest of the Cairngorms in the north-east, and Ben Nevis (1,344 metres) in the west are the highest mountains in the whole of the Isles.

The mountains continue all the way to the northern coast of Scotland, especially on the west side, where millions of years of erosion, compounded by the gouging action of the glaciers, which covered the whole of Scotland in the last Ice Age, have left a dramatic landscape. In the far north-west, Old Red Sandstone peaks like Suilven and Stac Pollaidh stand isolated above featureless country of bog and lochan. In the extreme north, the mountains relent, leaving a fertile coastal strip where the thin, acidic soil of the Highlands is invigorated by calcium-rich limestones and sandstones.

The effect of limestone, wherever it occurs, is always dramatic. It neutralizes the otherwise acidic soils and in so doing transforms the colour of the landscape from a yellow-brown to a vivid green. In the Highlands and the Hebrides, the occasional limestone outcrops are marked out by the rich growth of grass and wild flowers. But nowhere is the effect of neutralizing the soil more noticeable or more delightful than in the Western Isles, the long chains of islands that protect the mainland from the full force of the Atlantic. On the western edge of these islands are some of the most beautiful beaches in the world. Brilliant white in the sunlight and lapped by turquoise, translucent seas, they are not made of the usual sands to be found on the crowded holiday beaches of southern England. The white beaches of the Western Isles are composed of the pulverized shells of countless billions of sea creatures that have been ground to a coarse powder by the pounding waves of the Atlantic. The wind, which for 300 days out of 365 roars in from the ocean, has blown the shell sand inland for a mile or two. And there it works its magic on the soil, neutralizing the acid and supplying essential phosphates that are otherwise entirely lacking. The result is the *machair*, a thin strip of meadows and grassland which, so long as the sheep don't get there first, is full of wild flowers – purple orchids by the hundreds, blue harebells and the purple and yellow flowers of heartsease, the wild pansy. A couple of miles further inland, beyond the reach of the wind-blown shell sand, the moss and dark rushes are back, signalling the return of the acid lands.

The white beaches are also spread along the north coast, but there they are not needed to help the soil. The older gneisses and schists of the Highlands, among the oldest rocks in the world, are replaced by alkaline sandstone. Green grass grows far inland in Caithness at the extreme north-east tip of the mainland, and is rich enough to support large herds of sleek black cattle. The fertility of the sandstone soil is even more remarkable in the Orkneys, now a few miles from the Caithness coast but joined to it until 7,000 years ago. On the east coast, there is good low-level farmland around the Moray Firth near Inverness and inland of Aberdeen, at the eastern edge of the Cairngorms. One deep geological fault divides the Highlands along the Great Glen, running between Inverness and Fort William. Another fault line runs between Stonehaven, on the east coast just below Aberdeen, and Loch Lomond to the north of Glasgow. This southern fault line separates the Highlands from the rich farmland of the Central Lowlands, which is also the location of the major cities of Dundee, Stirling, Glasgow and Edinburgh. Most of the 5.2 million Scots live in this Central Belt, a great many having moved there from the Highlands. Further south the ground rises again to form the hills of the Southern Uplands. Lower and less rugged than the Highlands, these hills have been eroded by glaciers into smooth-topped plateaux separated by narrow, flat-bottomed valleys. Beyond the hills, the valleys open out into the rolling farmland that surrounds the River Tweed, which flows into the North Sea at Berwick on the east coast. On the west side of the Southern Uplands, the hills give way to the Galloway peninsula and the flat lands bordering the Solway Firth.

Since the whole of Scotland was under thick ice until the end of the Ice Age and again during the cold snap of the Younger Dryas, it isn't surprising that no evidence, yet, has been found in Scotland of Palaeolithic settlements such as remain in the Cheddar Caves in south-west England. The first signs of human occupation are not found until well after the cold snap and, as in Ireland, these are Mesolithic settlements at or near the coast. The earliest dated site is at Cramond, on the southern shore of the Firth of Forth, only 3 miles from the centre of Edinburgh. It is a picturesque spot, with a small terrace of old houses on one bank of the River Almond, where it flows into the Firth. Swans and ducks bob around in the quiet tree-lined bay and, when I visited on a crisp sunny day in November, I could not have imagined a better spot for a bit of hunter-gathering. A seashore for shellfish and wading birds, a medium-size freshwater river for salmon. All that would have been missing was the cappuccino that was steaming on the table in front of me. The Cramond remnants, a few microliths and the bony evidence of past meals, are dated to about 10,000 years ago. There are no signs of permanent settlement at Cramond, no post-holes as at Mount Sandel in Ireland, so it was probably just one of many places where the small bands of humans used to camp for a while as they moved around the country in search of food.

The seasonal movements of the Mesolithic hunter-gatherers from one site to another are nowhere better illustrated than on the island of Oronsay, off the opposite coast of Scotland from Cramond. Oronsay is a small island, roughly triangular in shape and each side only 3 kilometres long. Despite its small size, no less than five Mesolithic shell middens have been discovered, each containing vast numbers of mollusc shells. Limpets, winkles, whelks, oysters and scallops were all on the menu. Curiously shaped implements, made from the antlers of red deer, have also been found. Their use is immediately obvious when you watch the staff at work in an oyster bar. They are shaped exactly like the knives which, inserted between the two shells of an oyster, then twisted, open it to reveal the silver-grey flesh inside. It is a sight to behold – as it must also have been for the children of Oronsay, 8,000 years ago, for that is the date of the Oronsay midden.

The seasonality of the Oronsay middens has been discovered in a very curious way. As well as huge numbers of mollusc shells, the middens also contain the bones of saithe, a relative of the haddock that is still plentiful in the waters off the west coast of Scotland. The saithe grows rapidly in its first years of life and the age of a fish can be worked out from, of all things, the length of the ear bone or *otolith*. Otoliths within the same midden tend to be about the same length but there is a big difference in average otolith size between one midden and the next. The conclusion is that the middens marked different seasonal camps where the fish caught were at different stages of their development. What we do not know is if Oronsay was a permanent home or, like Cramond, another seasonal camp, occupied at the same time each year to take full advantage of the harvest of the sea.

Oronsay and its close neighbour Colonsay lie about 15 miles from the larger islands of Islay and Jura, themselves 10 miles or so from the long finger of the Kintyre peninsula. Clearly, the Mesolithic hunter-gatherers – an epithet to which we must surely add fishing – were well used to making these quite substantial sea crossings between the islands and the mainland. No boats remain, destroyed by millennia of decay, but they were probably made from animal skins stretched across a framework of hazel branches. They would have resembled the coracle, still, just about, used for fishing in the rivers of west Wales, and the more substantial curraghs of the west of Ireland. Whatever they used, these boats were perfectly good enough for coastal work and island hopping.

The sea has never been a barrier to the people of the Atlantic. It was their highway, just as the Pacific was to the Polynesians. There are confirmed Mesolithic sites on many of the islands lying off the west coast of Scotland, and where no evidence has yet been found there is a feeling among archaeologists that, with more field work, every island will be shown to have been occupied, if only for one part of the year. There is even indirect evidence, in the form of unusual patterns of soil erosion, that the Mesolithics reached Shetland, which would have involved a voyage on the open sea of 60 miles from Orkney, the nearest point. Valuable materials were also transported over long distances by sea. Flint is unknown in Scotland and other stones were used for making tools. Bloodstone quarried from the Isle of Rum, where there is a very early Mesolithic settlement, has been found in many sites around the west coast. The Mesolithic was a time of plenty for those bands who lived on the coasts of Scotland and Ireland. There was ample food within easy reach, both in the sea and in the dense woodland that lay behind the shoreline. It certainly wasn't crowded. One recent estimate puts the total population of the whole of the Isles during the Mesolithic at less than 5,000.

There is one tantalizing fragment of evidence – a grain of wheat pollen from the Isle of Arran in the Firth of Clyde – that the Mesolithics were already experimenting with growing their own plant food, well before the arrival of agriculture proper. However, it is only with the arrival of farming that the whole way of life begins to change. Curiously enough, despite the major effect this transition from the Mesolithic lifestyle of thinly dispersed hunter-gatherers to full-blown farming must have had on the early inhabitants of Scotland, there is a distinct lack of material evidence from the early stages. Part of the reason is probably the later growth of thick layers of moss which have buried early field systems. In Ireland a whole patchwork of fields has been discovered at Ceidi, near Ballycastle, County Mayo in the north-west, lying under several feet of peat and visible only when this layer was cleared away. Even the megaliths suffered from the accumulation of moss and peat. The stone circle at Callanish on Lewis, where the stones reach nearly 5 metres in height, had been almost swallowed up by the peat before it was excavated in the nineteenth century. Only the tips of the tallest stones protruded above the peat.

Covering of a different kind obscured what, in my opinion, is the most remarkable archaeological site in the whole of the Isles. The settlement at Skara Brae in Orkney does not have the grandeur of Callanish or Stonehenge. It is altogether more domestic. Following a violent storm in the 1850s, the sand dunes which back on to the beach in the Bay of Skaill, on the west coast of the largest island, were stripped back to reveal the walls of houses. Unlike today, when such a discovery would precipitate an immediate excavation, nothing much was done either to excavate or even to protect the site until the early years of the twentieth century. Hidden beneath the sand was a small group of interconnecting stone houses, each about 5 metres in diameter and complete with stone beds, stone dressers, even waterproofed stone basins sunk into the floor to keep live lobsters and to soften limpet flesh for fishing bait.

That Skara Brae is still standing and not strewn about the countryside has a lot to do with the remarkable rock found all over Orkney and Caithness. The sandstone comes in flat slabs, about 5–10 centimetres thick. Even without mortar, anything built with Orkney flagstones is not going to fall down. Ruined buildings, 100 years old, which are a not uncommon sight all over rural Scotland, are still standing. Their roof timbers have decayed and collapsed, but the walls of flagstone houses are as solid as ever. Metre-square flagstones, split even thinner, are even used as roof tiles or stuck upright in the ground as fencing.

The charm of Skara Brae is in its ordinariness. I have to admit that, though I enjoy standing in awe amidst the great monuments from the past, I feel strangely detached from them. But at Skara Brae I really *can* imagine people living there, coming in from the wind to the warm, snug interiors, recounting, in whatever tongue, the events of the day. The beach at Skaill just next to Skara Brae is strewn with broken flagstones and when I was there, during the school summer holidays, families were playing on the beach. But instead of building sandcastles – and there is plenty of good sand – the children were constructing their own miniature stone circles. These rocks are just asking to be stood upright, and that's exactly what has happened all over Orkney. The Ring of Brodgar, about 5 miles inland from Skara Brae, was originally a circle of sixty stones 7 metres high and 100 metres across. Twenty-one remain in position. A mile in one direction is the stone circle of Bookan, while the same distance in the other direction is another, Stenness, and half a mile further lies the astonishing passage tomb of Maes Howe. Like the tomb at Newgrange on the Boyne, Maes Howe is aligned so that the sun shines along the low passage at the winter solstice and floods the inner chamber with light. Once again, the wonderful building quality of the rock makes Maes Howe appear much younger than its 5,000 years, the stone slabs neatly laid and corbelled at the top to form a roof. These are only the major structures. All around are burial mounds, many not yet excavated, single standing stones and other remnants of a vibrant ritual past.

The sheer scale of the Orkney megalithic monuments, and the equivalents in Ireland and all along the Atlantic coast, is a testament to the economic effects of agriculture. However like us they may have been, the Mesolithic hunter-gatherers who first settled in Scotland simply could not have assembled the manpower to build these great monuments. There just were not enough of them. The easy life on the shoreline could support only a few thousand people. It was the coming of agriculture to Scotland, beginning about 6,000 years ago, that boosted the population so that, only a few centuries later, there was enough manpower to construct these vast monuments. But did this evidently greatly increased population mean the immigration of large numbers of people, or did the original Mesolithic inhabitants adapt and proliferate? Were the descendants of the fishermen of Cramond and Oronsay replaced, or at least overlaid, by new arrivals? There is no firm archaeological evidence either way, and it is one of the principal questions to ask of the genetic evidence.

There is, however, on Orkney, ample evidence that, whether or not the inhabitants of Skara Brae and the builders of Maes Howe were descended from the original stock, they were not by any means the last people to take an interest in this green and fertile land. In the centre of

Kirkwall, the capital of Orkney, stands the magnificent medieval cathedral of St Magnus, built in the mid-twelfth century. It is as impressive a piece of late Norman architecture as anything in England. But Norman it is not. This is a Viking cathedral, started in 1137 by Rognvald, Earl of Orkney. Vikings began to arrive in Orkney, and in Shetland to the north, at the end of the eighth century. There is no exact date, but this coincides with the first of the Viking raids in England on the undefended monastery of Lindisfarne off the Northumbrian coast of England. The date of that raid is known very precisely. It took place on 8 June 793. The raiders carried off the rich monastery treasures and returned whence they came. That may have been Norway, but it is more likely that the base for the raid on Lindisfarne was Orkney.

Lindisfarne was the first of many raids. The next year a Viking fleet attacked Jarrow, down the coast from Lindisfarne. The following year, 795, the raids switched to the west coast of Scotland and St Columba's church on Iona was attacked. Iona suffered twice more, in 802 and 806. Enough was enough and the monastery was evacuated back to Kells in Ireland – well away from the coast. The Viking raids were only the first flurries in a campaign of invasion and settlement that dominated the Isles for the next 400 years. By the time Rognvald began to build his magnificent cathedral, the Vikings had long been in control of Orkney and Shetland. They had established bases in Ireland at Dublin, Waterford, Wexford and Limerick, though their hold there was always precarious and they never managed to get control of Ireland from the High

Kings. But that was not for lack of trying. In the 830s a large Viking raiding fleet appeared regularly around the Irish coast and by the 840s they had built Dublin up as a major base for slaving and for attacking Britain. The Dublin Vikings took sides in the ceaseless wars between the feuding Irish kings, but made the bad mistake of joining the losing side and, in 902, quickly evacuated Dublin and retreated to the Isle of Man to escape the advancing army of their conquerors. But they were back in force by 907.

The Irish bases were at the end of a supply chain of men and weapons, based on Orkney and extending from the Hebrides to the Isle of Man and, on the mainland, to parts of Argyll. By AD 1000, Norse power had reached its peak and the Vikings were gradually forced back towards Orkney. They lost Limerick in 965, Dublin in 999 and were finally beaten at the battle of Clontarf in 1014. This famous battle is remembered not only for the Irish victory but also for the death of Brian Boru, King of Cashel and High King of Ireland. The Norsemen maintained their grip in Man and the Western Isles until well into the twelfth century, when they were driven out by Somerled, a Celtic hero we will hear more about. Eventually they lost Orkney and Shetland when the two island groups were annexed by James III of Scotland in 1468.

Although the initial Viking raids on Lindisfarne and the other coastal monasteries were motivated by material avarice, and the glory of returning home with conspicuous wealth, it was not long before the Vikings began to settle. Confined to a coastal strip of western Norway between the mountains and the sea, it is not hard to understand the attraction of the rich farmland of Orkney and the northern Scottish mainland. Shetland, too, which was much nearer home, was also attractive for settlement, though less fertile than Orkney. As well as being scarce, farmland in Norway was handed down to the eldest son. Younger sons had few prospects at home and the chance of getting land overseas was a great temptation. How extensive the Norse settlement of Scotland eventually became is one more question I hoped to answer using genetics. Certainly their cultural influence has been overwhelming. All place-names in Orkney and Shetland have a Norse origin, and *Norn*, a hybrid Scots/Norse dialect, was spoken there until the end of the eighteenth century. And yet positively identified Viking archaeological remains are few and far between in Scotland.

An exception is the site at Jarlshof on the southern tip of Shetland, where a small indigenous community was replaced by a series of Viking longhouses some time in the ninth century. These were impressive structures. Though only the base of the walls survives – the building stone is far more irregular in Shetland than in Orkney – the typical layout of a Norse longhouse is easy to see. Built of stone with an earth core, the houses are typically 20 metres long by 5 across, with door spaces opposite each other in the long wall. There are two or possibly three houses at Jarlshof and their position on the site of early, circular, houses might indicate a violent settlement, although that cannot be taken for granted. Grouped longhouses, as at Jarlshof, are unusual; single isolated farmhouses are more the rule, giving no indication of whether the settlement was amicable or violent.

If the genetics proved that the Norse settlement in Scotland had been extensive, then who was it that had been replaced? This is the time to introduce the people who, above all others in the Isles, are surrounded by the greatest mystery – the Picts.

11
THE PICTS

On 15 July 1995 the final section of the Skye Bridge was lowered into place. Three months later, at 11.00 a.m. on 16 October, the Secretary of State for Scotland declared the bridge open and, for the first time since the Ice Age, the Isle of Skye was joined by solid connection to the mainland. The very next day the protests started. The target of the protesters was a combination of the very high toll, the loss of the ferry and the suspicion that the main financial backers, the Bank of America, were making far too much money. By 1.00 a.m. there was a queue of thirty-five cars all refusing to pay. Welcome to the spirited world of island protest. There followed years of active opposition, non-payment, even one imprisonment. Hilariously, those charged with refusing to pay the toll had to make the 140-mile round trip to the Sheriff Court at Dingwall, which once again meant crossing the bridge, where they of course refused to pay, thus incurring further criminal charges. The Skye Bridge toll became a *cause célèbre* until eventually the Scottish Executive bought the bridge and the tolls were scrapped on 21 December 2004.

Though Skye is firmly Gaelic, the protests were co-ordinated by one Robbie the Pict. Not just a sobriquet but a formal change of name. Born Brian Robertson, Robbie the Pict is a celebrated campaigner against all kinds of modern evil. He has been arrested over 300 times, refuses to pay road tax and has formed his own sovereign state on one acre of land in the north end of Skye. There are one or two other people who choose to link their name to this obscure ancient people. I am regularly contacted by one 'Nechtan the Pict', eager to enlist my help in recovering DNA from an allegedly royal Pictish body found in Perthshire. Clearly it means something to be thought of as a Pict. So who were they?

Although the Picts have been garlanded with an air of mystery, with book titles such as *The Puzzle of the Picts* that capture the imagination with hints of a lost people, the answer is almost bound to be more prosaic. The derivation of the name is *Picti*, the generic nickname the Romans gave to the indigenous inhabitants of the Isles. It was not just the northern tribes that were given this description. Any tribes the Romans encountered who either wore tattooes or adorned their bodies with wode earned the un-complimentary nickname. *Picti*, literally 'the Painted People', is also from the same root as *Pretani*, the Gaelic term which, according to the Romans, the islanders used to describe themselves and from which, so some historians believe, the name Britain itself derives. As the Romans occupied more and more of the Isles and developed separate names for the tribes they conquered, the only peoples left with the original nickname were the tribes living in the far north. All tribes north of the Antonine Wall, which ran between the Clyde and the Forth, were automatically Picts.

The material remains of the Picts are extremely impressive, though nowhere numerous. About 200 carved symbol stones and rock inscriptions have survived, mainly in the north and east of the Scottish mainland and on Orkney. Even though they are for the most part badly weathered, the symbol stones reveal a mastery of naturalistic relief and abstract carvings. Most of the inscriptions and carvings date from the fourth to the seventh centuries AD, the later ones incorporating Christian symbols in the wake of St Columba's conversions. They are not close to any of the other contemporary styles to be found in the Isles, not Roman, Saxon or even Irish, adding further mystique to the Pictish enigma.

The Picts also left behind a collection of remarkable stone structures unlike any other in the Isles – the brochs. These take your breath away, especially when you realize that they were built over 2,000 years ago. Their form is similar wherever they are found. Round towers, tapering inwards at the top rather like a power station cooling tower, these huge stone buildings were once the largest structures in the whole of the Isles. Brochs typically enclose a central area 10–12 metres in diameter, with walls only slightly lower. They have double-skinned walls, held together by flat stones which form inner galleries within the walls. As well as providing storage space, these gaps, just like cavity walls in modern houses, would have insulated the interior and kept the heat in. This is easiest to see where there has been a partial collapse, such as at Dun Telve, near Glenelg on the mainland opposite Skye, or at Dun Carloway on the west coast of Lewis, a few miles north of the stone circle at Calanais. From gaps left in the inner walls, it looks as if the central area was fitted with wooden galleries, the whole structure resembling Shakespeare's Globe Theatre in miniature. The brochs were not roofed, so fires in the central living area could vent straight into the open air.

At first sight brochs appear to have been built for defence and they would certainly have been extremely difficult to attack successfully. The view from the ramparts would have given plenty of warning of any hostile approach and the blank, windowless external walls were impregnable. However, it is not at all certain whether brochs were built to withstand attack – or just to show off. Some archaeologists believe they are simply a natural evolution of the much smaller Pictish roundhouses typical of the region. Since there is no evidence of attacks, such as the reddening that discolours the stone of buildings that have been set alight, it is more likely that their impressive bulk was valued for just that purpose – to impress. The standard design, and the relatively short time over which the brochs were built, in the first and second centuries BC, suggests that there may have been mobile teams of masons and labourers who toured the Highlands and Islands and built brochs to order. That in turn must mean that the local landowners were wealthy enough to afford it – and it isn't hard to imagine how rivalry between them would be a spur to taller and taller brochs. Finds at the broch at Gurness on Orkney show that the local aristocrat who lived there was not merely active locally. Fragments of Roman amphorae, or wine carriers, link Gurness to a recorded visit of submission by a Pictish king to the Emperor Claudius at Colchester in AD 43. Whoever the Picts were, they were certainly not primitive relics of the Stone Age.

There has always been a lingering question about what language the Picts spoke. For many years, some linguists believed they may have spoken an ancient tongue unrelated to the Indo-European family which embraces almost all other European languages. To me, and probably to you, while I can see there might be a family connection between, say, Italian and Spanish, it is not at all obvious that German, Portuguese and French are all related. However, be assured that they are and that, along with practically every other European language and others, like Sanskrit from the Indian subcontinent, their grammatical structure shows that they have evolved from a common root. The only living exception in western Europe is *Euskara*, the language of the Basques of north-east Spain and south-west France. Euskara is totally different from any other European language. The grammar is different and the words have quite different roots.

Some scholars, keen to mark out the Picts as an ancient people, relics of the Old Stone Age, have pointed to the few examples of ambiguous runic carvings as evidence that they spoke a language unrelated to any other Indo-European tongue. The truth is that, unless we have more evidence, we may never know. Since there are no written Pictish texts, and so very few surviving stone inscriptions, the language of the Picts enters the realms of the unknowable. Which all adds to the mystery.

Unfortunately, there is virtually no guidance from mythology as to the origin of the Picts. Unlike the rich mythologies of the Irish, the Welsh and the English, the mythology of the Picts is almost non-existent. That does not mean it *never* existed; it surely must have done. It is more a reflection of the absence of writing or, more accurately, the absence of anyone else to write it down until it was too late. In the rest of the Isles, it fell to Christian monks to record, or rather to mould, oral myths. For some reason, this did not happen with the Picts, even though they were among the first people in Britain to have been converted to Christianity after Columba arrived from Ireland in the mid-sixth century. However, the majority of modern scholars now consider that Pictish was closely allied to the strand of Gaelic spoken throughout the rest of Britain and surviving in modern Welsh. If Gaelic was the language of the Picts, it would have been the P-Gaelic of Britain and not the Q-Gaelic of Ireland. If so, then why is the Scottish Gaelic spoken in the Hebrides and now taught in schools in the Highlands and Islands so closely allied to Irish Q-Gaelic and not to the harsher P-Gaelic of the Welsh? For the answer we must look to the west, and to the peninsula of Kintyre, the long finger that reaches almost as far as Ireland itself.

Across the sea from Kintyre, in County Antrim, close to the Giant's Causeway, the Irish kings of Dál Riata began to look for new conquests, and the lands visible across the sea were the natural target. In the first centuries of the first millennium AD, the Dál Riata founded three colonies – on the islands of Islay and Mull and on the Kintyre peninsula. They called their possessions *Ar-gael* – hence Argyll.

The Picts briefly regained Argyll in the sixth century. When Columba arrived we know that it was a Pictish king who gave him the land on Iona in 563. Shortly afterwards, the Dál Riata got a new king, Aidan, who set out to re-establish the colonies in Argyll. If this wasn't enough to upset the Picts, he made matters worse by attacking their possessions on Orkney and on the Isle of Man. He also annoyed the Ui Neill High King of Ireland by these unauthorized adventures. Matters came to a head in 575 when Columba, himself a member of the Ui Neill clan, arbitrated the treaty by which Aidan agreed to pay the High King a military tribute while keeping his maritime revenue for himself. To make the most of this outcome, Aidan built up a strong navy, which is just as well, because he lost most of his land battles. The treaty of 575 kept the peace in Ireland for fifty years, but the Dál Riata never fully recovered their Irish possessions. Their centre of power switched to Argyll and their territorial ambitions were directed north and east towards the lands of the Picts.

For the next two centuries the balance of advantage see-sawed between the Gaels of Dalriada (just another spelling of Dál Riata) and the Picts, with each side alternately gaining ground only to lose it again. Eventually the Gaels gained the upper hand and in 843 the Gaelic king Kenneth MacAlpin was crowned the first king of Alba, a unified country covering both the land of the Picts and Dalriada.

Kenneth MacAlpin's claim to the throne was a combination of the Gaelic patrilineal succession of Dalriada and the matrilineal inheritance system of the Picts. These rules did not mean that women became rulers themselves, but that a man would be able to claim the throne through his mother's genealogy rather than his father's. The land came to be called Scotland because *Scotti* was the label the Romans gave to all Irish immigrants into Britannia. As we have already seen, that name has its own, deeper origins in the mythology of Scota, wife of Mil.

The unification of Scotland under a single king came shortly after the Vikings began their attacks on the coast and is widely seen as a response to this external threat, when unity against a common enemy was more prudent than being weakened by continued feuding, a solution that eluded the Irish. Kenneth MacAlpin moved his centre of operations from Dalriada to the Pictish capital near Perth on the eastern side of Scotland. To emphasize that he was there to stay, he brought the ancient 'Stone of Destiny' from the west and installed it at Scone, near Perth, for his coronation. These decisions, no doubt diplomatically and politically sound at the time, did mean that the centre of power shifted away from the Gaelic west. In later centuries Argyll and the Hebrides consistently refused to be governed by the kings of Scotland, and even now still see themselves as different.

Kenneth was the first of a dynasty of Scottish kings that ruled in patrilineal succession until 1286. Towards the end, Robert the Bruce emerged victorious from a confusion of claimants. His grandson Robert II, the son of Walter, the

High Steward of Scotland, and Bruce's daughter, began the Stuart dynasty, which ruled in Scotland until 1603. This was when James VI, on the death of the childless Elizabeth I, also became King of England, and, though it is often forgotten, King of Ireland as well.

The Stuarts were not Scottish in origin at all, but Anglo-Normans. Just as territorial ambition had spurred Richard de Clare, Earl of Pembroke, to invade Ireland in 1166, so other Anglo-Norman lords had their eyes on Scotland. However, unlike Ireland, where the chaos of rival kings made it easy for de Clare to divide and conquer, the relative stability of the unified Scottish royal house required more subtle tactics. Anglo-Norman barons sided with the Scottish kings against the unruly Gaels of the west and it was the contingent of armoured Norman knights on horseback that defeated the Celtic chieftain Somerled's attempted invasion of Scotland at the battle of Renfrew in 1164. Walter the Steward, whose son was to become, as Robert II, the first of the Stuart dynasty, was himself a member of the Norman Dapifer family from near Oswestry in Shropshire, where they had been granted land by Henry I. This is relev-ant in the genetic context because, although there was no invasion as there had been in Ireland, the Anglo-Norman presence in Scotland was very influential. It may have affected the nature of the Y-chromosome pattern that we find in much the same way that Gaelic and Anglo-Norman Y-chromosomes are distinctly different in Ireland.

So far, we have four possible influences on the genetic structure of the people of Scotland: firstly the Picts; then the

Gaels of Ireland, synonymous with the Celts; the Vikings; and, in the south of Scotland particularly, the Anglo-Normans. As we shall see later, the south of Scotland was originally the British Celtic kingdom of Strathclyde. It is known that from the fifth century AD onwards this came under pressure from Anglo-Saxons, but we will leave that to a later chapter. With the Picts, Celts, Vikings and Anglo-Normans to sort out, there is already more than enough to keep us occupied.

12
THE DNA OF SCOTLAND

'We have just had a message,' the pilot's voice came over the intercom, 'that Sumburgh is fogbound.'

It looked as though our trip to the Shetland Isles was going to be cancelled. 'But we'll carry on and see if we can find a gap in the clouds.'

This was not the sort of thing that I, not at my very best in the air, really wanted to hear. We were heading north from Edinburgh airport over the thick layer of sea mist that was covering Scotland for as far as the eye could see. The plane was not a regular jet, but a twin-engine propeller plane, small, cramped and very noisy. Strangely, though, because the plane was small and was driven by propellers, it felt as though all of us, passengers and crew, were part of an adventure. Sure enough, when we reached the Shetlands, after a couple of circuits, the pilot did find a gap in the clouds and he dived through it to make a perfect landing. The team for Shetland was made up of Jayne Nicholson and Sara Goodacre from my research group, my son Richard, then aged eight, whose half-term it was, and me.

For the week we were in Shetland it never really got dark at all. The sun rose at 3.30 in the morning and set at 10.30 at night. But even for the five hours that the sun dipped below the horizon, everything was illuminated by the ethereal northern twilight. It is easily light enough to walk around, and even to read a newspaper, right through the night. And everywhere the air was full of the sound of birds, the raucous clatter of terns and kittiwakes on the coasts and the sweet bubbling of curlews across the moorland away from the sea.

Shetland is nowhere near as fertile as Orkney, but both places – to an outsider – are very different from anywhere else in the Isles. There is a tangible air of Scandinavia about both archipelagos, stronger in Shetland than in Orkney, but unmistakable in both. And it isn't just obvious things like the 'Viking Coach Station' in Lerwick, the capital of Shetland, or signs in shop windows saying 'Norwegian spoken'. It is there in the domestic architecture – the wooden A-frame houses painted with the same rust-red shade that is everywhere in Scandinavia. It is in the undemonstrative, no-nonsense feeling of the place. Although, even recently, anthropologists have written that in Lerwick, and in Kirkwall, the capital of Orkney, practically everyone they saw was blond, I have to say that was not my experience of either place. I could not see an overwhelming presence of the blond Scandinavian archetype which is such a feature of John Beddoe's descriptions, but then I haven't seen it in my visits to Norway and Sweden either. However, the reason we had come to Shetland was not primarily to gaze at the exterior features of the islands' inhabitants but to look for evidence of history hidden from view, hidden in the DNA.

Unlike the rest of Scotland, where most of our DNA samples came from blood-transfusion donor sessions, there are none of these in Orkney or Shetland so we had to arrange other methods of getting our samples. Jayne Nicholson discovered that the Shetland Science Festival was being held in May, so she arranged for us to have a stand at the Festival and also organized a series of visits to schools for the same week. This worked extremely well: while two people manned the booth at the Festival, the others went to schools around the islands. The Festival itself was held in a smart new sports hall on the outskirts of Lerwick, one of many around the islands. The same is true of schools, all of which have brand-new buildings. Shetland Council spends a lot of the revenue it gets from the Sullom Voe oil terminal on upgrading the island infrastructure. The roads are excellent, the inter-island ferries are well equipped and run on schedule. I saw neither poverty nor extravagant wealth on Shetland.

The Science Festival was a jolly affair. Groups from all over Scotland, including a strong contingent from the University of Aberdeen, put on displays of such varied nature as an artificial tornado generator, a giant bubble machine and a practical course in making plaster casts of fossils. Although the Festival was aimed primarily at schoolchildren, there was a healthy flow of adults coming to our stand and we had no difficulty enrolling volunteers in the Genetic Atlas Project. We were not taking blood, only cheek swabs, and I am sure that helped. For this we use a small brush like a miniature bottle-brush, 1 inch long at the end of a 5-inch plastic handle. The bristles on the brush collect cells from the inner cheek as they are rubbed gently over the surface. There is plenty of DNA in these cells and the brushes can be stored for weeks, or posted, without the DNA suffering. It is one of those seemingly unimportant practical changes that actually make all the difference. Now, instead of collecting blood samples, we can send brushes to anywhere in the world and receive DNA back through the post. These brushes can hold DNA safely under even the most extreme conditions. I have equipped a number of university expeditions with DNA brushes and nearly all of them are returned with the DNA intact, even when they have been carried for weeks in a rucksack through deserts and across mountains.

When we began to use the brushes to collect DNA, we would often help the volunteers by doing it for them. However, we have now had to stop this, and volunteers must do it themselves. This is not for fear of breaking new Health and Safety regulations but for a far more delicate reason. False teeth. It was at the Shetland Science Festival that I learned this painful lesson. An elderly lady, eager to join in the project, opened her mouth to allow me to rub the inside of her cheek with the brush. No sooner had I begun to guide the brush across her cheek than it suddenly stopped moving. I let go. I looked at her. She blushed and turned away. After regaining her composure, she returned with the brush and the explanation. I had inadvertently dislodged the top set of her dentures, which had dropped down and clamped the handle of the brush to the lower set. After this, we let people do their own brushing.

The Science Festival was also the scene of another humiliation. One of my obligations in exchange for the display space was to give a public lecture during the Festival, to which I was happy to agree. As usual I spent the previous evening preparing my talk and organizing my slides. With five minutes to go before my talk, I went over to the screened-off section of the hall that had been set aside for public lectures. There was no one there. I checked the time on the Festival programme. This was definitely the right time, and the right place. I waited, but still nobody came, so I thought there must have been some sort of rescheduling that I had not got to hear about. As I was unloading my slides, a lady came in and sat down. I asked if she had come to hear my lecture. She had. Having no audience is bad enough. Having an audience of one is far worse. Unable to slink quietly away, I was honour-bound to give the lecture, all forty-five minutes of it, slides and all. The sole member of the audience sat there quietly, paying attention and, when I had finished, she picked up her handbag and, without a word, left the area. Field work is full of surprises.

One last reflection of Shetland came from talking to men and women at the Festival. I wanted to know whether they felt closer to Scandinavia or to Scotland. On this question, the answer was clear-cut. It was Scandinavia without a doubt. Very few felt any connection with Scotland, let alone with the new Scottish parliament in Edinburgh. It was as if they even preferred to have their affairs governed from

Westminster than from Edinburgh. This allergy to Scotland extends to their own individual desires for a Viking ancestry, especially among the men. Where there was any uncertainty, and most people did not know where their ancestors had come from, they wanted to be Vikings. Scots came a very poor second and, to my surprise, an Irish ancestry was even worse.

I know hardly anybody from among my friends and colleagues who has been to Shetland. Only one, who is on the maintenance staff at the Institute where I work, visits regularly. He goes there to witness the festival of Up Helly Aa. This annual event is held on the last Tuesday in January, in the depths of winter darkness, and is a very real reminder of Shetland's Viking affiliations. The day begins with the year's elected Jarl, or leader, and his fifty-seven-strong retinue of *guizers* marching through the streets of Lerwick dressed in scarlet velvet, wearing winged helmets and carrying elaborate shields and heavy war axes. Becoming the Jarl of Up Helly Aa is a great honour for a Shetlander. It is the culmination of an induction and selection process that can last twenty years and that begins as a teenager with a minor role in the pageant. The Jarl assumes the name Sigurd Hlodvisson for the day and receives the freedom of Lerwick for the duration of his twenty-four-hour reign. The culmination of Up Helly Aa is the ceremonial torching of Sigurd's galley *Asmundervag*, specially made for the occasion. The real Sigurd Hlodvisson, also known as Sigurd the Stout, lived from 980 to 1014. Sigurd was the Norse Earl of Orkney and divided his time between visiting his overseas dominions, in Ireland

and the Isle of Man, and summers spent raiding the Hebrides and the Scottish mainland. His reign as Earl of Orkney came to a sudden end when he was killed at the battle of Clontarf when, as you may recall from the last chapter, Brian Boru finally forced the Vikings out of Ireland. Maybe that is why the last thing a Shetland man wants to be thought of is Irish.

We left Shetland after a busy week. The take-off was as alarming as the landing. In certain wind conditions the elected runway faces south, straight at the cliff of Sumburgh Head. I thought we were taxiing to another part of the airport, when the engines went to full throttle and we accelerated down the runway – straight towards the cliff! Needless to say we banked sharply as soon as we left the ground. We had with us over 600 DNA samples, a magnificent total.

We realized that we had the best chance yet of finding genetic evidence of Viking settlement in the Northern Isles. If we could detect the signal anywhere it would be in Orkney and Shetland. And if we could only identify Viking DNA in the Northern Isles, we could look for it elsewhere. According to everything we are told about the Vikings, and which is reinforced by re-enactments like Up Helly Aa, this was a society dominated by warlike chieftains and their blood-thirsty acolytes, raping and pillaging their way around Europe. These being men, it seemed only sensible to begin our search for Viking genes with the Y-chromosome. If these stories were true, then that would be the place to look. Recalling the Irish results, where almost 100 per cent of men with Gaelic surnames are in the same Y-chromosome clan – that of Oisin – what is the paternal clan make-up of Orkney and Shetland? The answer is, very different from Ireland. Although there are still plenty of Oisins in the Northern Isles, the proportion is very much lower than it is in Ireland. Even so, Oisin is still the major clan in both Shetland and Orkney, with just under 60 per cent of men in this paternal clan. That is a very big difference from the situation in Ireland, so this was a very promising start. Almost all the remaining 40 per cent was made up equally of the two clans Wodan and Sigurd, with just a smattering from the minor clans Eshu and Re.

Even without delving any further into the detail of the Y-chromosome genetic fingerprints, it was clear that Ireland and the Northern Isles had a very different genetic history if we listened only to the version told by men. But it wasn't completely different. Oisin still dominated, as it did in Ireland, but nowhere near as much. Our first thought, when we saw these results, was to draw the conclusion that in the Northern Isles Oisin represented the descendants of the indigenous Pictish ancestry, while the men in the clans of Wodan and Sigurd had Viking ancestors who had come from Norway. That would put the ancestral proportions in present-day Shetland at roughly 65 per cent Pict and 35 per cent Viking. The indigenous Pictish ancestry would still be in the majority but with a big slice of Viking male ancestry.

The first test of this theory was to see what things were like in Norway. To prepare for this comparison, two of the team, Jayne Nicholson and Eileen Hickey, had already been collecting in Norway. Thanks to the co-operation of the Norwegian Blood Transfusion Service, we had 400 blood samples from all over the country, from Finnmark in the far north to Rogaland in the extreme south. If Norwegian Y-chromosomes were all either in the clans of Wodan and Sigurd, with no Oisin, then it would back up this first conclusion – at least to the coarse level of detail embraced by simple clan membership. However, as it turned out, there were plenty of Oisins in Norway as well. Altogether, nearly a third of Norwegian men were members of the clan of Oisin. The straightforward link between Oisin = Pict and Wodan and Sigurd = Viking that we had begun to hope for in our first run through the Shetland Y-chromosomes had obviously been an oversimplification.

However, when we looked at the clan make-up in the different regions of Norway, the concentration of Oisins in the western provinces, the traditional homeland of the Vikings, was much lower than in other parts of Norway. Around Bergen, on the south-west coast, only 15 per cent of men had Oisin clan Y-chromosomes. The other two thirds of Norwegians were split between the clans of Wodan and Sigurd, with Wodans outnumbering Sigurds by roughly two to one.

We were faced with two questions before we could be sure of interpreting our Shetland results correctly. The first was this. Were the Norwegian Wodans and Sigurds genetically similar, at the more detailed fingerprint level, to the men in the same clans from the Northern Isles? In other words, did we find the same detailed Y-chromosome fingerprints in Norway and the Northern Isles within each of the clans? We checked each one, looking for matches in the Norwegian men. To our great relief, we found exact or first-generation matches to almost all the Sigurds and to about two thirds of the Wodans. This certainly looked like a good indication that most, if not quite all, of the Y-chromosomes in these two clans had arrived from Scandinavia. But how about the Oisins? Here again there were matches between the Norwegian and Shetland samples, but nowhere near as many. There were far more Shetland Oisins whose Y-chromosome signatures were unmatched in Norway than in the other clans. We expected some similarities, since the Viking ships would not have distinguished between genetic clan when choosing their crews and there were plenty of Oisins in Norway. When we took this into account it was clear that our initial estimates of Viking ancestry had been a bit low. Some of the Northern Isle Oisins had almost certainly come with the Vikings. Including them pushed our estimate of Viking ancestry in men from Shetland up to 42 per cent. The proportion of Orkney men with a Norse Viking ancestry, which we estimated in the same way, was slightly lower, at 37 per cent. But please do not concern yourself with exact proportions; just take from this that the male Norse ancestry of Orkney and Shetland is substantial, but was never complete.

I began our interpretation of the Northern Isles DNA with the Y-chromosome because of the Vikings' reputation, but I also wanted to see what the maternal DNA told us as well. At the time we were analysing the DNA from the Northern Isles we had just completed a study with Agnar Helgason, an Icelandic anthropologist, on the genetic ancestry of his native land where we had asked a similar question about the paternal and maternal input. The histories of Iceland and of the Northern Isles were quite different in that, when the Vikings began to settle Iceland from around AD 860, it was uninhabited. The few Irish monks who had settled there in the quest for a life of contemplation sensibly left as soon as they saw the first sails on the horizon.

Over the next fifty years large numbers of Norse settlers arrived in Iceland, most from around Bergen but some from Viking settlements in Britain. This was large-scale, planned immigration to a land with no indigenous opposition and by the beginning of the tenth century there were 60,000 people living in Iceland. The population has grown to 250,000 today, but there has been no recorded large-scale immigration since the original settlement. Agnar and I wanted to find out whether this had been a predominantly male-driven settlement, with females brought in from elsewhere, or whether roughly equal numbers of Norse men and women had arrived. There have been persistent stories that Icelandic men raided the coasts of Scotland and Ireland for wives. Agnar and I thought we could check these stories by comparing modern Icelandic Y-chromosomes and mitochondrial DNA with the equivalent DNA from Scandinavia, Ireland and Scotland. By going through the Icelanders' DNA results one by one, we assigned their most likely origin from comparison with British, Irish and Scandinavian samples.

We discovered that roughly two thirds of Icelandic Y-chromosomes were Scandinavian, while the remaining third were from Ireland and Scotland. However, the origin of maternal DNA was reversed, with only a third from Norway and two thirds from Ireland and Scotland. This confirmed the stories that, while most of the men had settled in Iceland from Norway, they relied heavily on women imported from Ireland and Scotland. It doesn't necessarily mean they were taken there against their will, as the results could not distinguish between settlers who had arrived straight from Norway and the male descendants of Vikings who had spent a generation or two in Scotland. Even so, it is hard to account for the Gaelic origins of a third of Icelandic Y-chromosomes without contemplating that these men were taken to Iceland as slaves. The Iceland study gave us a very interesting result, and also helped us to develop the way of assigning the Icelandic DNA to a Norse or Gaelic/Pictish origin, which we then used for Orkney and Shetland and then, in modified form, for the rest of the Isles.

When we tried the same treatment on the Northern Isles, expecting a similar result to what we had found in Iceland, we were in for a major surprise. The maternal clans in Norway and in Orkney and Shetland were superficially quite different. Katrine was common in Norway but rare in Orkney and Shetland, and the same was true for Tara. But when we looked more carefully at the detailed sequences, the matches leapt out. Within each of the seven major clans, and the minor ones too, the similarities in detailed sequence were remarkable. I had initially expected to find hardly any Scandinavian mitochondrial DNA in either Orkney or Shetland. I had imagined that the Viking reputation for rape, pillage and general destruction recalled in Up Helly Aa, in atmosphere if not in fact, would have had the expected genetic consequence – kill the men and keep the women. When it came to permanent settlement, these same women, I had expected, would have become the wives of Viking men. That is the usual pattern of conquest and settlement that I have seen many times throughout the world. It is all too obvious in the genetic consequences of the European colonization of Polynesia and South America, where European Y-chromosomes are extremely common, while European mDNA is virtually unknown. This is a record of great success for the incoming Y-chromosomes at the expense of the indigenous, but with no effect at all on the aboriginal mitochondrial DNA. Orkney and Shetland had all the right ingredients, but the genetics said otherwise. Amazingly, there was as much Norse mitochondrial DNA in the Northern Isles as there were Norse Y-chromosomes. This could mean only one thing – anathema to the Jarls for the day of Up Helly Aa and their retinue of axe-wielding *guizers*. The Viking settlement of Orkney and Shetland had been peaceful! The Scandinavians had brought their women with them.

The 60 per cent of Orcadians and Shetlanders who do not have a Viking genetic ancestry are most likely to be the descendants of the indigenous Picts. However, there is a proviso. After the islands were eventually ceded to Scotland in the fifteenth century there was a substantial immigration of Scots, which would have diluted the genes of the islanders, whether of Viking or Pictish ancestry. Since we had been successful in identifying Viking genes, both male and female, the next question was whether we could do the same for the Picts, and for that we must head south to the heart of Pictland.

Close by the small town of Dunkeld, a few miles north of Perth on the banks of the River Tay, is the site of the Abbey of Scone. It was here that Kenneth MacAlpin was crowned as the first king of a united Scotland in 843. The area around Dunkeld was the central stronghold of the Pictish kings and Kenneth, a Gael from the west, deliberately chose Scone for his coronation to symbolize the unity between Pict and Celt which his reign proclaimed.

Beneath the coronation throne lay *Lia Fail*, the Stone of Destiny, a rectangular block of sandstone. It is said that *Lia Fail* could talk and that it spoke the name of the next king. The Stone itself has a mythical history linking it to Egypt, Spain and Ireland, reminiscent of the Irish origin myths of Mil. However, geologists who have examined the Stone say it comes from the neighbourhood of Scone itself. But there is an explanation for that. The kings of Scotland continued to be crowned above the Stone of Destiny until 1296 when Edward I, always aware of the power of symbolism, carried off the Stone and installed it in Westminster Abbey. But, according to the legend, he was duped. Monks from the abbey, warned of the approach of Edward and his army, hid *Lia Fail* nearby and replaced it with a slab of local sandstone. It was this replica which Edward took back to England while the real Stone lies hidden somewhere close by.

This neatly explains the geological similarity of the Stone to local rocks, and also why there continued to be a long succession of Scottish kings even when the Stone was lying in England. It could hardly be expected to speak the name of the next king of Scotland if it was installed in Westminster Abbey. Why didn't the monks recover the Stone from its hiding place once Edward had departed? For fear of retribution once he knew he had been tricked is the rationalization of the myth. By the time it was safe to bring it out of hiding, the monks had forgotten where they put it. In the eighteenth century there was a local legend that, after a violent storm, a farm lad discovered an underground cavern which had been exposed by a landslide triggered by the torrential rain. The lad entered the cavern and found a stone covered with inscriptions, as indeed the original *Lia Fail* was recorded to have been. Thinking it of no importance he did not speak of it until years later when he heard the story that the monks had switched the stone. Alas, when he returned to the spot, he could not find the cavern entrance, presuming it to have been once more covered by a landslide. This all sounds very unlikely, but stranger things have happened and I am reminded how the prehistoric caves at Lascaux, in the Dordogne, the walls of which are covered with the ancient paintings of bison and reindeer that our ancestors hunted 20,000 years ago, were discovered by accident by another farm lad at about the same time. So perhaps *Lia Fail* really is still there, waiting to be rediscovered.

Meanwhile, the Stone in Westminster Abbey remained resolutely where it was, beneath the coronation throne for every English monarch since Edward II, up to and including the present Queen Elizabeth II in 1953. That will be the last time, for in 1996, 700 years after it was taken to London, *Lia Fail* was returned to Scotland. In an elaborate procession along the Royal Mile, lined by 10,000 people on St Andrew's Day, the Stone was taken from the Palace of Holyroodhouse to its new home in Edinburgh Castle. To the sound of a twenty-one-gun salute from the castle ramparts, the Stone was laid to rest in the Great Hall. The strength of feeling which energized the campaign to return *Lia Fail* to Scotland after 700 years was formidable. The ceremony which attended its return was in many respects the assertion of an ancient Pictish connection, in the same way that Up Helly Aa celebrates the Norse identity in Shetland.

From a genetic point of view, I wanted to see whether I could find a parallel in the living descendants of the ancient Picts. Was there, hidden deep within the cells of Scots still living in the Pictish heartland, a signal of their ancient identity every bit as real, or perhaps more so, as the Stone of Destiny itself? We began our search for Pictish genes at Auchterarder, 15 miles south-west of Perth and temptingly close to the famous golfing hotel of Gleneagles, but I am sad to report that our research budget did not stretch to that level of subsistence. Auchterarder was the first of many visits that my research team paid to blood-donor sessions.

Three months before, in the spring of 1996, I had spent a week travelling all round Scotland visiting the directors of all the Scottish Blood Transfusion Service centres, enlisting their help in our project. It was never difficult to explain why we wanted to do this work, but there were a lot of details to be sorted out in getting permission from the donors' representatives, as well as formal permission from the Transfusion Service itself, ensuring we did not compromise the confidentiality of the donors. We also had to agree a way of collecting the blood that would not interfere with the smooth running of the donor sessions. There was one thing both I and the directors were agreed on. We must attend the sessions in person. Too many researchers ask for blood to be collected on their behalf, without actually going to the sessions. This makes extra work for the donor nurses. I also wanted to be sure we were there to explain our project to the donors and get their consent, and also to talk to them about their own backgrounds and to get the feel of the place.

You may be a blood donor yourself, in which case you will know how the sessions work. As each donor arrives, they wait to be checked in. This, we jointly decided, was the best time for us to introduce ourselves and to ask for their consent to having us analyse their DNA. I was extremely fortunate in having a team of researchers in my group at the time who were absolutely brilliant in the art of persuasion. To the waiting donors, we explained that we were creating a new genetic map of Britain and trying to work out from it our Celtic, Pictish and Viking roots. That was about all the explanation anyone needed before agreeing to take part, especially when they realized we would only be taking a sample of blood from their donation, so there was no need for another needle. Donors told us where they were from, as far back as their grandparents. Those who didn't know, generally the men, took a purple form home with them to ask someone in the family, invariably a woman, and sent it on to us.

By the end of the session in Auchterarder we had collected 187 blood samples, a wonderful start. Over the next two years we visited almost all of the donor sessions throughout Scotland, from Galashiels and Thornhill in the Borders, to Thurso at the very top of Caithness, to Stornoway in the Western Isles, to Campbeltown on the tip of the Kintyre peninsula. Everyone in my research lab joined in, even if they were working on different projects. Itineraries were prepared so that, with luck, several different sessions in different regions could be covered in one trip. We travelled to Scotland by road, by air or by the Highland sleeper from Euston. We set aside a small office at the Institute as a planning room, with donor-session schedules on the wall and a large map of Scotland next to them. By the time we went to our last Scottish session, two years later in Fort William, we had collected over 5,000 blood samples and clocked up over 50,000 miles between us. It is a testament to the team's powers of persuasion that we only ever had one person decline to take part in the project – a farmer from Callander in the Trossachs, north of Stirling – who had to rush off because one of his cows was about to give birth and he didn't have time to fill in our form. It says a lot about him, and donors in general, that they take their blood donations very seriously. None of the donors is paid a penny and the sessions have a tangible atmosphere of selfless community service. Most sessions are entirely run by women, with the only men present being the drivers of the vans that bring the teams and the equipment. It was friendly, calm and efficient. Very impressive all round.

To begin looking for the genetic signatures of the Picts on the mainland I began by dividing Scotland into regions. It was easy to decide where to draw the line on Orkney, Shetland and the Hebrides – they were islands – but on the mainland I needed to draw boundaries. These are shown on the map on page 14. Pictland was covered by two of these: the Grampian region and Tayside and Fife, which for convenience we will henceforth refer to simply as Tayside.

Since we began our analysis of the Northern Isles with the Y-chromosome, and also in deference to the Pictish tradition of matrilineal inheritance, we began the search with mitochondrial DNA. The clan proportions for both Pictish regions were remarkably similar to one another – again you can see this in the Appendix. When I put the results through a statistical test, the only clans that had a significantly different frequency in the two regions were Jasmine, higher in Grampian, lower in Tayside, and Tara, higher in Tayside, lower in Grampian. Otherwise there was no difference. It looked, at this level of scrutiny, as if the maternal ancestry of the two Pictish regions was almost indistinguishable one from the other.

When it came to analysing the detailed sequences, though, I could see plenty of differences. That is always to be expected, because a large proportion of mitochondrial sequences are unique to one region. At the risk of being technical, of the 170 different sequences we found in the two Pictish regions of Grampian and Tayside, 70 occurred only once. I used our experience with disentangling the Norse and Pictish components in the Northern Isles to devise a simple score between 0 and 100 which would summarize the similarity between the two regions. If all the sequences in one region have an exact match in the other, then the score is 100. If none of them matches, the score is 0. On this scale the match score for Grampian and Tayside was 77. Of course that doesn't mean a great deal without anything else to compare it with but, as we shall see, 77 is a very high score compared to most others. It is high enough to consider both regions as one for the purpose of searching for Pictish genes.

When I began to look in detail, it was immediately obvious that the DNA from these two regions was not really all that different from much else in Britain. There was no sign at all of the exotic sequences one might associate with a truly relic population that had been somehow isolated from the rest of mankind. Lots of sequences were unique to the two regions, but that isn't unusual, as we have just seen. Looking through these unique sequences, I could see they were closely related to mDNA sequences from other regions, differing from them by just a single mutation. There was nothing very special about the Pictish DNA, at least on the maternal side. It didn't seem to me that, on this evidence, a case could be made for treating the Picts of Tayside and Grampian as being particularly unusual. But that was just how they appeared to me at the time. We would certainly need to compare them with the rest of the Isles to gauge their true nature. That was my impression from the maternal signal, but what would the Y-chromosomes look like?

Once again the overall Y-chromosome clan structures in Grampian and Tayside were, like the maternal signals, remarkably similar to each other. The clan of Oisin predominated in both, rising to 84 per cent in Grampian – not quite as high as the west of Ireland, but much higher than in Orkney or Shetland. Wodan was quite high in both, at 12 per cent in Grampian and 18 per cent in Tayside respectively, but Sigurd was very low indeed. Only 2 per cent of men in both Pictish regions belonged to Sigurd's clan. You will recall that, in Orkney and Shetland, we assigned all the Sigurds to a Norse Viking origin. On the evidence from the Pictish regions, with low numbers in the clan of Sigurd, it looked as if Grampian and Tayside had virtually no Viking ancestry. This is precisely what we would have expected from the history and the archaeology of both regions. There are no remains of Viking longhouses and no Norse place-names. In fact, some of the place-names have recognizably Pictish origins, notably Pitlochry on the River Tummel a few miles north of Dunkeld. In Orkney and Shetland the reverse is the case. All the place-names have Norse origins.

In Pictland, the genetics suggests a very low level of Viking ancestry among the men. However, if we accept that, as I think we should, what can explain the substantial percentages of Wodan in both regions? In the Northern Isles the proportions of Sigurd and Wodan were roughly equal. If, as we had done, we attribute both clans in the Northern Isles to Viking settlement, based on the close affinities with Y-chromosomes we know exist in Norway, how do we explain the Wodan presence in Pictland? If Viking settlers in Orkney and Shetland were composed of roughly equal numbers of Wodans and Sigurds and these reflected the composition of a typical Viking immigration anywhere in the Isles, then only 2 per cent of the Pictland Wodans could have a Viking origin, leaving the other 12–16 per cent unaccounted for. When I checked through the detailed signatures of Pictland and Northern Isles Y-chromosomes from the clan of Wodan, there were plenty that matched – and plenty that didn't. This was a puzzle. The Pictland Wodans could not all have arrived as Vikings, but where had they come from? Certainly not Gaelic Ireland, where they are almost unknown. Perhaps these men in the clan of Wodan really were the surviving descendants of the Picts.

I made the settlement date calculations, as I had in Ireland, for both the paternal and the maternal ancestors. There was still a wide gap between the male and the female side. The ages of the mDNA clans varied between Ursula at 9,200 years, slightly older than in Ireland, and Jasmine, again the youngest at 5,000 years. The paternal clans were slightly older than in Ireland, but still much younger than the maternal dates. There was no immediate answer to what this meant; indeed by this time I had more or less decided to wait until I had surveyed the entire Isles before trying to make sense of it all. But to what extent had the Picts been replaced by the Dalriadan Celts, the Gaels from Ireland? To try to find out we need to move away over the mountains that separate Pictland from our next destination – the Celtic west.

The gradual colonization of the west from the Irish kingdom of Dál Riata during the first half of the first millennium AD, and the consolidation of their Gaelic kingdom in Scotland following their defeat by the Ui Neill, had an immense cultural impact in Scotland. As we have seen, the language changed from the P-Gaelic of the Picts to the Q-Gaelic of the Irish and, on the accession of Kenneth MacAlpin in 843, Gaelic political dominance was complete.

In the west, one question which our genetic analysis could hope to answer was the degree to which the arrival of the Dalriadan Celts from Ireland displaced the Pictish inhabitants of the region. But there is also another factor to bear in mind, and that is our old friends the Vikings. The whole of the west coast and the Hebrides were repeatedly raided by Vikings from the first attack on the monastery of Iona in 795. If the experience in Orkney and Shetland is anything to go by, we should expect to see evidence of a Viking presence among today's inhabitants of the west coast and the islands.

When we were collecting our samples from the west coast and from the Hebrides, there was a distinctly different response to my questions about people's own ancestry. In Shetland the last thing men, in particular, wanted to see in their genes was the signal of an Irish ancestry. In the Western Isles, and along the west coast, there was still a certain arcane thrill at the possibility of a Viking ancestry, but this was eclipsed by an affiliation with a Celtic past, whatever that actually meant. People were keen to expose an Irish ancestry, if there was one, but most showed no real interest in the prospect of being of Pictish descent. And yet that was the most likely outcome, since it is almost always, in my experience, the earliest occupants who dominate the gene pool of a region. The later arrivals may get all the headlines, but it takes a lot to displace indigenous genes, especially on the female side. Thanks to the Scottish Blood Transfusion Service, we travelled to donor sessions from Thurso in the far north, along the west coast to Ullapool, Gairloch and Fort William, then south to Oban, Lochgilphead at the top of the Kintyre peninsula and right down to Campbeltown at the very end. We travelled over the sea to the Western Isles and across the bridge to Skye. We saw the land in all its moods, from brilliant sunny days when the bright hills shone in the sunlight to furious tempests when wind and rain lashed along streets and through doorways.

Not even the foulest weather prevented the calm progression of the donor sessions, even when the rain was coming in through the windows of community centres that had seen better days. Attendance by the donors was just as high in the bad weather as in the good. In Grampian, almost everyone coming to the donor sessions had been born nearby, and so had their grandparents. In this respect, the most stable place we visited was Huntly in rural Aberdeenshire, where 78 per cent of donors had all four grandparents born close by. In the west this figure was quite a bit lower, and there was a noticeable proportion who had moved into the area in the recent past, mainly from the towns of the central lowlands or from England. Since the project covered the whole of Britain, practically everybody could contribute to the outcome, even if they had only recently arrived in their current locality. It also worked both ways. In and around Glasgow, Edinburgh and London we often encountered donors whose ancestors had come from the west of Scotland and where, for the purposes of the genetic map, they could be confidently placed.

What of the results? We were becoming very adept at identifying Viking DNA and, sure enough, we found plenty of it. In Caithness and along the stunningly beautiful north coast from the Kyle of Tongue to Loch Eribol and Durness we found, by the same tests we had used in Orkney and Shetland, that 15 per cent of the DNA was Norse in origin. Like the Northern Isles, this was true both of Y-chromosomes and of mitochondrial DNA, so it looked as though it was by establishing family-based communities that the Vikings came to settle here, however unlikely this sounds in relation to their folk memory as bloodthirsty plunderers. However, in the Western Isles and Skye, the genetic evidence for a more typecast male-dominated Viking colonization began to emerge when we looked at the results.

There are twice as many Norse Y-chromosomes in Skye and the Western Isles as there are Norse mitochondria; 22 per cent of Hebridean Y-chromosomes, but only 11 per cent of mitochondrial DNAs, had a Norse origin. The further down the west coast, the lower the Viking component became until, in Argyll, it was down to 7 per cent for Y-chromosomes and only 2 per cent for mitochondria.

The diminishing Viking input and its increasing asymmetry between the sexes as we travel down the west coast seems to me best explained by a gradual process of Viking settlement from the early bases in Orkney and Shetland. Some men took their women with them, or returned to Orkney to bring their families once they had laid claim to a plot of land; others intermarried with local Gaelic or Pictish women. In general we found the same detailed Norse Y-chromosomes along the west coast and in the Hebrides as we had already discovered in the Northern Isles. It really didn't look as though there had been a rush of fresh arrivals from Scandinavia.

If that was the level of Norse DNA, what of the rest? Could we assign this to Celtic or Pictish origin? For this, I made a start by comparing our results from the Pictish regions of Grampian and Tayside with the west coast locations. I could tell straightaway that they were substantially different. Not only that – there was also a big difference between the three regions of the west. Much as I had divided Pictland into Grampian and Tayside, so I split the west into three. They were the Highlands from Durness to Fort William, then from Oban south to Kintyre, which I grouped together as Argyll, and, thirdly, the Hebrides, which combined Skye and the Western Isles.

On clan comparisons alone, the Hebrides stood out as very different from the other two. Argyll, at this crude level, was far more like the Pictland regions of Grampian and Tayside than the Hebrides. The Highland coast was somewhere in between. Even when I removed the Norse DNA, the picture was the same. At the greater level of detail revealed by the precise sequences, in the case of the mitochondria or the profiles of the Y-chromosomes, the stark differences between the regions still stood out. For the mitochondrial comparisons, on the scoring system of similarity that I introduced in Pictland, which goes from 0–100 (the higher the score, the greater the similarity), Argyll vs Pictland scored 60, the same score as Argyll vs Highlands but much higher than the Hebrides scored in this equation of similarity with either of them. However, the Y-chromosomes told a different story. The Argyll Y-chromosomes were much more like their Hebridean counterparts than those in the Highlands.

If your head is spinning, you are feeling just as I did when I first tried to decipher these results. It seemed to be going so well. We had identified the genetic legacy of the Vikings and we had found that, just as the archaeology and history leads us to expect, they did not settle in Pictland to any extent. We had seen their diminishing genetic impact as we travelled further and further away from their forward bases in Orkney and Shetland. Until then everything made good sense. But then, the simple story, based on our historical assumption, began to unravel. Far from Pictland being genetically distinct from the Celtic heartlands of Dalriada and Argyll, they were remarkably close, on the maternal side at least. However, this similarity is not reproduced by the Y-chromosome, where Argyll has a low gene-sharing score with Grampian, even after the Norse component has been subtracted.

To me this is the familiar signal of maternal continuity. What we have here, I think, is the imprint of Scotland's Pictish ancestry, on the maternal side, spread more or less uniformly across the land. This is the bedrock of Scottish maternal ancestry on which more recent events have been overlaid. The maternal gene pool is more or less the same in Pictland, in 'Celtic' Argyll and in the Highlands. In Orkney and Shetland, the Pictish bedrock has been overlain by a more substantial and identifiable Norse settlement than anywhere else in Scotland, but it is still there nevertheless.

On the male side, we can see plainly what must be the Pictish bedrock in Grampian and Tayside, but in Argyll it has been substantially overlain by new arrivals. The Argyll Y-chromosomes are in between the Irish and Pictish values and, although these estimates are approximate, a 30–40 per cent replacement of Pictish by Gaelic Y-chromosomes would account for this. It is much harder to be accurate in this case than it was in judging the Norse contribution to the Northern Isles because of the basic similarity between Irish and Pictish Y-chromosomes which, incidentally, makes it almost impossible to detect any genetic effect of the Ulster plantations. However, the genetic signal, as far as I can judge, points to a substantial and, by the look of it, hostile replacement of Pictish males by the Dalriadan Celts, most of whom relied on Pictish rather than Irish women to propagate their genes. The reason I cannot be more certain is itself very relevant to the myth of the Picts. It is precisely because they are genetically close to the Gaelic Irish that these estimates are so difficult. If they had been a relic people, a genetic isolate, then it would have been easy to distinguish them from Irish Gaels. But on the contrary, it is extremely difficult, from which we can confidently conclude that the Picts and the Celts have the same underlying genetic origins.

Which leaves the Hebrides. Their genetics stand out from the Picts and the Celts and the Norse of Shetland or Orkney. Their DNA-sharing scores are low for all comparisons, and for both maternal and paternal genes. Take away the attributable Norse component and the differences remain. What can be so special about the Hebrides? Let's take a closer look.

The long line of islands of the Western Isles are battered on their western sides by the pounding of the Atlantic. These islands protect the Inner Hebridean islands of Canna, Rum, Eigg and Skye from the worst of the Atlantic swell – though when I was caught on an inter-island ferry in a gale I thought the violently bucking boat could have done with a lot more protection. The islands are the last stronghold of the Gaelic language in Scotland and had suffered from decades of depopulation even before the Highland Clearances of the eighteenth and nineteenth centuries. The sight of an abandoned village, with the outlines of stone-walled cottages collapsed and overgrown, is always a sad one. But the sheer scale of it only struck me one day last December when I was taking advantage of the few hours of sunlight to have a trip in the car around Skye.

I went, for the first time, to Glen Eynort, near the Talisker whisky distillery at Carbost. The road to Glen Eynort rises from Carbost and then crosses a low pass which leads to the glen with its two or three inhabited cottages, each with a plume of smoke rising straight up into the cold and, for once, still air. As I descended, the sun, very low in the sky, came out and lit up the hillsides which surround the glen. What I saw utterly amazed me. The low angle of the sun transformed every patch of hillside into lines of light and shade. It took me a moment to realize that these were abandoned fields, with the sun striking the ridges and casting a shadow in the furrows. This ancient landscape, glimpsed only because of the low angle of the sun and normally impossible to make out, covered hundreds of acres. The valley must once have been teeming with life but now, save for the three cottages, it was empty, the crofters dispersed to the far-flung corners of the world.

Luckily the depopulation was not complete and the Hebrides are once again thriving. But why are the genetics so unusual? On the maternal side, the striking thing, compared to other regions, is the much higher proportions of clans that, though they certainly occur elsewhere, are much less frequent. These are the two clans of Jasmine and Tara. And these clans carry the unmistakable signature of agriculture. As we saw in an earlier chapter, Jasmine herself lived in the Middle East and her descendants accompanied the spread of farming into Europe. The clan divided into two around the Balkans. One branch followed the Mediterranean and Atlantic coasts, the other crossed Europe overland. The two branches can be told apart by a series of mutations which must have happened after the split. Both branches have the characteristic mutation of all members of Jasmine's clan of 069 and 126, plus two others at 145 and 261. On its way round the Mediterranean, one branch acquired two more changes at 172 and 222, while on its trek through Europe the other branch gained one extra change at position 231. It is still amazing to me that these tiny changes can tell us so much about the journeys of our ancestors. How one line, hugging the Mediterranean coast, reached Spain then headed north up the Atlantic coast of France, while the other forced its way through the forests and valleys of continental Europe. These mutations illuminate such different journeys. In Ireland, and all along the west coast of Scotland, only the Mediterranean branch of Jasmine is found. The same is true of the Hebrides, and the concentration of these Mediterranean Jasmines in Skye and the Western Isles explains one of the differences.

The other difference is in the clan of Tara. When I first discovered the clan, with my colleagues, it had all the characteristics of a hunter-gatherer origin: a founding date of 17,000 years ago, and a location to the north of Italy among the hills of Tuscany.

When my research group were defending our conclusions about the human past in Europe, and had gathered lots more samples in the process, it gradually became clear that the clan of Tara had, within it, a branch that looked much younger than the rest of the clan. As well as the signature Taran changes at 126 and 294, this branch had additions at 296 and 304. We dated this branch at slightly younger than Tara herself, possibly just within the scope of the spread of agriculture, possibly at the end of the Mesolithic. And it is this Taran branch that dominates the Hebrides.

It seemed to be these two young branches of the two clans, Jasmine and Tara, that were responsible for the unusual genetics of the Hebrides. And both of these branches, the Mediterranean Jasmines and the younger Tarans, had a distinctly seaborne flavour about them. They are spread all along the Atlantic fringe, but rarely inland. This was a definite clue, but the solution was not yet clearly visible. The Hebrides are also unusual in having a very high concentration of members of the Katrine clan, especially on Lewis, where they reach the highest frequency of anywhere in Scotland.

It was during my research on Skye that I stumbled across a genetic phenomenon which, with hindsight, I should have investigated much sooner. At that stage I had already discovered the link between my own surname and a particular Y-chromosome profile. Foolishly imagining that such a link to a common founder would only be found in comparatively uncommon English surnames, it took another year before I realized the same might be true, albeit in diluted form, among Scottish clans as well. My research student Jayne Nicholson and I found a rare Y-chromosome profile in our Skye samples and, when we compared it to others collected at donor sessions elsewhere in Scotland, we noticed that we found it almost exclusively among men with the surnames Macdonald, McDougall and Macalister. It was Jayne who remarked that all three names were said to be descended, according to traditional clan genealogies, from Somerled, the Celtic hero whom we have already encountered. It was Somerled who was responsible for ending the power of the Norse earls of Orkney in Argyll and the Hebrides, and who died at Renfrew during his ill-fated invasion of Scotland in 1164. Jayne set about writing to men with these three names asking for DNA samples, while I contacted the five living clan chiefs whose genealogies traced back to Somerled. They all agreed to help and, I'm very glad to report, all five had inherited the same Y-chromosome that we had seen in the men with the three surnames. Somerled's Y-chromosome had done extremely well and, thanks to its association with a powerful and wealthy clan, has become very common indeed in the Highlands and Islands, and among Highlanders who have emigrated overseas. Roughly a quarter of Macdonalds, a third of McDougalls and 40 per cent of Macalisters are direct paternal descendants of Somerled. This is not just true in Scotland, but throughout the world; it has been estimated that there are 200,000 men who carry Somerled's Y-chromosome as proof of their descent from the man who drove the Norse from the Isles.

I am only summarizing here what was an exhilarating search for the legacy of this illustrious Celtic hero because I have written about it at length in *Adam's Curse*. Soon after this discovery – which was also paralleled by the Macleods of Skye, though there the linkage was to a different chromosome – I heard about the research on Genghis Khan's profligate genetic legacy. His Y-chromosome, passed down through generations of emperor sons, is now found in an estimated 16 million male descendants. This might put Somerled's 200,000 descendants in the shade, but the feeling has grown among geneticists that the Genghis effect could be an important factor in the rise and fall of Y-chromosomes, not only in Asia but in other parts of the world, including the Isles. Recently Brian McEvoy and Dan Bradley from Dublin have found an Irish equivalent to the Macdonalds and the Macleods. Again starting with an unusual Y-chromosome, they noticed its occurrence in a related set of surnames that were linked to branches of the Ui Neill, the clan that had held the High Kingship at Tara, and had expelled the Dál Riata to Argyll. The Ui Neill equivalent of Somerled was Niall Noigiallach, better known as Niall of the Nine Hostages, who lived in the second half of the fourth century AD. This was a time when the Romans were beginning to withdraw from mainland Britain. According to legend, Niall raided and harassed western Britain and specialized in capturing and then ransoming high-ranking hostages, hence his soubriquet. His most famous captive was one Succat, who went on to become St Patrick. Niall's military exploits carried him over the sea to Scotland, where he fought the Picts who were trying to retake the recent Irish colonies of Dalriada. It was during a raid even further afield, in France, that an arrow from the bow of an Irish rival killed Niall on the banks of the River Loire in AD 405.

Niall was succeeded in the High Kingship by his nephew, Dathi, his brother's son. This was typical of the Gaelic tradition of *derbhfine*, the rules of inheritance that chose the new king from among the direct male relatives of the old. This served to ensure the patrilineal inheritance of the High Kingship itself and of the whole clan of Ui Neill. Their hold on the High Kingship was remarkably durable, lasting from the seventh to the eleventh century AD. Brian McEvoy's and Dan Bradley's Y-chromosome tests on the Irish showed that a high proportion of men with Ui Neill surnames – names like Gallacher, Boyle, Doherty, O'Connor and even Bradley, as well as O'Neill – shared an identical or very closely related Y-chromosome signature, strongly indicative of direct descent from Niall himself. In the parts of Ireland most strongly associated with the Ui Neill, mainly in the north-west, the proportion of these Y-chromosomes reaches almost one quarter of the male population.

These bursts of Y-chromosome success over a few generations are something to be aware of in our interpretations of the genetic evidence from the Isles. The predictable effect will be to distort the Y-chromosome profile of a region in favour of the local chieftains and also to exaggerate the differences between the regions. We have already seen how this may be happening in that Y-chromosome similarity scores between regions are usually lower than the same comparative score for mitochondria. The only regions that we have so far encountered where the Y-chromosome similarity score is almost as high as the mitochondrial are the two Pictland regions of Tayside and Grampian. If inheritance and succession really were matrilineal, then this practice would indeed neutralize the Genghis effect, since no Y-chromosome could be linked to wealth and power for generation after generation. Another effect will be to reduce the age of a patrilineal clan. If one or a few Y-chromosome signatures come to predominate in a region due to the Genghis effect, they can do so only at the expense of others. These, it follows, are eliminated either because the men who carry them are actually killed, as was the case in the Mongol Empire, or because they do not have their fair share of children, since the Genghis male monopolizes the women in one way or another. The Genghis effect can substantially reduce the variety of Y-chromosomes, so the normal way of estimating the age of a clan in a region by averaging the number of mutations will be distorted. The fewer different Y-chromosomes there are, the fewer mutations will be found, the average will drop, and the age estimate will become artificially younger. The more pronounced the Genghis effect, the greater the distortion and the greater the difference between the true age of a clan and the estimate. To take things to extremes just to illustrate the point, were Genghis Khan's Y-chromosome the only one to have survived from thirteenth-century Mongolia, only the mutations along his line would have accumulated and the age estimates of Mongolian Y-chromosomes would come out around 800 rather than thousands of years.

Scotland has shown us a bit of everything. Vikings, Picts, Celts, the erratic effects of patrilineal kingship and the ancient bedrock of maternal ancestry. We have discovered that the Viking settlement of Orkney and Shetland was very substantial but also much more peaceful than was previously thought, with as many Norse women as men among the settlers. We now know how to identify a Norse Viking genetic presence anywhere in the Isles. Orkney and Shetland aside, there is a very close genetic affinity between Scotland and Ireland. There has certainly been a substantial settlement from Ireland at some time in the recent past, and the Irish Y-chromosome infiltration into the west of Scotland is almost certainly the signal of the relocation of the Dál Riata from Ulster to Argyll in the middle of the first millennium. We have also made an important discovery about the Picts. Their descendants are still in

Scotland in force, yet they are not the weird prehistoric relics that were once imagined. They fit very comfortably into the Celtic bedrock of the Isles and they have been here a very long time. The Y-chromosomes are more diverse in the Pictland regions of Grampian and Tayside than in, say, Argyll or Ireland, and the explanation may have something to do with the tradition of matrilineal inheritance. The Western Isles stand out as being a little different from the mainland. There are Viking genes there for sure, but also strange ratios of the maternal clans. The Western Isles have the highest concentration of Katrines in the whole of Scotland, twice that of the Pictish heartland of Grampian, along with large numbers of a maritime branch of the clan of Tara which has travelled from the Mediterranean.

We now have a very good idea of the basic genetic structure of Scotland and Ireland, two of the three regions of the Isles that are most closely identified with a Celtic ancestry. The third is Wales and to reach it we go south down the west coast, through the North Channel and into the Irish Sea. We sail past the Norse outpost of the Isle of Man and head further south to the distant peaks of Snowdonia, the highest point in the land of the Red Dragon.

13

WALES

The smallest in land area of the four regions of the Isles, Wales has a population of just under 3 million, occupying a country of 8,000 square miles. Like Scotland, Wales is a mountainous country, with a broad upland spine running down the centre from the high mountains surrounding the summit of Snowdon (1,085 metres) to the Brecon Beacons, which rise to 886 metres in the south. Between these, the upland plateaux of the Cambrian Mountains are intercut by river valleys radiating in all directions and emptying the abundant rainfall into the Irish Sea and the Bristol Channel. Like Scotland, Wales is bounded on three sides by the sea, backed by coastal lowlands, and shares a land boundary with England. And, also like Scotland, this border, the Welsh Marches, has moved backwards and forwards according to the successes and ambitions of the rulers on either side.

The archaeological evidence for the earliest settlers is comparatively thin on the ground. There is the ancient tooth from the cave at Pontnewydd in north Wales that we met in Chapter 1, but at 300,000 years it is far too old to be from a modern human species. At the other end of the country, at Paviland Cave on the Gower Peninsula, the remarkable burial of the ochre-tinted body of the Red Lady showed that *Homo sapiens* had reached Wales before the last Ice Age, but had been forced to retreat south as the temperature dropped and the great herds left the slowly freezing land.

Precisely when humans returned to Wales is uncertain, but considering how close it is to the Cheddar Caves across the Severn, it is surely likely that Palaeolithic hunters got that far, though they left no trace. There are just a handful of late, coastal Mesolithic sites around the Irish Sea, where conditions were similar to sites in Ireland and on the west coast of Scotland. Life for the early Welsh followed the familiar pattern we have already seen elsewhere in the Isles: a life of gathering shellfish, offshore fishing in coracles and hunting in the wooded slopes behind the seashore. There are Neolithic megaliths in Wales, though none matches the magnificence of the Irish passage graves at Newgrange or the great monuments in Orkney or at Stonehenge. Neither have any Neolithic villages like Skara Brae yet been discovered. The earliest houses, round in outline, are isolated. There is some evidence of communal activities around the sites of chambered tombs, the *cromlechs*, whose stark stones have been stripped of their protective mounds of earth.

The history of Wales reads like a catalogue of struggle and resistance against invasion. The Romans were the first to make a serious attempt to subdue the Welsh after the

Claudian invasion of Britannia in AD 43. There were, of course, no national boundaries in those days. There was no country called Wales, or Scotland, or England. The only defined territories were those occupied by Celtic tribes, in Wales the Silures in the south, the Demetae in the south-west, the Cornovii in mid-Wales, the Deceangli on the north coast and the Ordovices in the mountains of Snowdonia and Cader Idris. Our only knowledge of these tribes and the lands they occupied comes from what the Romans themselves recorded on their campaigns. How accurate this is, we cannot know.

The relentless expansion of the Roman Empire was nowhere near as well thought out as we might imagine. It was much more of a hit-and-miss affair, and when the invasion was launched, the Romans had very little idea of the extent or the geography of Britannia. They probably did not even realize that beyond the easily subdued fertile lowlands lay barren mountain tracts which were far more difficult to conquer and then to hold against stubborn and spirited resistance. The mountains were also hardly worth having anyway, since the land was so poor that it could never yield much in the way of taxes. Everywhere there was the problem of secure frontiers.

The first frontier in western Britannia between the Romans and the unconquered tribes followed the diagonal course of the Fosse Way from Exeter to Lincoln. This proved to be an unstable border and was repeatedly attacked by the Silures in AD 47 and 48, encouraged by Caratacus, the fugitive chieftain of the defeated Catuvellauni who had taken refuge in Wales. To contain the Silures, the

Romans built fortresses at Gloucester and Usk. Caratacus moved north to the Ordovices in Snowdonia, and after their defeat in AD 51, and the capture of his wife and children, he fled to the court of Queen Cartimandua, leader of the Brigantes in northern Britannia. There his flight ended and he was handed over to the Romans by Cartimandua and taken to Rome in chains. Rather than execution, which captured 'rebels' could usually expect, Caratacus was released by Claudius after a defiant speech in which he is said to have exclaimed, referring to the grandeur of Rome, 'Why do you, who possess so many palaces, covet our poor tents?'

Welsh resistance to Rome did not end with the capture of Caratacus. The Silures resumed their attacks and defeated the twentieth legion in AD 52. Eventually the Emperor Nero, who had succeeded Claudius in AD 54, issued instructions to subdue the entire island of Britannia and in AD 58 a new governor arrived in Britannia to carry out the orders of the Emperor. Suetonius Paulinus was a professional soldier with campaign experience in the Atlas Mountains of Algeria, so he was used to dealing with independent-minded tribesmen the hard way. In two years of campaigning he had Wales in an iron grip. Refugees fled to Anglesey, the centre of the Druids, and Suetonius launched an attack. Tacitus records the scene with the British lining the shore of the Menai Straits: 'Among them were black robed women with dishevelled hair like the Furies, brandishing torches. Close by stood the Druids raising their hands to the heavens and screaming dreadful curses'.

Tacitus was a historian, but he needed to sell books, so

his popular histories were always written to appeal to his readers in Rome. His description of the Druids' habit of 'drenching their altars in the blood of prisoners and consult[ing] their gods by means of human entrails' was bound to boost sales.

Neither the sight of wailing women nor the threat of evisceration on a Druid altar was likely to deter Suetonius Paulinus. His troops swam across the Straits and easily defeated the Celtic refugees and the Druids, not only killing all they could find but destroying the groves of trees that were sacred to their religion. However, Suetonius was forced to withdraw immediately to deal with the revolt of the Iceni under Boudicca and it was left to Tacitus's father-in-law, the general Julius Agricola, to complete the subjugation of the Ordovices in AD 78, which he did, according to Tacitus, by killing them all, before moving off the following year to deal with Caledonia.

Containing the Celtic tribes of Wales proved to be a long and costly operation for the Romans. Legionary forts at Chester, at Wroxeter near Shrewsbury and at Caerleon near Newport in south Wales defined the boundary between the rebellious uplands and the subjugated lowlands. Smaller forts at Caernarfon in the north-west and Carmarthen in the south-west contained Wales within a fortified rectangle, supplemented with a network of camps and smaller forts placed one day's march apart and connected by straight roads. The military presence was strongest in the lands of the most belligerent tribes, the Ordovices in Snowdonia – so some must have survived Agricola – and the Silures of the south. The other Welsh tribes, the Deceangli along the north-western coastal plain between Conway and Chester, and the Demetae of Dyfed, showed less appetite for resistance and their territories were accordingly less densely garrisoned. Eventually the Celtic tribes of Wales settled for the life of a distant outpost of the Empire. The Romans took gold from Dolaucothi in mid-Wales back to Rome to be minted into coins and mined copper from the Great Orme near Llandudno. The Romans began to withdraw their garrisons from Wales by the beginning of the second century, indicating that the inhabitants were coming to terms with the Roman occupation, the last to succumb being the Ordovices.

What might have been the genetic consequences of the Roman occupation that we should look out for? After the initial campaigns of subjugation, which may well have resulted in the deaths of thousands of men, the military outposts became important centres of economic activity. Around Caerleon, for example, a small township or *vicus* grew up outside the walls of the fort. By AD 100 there were 2,000 people living in the Caerleon *vicus*, attracted from far and wide by, and dependent on, the great wealth, in comparative terms, of the garrison. Even though there were rules which banned official Roman marriage between the legionaries and the indigenous people before AD 190, unofficial liaisons were tolerated. Indeed, as the threat level fell, garrisons were reduced in size and troops were withdrawn to be redeployed elsewhere in Britannia; this had a severe effect on the economy of the *vici*. And not only on the economy, according to one historian, who points out the effect that the redeployment of the garrison would have had on the women who had borne children. They had to stay behind.

As usual, if there is one, it will be the Y-chromosome that is the witness to this activity. But who were the soldiers of the Roman army? Not all from Rome, that's for sure. After the initial campaigns, when there would have been a substantial Italian contingent in the legions, the occupation itself was left in the hands of the auxiliaries. In Wales these troops, who would be granted citizenship when they retired, were drawn largely from the valleys of the Rhine and the Danube. It is for Y-chromosomes from that part of Europe that we should keep an eye out as a sign of the genetic influence of the Roman occupation.

After the withdrawal of the Roman army from Wales in the fourth and fifth centuries AD, the demilitarized population came under attack from the Irish, including the infamous Niall of the Nine Hostages. In a mix of raiding for slaves and settlement, reminiscent of the first decades of the Viking age in Scotland, the coast of Wales facing the Irish Sea endured continual attacks. This period of attempted Irish colonization coincides with the expansion of the Dál Riata into Argyll, only 100 miles to the north. It may even have been carried out by the same people, and for the same reasons: the ambitions of the Ui Neill. But the Irish never established themselves in Wales as successfully as they did in Argyll. There was no equivalent in Wales of the continuous friction in Scotland between the Picts and the Gaels of Dalriada. The Irish form of Gaelic never displaced the P-Celtic of the Welsh as it did in Scotland.

Within Wales, the people divided into a succession of

minor kingdoms and before long the disputed land frontier became a battle zone once again, as it had been during the first years of the Roman occupation. This time the enemy were the Saxons, who had arrived in England in the middle of the fifth century and who, like the Irish, took advantage of the power vacuum left behind when the Romans departed. There is more to come on the Saxons and their genetic legacy when we travel to England, but for the time being we need only know that their westward expansion was effectively halted at roughly the same frontier that the Romans had defined with their lines of legionary forts.

The boundary was formally marked out in the late eighth century by Offa's Dyke, named after the Mercian king responsible for its construction. Unlike Hadrian's Wall, Offa's Dyke was not a fortified frontier barrier with regularly spaced garrisoned forts, but an earthwork built to denote rather than to defend the frontier, though in its construction it was far more than a boundary fence. Offa's Dyke consisted of an earth embankment up to 3 metres high and backed by a ditch up to 20 metres wide. The boundary it defines stretched for 240 kilometres from Prestatyn on the north coast to Beachley near Chepstow on the Severn Estuary. The Dyke marks this boundary for 130 kilometres, the rest being defined by natural features like the River Severn. Though it is built only of earth, thousands of men must have been involved in its construction, proof of the level of organization in the kingdom of Mercia at the time.

The Saxons did not advance far beyond the Dyke but, as you might by now expect, it proved to be a fluid boundary.

Though the construction of the Dyke coincided with the beginning of the Viking Age, the Welsh kings did not respond by uniting under one leader as the Celts and Picts had done in Scotland. The Welsh never did regain the lost lands in England on behalf of the Britons, though not always through want of trying. In 633 Cadwallon launched a counter-attack against the Saxon King Edwin, whose title *Bretwalda* at least claimed control of the whole of Britain. Edwin had attacked Anglesey, but Cadwallon drove him back into England and eventually defeated and killed him at the battle of Meigen near Doncaster. He then killed Edwin's heirs, Osric and Eanfrith, and, according to Bede, it was his intention to exterminate the whole English race. He had his best and only chance in 633 for, the following year, he was himself killed by Eanfrith's brother. As we shall see, the memory of Cadwallon's near success was to shape things to come.

We have seen what a significant genetic effect the Viking settlements from the late eighth century onwards have had in Scotland. Can we expect the same in Wales? Although the Vikings soon dominated the western seaways and had, by 830, begun to set up colonies at Dublin and other Irish coastal towns, there is very little evidence of them having succeeded in colonizing Wales. In the north they were actively repelled by Rhodri Mawr (Rhodri the Great), King of Gwynedd, who defeated a Danish attack on Anglesey in 856.

Only in the far south-west is there any suggestion of Viking settlement. It is there, as we saw in an earlier chapter, that the high levels of blood group A have been used to argue for a substantial Viking settlement in what is now Pembrokeshire. We shall certainly see if we can find corroborative evidence when we look at the genetics. Based on the experience in the Northern Isles, if Viking genes are there in large numbers we will certainly find them.

The Welsh kings continued in their internecine wars, sometimes making alliances with the Saxon kings against one another. So long as they were busy fighting between themselves, they were no threat to England. Only once did they unite under a single ruler, and then only for six years. Gruffudd ap Llywelyn began as the King of Gwynedd and it was from this position that he launched a campaign of murder and usurpation against the other kings that culminated in his recognition as the King of all Wales by 1057. Gruffudd's campaigns against Mercia on the border with England revived the memories of Cadwallon, the last Welsh king to interfere in English affairs, so in 1063 the English decided to do something about it. Harold, Earl of Wessex, went after him. Gruffudd was pursued back to Snowdonia, where he was killed by the son of one of his royal victims. To show there were no hard feelings, Harold married Gruffudd's widow, Ealdgyth, the granddaughter of Lady Godiva. When Harold became king in January 1066, Ealdgyth became Queen of England after six years as the first, and only, Queen of Wales. Her reign as Queen of England was even shorter: it came to an abrupt end when Harold was himself killed by the Normans at the Battle of Hastings the following October.

The Norman Conquest had immense repercussions for life in England almost immediately. For Wales, the old

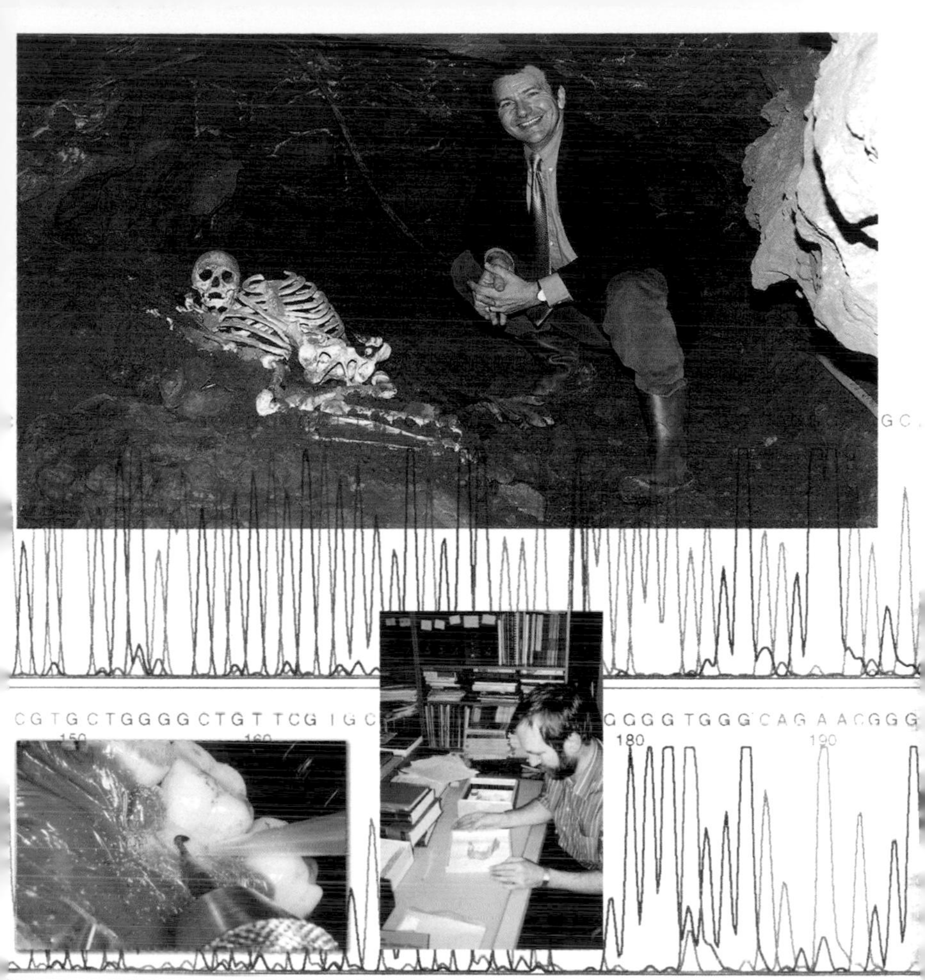

Top: History teacher Adrian Targett meets Cheddar Man. Tests on mitochondrial DNA showed they are related to each other over a span of 9,000 years.

Middle: The readout from a DNA sequence analyser that provides the raw material for *Blood of the Isles*. Coloured peaks on the trace denote the order of the four DNA bases, A, C, G and T, in a segment of DNA.

Inset left: Extracting dentine powder, which contains DNA, from a molar belonging to a young man who died over 12,000 years ago in Cheddar Gorge, Somerset. The teeth are in excellent condition and the enamel has protected the DNA during the intervening millennia. The pink material is a dental mastic, which I used to protect the rest of the jaw.

Inset right: Professor Chris Stringer of the Natural History Museum, London, takes the 12,000-year-old lower jaw from its storage case prior to my attempts at DNA recovery.

Above: The Priory at Lindisfarne. The ruins occupy the site of the undefended monastery which was attacked on 8 June 793 in the first recorded Viking raid in the Isles.

Left: Viking longship of the type that terrorized the Isles for 500 years. The sleek lines and shallow draught made for both speed and stealth. Longships like this could be swiftly beached on almost any coastline for a lightning raid.

Below: The beach just below the monastery at Lindisfarne – perfect landing for the Viking longships in advance of their attack.

Above: Jarl squad members in full Viking dress celebrate Up Helly Aa in Lerwick, Shetland. The annual pageant, held on the last Tuesday in January, celebrates Shetland's Viking past and culminates in the burning of a replica Norse longship.

Below: Beddoe describes the inhabitants of northern Lewis as a 'large, fair and comely Norse race, said to exist pure in the district of Ness at the north end of the island'. Plainly they are still there.

Right: The 5,500-year-old Neolithic *cromlech* at Carreg Sampson in Pembrokeshire, south-west Wales. Originally a covered grave, the earthen mound has eroded to reveal the megalithic internal structure.

Left: The Roman fort at Caerleon in Gwent. The Romans spent huge amounts of time and effort trying to subdue the Welsh, with only moderate success.

Below: Offa's Dyke, near Knighton in mid Wales, constructed in the late eighth century in yet another attempt to confine the troublesome Welsh and prevent them from raiding England.

Right: The head of Offa, King of Mercia, who considered himself to be in the same league as his eighth-century contemporary Charlemagne.

Left: Pembroke Castle, built by Arnulf de Montgomery, Earl of Shrewsbury, the first of the Norman Marcher Lords to make significant inroads into Wales in 1093.

A young Welsh fan cheers on his team at the 2003 Rugby World Cup finals match against Italy. Merlin's Red Dragon is still a prominent feature of Welsh identity.

The sun streams into the Neolithic passage grave at Newgrange, County Meath, at the midwinter solstice. The massive tombs clustered around Newgrange on the Boyne were constructed about 5,200 years ago.

Left: The rocky coastline of south-west Ireland, near the river Kenmare, the first landfall for Mil on his way from Spain to defeat the Tuatha Dé Danaan.

Above: The sacred hill at Tara, seat of the High Kings of Ireland.

Left: A delicate model of a sea-going vessel, made of solid gold between 1,900 and 2,100 years ago, and probably a votive offering to Manannan mac Lir, King of the Ocean.

Below: St Patrick's Day, the most vigorously and widely celebrated of the four national Saint's Days. Here crowds throng Fifth Avenue, New York, for the 2006 parade, the 245th in the city's history.

Below: This bronze statue of Cú Chulainn, Celtic super-hero and the saviour of Ulster in the war with Connacht, stands in Dublin's main Post Office, the scene of the most intense fighting during the Easter Rising of 1916.

Above: The resurgence of the Celt. The dramatic entrance to Canolfan Mileniwm Cymru, the newly opened performing arts centre in Cardiff, with two lines of poetry by Gwyneth Lewis, one in Welsh, the other in English.

Below: Once more, young children, like these from Lahinch, County Clare, are having lessons in the ancient languages of the Isles.

border held the Normans at bay – for a while. Compared to Scotland, with its 200 years of unified rule under the descendants of Kenneth MacAlpin, Wales was in a shambles after the downfall of Gruffudd ap Llywelyn. Feuds between claimants to the now vacant kingdoms had created a chaos of murder and betrayal which culminated in the battle of Mynydd Carn in 1081. Two royal houses emerged: Gwynedd in the north and Deheubarth in the south.

Again the perpetual problem of a secure border with Wales presented itself to the first Norman king, William the Conqueror, just as it had to the Romans and the Saxons before him. He had no interest in the conquest of Wales, but he did want a stable frontier. His solution was to grant lands along the frontier to his most reliable barons and, without positively encouraging them, to turn a blind eye if they felt like expanding their holdings into Wales. These men, the Marcher Lords, began by building castles along the frontier, first of earth and timber, then of stone. Then they really let rip and spilled over the border in deadly earnest.

By 1093 the most aggressive of the Marcher Lords, the Earl of Shrewsbury, reached the Irish Sea coast at Cardigan at the mouth of the River Teifi. Up went a castle. From there he pushed south into Dyfed and built the huge castle at Pembroke. Another Marcher Lord launched an attack against Rhys ap Tewdwr, the ruler of Deheubarth, who was killed at Brecon in 1088 resisting the advance. It was the death of Rhys ap Tewdwr that, to later historians, marked the final demise of the Welsh kingship. It looked as if nothing could save the Welsh from the Norman threat. However, the Welsh did manage to fight back. The forces of the Marcher Lords were expelled from Gwynedd, Ceredigion around Cardigan and from most of mid-Wales, but they hung on around Pembroke, Glamorgan and Brecon. The Norman domination was never complete and there was a resurgence in the position of the Welsh princes. In the Treaty of Montgomery in 1267, Henry III recognized Llywelyn ap Gruffud as the first 'Prince of Wales' with control over several of the old Welsh kingdoms.

However, Henry's successor, Edward I, decided to conquer Wales once and for all and in 1277 led his army of 800 knights and 15,000 infantry into the heartland of Gwynedd, stronghold of Llywelyn, and forced his submission. Edward continued his campaign through Wales, building a new series of castles, including the impregnable structures at Conway, Harlech, Beaumaris and Caernarfon. A revolt in 1282 gave Edward the excuse for another campaign. This time the Welsh fared better and defeated Edward's army on more than one occasion. However, Llywelyn himself was killed near Builth in December 1282 and resistance had collapsed by the following summer. In 1284 the Statute of Rhuddlan set out England's sovereignty over Wales and in 1301 Edward's son, who became Edward II, was invested with Llywelyn's title 'Prince of Wales' at an elaborate ceremony at Caernarfon Castle. With the exception of Edward II himself, every subsequent British monarch has given the title 'Prince of Wales' to their eldest son.

The Welsh made one final attempt to free themselves from English domination. In 1400, taking advantage of the confusion caused by the overthrow of Richard II, the Welsh rose up in revolt under Owain ap Gruffydd Glyn Dwr of Glydyfrdwy, better known outside Wales by the English translation Owen Glendower. On 16 September 1400 he was proclaimed Prince of Wales at Bala and his followers began their quest to regain the independence of Wales by attacking nearby English settlements at Ruthin. Intriguingly, Owen Glendower used his alleged descent from the legendary Brutus, first King of the British, to back his claim. He reigned for twelve years, even convening a Welsh parliament at Machynlleth in mid-Wales and he was recognized as sovereign of an independent country by the King of France. The revolt was eventually ended by England's military superiority. Many of the great castles built 100 years earlier by Edward I had never surrendered, and by 1414 the army of Glendower surrendered at Bala. Owen Glendower himself was never captured and, rather like his 'ancestor' King Arthur, he vanished into the mists. Finally, in 1563, the Act of Union formally combined th political fortunes of England and Wales.

14
THE DNA OF WALES

Wales is the only part of mainland Britain where the original language is still spoken. We might take that as an indication that there has been very little disturbance of ancient Welsh culture, and maybe very little disturbance of the indigenous genetic make-up. But it is clear from Welsh history that there have been very many foreign intrusions on to Welsh soil from the Roman period onwards. What we do not know is the magnitude of their genetic effect. Traces of Viking DNA are a strong possibility in Pembroke, and the effects of the Saxon and Norman incursions may have had substantial genetic consequences.

Our campaign in Wales, for that is how it seemed, began in the early days of the Genetic Atlas Project. Four of us set off by car in a planned series of swoops on secondary schools throughout the Principality. This was in the days before we had discovered the easy delights of the DNA brushes. We needed blood. But we had not arranged to visit

blood-donor sessions in Wales. We had yet to refine that approach. The blood samples we used in the early days were taken from fingerpricks, the collection of which had unintended consequences. One of my research team, Kate Smalley, had once been a teacher and she realized that hard-pressed sixth-form Biology teachers might welcome a visit from outside scientists if we gave a lecture and, in return, we might be able to ask for volunteers. That would give the teacher a double period off, if nothing else. We chose Oswestry, a market town on the English–Welsh border not far from Shrewsbury, as our first destination. My main concern was that, however well the lecture on our project went down, it might be hard to get volunteers to submit to a fingerprick blood test. The automatic lancets, the ones diabetics use to take a sample for blood-sugar measurements, drive a short needle into the skin. It isn't painful, but neither is it completely painless.

I had been through my presentation and the time to ask for volunteers had arrived. I was met by a sea of blank faces. 'It really doesn't hurt,' I entreated. There was no reaction. I suddenly realized what I needed to do. I got out a lancet and pulled back the spring-loaded trigger. I wiped the tip of my left index finger with an alcohol swab to sterilize it and, 'ping', lanced it, trying not to wince. That did the trick and soon we had everybody lancing their own fingers or, better still, their friends'. The drops of blood were soaked up on special cards, which we knew would keep the DNA safe until we got back to the lab. I don't think we would be allowed to take blood these days. Everyone is so scared of it.

After Oswestry we divided into two teams of two, one heading north to Anglesey while Kate and I set out for Bala and Dolgellau. At Bala I discovered the unexpected advantages of the fingerprick technique as a way of collecting DNA in schools. It is this. Because there is some discomfort involved, to take the test is a mini-act of bravery. And once the children had done it, what better thing to do, at the break after the lesson was over, than to run to their friends in other classrooms and taunt them into having the test. It certainly worked. Once they had given the blood sample, the children were running off round the school, to the staffroom and the canteen, collecting more volunteers. They had started a chain reaction. A queue of children, teachers and dinner ladies formed and we were busy for at least another hour. By the end we had over 200 samples from Bala, practically the entire school. By the end of the week, we had been to twenty schools and collected over 2,500 samples. Fantastic.

What are we on the lookout for in Wales? The early blood-group work, as well as proposing the Viking settlers/Flemish weavers solution to the elevated blood group A frequency in Pembrokeshire, also noted very high levels of blood group B around the Black Mountains at the western end of the Brecon Beacons south of Llandovery. There is also abundant work from the early twentieth century by H. J. Fleure, an eminent anthropologist based at Aberystwyth University, on the unusual head shapes and Neanderthal-like faces of people living in the remote mountains near Plynlimmon in mid-Wales at the headwaters of the River Severn and the River Wye.

Plynlimmon is not very far from the market town of Tregaron, where, while staying at the Talbot Inn in the market square one October night on another visit to collect DNA samples, I was told the fantastic story of the Tregaron Neanderthals. The Talbot Inn is an old drovers' inn dating from the thirteenth century, complete with stone walls, oak beams and open fires. It was a dark night and the rain had not stopped all day. The fire was blazing away and there were a few local men at the bar, staring at their pints of bitter and glad to be out of the rain. We got talking, and before long I was telling them about what I was doing in that part of Wales and about the Genetic Atlas Project. We had evidently been overheard by a man sitting alone at a small table. He beckoned me over and I sat down. And then he began to tell me about the elderly twin brothers, both bachelors, who had lived at the end of a long track leading into the Cambrian Mountains behind the ruins of the Cistercian monastery at Strata Florida, further up the Teifi from Tregaron. I knew this track, as once in my youth I had been up it looking for an incredibly rare bird, the Red Kite. Now, thanks to successful reintroductions to the Chilterns, anyone can see these beautiful birds gliding and twisting every time they travel on the motorway between Oxford and London. But, back then, there were only a few pairs left, all of them in mid-Wales. I had heard that a pair was nesting in the woods behind Strata Florida and I remember walking for several miles up into the hills, first through the woods then up on to the grassy uplands. I did not see a Red Kite, but I do remember seeing a cottage, up a side track, which, from the washing on the clothes line, was clearly inhabited. I think this must have been the place. I don't remember any other dwellings.

My companion at the Talbot told me that the men who lived in this cottage in the 1950s and 1960s were Neanderthals. This fact was well known. So well known that a visit to the brothers was on the history syllabus at Tregaron school. Every year, in the summer term, the third-form History class would take the school van as far as they could up the track and the children would walk the rest of the way to the cottage. The Neanderthals obviously looked forward to the visits because, on the appointed day, they made sure they had plenty of cakes and lemonade. The children stayed for an hour while the teacher explained about human evolution and where the Neanderthals fitted into the scheme of things. Then they left and walked back down the hill to the van.

Of course I didn't actually believe these men were Neanderthals any more than I am. But I do still hope one day to find just one person with Neanderthal DNA. It is a vanishing hope as more and more DNA is tested from around the world. But could I recognize it if I found it, whether around Tregaron or Cardiff, or London or California? The answer is definitely yes – so long as it is mitochondrial DNA.

I had once attempted, but failed, to recover Neanderthal DNA from the Tabun skull from the Natural History Museum in London. The Tabun skull was dated to 100,000 years ago and the teeth looked in fairly good shape. But when I tried to drill into a molar tooth, it was rock hard and I was terrified it would fracture. I did get a little dentine powder from the inside, but I did not smell the reassuring scent of burning flesh, the smell that meant success. However, I did manage to recover a few molecules of DNA from the Tabun tooth. When I put them through the DNA analyser, the mDNA sequences looked distinctly modern, with their closest matches in Israel, where the skull had been excavated. The big debate at the time, in the early 1990s, was whether Neanderthals were an extinct species of human, in which case their DNA should be very different from ours, or whether they were just a phase in the evolution of modern humans, in which case the DNA should be reasonably similar. I never felt confident enough about proclaiming that the modern-looking DNA that I had recovered from the Tabun skull was really from the skull, rather than from the archaeologists and museum curators who had handled it over the fifty years since it was excavated.

I am glad I was cautious, because two years later what did appear to be genuinely ancient DNA was recovered from the Neanderthal-type specimen, the original one that had been found in the Neander Valley in Germany (*Tal* is valley in German) in 1863. This DNA was very different from any modern DNA. It had 27 mutations in comparison to the mitochondrial reference sequence, while even the most distinct modern DNA only varies from the reference by 12 changes. When similar DNA was found in two further Neanderthal remains, from Croatia and the Caucasus mountains, it provided reasonable proof that Neanderthals were indeed an extinct species of human. The last Neanderthal died in southern Spain about 27,000 years ago;

at least that is where the most recently dated remains have been found. But that was before the world knew about the Tregaron twins!

The brothers had passed away in the 1980s, so another trip up the track into the hills would be pointless. Since they were men, and bachelors at that, their mitochondrial DNA could not have been passed on to their children, even if they had any. And neither the man at the Talbot Inn, nor anyone else I spoke to in Tregaron, knew where the brothers had come from, so I could not track down a relative. The only chance was that, among the smiling children at the local school, there was one who, through maternal connections, would carry the tell-tale Neanderthal DNA. There was a lot to look out for in Wales.

Examining first the matrilineal DNA from Wales, the living record of the journeys of women to this part of the Isles, the pattern of maternal clans is very similar to Ireland, and to what we have also seen in the two Pictland regions of Scotland, Tayside and Grampian. The clan of Helena predominates, as always, with 47 per cent of people in both regions belonging to that clan. When Ireland is compared to the whole of Wales, this close similarity extends to the other clans as well. When I divided Wales into three regions, north, mid- and south Wales, a few differences did emerge, mostly ones that showed a closer genetic link between north and mid-Wales than either did to the south of the country. But the overall pattern was one of continuity with Ireland and, to a lesser extent, with the Pictland regions of Scotland. But, unfortunately, there was no sign of any Neanderthal mDNA.

When I looked at the patrilineal Y-chromosomes in the three regions of Wales, the pattern was extremely interesting. There were two outstanding features. First, there was practically no sign of Norse Viking settlement. If you recall from the Northern Isles and from Norway itself, there is a high concentration of members of Sigurd's clan; 20 per cent of Shetland men are in this clan. And yet in Wales there are virtually no men from Sigurd's clan. I interpret this as strong evidence against any substantial Norse Viking settlement in Wales. The only hint of Viking ancestry is in the north, where just three men, Mr Roberts from Bangor, Mr Owen from Llanfair and Mr Davies from Meifod, are in the clan of Sigurd. At such low frequencies we must doubt whether they have inherited their Sigurd chromosomes from Vikings directly or in their transmuted form in the blood of a Norman. Since there were no Sigurds at all in our samples from south Wales, which was far more heavily occupied by Normans than was the north, I tend to think that these three gentlemen are more likely to be of direct Viking than Norman ancestry. You will recall that there were Viking raids on Anglesey which were actively repelled by Rhodri Mawr in 856. Perhaps it was from action around this time that Messrs Roberts, Owen and Davies acquired their Viking ancestors. Their detailed fingerprints are certainly matched in Norway.

There was just one Sigurd in mid-Wales, Mr Jones, from the small village of Garthmyl near Rhyader. And none at all in south Wales, even in Pembrokeshire where the high level of blood group A was explained by a Viking settlement in the area. There would need to have been a very large influx of Vikings into Pembrokeshire to alter the blood-group proportions of the whole region and we would have been bound to find several Sigurds in the vicinity. But we did not find a single one. I think that has to mean that the Viking explanation of Morgan Watkin for the high frequency of blood group A in 'Little England beyond Wales' is wrong.

Turning to the clan of Wodan, this hovers around the 10 per cent mark in all three regions of Wales. However, when I looked at the detailed fingerprints, I found a small cluster in mid-Wales that caught my eye. There were only half a dozen of them, but they were unusual. Mr Rees from New Quay, a picturesque fishing port on Cardigan Bay, Mr Jones from Mynachlog near Tregaron, and finally Mr Davies from Lampeter.

Before I draw any profound conclusions, may I recommend Lampeter as the best place in Wales for ice-cream. At the junction of the High Street and the Tregaron Road stands the ice-cream emporium of Conti's Café. Going inside, when I was last there, was like returning to the cafés of my youth. No cappuccinos or lattes here, just weak milky coffee in one of those unbreakable glass cups, served by a waitress in a blue tabard. A rare experience indeed these days. Alas, I've heard that the interior has been recently revamped, but the ice-cream is still wonderful. Made every day on the premises by the owner, Leno Conti, not brought in ready-made. Perish the thought.

Now for the profound conclusions. I think this Wodan

Y-chromosome has been in mid-Wales for a very long time. There are first-generation derivatives nearby, by which I mean Y-chromosomes that have diverged away by one mutation. And it is only one mutational step removed from a chromosome cluster in Pictland. I have not found this chromosome in Ireland or in England, except in one place. Mr Roach, from Sidmouth in Devon, has it. I could be wrong, but I don't think this is a Norman chromosome. If it were, I would have expected to find similar chromosomes in other parts of England, which, with the exception of Mr Roach, I have not. I couldn't help wondering if this is a very ancient Welsh chromosome. After all, Tregaron and Lampeter are not that far from Plynlimmon where H. J. Fleure was convinced from his work on skull shapes that he had found a relic population, and where there was also a very high frequency of blood group B. I wonder, as I write this, whether the great anthropologist ever tasted Conti's ice-cream on his travels.

Of course, we must not forget the clan of Oisin. This is far and away the most common clan in all the three regions of Wales, which it also is in the whole of the Isles. In fact, at 86 per cent, mid-Wales has the highest proportion of Oisin in the Isles outside Ireland. Interestingly, the Pictland region of Grampian is only just behind, with 84 per cent. Only Munster and Connacht in the west of Ireland have higher proportions of Oisin. The Atlantis chromosome, the prevalent Y-chromosome in the clan, is very frequent in Wales, more so even than in Ireland, as a proportion of Oisins as a whole.

There is one other interesting thing to point out. The

diversity, that is the variety, of different Oisin Y-chromosomes is lower in Wales, especially mid-Wales, than anywhere else in mainland Britain. Geneticists usually put that down to a recent arrival date, there having been less time for mutations and diversity to have arisen. But to find the lowest diversity in mid-Wales of all places seems very peculiar to me, since all the other historical indicators suggest that mid-Wales has been among the most stable and longest settled of any region in the Isles – even if I did not find any evidence of Neanderthals. The lower than expected amount of accumulated mutations in the Y-chromosomes is beginning to be a recurrent feature of most of the Celtic regions of the Isles. Whether this is also true of England, we are about to discover as we push east over the hills.

15
ENGLAND

As we cross the long-disputed boundary into England, the land spreads out in all directions, undulating certainly but without the mountains that insulated Wales, and Scotland, against the full force of foreign invasion which began with the Romans and continued for more than 1,000 years. Geography, as always, led history by the hand. It was the fertile lowlands of England, not the barren hills of Wales or Scotland, that made the Isles such a tempting target from the Roman invasion of AD 43 to the Norman Conquest of 1066 and beyond. But the settlement of England and the Isles began thousands of years earlier.

England is home to 49 million people, which is almost 80 per cent of the entire population of the Isles, packed into 50,000 square miles, which is 40 per cent of the space. England has examples of almost every kind of geological structure, from extremely old volcanic rocks in Cornwall and Cumbria to very recent, reclaimed soils in the fenlands of East Anglia. Between these extremes of age and distance lie successions of sandstones and limestones from different geological eras which cross the country diagonally from the south-west to the north-east. As a rule of thumb, the further east, the younger in geological time the rocks become. These sedimentary bedrocks, built up over hundreds of millions of years when England lay beneath a warm and shallow sea, are mainly alkaline. They erode to very fertile soils, and almost all of England is now intensively farmed. It was always the agricultural wealth of England and the opportunities this provided for taxation and tribute, as well as settlement, that attracted the attention of foreign invaders.

Beyond the fertile plains and rolling downland, England is surrounded by mountains and high hills. Along the centre, the spine of the Pennines in the north of England rises to 893 metres at Cross Fell. Forty miles to the west, among the picturesque mountains of the Lake District, is Scafell Pike (977 metres), England's highest peak. The garland of mountains and hills which form the boundaries with Wales and Scotland have preoccupied all invaders as they tried, and usually failed, to protect England behind stable frontiers.

The first people to reach England after the Ice Age were the big-game hunters of the Old Stone Age, colonizing the Isles directly over the land bridge from continental Europe. By 12,000 years ago, hunters were living in the caves at Cheddar. After the cold snap of the Younger Dryas forced a temporary retreat, the Mesolithics returned 10,000 years ago. They were confined to the coasts and riverbanks by the dense woodland that soon covered the warming Isles.

Like the occupants of Mount Sandel in Ireland and Oronsay off the coast of Scotland, they were semi-nomadic, with winter and summer camps alternating between woodland and shore to make the most of the wild food: fish and shellfish in winter, birds' eggs in spring and summer, hazel and other nuts in the autumn – and red deer at any time they could be killed. The Mesolithic life in England was no different from that in the rest of the Isles, and is nowhere more completely documented than at Starr Carr in the Vale of Pickering in North Yorkshire, 5 miles to the west of the seaside resort of Scarborough.

At the marshy edge of a lake, this was a site where, 9,500 years ago, the elusive Mesolithics brought their kills from the nearby high ground of the North Yorkshire Moors to be butchered and distributed. Thanks to the marshy, waterlogged conditions, all sorts of things have been preserved which on dry sites would have been lost. Pollen, insects, charcoal, wood and animal bones are all preserved in the damp and airless peat. From an analysis of the bones left at Starr Carr, most of the meat came from wild cattle, the enormous aurochs which roamed through the dense woods. There were elk and red-deer bones too, sometimes with marks to show where a flint-tipped arrow had cut through the skin on its way to the beast's heart. Badger, red-fox and pine-marten bones show that even smaller mammals could be killed, perhaps for food, perhaps only for their skins. The Mesolithic occupants of Starr Carr were extremely skilled in working deer antler, making not only large objects like spearheads, but also smaller, but still deadly, arrowheads. The flints they used to work the antlers lie all around the site. But perhaps the most remarkable revelation at Starr Carr is the evidence of domestic dogs. The hunters, we can assume, used these dogs to round up deer and wild cattle or to pursue a wounded animal if an arrow had failed to find the heart.

Farming arrived in England a little before it did in the rest of the Isles. Bit by bit the wild woods were cleared. The Mesolithics already knew how to kill trees by ring-barking, so they created glades to encourage the growth of hazel bushes. The Neolithic farmers killed trees in the same way, and may have been descendants of the same people. They targeted elms in particular, because they understood that they grew in the most fertile soils. Gradually, more food was grown than was strictly necessary for survival, which meant that not everyone had to spend all their time looking for food. Thus began the social revolution that culminated in the rise of chieftains and then minor kings, each battling it out for supremacy and ownership of land. Megalithic monuments, like the stone circles at Stonehenge and Avebury, took pride of place in a landscape rich in burials and tombs. The newly discovered metals of copper, bronze and iron, in that order, replaced bloodstone and flint as the principal materials for axes, knives and other agricultural implements. They also found their uses as weapons, cast or beaten into daggers, swords and spears as warfare became endemic. Iron tools, much stronger than bronze and with a much sharper cutting edge, made woodland clearing easier. The increase in the acreage of agricultural land led to a big rise in the population of the Isles.

By the fourth century BC, the archaeological evidence points to an increase in inter-tribal warfare. Hill forts became more numerous and their defences more elaborate. Swords replaced daggers in a sign of more organized fighting. By the third century BC, the style of metal-working for both weapons and jewellery had changed to the second Celtic phase of La Tène, but always with a distinctive British dialect. The export of Cornish tin, an essential ingredient in the manufacture of bronze, continued apace, with the export trade to the Mediterranean dominated by Phoenicians.

One of the very first accounts of the Isles of the time, by Pytheas from the Greek colony of Massilia (now Marseilles) in southern France, was written around 320 BC. His original work, *On the Ocean*, has not survived and we only know of his remarkable journey through references to it from other classical writers like Eratosthenes and Pliny. Pytheas probably travelled overland from Massilia to the mouth of the Gironde, near present-day Bordeaux, and boarded a ship bound for the north. It took him three days to sail up the coast of France and around the edge of Brittany. From there, his journey took him across to Cornwall and the *Prettanic Isles*, as he calls Britain. He noted the lengthening day as his voyages took him right up the eastern side of Britain to the Orkneys. From there he travelled even further north to a land of frozen seas and volcanoes. This must have been Iceland, though whether he actually went that far north himself or only sailed as far as the Shetlands and recorded the tales of sailors he met there is still keenly contested among historians. *On the*

Ocean is important in two ways. It brought the Isles to the attention of the classical world, and it also showed how active were the sea lanes up and down the Atlantic coast of France and all round the British coastline as well. Pytheas seemed able to pick up a sea passage whenever he wanted one.

The need to impress and confirm status with material objects was at least as prevalent then as it is now. The desire for displays of wealth led to the creation of astonishingly beautiful objects and ceremonial weapons. The finds from the royal burial at Sutton Hoo near Woodbridge in Suffolk, from the seventh century AD, in the middle of what we now refer to as the Dark Ages, are delicate and beautiful beyond belief. This was almost certainly the tomb of King Raedwald, a Saxon king from the 620s. Buckles and strap-mounts of gold inlaid with garnets and *millefiori* glass, so fresh and so delicate that, when I saw them on display in the British Museum, it was very difficult for me to believe that they were the originals and not modern copies. The ceremonial shield, the inlaid helmet – these were not objects to be used in battle; they were strictly for display only. Even the sword, its blade forged from eighteen laminated iron rods twisted together and beaten flat, was purely for show. There the display is a modern replica. The original lies with its iron blade rusted, peeled and pitted. But the handle ends with a gold and garnet cloisonné pommel as bright and fresh as new.

In the centuries preceding the Roman conquest, life in the Isles followed the progression widely found across continental Europe. Iron replaced bronze as the principal metal. Fortified encampments developed on the hills. Although there were still extensive forests, much of the land had been cleared for grain or pasture. In the centuries before Caesar's expeditions in 55 and 54 BC, the Isles, and England in particular, had adopted many of the artistic styles of the continental Iron Age. The perennial question as to whether these cultural changes were the consequence of large-scale immigration or of the indigenous people copying and adapting new styles has never yet been confidently answered – and is one that genetics should be in a better position to explore than most disciplines.

Caesar's expeditions set the pattern for the Roman invasion proper a century later. What prevented Caesar himself from embarking on a full-scale invasion, or even if this was his intention, is not known. Certainly he had his hands full in controlling rebellions in Gaul and his ambitions may have been curtailed by such practical considerations. Nevertheless, his expeditions set the pattern for the later invasion. Caesar had forced the surrender and submission of tribal leaders in Britain and had exacted annual tribute payments from them. He also installed puppet kings. So, although there was no permanent occupation, the political influence of Rome was already substantial well before the invasion proper. The British aristocracy began to adopt the trappings of Roman civilization, particularly in the south-east where there was vigorous trade with the nearest parts of Gaul. Britain was exporting corn, iron and cattle to the Roman Empire across the busy sea routes to the ports of Gaul, while Roman luxury goods flowed in the opposite direction. Even if

Britain was not part of the Empire, it certainly benefited from the proximity and the requirements of its armies.

The full integration of Britannia into the Empire was only a matter of time. Under Caesar's successor Augustus, and even under Tiberius who came after him, there was no appetite for invasion, even though it would have been comparatively easy. But the taxes were flowing in and Britain posed no military threat. A few troublesome Gauls might have crossed the Channel to escape the wrath of Rome, but that was all. One British tribe, the Catuvellauni, centred on Hertfordshire, began to expand their territories into the lands of neighbours who had thought they enjoyed Rome's protection. But the Romans, now under Augustus, turned a blind eye to these infringements, enabling Cunobelinus, King of the Catuvellauni, to move his headquarters to Colchester, the former base of the Trinovantes, from where he could control the trade routes across the North Sea to the Rhine.

In a re-run of the age-old story, a disgruntled prince – in this case it was Amminius, one of the sons of Cunobelinus – fled to the emperor for assistance. By now the emperor was the notoriously unstable Caligula, who claimed that by accepting the formal submission of Amminius he had actually negotiated the surrender of the whole of Britain, and he issued orders for an invasion to consolidate the surrender. That was abandoned at the last minute, but only after Caligula had reached the Channel coast with his armies. He collected some sea shells and ordered a withdrawal back to Rome.

Although this was a farce, all the ground work had been

done. The military build-up, the logistics of invasion, the public relations with the citizens of Rome: everything was in place, so it was an easy matter for Caligula's successor – after his welcome murder – to give the signal to invade. The new emperor was Claudius, Caligula's uncle. Widely thought of at the time as mentally retarded, he was nothing of the sort. Claudius needed a military triumph to cement his authority and Britain was the obvious target. The excuse was an invitation from Verica, King of the Atrebates, who had been expelled following an internal palace coup. The invasion force that assembled on the Channel shore comprised four legions: the II Augusta and XIV Gemina from the upper Rhine, the XX Valeria from the lower Rhine and the IX Hispania from Pannonia in modern Hungary, each with about 5,000 men and an equal number of auxiliaries. The legionnaires were all Roman citizens, mainly drawn from Italy at this period, while the auxiliaries were recruited from native fighters from previously conquered regions of the Empire and organized into regular regiments with Roman commanders. Forty thousand men in 600 ships, under the command of Aulus Plautius, who had seen service in the Balkans, crossed the Channel from Boulogne in Gaul to land on the shingle at Richborough, near Sandwich on the east coast of Kent.

The landings were unopposed and, after digging defensive ditches at Richborough, the troops advanced rapidly to the River Medway, 20 miles to the west, where the British defence under Caratacus and Togodumnus, joint leaders of the Catuvellauni after their father Cunobelinus's death, lay in wait. The British assumed that a major river crossing would deter the advancing army. But Paulinus sent across a contingent of Batavian auxiliaries who were trained in swimming across rivers in full armour. The Britons wore little or no body protection and their long, slashing swords were no match for the short, stabbing *gladius* of the Romans in close combat. Unable to halt the Roman advance at the Medway, the Britons withdrew to the Thames and prepared to defend the crossing at London. Instead of launching his attack at once, Plautius sent word to Rome so that the Emperor could witness the decisive battle. Claudius hurried to join his legions, accompanied by a retinue of Roman aristocrats and a troop of elephants. Once he had arrived, the fighting could begin. It did not last long. Togodumnus was killed and his brother Caratacus fled to Wales. Within days, Claudius entered Colchester, capital of the Catuvellauni, surrounded by his elephants, to receive the submission of eleven British kings, including the Pictish King from Gurness in Orkney.

Claudius stayed in Britain for just over a fortnight, then returned to Rome, where he insisted the senate proclaim an official 'victory' and commission the building of a triumphal arch. From then on he insisted on being called 'Britannicus'. It did the trick. Claudius had gone from despised idiot to military hero in only six years. Even though the Emperor had returned to Rome, the invasion continued on and off for another forty years. As far as possible, actual fighting was restricted to tribes who did not submit voluntarily. In fact, this was easier than it seemed. The defeat by the Romans of the expansionist Catuvellauni was a cause for celebration among rival tribes and many of them viewed the Romans as liberators rather than conquerors. The Atrebates of Hampshire, the Iceni of Norfolk and the Brigantes of Yorkshire were happy to submit and pay their taxes rather than fight. After four years, Plautius had enlarged the frontier to the Fosse Way. The only real resistance came in the Isle of Wight and Dorset, where the II Augusta, under the command of the future Emperor Vespasian, was forced to storm and capture some twenty hill forts from the Dumnonii before Vespasian could build his own legionary fortress at Exeter.

The first phase of the invasion was finished and, were it not for the perennial difficulty of establishing a stable frontier, it may have settled at that. To celebrate the orderly incorporation of Britannia into the Empire, an enormous monumental arch, 26 metres high, was built at Richborough where the Romans had landed. It was dressed in white Carrara marble and decorated with statues and inscriptions. Richborough stood on a promontory, so the arch must have been visible for miles out to sea. Its purpose was to emphasize that the Romans had tamed Britannia and every official visitor to the province entered through this arch before making his way inland along Watling Street.

However, further west things did not go so smoothly. The repeated attacks by the Silures, inspired by the fugitive Caratacus, persuaded the Romans that they must invade Wales. The first attempt was stalled when Suetonius Paulinus, who had routed the Druids on Anglesey, was forced to divert his troops to put down the far more serious revolt of the Iceni under Queen Boudicca. The Iceni had been a relatively quiet client kingdom under Boudicca's husband, Prasutagus. As a willing ally of Rome, it was his expectation that his kingdom would remain intact after his death. This did not happen. His property was seized, the aristocracy expelled from their estates and crippling taxes enforced. When she protested, Boudicca was flogged and her daughters raped. Her vengeance was swift and terrible. Rallying her own tribe, the Iceni, and the neighbouring Trinovantes in revolt, she swept through southern Britain, sacking and burning Colchester, London and St Albans. She tortured and killed every Roman and every Roman sympathizer that she could capture. The IXth legion, which tried to halt her advance, was cut to ribbons.

At the time of Boudicca's uprising, the south-east was considered to be well on the way to submission, so the bulk of the Roman army had been moved to the western front, from where Suetonius Paulinus was forced to abandon his invasion of Wales and return to deal with the revolt with the three remaining legions. If the uprising had been bloody, the retribution of Suetonius was even more so. Tacitus reckons 70,000 were killed on both sides during the revolt itself, and 80,000 during its suppression. Nero, who had succeeded Claudius as Emperor, seriously considered abandoning Britannia as a colony altogether.

After Boudicca's revolt had been put down, Roman control recovered. The crippling taxation was relaxed a little and those parts of Britain that had been conquered began the long process of assimilation into the Empire. But the stability of the northern frontier was beginning to crumble. Cartimandua, Queen of the Brigantes and the woman who had handed over the fugitive Caratacus, lost control of the loose federation of northern tribes. Agricola responded to this instability by pushing the frontier back to the very edge of the Scottish Highlands. He took his army even further north in his campaign against the Picts, inflicting a crushing defeat at the battle of Mons Graupius in AD 83. The location of Mons Graupius has eluded historians and archaeologists alike. The best guess is at Bennachie, near Inverurie on the banks of the River Don, 15 miles north-west of Aberdeen.

For the Romans it was a long way from home – 'the place where the world and nature end', according to Tacitus. But even with this defeat, the Highland Picts avoided being forced to submit to Rome in the way the Welsh did not, although the intention to complete the invasion of Scotland was there. At Inchtuthil, near Blairgowrie, a huge legionary fortress began to take shape, the equal of Chester or of Caerleon on the Welsh frontier. But reverses on the continent forced the Emperor Domitian to withdraw his troops from Scotland. The fortress was carefully dismantled and the materials taken south. It had been a lucky escape for the Picts.

By AD 120 the frontier had moved south to the line between the Solway Firth in the west and the mouth of the Tyne in the east. At first only a turf rampart, the frontier was turned into the impenetrable stone barrier of Hadrian's Wall, on the orders of the Emperor. Under Hadrian's successor, Antoninus Pius, the frontier moved north again. This time it was defined by the eponymous Antonine Wall, a barrier of rock and turf 20 feet high running between the Firths of Clyde and Forth. This was a much shorter boundary and many military historians think Hadrian should have built his wall here in the first place. But more trouble with the Picts convinced the next Emperor, Marcus Aurelius, to bring the frontier back down to Hadrian's Wall in 163. Even that great barrier was not impermeable and there were repeated raids across the wall as far as York.

Further south the fighting was less intense and the native population became drawn into the seductive and deliberate process of civilization. Towns were planned and built. Urban life, unknown in the whole history of the Isles, was born. People began to learn Latin and Roman dress became popular. As Tacitus shrewdly observed, 'Little by little there was a slide towards the allurements of degeneracy; assembly rooms, bathing establishments and smart dinner parties. In their inexperience the Britons called it civilisation when it was really all part of their servitude.'

In the south, cities like Lincoln, Colchester and Gloucester grew up explicitly to accommodate army veterans on their retirement. Britons joined the army as auxiliaries and retired as citizens. In the towns, administrators mixed with craftsmen and artisans. Slaves were freed and were set up in business by their former masters. In the countryside, undefended villas of sumptuous magnificence sprang up, complete with wood- or coal-fired central heating, windows and glazed tile flooring. But even as these outward signs of affluence amused their owners, the seeds of destruction had been sown. The traumas of the

Empire, its division into eastern and western sectors, the movement of the centre of the western Empire from Rome, first to Milan, then to Trier in eastern France, the deadly rivalries and murderous conspiracies all spelled the eventual end of the Roman occupation of Britain.

The surprise is that the Empire in the west lasted as long as it did. Even after extremely serious reverses – such as in AD 367 when a concerted assault by Picts, Saxons and Franks attacked the Roman provinces of Britain and Gaul, ranging at will, burning, killing and looting as they went – still the Romans managed to stage a comeback, this time under the Emperor Valentinian. By then the Roman army had changed its composition, no longer relying on Italian legionnaires or auxiliaries from the east. A quarter of the regular army was Germanic. By the beginning of the fifth century, the signs of weakening central direction were growing. There were no more bulk imports of coins, a sure sign that the army was not being paid as it once had been. The thriving pottery industry suddenly ceased. By AD 430 coins were no longer in regular use – another indicator of an ossifying economy. Even though there is evidence of one last attempt to reclaim Britain around 425, it came to nothing. By 450 Britain was well and truly on its own.

What lasting genetic legacy of the Roman occupation should we look out for? Whatever it is, we must expect it to be more pronounced in England, which was far more integrated into the Empire than Wales or Scotland ever were. And in Ireland we should not expect any significant traces at all. If Tacitus and other historians are to be believed, tens of thousands of Britons were slaughtered in the early years of the occupation – at least 80,000 as a result of Boudicca's revolt, 30,000 at Mons Graupius. These are large numbers for a relatively small population. The genetic legacy of wholesale military slaughter will be found, one imagines, mainly among men. The effect will be to reduce the diversity among Y-chromosomes. Population numbers can recover quickly if the women are spared, with men taking advantage of the surplus of women to bear their multiple children. But, with a smaller number of fathers, the Y-chromosomes that are passed down to future generations will not be as varied as if there were equal numbers of men and women.

The genetic origin of the Roman army itself is also something to be aware of when we examine the genetics. It was certainly not 100 per cent Roman, in the Italian sense, and drew its recruits from many different parts of the Empire, particularly from the lower Rhine. But nothing from the Roman occupation, save perhaps the import, and export, of female slaves, seems likely to have had a big impact on the maternal genealogy of England.

16

SAXONS, DANES, VIKINGS AND NORMANS

The end of the Roman occupation of Britain was quite unlike our own recent colonial goodbyes. There was no lowering of the flag, no salute from a member of the imperial family, no tear brushed away from the eyes of the last governor and no dignified departure on a warship. That was Hong Kong in 1997, not Britain in the fifth century AD. The Romans left a country already accustomed to the intermittent attention of raiding war parties from across the porous land borders to the west and north. In the great attack of 367, Picts from Scotland had joined Saxons from across the North Sea in rampaging through the countryside, killing and looting at will. The final withdrawal of the Roman army, some fifty years later, left England completely undefended and the population unprotected. Four centuries of occupation, during which citizens and slaves alike were forbidden even to carry arms and all weapons and military equipment were in the hands of the army, had left a population unaccustomed to warfare. That is not to say that the population was necessarily completely defenceless. Everyone must have seen this coming, and there were unknown numbers of retired veterans living in the towns and countryside. There may even have been remnants of a command structure at York and around Hadrian's Wall. The wall was not breached by the Picts, who must, therefore, have taken to the sea to attack the North Sea coasts in the great rising of 367. There were already Germanic settlements in eastern England based on former auxiliary units of the Roman army.

It takes only a little imagination to see these men using even their small advantages to establish themselves as minor kings in the confusion. But what actually happened is shrouded in mystery for one very good reason. There are simply no contemporary records. Even allowing for their exaggerations and creative imagination, the histories of Tacitus and others were some sort of record. After AD 410 there is nothing. We have to wait over 100 years for the next account – and that makes Tacitus sound as reliable as the *Encyclopaedia Britannica*. *The Ruin of Britain*, written by the monk Gildas in about 540, which we encountered in an earlier chapter, is little more than an indignant rant against the corruption and godlessness of his own time. This is how he describes the incursions of the early fifth century:

> As the Romans went back home, there eagerly emerged from the coracles that had carried them across the sea valleys the foul hordes of Scots and Picts, like dark throngs of worms who wriggle out of narrow fissures in the rock.

As to their appearance, Gildas writes, 'They were readier to cover their villainous faces with hair than their private parts with clothes.'

Here he describes the emergence of Vortigern from the chaos as a leader of the British and his invitation to the Saxon Hengist to protect him against Pictish attacks:

> To hold back the northern peoples, they introduced into the island the vile unspeakable Saxons, hated of God and man alike ... of their own free will, they invited in under the same roof the enemy they feared worse than death.

The Ruin of Britain is certainly colourful stuff – and totally unreliable. But what a great title. It is largely through the writings of Gildas that the central enigma of the Saxon age and its genetic effect on the British has been formed. Were they all killed or driven to the hills? This is what Gildas has to say about the effect of Saxon attacks in Norfolk:

> Swords flashed and flames crackled. Horrible was it to see the foundation stones and high walls thrown down ... mixing with holy altars and fragments of human bodies, and covered with a purple crust of clotted blood ... There was no burial save in the ruin of houses or in the bellies of the beasts and birds.

However, the archaeological evidence for immediate and wholesale destruction is conspicuously absent. London was not sacked, York and Lincoln were evacuated, then quickly recovered. In the far west the former legionary town of Wroxeter near Oswestry in Shropshire was completely untouched.

The far more dependable Bede, writing from the monastery at Jarrow, completed his *Ecclesiastical History of the English People* in 731. It is thanks to him that we are able to differentiate between the three tribes of 'barbarians', namely Saxons, Angles and Jutes. According to Bede, Jutes from the Jutland peninsula of northern Denmark occupied Kent and the Isle of Wight, while Saxons from Saxony in north-west Germany settled in southern England. They eventually differentiated into the East Saxons, in Essex, the Mid-Saxons farther west (and remembered in the now vanished county of Middlesex) and the West Saxons of Wessex, which was much later divided into Hampshire, Wiltshire and Dorset. The Angles, originally located in Angeln in southern Denmark, between Saxony and Jutland, took over East Anglia, as well as the Midlands, which became Mercia, and Northumbria in the north-east.

In very broad terms, archaeology confirms Bede's account of the origins of the invaders, as far as the general area goes, with objects found in English graves of the period very similar to the styles of northern Germany and southern Denmark. But the neat division between Saxons, Angles and Jutes and their various destinations in England almost certainly applies only to the leaders, not the mass of settlers.

Unlike the 'barbarians' who finally defeated the Roman Empire within Europe, the Saxons, if I may use that term to embrace the three 'tribes' of Bede, came from well outside the frontiers of the Empire. They had completely different customs, and social organizations which emphasized kinship and loyalty to the chieftains. Honour was to be found in avenging the death of relatives, or accepting a payment, the *wergild*, in its place. The Gods were Norse – Tiw, Woden, Thor, Freya, and are remembered in the days of the week – Tuesday, Wednesday, Thursday, Friday – and also in English place-names like Tuesley in Surrey and Wednesbury in Staffordshire.

There was stiff resistance to the Saxons, culminating in the British victory around AD 500 at Mons Badonicus, an unknown location in the West Country where Geoffrey of Monmouth has King Arthur lead the victorious Britons. In the century that followed, the Saxons advanced only very slowly into territory still held by the Britons. By 600 the Saxons had moved north from Northumbria to defeat the Britons of southern Scotland. The Saxon victory at the battle of Chester in 616 severed the land link between the Britons of Wales and the Britons of the north, preventing them from helping each other. The British kingdoms of Rheged on the Solway Firth and Elmet around Leeds were extinguished, while Strathclyde, with its base in Dumbarton on the Clyde, survived. At the other end of the country, Cornwall resisted until the beginning of the ninth century. Saxon lands coalesced into larger kingdoms – East Anglia, Kent, Sussex, Essex, Middlesex, Wessex, Mercia, and Bernicia and Deria, both in Northumbria. Gradually, through conquest and alliance, kings of one region claimed sovereignty over one or more of the others. Raedwald of East Anglia, whose treasures were found at the burial site at Sutton Hoo, was one of these, claiming supremacy over Mercia and Northumbria.

Life in the court of Raedwald and other Saxon kings centred around the Great Hall and Bede gives a captivating account of what it was like: 'the fire is burning on the hearth in the middle of the hall and all inside is warm, while outside the wintry storms of rain and snow are raging.' The king, his earls and household listen to the songs and poems of their bards. This is the world of *Beowulf* – heroic, courageous and at the same time sensitive to literature and beauty, as even a brief glimpse at the Sutton Hoo treasure confirms.

One enduring question is why it was that the Britons did not simply absorb the invaders. This is what happened in France, where the Germanic invaders were quickly assimilated into the culture of Roman Gaul. Their language was almost entirely lost as Gaul slowly moved from Latin to French. But in England the reverse happened. English owes very little to Celtic, but almost everything to its Germanic roots. The abrupt change of language, the reason indeed that I am writing this book in English rather than a form of Welsh, is a major reason among historians and archaeologists for supporting the extermination scenario. Reading the bloodthirsty accounts from Gildas and faced with the extinction of the Celtic language and its replacement by English, it is tempting to explain them as variations on the theme of genocide. The English Celts were simply wiped out, or driven to the hills. Whether this is true or not is certainly something I hoped genetics would be able to discover, but is it really very likely?

There certainly were civilian massacres, on the eve of the battle of Chester in 616 for example, but there is also plenty of evidence that the British were living peacefully in Saxon kingdoms. A set of laws promulgated by a seventh-century king of Wessex specifically provides for Britons living in his territory. There is also the question of numbers. Is it realistic to think that there were enough invaders coming across the sea completely to supplant the native population? The genetics should provide a big clue towards resolving the perennial Saxon/Celt debate, and it is the main question to be answered about England. Or is it?

In the year 789 it is recorded that the King of Wessex married the daughter of the Mercian King Offa. Almost as an afterthought is added this ominous sequel:

> And in his days came first three ships from Horthaland and then the reeve [the King's sheriff] rode thither and tried to compel them to go to the royal manor, for he did not know what they were; and then they slew him. These were the first ships of the Danes to come to England.

This was a chilling prelude to yet more raids, invasions and warfare by the mixed hordes of Vikings and Danes. After two centuries without any substantial foreign invasions in England, it looked as if it was starting all over again. After the killing of the king's sheriff in 789, on what has all the appearance of a reconnaissance mission, the Vikings paid most attention to the north of Britain and to Ireland, as we have already seen. But this was only a temporary respite. In 835 there was a large raid in Kent, then annually after that until, in 865, there was a full-scale invasion. The Danish Great Army landed in East Anglia led by Ivar Ragnusson, better known as Ivar the Boneless. I have rather a soft spot for Ivar the Boneless, because he was said to have suffered from the same genetic disease which I once researched myself. He was born, so it is said, with 'only gristle where his bones should have been'. From this description, Ivar almost certainly suffered from osteogenesis imperfecta, an inherited form of severe brittle-bone disease. If Ivar was anything like the osteogenesis patients I got to know he would have been very short, unable to walk without aid and with badly deformed limbs and spine. His head, however, would have been of normal size and his mental functions not impaired in the least.

The mystique of a fully mature mind in the broken body of a child is very powerful. I am not surprised that, even with this great physical disability, which would have prevented him from any combat himself, he was able to command an army by his legendary wisdom and force of personality alone. He was carried into battle on a shield. It must have been a disconcerting sight for the enemy.

Ivar forced the East Anglian king to supply him with food, horses and winter quarters, and next spring marched his troops north and captured the Northumbrian capital of York, beginning the long association between this city, renamed Jorvik by Ivar, and the Vikings. The Great Army then moved south to invade Mercia, then east to complete the invasion of East Anglia, which culminated in the brutal murder of Edmund, the Anglian king who had supplied the Great Army when it first landed. In three short years the Saxon kingdoms of Northumbria and East Anglia had been utterly destroyed.

The rampaging Great Army then turned south and prepared to invade Wessex. For the first time, the Danes were defeated, on the Berkshire Downs near Reading by Alfred and his brother Aethelred. The Danes withdrew and attacked again, this time beating the Saxon force near Basingstoke. The Danes were reinvigorated by the arrival of a new army in 871 and then prepared for the final showdown with the Saxons, with Alfred at their head. Alfred's Wessex and Mercia under King Burgred were the only Saxon kingdoms left in England that were not under Danish control. The Danes left Alfred alone for five years, and headed north, conquering Mercia *en route* to Yorkshire, which they began to divide up into permanent settlements. Then, at last, the Great Army turned south to attack the remnants of Saxon resistance in Wessex. They crushed Alfred at Chippenham in 878 and forced the king to retreat to his refuge in the marshes of Somerset, where he spent the winter arranging reinforcements. In the spring of 879 he headed towards Wiltshire and engaged the Danes at Edington Down on the slopes of Salisbury Plain near Warminster. He crushed the Great Army completely and forced their commander Guthrum to come to terms. The treaty separated England into two halves, with the dividing line running roughly north-west from London to the coast near Liverpool. East of the line was the Danelaw, to the west was Alfred's Saxon England. Schoolchildren learn that Alfred the Great saved England from the Danes. He clearly did not, as the Danes won control of half the country. Unsurprisingly, the peace did not last. Another army landed in 893, but restricted its campaign to the Danelaw and left Alfred's kingdom undisturbed.

From the genetic point of view I could see it was going to be hard to distinguish between Saxon and Dane. They both came from roughly the same place, their cultures were very similar, built around the Great Hall ideals of *Beowulf*. It was beginning to look, from the genetic point of view, like just another layer of north Germans and Scandinavians.

The next century saw the gradual reconquest of the Danelaw by the Saxon kings of Wessex. There were the inevitable setbacks. Norse armies recaptured York in 939 and 947, on the latter occasion under the command of the colourfully named Eric Bloodaxe. Another Danish army, under the equally chromatic Harold Bluetooth, had to be bought off after defeating an English militia in Essex. That only encouraged more raids, and by the turn of the first millennium huge amounts of cash had been paid to the Danes as what amounted to protection money.

The Vikings also used the same methods on the other side of the Channel. In 911 Hrolfe of Norway, or Rollo as he is more commonly known, sailed up the Seine and blockaded the river. In exchange for lifting the siege and withdrawing the threat to attack Paris, Rollo demanded, and got, a grant of land on the north-west coast from the French king. He became the first Duke of Normandy. He, his followers and descendants soon immersed themselves in French language and culture, though never forgetting their Viking roots.

Meanwhile, in England, the endless wars between Saxon and Dane continued. King Aethelred ordered a massacre of all Danes in England in 1002 – an impossible task, but serving to spread more hysteria and violence. Danes in Oxford took refuge in a church, but the citizens burned it down with the Danes still inside. The attempted ethnic cleansing forced Sweyn, the King of Denmark, to intervene, which he did on two unsuccessful campaigns until, in 1013, he launched a full-scale invasion. Aethelred fled to Normandy and thus began the fateful alliance that was to lead directly to the Norman Conquest. On Sweyn's death the following year his son Cnut, or Canute, inherited the Danish throne. By 1016 he had crushed Saxon resistance and become King of England as well. Notoriously he is the monarch who sat on the beach commanding the tide to retreat as a show of strength, but it was actually done to demonstrate his limitations in the face of nature. He was, in fact, a surprisingly good king, even though he divided his time between England and Denmark. But the fortunes of Wessex, whose regal supremacy Cnut had terminated, revived as Godwine, the Earl of Wessex, rose to prominence, even though he was not of the royal house.

Cnut died in 1035 and was succeeded by his son Harold. When Harold passed away five years later, his brother Harthacnut reigned for two brief years before he too died in 1042. That was the end of three decades of direct Danish rule and the kingdom was once more under a Saxon king, Edward (the Confessor), the son of Aethelred. Edward had grown up in Normandy at the court of his father-in-law, Richard, Duke of Normandy, after Aethelred had fled to

France to escape the Danes in 1013. Already the Saxon royal family owed a debt to the Normans, a debt which only increased when the Earl of Wessex, Godwine, defied the king and threatened to seize control. To deflect this ambition of Godwine, according to Norman propaganda, Edward, who had no children, promised the succession to William, Duke of Normandy. When Godwine died, he was succeeded to the earldom of Wessex by his son Harold who, again according to the Norman version of events, promised to back William of Normandy's claim to the English throne.

However, as he lay dying, Edward named Harold as his successor and England's last Saxon king came to occupy the throne on 5 January 1066. As William, Duke of Normandy, prepared the ground for invasion to press his claim to the Crown of England, the Danes were getting ready to do the same. Harald Hardraade, whose claim to the throne came through Cnut, was the first to attack. He invaded Northumbria and occupied York. King Harold, whose main army was in the south anticipating William's invasion from Normandy, was forced to move north to deal with Hardraade. This they did, and destroyed the Viking army at the battle of Stamford Bridge, close to York, on 25 September. Hardraade was killed. Three days later, on 28 September, William landed with his army at Pevensey Bay on the Sussex coast. Only nineteen days after defeating the Danes at York, Harold's exhausted army arrived to confront William at Senlac Hill, near Hastings. On the morning of 14 October 1066 the battle forces lined up. Harold's Saxon army massed behind a wall of shields on the crest of the hill and threw back charge after charge by William's heavy cavalry. In mid-afternoon, sections of Harold's army broke away to pursue a feigned Norman retreat and, without the advantage of the high ground, were cut off and overwhelmed. Harold was killed by an arrow and the day was lost. His men did not surrender, but fought to the death. They were all killed.

Having survived nearly three centuries of almost continuous attack by Vikings from Norway and Denmark, the Saxon dynasty of Alfred eventually succumbed to the Vikings from France. The resistance had lasted from the day in the summer of 789 when the king's sheriff was murdered on the Dorset coast, to the death of the last of Harold's huscarls on an autumn afternoon 277 years later. In the 940 years since the Norman Conquest many have tried to invade the Isles, but none has succeeded.

17
THE DNA OF ENGLAND

Our strategy for recruiting volunteers for the Genetic Atlas Project in England was at first the same as our successful campaigns in Scotland, through blood-donor sessions. We did try one or two other methods, like setting up stalls at agricultural fairs. This worked very well in Cornwall, where a team at the nearby University of Plymouth was conducting a medical research project which involved taking blood samples. In other places it was less successful, mainly because we had not developed our cheek swab method for collecting DNA and were asking for blood. A further factor was that the majority of visitors to agricultural shows were farmers. On the one hand, this was why we had originally thought of the shows as a good place to collect DNA samples, reasoning that we were more likely to encounter families whose roots in the surrounding countryside went back a very long way. That part of the logic turned out to be true. But the flaw was that most farmers are men. If there is one universal truth which many years of fieldwork has taught me, it is that men are far more reluctant to give a DNA sample in unfamiliar surroundings than are women. In the blood-donor clinics it was different. We were part of the main event, not separate as I felt we were at the shows. If we had been a little more patient and perfected our approach, and if we had tried again with our cheek swab method, it may have worked. I think the reasoning was right; in Cornwall, where this worked really well, practically everybody whose DNA was sampled had at least two grandparents from the local area.

Our first English blood-donor sessions were in East Anglia and over a couple of months we collected almost 1,500 blood samples in ways with which you are now familiar. I well remember travelling over the flat lands of the fens, where the soil is almost black and raised dykes drain the excess water to the sea. Scattered farmhouses and the occasional windbreak of Scots pine are all that protrude above the deadpan flatness. I know many people love the feel of openness and the big skies of East Anglia, but I need hills. When asking donors about their own origins, I was surprised how little movement there had been in the fens, even at places only a few miles from cosmopolitan cities like Cambridge. On one visit to a blood-donor session at the market town of Chatteris, 15 featureless miles north of Cambridge, the insularity of the fens came home to me when I was sitting next to a man in his forties, a farmworker, and going through my introduction of why we were there and why we wanted some of his blood. I explained how we were building up a genetic map and that was why we needed to know where people came from, so we could locate them properly on the map. When I had finished, he said he thought he probably shouldn't take part. That was unheard of, so I asked him why. He said it was because he had moved into Chatteris only recently.

'That's no problem,' I replied cheerfully. 'We can put you on the map wherever you're from, so long as we know. Where did you come from, before you came to live in Chatteris?'

'From Wimblington,' he replied.

'And where is Wimblington?' I enquired, ready to be told it was in Yorkshire or Dorset or somewhere else a long way away.

'It's up the road towards March,' he replied. And so it is, by 5 miles!

I think of that episode from time to time. The man is almost certainly still living in Chatteris and whenever I am asked how on earth I could ever expect to compile a genetic map from today's inhabitants that will reveal anything about the distant past, since people are so mobile these days, I tell them about the man from Chatteris.

Things were going nicely. We had more or less completed our DNA collections from Scotland, Wales and East Anglia and we had just been awarded another two years' funding from our major sponsors, the Wellcome Trust, which would give us ample time to complete our collections from the rest of England. I had arranged with other blood-transfusion regions in England to continue our work along the same lines. Word had got round that we did not interfere with the smooth running of the donor sessions. Indeed, donors on the whole enjoyed hearing about our work and it added a little more interest to their visit. I had a wonderful team who had honed their skills with, by now, three years of practice. In particular two of them, Emilce Vega and Eileen Hickey, who were assigned full time to the Genetic Atlas Project, were literally irresistible.

Nobody, male or female, young or old, could refuse Eileen and Emilce. They were, and still are, both striking young ladies, but in utterly different ways. Both are tall and slim, but while Eileen has the bright blue eyes, pale skin and auburn hair of her Irish ancestors, Emilce has the dark hair and deep brown eyes of her Argentinian forebears. Travelling to donor sessions with Eileen and Emilce was always interesting and our arrival at the small hotels we regularly used was always eagerly anticipated, and not because the owners were glad to see me again. Yes, things were going very well. Then disaster struck.

In scientific research the way is rarely smooth. Funds can be withdrawn, labs may have to be moved, extra duties of teaching or administration can be suddenly announced. It was none of these things. I put it all down to Ally McBeal. She, for those of you who do not know the TV series, was a glamorous Boston lawyer, though prone to fits of hysteria and some very strange dreams. Suddenly a career in law became a very attractive option for young women. Two of my team announced that they were abandoning their scientific careers to retrain as lawyers. And one of them was Emilce. It's always sad to see that happen, but it is also very understandable. Despite all the publicity about how badly the country needs scientists, the prospects for young scientists are actually pretty dismal. Even if you succeed against very stiff competition in landing a junior academic position with the chance of a career in science, the pay is not good. With the upsurge in biotechnology in the late 1990s, law firms were keen to recruit and retrain geneticists for work in that sector as either patent or commercial lawyers. I could hardly object, and I did not. Soon afterwards, Eileen decided to move into forensics, which at least offered the prospect of long-term security, which young scientists crave. Of course, I cannot really blame Ally McBeal, but the loss of my two best field-workers was a blow. By the time I had recruited replacements for Eileen and Emilce, there were only ten months for the project to run. It was too late to get the new recruits up to speed on the delicate technique of charming the DNA out of blood donors.

So I decided to fall back on Plan B. This had its origins in an unexpectedly fruitful visit a few years previously to a service station on the M6 motorway, where I had first seen an advertisement for the electoral roll in electronic form. As this ad was in the toilets I was a little doubtful, but I ordered a copy anyway. It has been extremely useful and I have used it extensively in my genealogy work, tracing the names and addresses of men who share the same surname. Plan B aimed to recruit volunteers for the Genetic Atlas Project in parts of England we now no longer had the time to visit through blood-donor sessions. We could have written to people in the regions of England we needed to cover and asked for their help directly. But there were two predictable drawbacks here. First, this would be unsolicited mail with very little context and likely, as with other unexpected material, to dive head first into the wastepaper bin. The second problem was that we would have been unable to tell by their addresses alone whether people were new arrivals to an area or whether they had lived there all their lives. Although we could have placed the origins of new arrivals elsewhere in the Isles, which would still have been useful, we really needed people with deep roots in the area, like Chatteris Man, to fill in the large gaps that we still had left in our coverage of England.

We got round this by combing the electoral role for surnames. By choosing names which we could tell from their geographical distribution were local to the areas where we needed coverage, we stood a good chance of getting hold of volunteers who had, at least on their father's side, been there for several generations. Thanks to the strictly enforced feudal system instigated all over England after the Norman Conquest, estates had insisted that men adopt surnames. This was so that they could be told apart and so that inheritance of land tenancies from father to son could be properly controlled. By the end of the thirteenth century the practice had spread throughout the land, and practically everyone in England had a forename and a surname.

The logic of Plan B was that if we had a DNA sample from a man whose surname we knew was concentrated in an area we needed to cover, his Y-chromosome had probably been in the vicinity since the thirteenth century. For this to work, we needed a lot of names, for the following reason. Men with the same surname often have the same

Y-chromosome signature, precisely because they are related to a common ancestor. It would be no use recruiting lots of men with the same surname just because they all lived in an area we needed to cover. Like as not, most of them would have the same Y-chromosome. To give you an extreme example, we could have got more than enough DNA samples from the Colne Valley in West Yorkshire just by writing to men with the surname Dyson. But 90 per cent of Dysons have the same Y-chromosome, owing to their common ancestry. We would get plenty of one particular Y-chromosome fingerprint and precious little else, and so our impression of Colne Valley genetics would be very misleading. For Plan B to give results for the Colne Valley that did give a representative picture of the whole area, we had to get DNA from all the local surnames. We would need to write to Dysons, Bamforths, Sykeses, Hirsts, Sutcliffes, Hills, Woods, etc., etc.

We worked our way through England, region by region, picking out scores of different surnames that, from directories and census distributions, were local to an area. We wrote to ten of each with an explanation of our project, a DNA sampling brush and return envelope. It was an exercise of, for us, military proportions. We sent out over 15,000 DNA brushes and got just over 3,000 back, a return of a little over 20 per cent, which proved to be a remarkably consistent average whichever region we tried. We also sent out 5,000 brushes to addresses in Wales, with a similar 20 per cent return rate. The DNA from our earlier blood spots from Wales had proved difficult to extract for Y-chromosomes. Plan B was no substitute for collecting in person, but we were left with little alternative if we were to complete the project on time. We did eventually manage to fill in all the gaps in our coverage of England. Fortunately, the DNA brushes kept their precious cargo in good condition, even after several days in the post, and we had barely a failure when we set out to recover it in the lab. What did we find?

We were expecting, as you would too knowing its turbulent history, that England would be the most mixed of all the regions of the Isles. That is largely how it turned out, with the exception of Orkney and Shetland. In these Northern Isles, the settlement of so many Vikings had an enormous influence on what, from the Pictland results, we might imagine the genetic make-up of the indigenous islanders to have been. In the Northern Isles, the great surprise had been that the proportion of Norse women who settled was on a par with the men. That unexpected result came from the comparison of maternal and paternal lineages. Would we see the same sort of family-based settlement in England? Or would the genetics parallel the more lurid histories in seeing a massive replacement on the male side and very little on the female? Let's take a look.

I first divided England into the rural districts shown on the map (page 14). The maternal clan pattern is stubbornly familiar wherever you are, but it does show a definite trend from the east and north to the south and west. It is literally as if the separation followed the line of the Danelaw. The Helena fraction is high, as usual, varying from 43 per cent in East Anglia to 47 per cent in the north of England.

Below the Danelaw line it is only fractionally higher, rising to 49 per cent in the far south of England. There is really nothing in it. But it is in the other clans that the differences stand out, particularly when you get down to the detail, from which I will spare you. The most striking are the differences within the Jasmine clan and the presence of some very unusual sequences in East Anglia and the north of England.

Taking the Jasmines, the 'farming clan', to begin with, there are two different branches, which arrived in northern Europe by separate routes, as we saw in an earlier chapter. Let's call one the Ocean branch. They travelled around the coast of the Mediterranean from the Balkans, round Italy, to Iberia and then up the coast of France. The other, which we will call the Land branch, made their way overland to the Baltic and North Sea coasts. In Wales, Ireland and Scotland, the only branch is the Ocean branch. Only on the eastern side of Britain do I find much of the Land branch, and that is not a great deal. The great majority of Jasmines are from the Ocean branch and they pepper the map of the west side of Britain from bottom to top. They also occur in Norway.

The other difference in the matrilineal DNA is the occurrence of the minor clans of Wanda, Xenia and Ulrike. Wanda, along with Isha and Xenia, was originally subsumed in the clan of Xenia, and Ulrike is, as we saw, the 'eighth' daughter of Eve. All three are found in East Anglia and the north of England, but hardly anywhere else. Mrs Archer from Great Dunmow and Mrs Peachey from Coggeshall, both in Essex, are descendants of Ulrike.

Ulrike's clan is particularly frequent in Scandinavia, so the hint is there that perhaps these two ladies are descended from that rare commodity, Viking women. Rare, that is, outside the Northern Isles. Xenia's clan originated in the steppes of Russia 25,000 years ago and travelled to Britain from the east. Wanda's clan is usually coupled with Xenia's, but has a more recent origin, 18,000 years ago, though she too came from the same vicinity. Mrs Lewis from Braintree in Essex and Mr Simmonds from Toft's Monk near Bury St Edmunds are both in Wanda's clan. They have certainly come a long way from the Ukraine.

In England there is a definite suggestion through detailed matches in most maternal clans of female immigration into the east from continental Europe, something which is undetectable in the west and north. How about the men? Here we do see a huge difference, even in the distribution of the clans, the crudest of indicators. Oisin's clan is down to only 51 per cent in East Anglia. The proportions increase as you travel west to Wales and north to Scotland. Where Oisin declines, Wodan increases and it reaches its highest proportions in the whole of the Isles in East Anglia, where Oisin is lowest. But there are virtually no Sigurds in East Anglia. However, there are plenty of Sigurds in the north of England, where they amount to 7 per cent of the total, which is a third of the Shetland total. In the south of England and in the Mercian territory of central England there are plenty of Wodans, and Sigurds too. The Appendix gives the figures.

The difference between the eastern regions and the rest intensifies when we look at the Y-chromosome diversity, which is much higher in the east, indicating a longer settlement if you follow the traditional way of interpreting genetic diversity. Diversity is much higher in the Wodan clan than in Oisin wherever you care to look.

By now there are so many threads in the air, so many facts to digest. And I have only been able to give you a tiny fraction of the detail. For every fact I have shown you, I have a hundred more in reserve. It has been a long tour, in time as well as in space. We have travelled to every corner of the Isles. At each step we have moved closer to an answer and now the time has arrived to distil the essence of our discoveries and draw our conclusions.

18
THE BLOOD OF THE ISLES

You have read the myths about the origins of the Isles that shimmer in the background, just out of reach; stories of brave kings and treacherous villains, fantastic monsters and invincible warriors. You have heard the ancient tales that have floated down the generations, stories that have been told and retold a thousand times around the campfire or in the flickering flame-light of the Great Hall. You have also heard how they were set down by Christian monks, transcribed from the world of the spoken and the sung to the realm of the written.

These same monks also wrote their own versions of our origins, histories that were sometimes an earnest attempt to pass on an impartial narrative of events and sometimes a fantastical torrent of loathing and contempt, fantasy and corruption. You have heard how these twisted histories were seized upon by kings, re-cast and put to work to bolster a fading reign or to right an ancient wrong and, in so doing, to inspire and justify a new conquest.

You have heard the chronicles of historians, from the amiable and conscientious Tacitus to the malignant architects of the Third Reich, each in their own way deriding and denigrating the people of the Isles as degenerate and barbaric. Yet archaeologists, whose account you have also heard, draw a sketch of the ancient Britons as masters of the shore and forest, able to fell the mighty aurochs with the well-directed flight of a flint-tipped arrow. You have heard how a medical man, the epitome of the Victorian amateur scientist, ranged through the Isles with card, tape and calipers searching for clues to our origins. You have heard how the search continued in the blood banks and laboratories of great hospitals.

I have introduced you to a new art and a new language. An art that is written in the codes of our DNA, those unseen architects of our bodies, even of our souls. It is a new art, not long tested and yet somehow irresistibly correct. How can anyone doubt that we are all our parents' children, as they also are the children of their parents? That is the simplicity of this art even though the language is new and obscure. I have tested you with talk of 'DNA sequences', 'haplotypes' and 'genetic diversity', of 'Y-chromosomes' and 'mitochondrial DNA'. I have impudently claimed that my art is oblivious to the prejudice of the human mind.

You have read the book, and I congratulate you on persevering through the technical sections. I have tried to make things as simple as I reasonably can, but it is no easy task to walk the tightrope between obsessive detail and arrogant patronage. My subject has been our history, the history written in our genes. Why, you might reasonably enquire, is this at all important in this day and age? What does it matter to me, you might say, whether my ancestor was a Viking, or a Saxon or a Celt? What difference will this make to my journey to work, what I eat for lunch or what I read on the way home? But if you really thought that, you would not have got this far. I hope you are by now just as fascinated as I am that within each and every one of our cells is something that has witnessed every life we have ever lived. I know that you can see the myriad threads of ancestry falling away beneath you into the abyss of the past.

I have introduced you to the brightest and strongest of these threads, one through which we are joined to our ancestral mother. An infinite umbilical cord which courses smoothly from mother to mother back into the mist of our ancestry. The other, which only men possess, thrusts its way from generation to generation. Erratic, illogical and passionate, it lives a life free from responsibility. But it enslaves its host and drives him to violence, murder and conquest. Follow this thread into the past at your peril. Sooner or later you will spend a generation or two in the testis of a warlord. We could not have any more different conduits into the depths of our ancestry.

The stories that these threads tell are completely individual. They are not composites or averages. I have been at pains to point out, even to the point of repetition, that to squeeze them through the mangle of mathematics risks robbing them of their vitality, silencing their murmurs. What I have tried to do is to listen to the whispered stories of thousand upon thousand of these threads and to divine patterns from the swirls. Enough of the philosophy – what are these patterns?

The first conclusion, blindingly obvious now I can see it, is that we have in front of us two completely different histories. The maternal and paternal origins of the Isles are different. And that should be no surprise, given the opposing characters of the chroniclers. The matrilineal history of the Isles is both ancient and continuous. I see no reason at all from the results why many of our maternal lineages should not go right back through the millennia to the very first Palaeolithic and Mesolithic settlers who reached our islands around 10,000 years ago. The average settlement dates of 8,000 years ago fit with that. But that cannot be the complete answer. That was well before the arrival of farming, and the presence, particularly in Ireland and the Western Isles, of large numbers of Jasmine's Oceanic clan, and her companions from the maritime branch of Tara, says to me that there was a very large-scale movement along the Atlantic seaboard north from Iberia, beginning as far back as the early Neolithic and perhaps even before that. The number of exact and close matches between the maternal clans of western and northern Iberia and the western half of the Isles is very impressive, much more so than the much poorer matches with continental Europe.

That is not to say this was a 'wave' arriving all at once and swamping the small numbers of Mesolithic inhabitants of Mount Sandel, Starr Carr and the like. They were well established, knew the land inside out and must have been easily able to adapt, gradually, to a less mobile agricultural existence. The change from hunter-gathering to agriculture may have taken centuries or millennia. There is no archaeological evidence of conflict and no reason to suppose that the arrival of the farmers would have been confrontational, at least not at first. We encountered the peaceful co-existence of Mesolithic and Neolithic communities in Portugal where the new arrivals from the Middle East cleared the woods for their crops well away from the coastal zones favoured by the residents. I think this pattern would have been reproduced all over the Isles. There was plenty of room, with the Mesolithic population only a few thousand strong and with plenty of land available for cultivation after the woods had been cleared. The mere presence of large numbers of Oceanic Jasmines indicates that this was most definitely a family-based settlement rather than the sort of male-led invasions of later millennia. I think the main body of the Neolithics arrived by this western route, since the Oceanic Jasmines reached right round the top of Scotland to the east coast and even inland to the Grampian region. There are far fewer Land Jasmines in the Isles. I found none in Ireland, only one in Wales, just five in Scotland, again in the Grampian region and in Strathclyde. The rest are in England and concentrated there in the Midlands and the east.

After that, the genetic bedrock on the maternal side was in place. By about 6,000 years ago, the pattern was set for the rest of the history of the Isles and very little has disturbed it since. Once here, the matrilineal DNA mutated and diversified, each region developing slightly different local versions, but without losing its ancient structure. Without agonizing over the precise definition, this is our

Celtic/Pictish stock and, except in two places, it has remained undiluted to this day. On our maternal side, almost all of us are Celts.

I can see no evidence at all of a large-scale immigration from central Europe to Ireland and the west of the Isles generally, such as has been used to explain the presence there of the main body of 'Gaels' or 'Celts'. The 'Celts' of Ireland and the Western Isles are not, as far as I can see from the genetic evidence, related to the Celts who spread south and east to Italy, Greece and Turkey from the heartlands of Hallstadt and La Tène in the shadows of the Alps during the first millennium BC. The people of the Isles who now feel themselves to be Celts have far deeper roots in the Isles than that and, as far as I can see, their ancestors have been here for several thousand years. The Irish myths of the Milesians were right in one respect. The genetic evidence shows that a large proportion of Irish Celts, on both the male and female side, did arrive from Iberia at or about the same time as farming reached the Isles. They joined the Mesolithics who were already here, having reached the Isles either by the same maritime route or overland from Europe before the Isles were cut off by the rising sea.

The connection to Spain is also there in the myth of Brutus, who came to the Isles from the Mediterranean and up the Atlantic coast to found New Troy in the land of Albion. This too may be the faint echo of the same origin myth as the Milesian Irish and the connection to Iberia is almost as strong in the British regions as it is in Ireland.

One myth that the genetic evidence certainly does not support is the relic status of the Picts. Their ancestors, just like the rest of the people of the Isles, have been there a very long time, but they are from the same basic stock. They are from the same mixture of Iberian and European Mesolithic ancestry that forms the Pictish/Celtic substructure of the Isles. It is very clear from the genetic evidence that there is no fundamental genetic difference between Pict and Celt.

This ancient matrilineal bedrock has been overlain to any substantial extent in only two places. In Orkney and Shetland there was a large settlement of women from Norway during the Viking period and the ancestors of roughly 40 per cent of today's Shetlanders and 30 per cent of modern Orcadians first stepped ashore from a Viking ship. But plenty of others in the Northern Isles can trace their ancestry back well before the Viking age to the sophisticated Picts who built the brochs at Mousa in Shetland and Gurness in Orkney.

The second overlay is in eastern and northern England, above the Danelaw line which ran from London to Chester. Above that line, and particularly in the east, there are clear signals of female settlement overlying the Celtic substratum. As we have already touched on, it is very difficult to distinguish Saxon, Dane and Norman on a genetic basis, since they are all from the same Germanic/Scandinavian origins, but the concentration of these signals above rather than below the Danelaw line makes me think they are more likely to be Viking than Saxon or Norman. The approximate extent of this overlay I estimate to be between 10 per cent in the east and 5 per cent in the north – substantial in terms of numbers, but really only denting the Celtic substructure.

Lastly, I have found a tiny number of very unusual clans in the southern part of England. Two of these are from sub-Saharan Africa, three from Syria or Jordan. These exotic sequences are found only in England, with one exception, and among people with no knowledge of, or family connections with, those distant parts of the world. I think they might be the descendants of Roman slaves, whose lines have kept going through unbroken generations of women. If this was the genetic legacy of the Romans, they have left only the slightest traces on the female side. I have not found any in Wales, or in Ireland and only one in Scotland. This is an African sequence from Stornoway in the Western Isles, for which I have absolutely no explanation. These exotic dustings, and the more substantial layers of Viking maternal lines, are the exception. Everything else in the Isles, on the maternal side, is both Celtic and ancient. But what about the men?

Here again, the strongest signal is a Celtic one, in the form of the clan of Oisin, which dominates the scene all over the Isles. The predominance in every part of the Isles of the Atlantis chromosome (the most frequent in the Oisin clan), with its strong affinities to Iberia, along with other matches and the evidence from the maternal side convinces me that it is from this direction that we must look for the origin of Oisin and the great majority of our Y-chromosomes. The sea routes of the Atlantic fringe conveyed both men and women to the Isles. I can find no evidence at all of a large-scale arrival from the heartland of the Celts of central Europe among the paternal genetic ancestry of the Isles, just as there is none on the maternal side.

The pockets of ancient Wodans in mid-Wales and the 'Pictland' regions of Grampian and Tayside are, I believe, the echoes of the very first Mesolithic settlers who arrived from continental Europe, perhaps even travelling by foot while there was still a land connection. They look old to me, and for an apparently contradictory reason. That is because they are all very similar. The same applies to the Oisins. And yet the customs of genetics state that the longer a gene has been in a place, the more diversity should have accumulated. That was how I was able to fix the homelands of the seven European clan matriarchs. Using that rule I placed them at the locations where the present-day diversity was highest, and thus where they had had longest to accumulate mutations away from the original.

But this rule does not seem to work with the paternal lines delineated by the Y-chromosome. The very striking thing about the clan of Oisin throughout the Isles is how very similar they all are. Or at least, how there are very large clusters of very similar chromosomes in one location, and not in others. For instance, the Ui Neill chromosome reaches a very high frequency in north-west Ireland but is rare elsewhere, and the Somerled chromosome is common in the Highlands and the Hebrides, but virtually unknown elsewhere – unless carried by a member of Clan Donald or Clan Dugall. This dramatically reduces the genetic diversity, and leads to very recent settlement dates, sometimes obviously incorrect. This has been noticed before with the Y-chromosome but has been attributed to what is called 'patrilocality'. This is the practice of men staying put, while the women move to marry. However, I don't think this works well enough to explain the amazing similarity in the Oisin chromosomes. The explanation is less cosy.

This is the 'Genghis effect' and it is not confined to the Mongol Empire. In the Isles very large numbers of men, perhaps all of them in the clan of Oisin, are descended from only a few genetically successful ancestors. All the conditions are here in the Isles. From the Iron Age onwards, and certainly during the first millennium AD, which we have covered here in such detail, the past is filled with the continual feuding between rival clans. One of the genetic consequences of the rise of powerful men is that they monopolize the women and have more children. I have even argued in *Adam's Curse* that therein lies the motivation for their procreative ambition. We can see the evidence in the Isles in the Scottish clans of Macdonald and Macleod and in the Irish Ui Neill. These are very dramatic examples of a process which has percolated throughout the history of the Isles. That is why the diversity has been lost. It is because only comparatively few men have left patrilineal descendants. So, the longer a clan has been in a place like the Isles, the more similar the Y-chromosomes become. That is the reason our Celtic Y-chromosomes are so alike.

It is also the reason why most of the Wodan chromosomes are the opposite. They are usually very diverse indeed in the Isles. Not because they have been here a long time, but because they are comparatively recent. There are pockets of 'old' Wodans in Wales and Pictland, but in the east and in the north above the Danelaw line, the Wodans, which reach 31 per cent in East Anglia, are extremely varied. I scarcely found any two the same when I looked at the detailed fingerprints, unless they had the same surname and were thus related to a common ancestor through that route. The clan of Oisin still predominates in every part of England, but the bedrock is substantially overlaid in the east. Because of the genetic similarity of Saxon, Dane and Norman, I cannot discriminate so easily between them. But I estimate that approximately 10 per cent of men now living in the south of England are the patrilineal descendants of Saxons or Danes, while above the Danelaw line the proportion increases to 15 per cent overall, reaching 20 per cent in East Anglia. Only a few of these men have surnames of Norman origin and, taking this into account, I estimate the Norman Y-chromosome legacy at 2 per cent or below even in the south of England.

From this evidence the succession of Saxon/Danish invasions during the turbulent centuries after the Romans departed did leave a mark on the stubbornly Celtic indigenous bedrock of parts of England. It is a real presence, but it is by no means completely overwhelming. The gory chronicles of Gildas do contain a grain of truth. The roughly twofold excess of Saxon/Danish Y-chromosomes compared to their maternal counterparts hints at a partially male-driven settlement with some elimination or displacement of the indigenous males. But the slaughter, if slaughter there was, was not total and still there are far more people with Celtic ancestry in England, even in the far east, than can claim to be of Saxon or Danish descent.

I have tried to find Roman Y-chromosomes, but they left very few traces that I can be sure were theirs. Only one very rare patrilineal clan, without even a name, may be the faint echo of the first legions. It is found in southern Europe, including Italy. What makes me think, as well as this link to Italy, that it might be linked to the Romans is that it is entirely restricted to England. There are no traces beyond the borders with Wales or Scotland. There may be others, but as was pointed out, the tradition of recruiting legionaries and auxiliaries from Gaul and other parts of the Empire, as well as from Britannia itself, makes them very difficult to spot among the descendants of later arrivals from the same areas. But true Roman genes are very rare in the Isles.

Overall, the genetic structure of the Isles is stubbornly Celtic, if by that we mean descent from people who were here before the Romans and who spoke a Celtic language. We are an ancient people, and though the Isles have been the target of invasion and opposed settlement from abroad ever since Julius Caesar first stepped on to the shingle shores of Kent, these have barely scratched the topsoil of our deep-rooted ancestry. However we may feel about ourselves and about each other, we are genetically rooted in a Celtic past. The Irish, the Welsh and the Scots know this, but the English sometimes think otherwise. But, just a little way beneath the surface, the strands of ancestry weave us all together as the children of a common past.

This genetic history has been read mainly from the surviving genes passed on by generations of ancestors who lived through the events described in *Blood of the Isles* and whose descendants carry them today. It is a new history, reconstructed from thousands of fragments from the past. The general conclusions in this and other chapters have been distilled from the DNA of hundreds of people from each region of the Isles. But to the people concerned, and to everyone else in the Isles, it is our own genetic ancestry that is the most important. It is the thread that goes back to our own deep roots that means the most. The proportions of one clan or another are vital and the detailed genetic comparisons are essential for arriving at any sort of general conclusion, but it is our own ancestry that understandably, and quite rightly, holds the most interest. Now that we know what the overall patterns mean and now that we can identify with confidence surviving DNA with the different ancestral signatures, it is open to anyone to find their place in this amazing story. For this is not the history told by fading manuscripts in dimly lit libraries, or by rusting weapons in glass cases. It is a living history, told by the real survivors of the times: the DNA that still lives within our bodies. This really is the history of the people, by the people.

APPENDIX

Within this appendix I have compressed just a small fraction of the genetic data from the Oxford Genetic Atlas Project that forms the foundation for *Blood of the Isles*. More details appear at www.bloodoftheisles.net.

Distribution of Maternal Clans in Scotland (%)

	Argyll	Borders	Northern Isles	Tayside	Grampian	Highland	Hebrides	Strathclyde	All Scotland
Helena	51.2	41.7	53.1	47.4	46.7	38.9	31.6	44.9	45.3
Isha	4.9	2.8	2.6	4.6	5.0	6.1	7.0	1.4	4.2
Jasmine	6.5	19.4	10.8	15.3	20.6	13.1	14.0	14.0	13.4
Katrine	9.8	5.6	5.1	6.1	6.1	4.5	14.4	7.2	7.2
Tara	9.8	2.8	7.7	10.2	6.1	10.6	13.6	15.5	10.1
Uma	0.8	0.0	0.0	0.0	2.2	1.0	0.0	1.0	0.6
Uta	0.8	2.8	0.0	0.5	1.1	1.5	3.5	1.9	1.2
Ulrike	3.3	8.3	4.4	2.6	2.8	2.0	0.9	1.4	2.8
Ursula	6.5	11.1	10.6	5.1	5.0	10.6	9.2	7.2	8.4
Velda	1.6	2.8	2.2	4.1	2.8	6.1	2.6	4.3	3.3
Wanda	0.8	0.0	0.4	1.0	0.0	1.5	0.4	0.0	0.6
Xenia	2.4	2.8	3.1	2.6	1.1	2.6	2.2	1.0	2.3
Other	1.6	0.0	0.0	0.5	0.6	1.5	0.4	0.0	0.5

Distribution of Maternal Clans in England and Wales (%)

	North-umbria	North	Central	East Anglia	London	South-west	South	All England	North Wales	Mid-Wales	South Wales	All Wales
Helena	51.0	47.1	45.8	43.0	40.9	45.8	48.6	45.7	52.1	42.7	47.2	46.3
Isha	3.0	4.7	3.8	4.6	3.7	2.6	3.4	3.9	6.3	7.3	0.0	6.1
Jasmine	15.0	13.7	11.0	9.1	13.4	13.7	12.3	12.2	11.5	8.5	2.8	8.8
Katrine	12.0	9.0	8.0	7.6	6.1	7.9	8.4	8.2	6.3	11.0	11.1	9.5
Tara	2.0	7.9	10.2	8.8	11.6	7.4	12.3	8.9	4.2	11.0	19.4	9.8
Uma	0.0	0.5	0.8	1.8	0.0	1.1	0.0	0.8	1.0	0.6	2.8	1.0
Uta	0.0	0.5	0.4	0.3	0.0	1.1	0.0	0.4	0.0	2.4	2.8	1.7
Ulrike	1.0	1.1	1.5	5.5	1.2	3.7	0.6	2.3	5.2	0.6	0.0	2.0
Ursula	10.0	8.8	13.6	10.7	14.0	11.1	8.9	10.9	10.4	11.0	11.1	10.8
Velda	5.0	3.6	2.7	4.3	3.0	2.1	1.7	3.2	3.1	3.7	0.0	3.0
Wanda	0.0	3.0	1.5	1.8	3.7	0.5	0.0	1.8	0.0	0.6	0.0	0.3
Xenia	1.0	0.0	0.8	2.4	0.0	1.1	0.0	0.8	0.0	0.6	0.0	0.3
Other	0.0	0.0	0.0	0.0	2.4	2.1	3.9	0.9	0.0	0.0	2.8	0.3

* The clans of Isha, Wanda and Xenia are minor clans subsumed within Xenia. Uma, Uta and Ulrike are minor clans in western Europe, but more frequent further east.

Distribution of Paternal Clans in Scotland (%)

	Argyll	Borders	Northern Isles	Tayside	Grampian	Highland	Hebrides	Strathclyde	All Scotland
Oisin	81.1	78.1	59.9	78.9	83.5	75.9	71.2	73.3	72.9
Wodan	3.8	12.5	16.8	17.5	11.8	16.5	17.8	20.0	15.4
Sigurd	7.5	3.1	19.8	1.8	2.4	6.3	11.0	4.2	8.8
Eshu	1.9	1.6	1.5	1.8	2.4	1.3	0.0	1.7	1.5
Re	5.7	4.7	1.5	0.0	0.0	0.0	0.0	0.0	1.2
Other	0.0	0.0	0.5	0.0	0.0	0.0	0.0	0.8	0.3

Distribution of Paternal Clans in England and Wales (%)

	North-umbria	North	Central	East Anglia	London	South	South-west	All England	North Wales	Mid-Wales	South Wales	All Wales
Oisin	68.3	62.8	65.8	51.2	57.6	57.7	78.2	64.0	78.5	86.4	84.2	83.2
Wodan	15.9	25.1	21.4	31.2	23.2	36.4	12.6	22.2	15.0	8.2	10.5	11.0
Sigurd	7.3	7.2	7.1	2.4	4.0	2.5	4.2	5.2	2.8	0.7	0.0	1.4
Eshu	1.2	1.9	0.0	3.2	3.3	4.9	1.3	2.1	3.7	2.7	2.6	3.1
Re	2.4	2.5	1.5	5.6	4.0	3.1	1.7	2.7	0.0	1.4	0.0	0.7
Other	4.9	0.6	4.1	6.4	7.9	5.5	2.1	3.6	0.0	0.7	2.6	0.7

Clan Distribution – Maternal

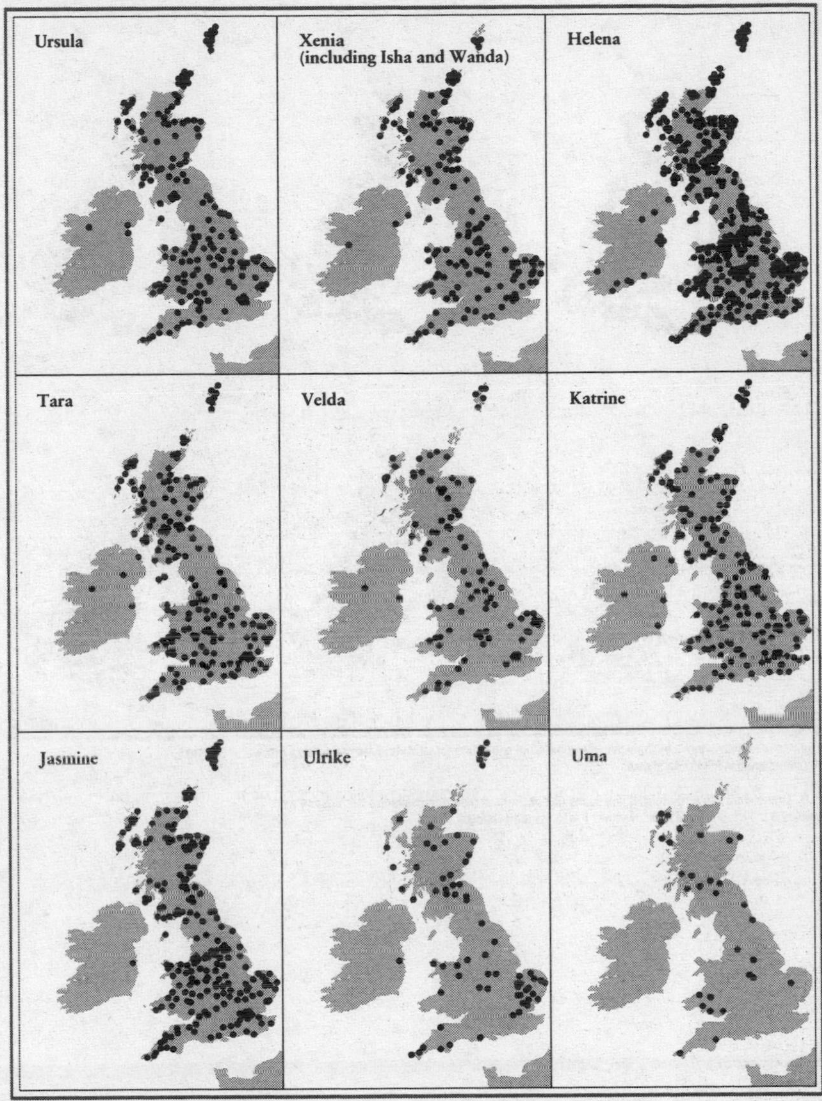

Locations shown are the birthplaces of the paternal grandfathers of Oxford Genetic Atlas Project volunteers.
No independent Irish data shown.

Clan Distribution – Paternal

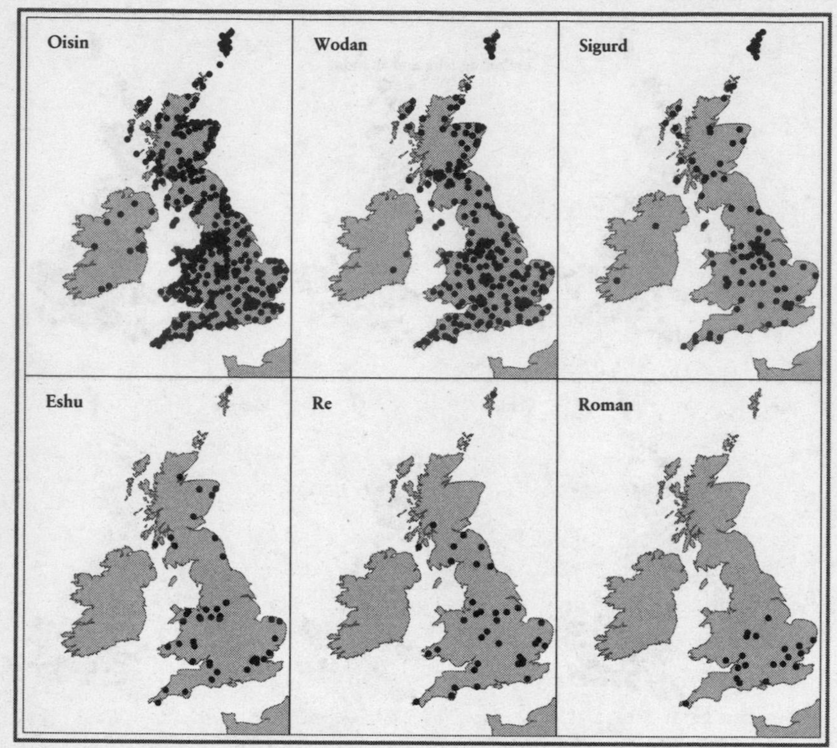

Locations shown are the birthplaces of the paternal grandfathers of Oxford Genetic Atlas Project volunteers.
No independent Irish data shown.

INDEX

Aeneas 43, 44, 45
Aethelred, King 311, 313–14
Africa 59, 158, 172, 334
Agricola, Julius 160, 267, 299
agriculture *see* farming
Aidan, King 222
Ailill, King of Connacht 167–8
Albion 41, 42, 44, 167, 332
Alfred, King 56–7, 311–12, 315
Amairgen 164
AMH *see* Atlantic Modal Haplotype
amino-acids 122, 123, 132
Amminius 294
Angles 86, 306
Anglesey 266, 271, 278, 283, 297
Anglo-Normans
invasion of Ireland 116, 154–5, 156, 162, 197–8, 201, 224
in Scotland 224–5
in Wales 272–4, 276
Anglo-Saxons 46, 56, 102, 225
Antonine Wall 218, 299–300
Antoninus Pius, Emperor 299
Aran Islands 94, 166
Argyll, Scotland 213, 222–3, 250, 251–3, 257, 259, 261–2, 269
Arnold, Matthew 61, 84–5, 87
Arran, Isle of 208
Arthur, King 38–9, 40, 47, 48, 49–52, 53, 54, 55, 56–7, 58, 162, 275, 307
Arthur, Prince of Wales 52
Aryan myth 63, 64
Ashmolean Museum, Oxford 67, 147–8

Atlantic Modal Haplotype/ 'Atlantis' chromosome 199, 285, 334
Atrebates, the 295, 297
Auchterarder, Scotland: blood donations 241–3
Augustus, Emperor 294
Aurelius, Emperor Marcus 300
Australia 75, 77–8, 114
Avalon, Isle of 50, 51

Bailey, Jill 184
Bala, Wales 275, 278
Ballynagilly, Ulster: Neolithic site 180
Balor of the Baleful Eye 166, 168
Barvas, Western Isles 100
Basques 113, 199, 220
Beddoe, Dr John 87–104, 227, 328
    Memories of Eighty Years (autobiography) 95
    The Races of Britain 95–7, 99–102, 103, 110, 113
Bede, the Venerable: *History of the English Church and People* 54, 271, 306–7, 308
Ben Macdui 202
Bennachie, Scotland 299
Ben Nevis 202
Beowulf 308, 312
Bernicia 307
Besu, Paul 75, 76
Bismarck, Otto von 64
Blackmore, R. D. 55
blood-donors 108–9, 228, 241–3, 249–50, 316–19
blood groups 105–8, 109–12, 113–20
    and DNA 121, 122–3, 125–6
    Rhesus 112–13, 114
blood transfusions 105–6, 108–9, 112
Bobbio, Italy: monastery 162
Boleyn, Anne 53
bone collagen genetics 24, 124
Book of Armagh 161
Boudicca, Queen 267, 297–8, 302
Boxgrove Quarry, Sussex: shin bone 29
Boyd, William 111, 113, 120
Boyne, battle of the (1690) 155
Boyne valley, Ireland: graves 179, 210
Bradley, Dan 10, 184, 186, 197, 199, 258, 259
Brecon Beacons, Wales 263, 278
Brennius 53
Brian Boru 213, 232
Brigantes, the 266, 297, 298
Bristol, Beddoe in 88, 92, 94, 95, 96

British Academy, London 182, 183
Britons 39, 42, 46–8, 52–7, 86–7, 101, 328
Brittany 46, 48, 66–7, 81, 178
brittle-bone disease 124, 310
brochs 218–20, 333
Brutus 41, 43, 44–5, 55, 275, 332
Buckland, Dr William 30
Burgred, King 311

Cader Idris, Wales 265
Cadwallader 41
Cadwallon 271, 272
Caerleon, Wales 267, 268
Caernarfon, Wales 267, 274
Caesar, Julius 45, 69, 293–4, 338
Cairngorms, Scotland 202, 204
Caithness, Scotland 100, 204, 209, 250
Caligula, Emperor 294–5
Callanish stone circle, Lewis 209
Camlan (Devon), battle of 50
Canadian Celts 75
Canna, Isle of 254
Canute *see* Cnut
Caratacus 265–6, 295, 296, 297, 299
carbon-dating 24, 27–8, 30, 33, 171, 176, 177, 179–80, 186
Cardigan Castle 273
Cartimandua, Queen 266, 298
Cassivelaunus 45
Catherine of Aragon 52, 53
Catuvellauni, the 148, 265, 294, 295–6
Ceidi Fields, County Mayo 209
cells 123, 126, 127, 128
  blood 106–9, 123–4
'Celtic Connections' (festival) 66
Celts 37, 42, 52, 66–70
  artefacts 66, 70, 79–80, 180–1
  Beddoe's views 102
  definitions 69–71, 83–4
  emigration and immigration 68, 72–8
  and genetics 67, 76, 78–9, 332–8
  in Ireland 65–6, 67–8, 72, 74, 84–5, 102, 180–1, 192, 332
  and language 66–7, 68, 72–3, 74, 308
  19th-century views of 61–2, 83–6
  in Scotland 224–5, 247–8, 253, 332–3; *see also* Somerled
  and spirituality 77–8
  in Wales 265–7
Charles, Prince of Wales 40
Chatteris, Cambridgeshire 317–18
Cheddar Gorge: tooth 22–4, 26–7

'Cheddar Men' 27–8, 29, 30, 33, 36–7, 171, 172, 264, 288
Chester 267–8, 333
battle of (616) 307, 309
Chippenham, battle of (AD 878) 311
chromosomes 126, 128–9
see X-chromosomes; Y-chromososmes
Church of England 53–7
Civil War, English 58
'clan mothers' 135–8
see Helena; Jasmine; Katrine; Tara; Ulrike; Ursula; Velda; Wanda; Xenia
Claudius, Emperor 45, 220, 265, 266, 295, 296, 298
Clontarf, battle of (1014) 213, 232
Cnut (Canute) 313
coins 147–8, 301
Colchester 294, 296, 298, 300
collagen 24, 122, 124, 128
Collins, Michael 153
Colne Valley, Yorkshire 322
Colonsay, island of 207
Columba, St 161, 212, 218, 221, 222
Columban, St 162
Conall Cernach 168
Connacht 167, 168–9, 192, 197, 285
Constans 46
Constantine, Emperor 46, 48, 53
Conti, Leno 284, 285
Cornovii, the 265
Cornwall 49, 66, 81, 96, 97, 99, 101, 287, 291, 307, 316, 317
Courcey, John, Baron de 162
Cramond, Scotland 205–6, 211
cromlechs 264
Cú Chulainn 168, 169
Cumbria 99, 287
Cunliffe, Barry 178
Cunobelinus 148, 294, 295
cytoplasm 126, 127

Dál Riata/Dalriada 221, 222–3, 248, 259, 261, 269
Dana 165
Danelaw, the 311–12, 323–4, 333, 336–7
Danes *see* Denmark
Dapifer family 224
Dartmouth, Devon 101
Dathi 259
Davies, Norman 39
Davis, Barnard 94
Dawson, Professor Geoffrey 116, 198
Deceangli, the 265, 268
de Clare, Richard *see* Pembroke, Earl of

Defoe, Daniel: 'The True-Born Englishman' 59
Deheubarth, Wales 273
de Lacy, Hugh 155
Demetae, the 265, 268
Denmark/Danes 49, 54, 58, 102, 271, 306, 311–13, 337
  Great Army 310–12
  see also Vikings
Deria 307
de Valera, Eamon 153
Diana 43, 44
DNA 76, 110, 121–5
  analysing 141–51
  and blood groups 121, 122–3, 125–6
  chromosome sequences 129–31
  collecting samples 139–40, 141, 228–30, 276–8
  'junk' 130
  male 128; *see* Y-chromosomes
  mitochondrial (mDNA) 126–8, 131–2; *see* 'clan mothers'
  and mutations 123–5, 127, 131–3, 134–5
  nuclear 126–9
  recovering from prehistoric teeth and bones 21–5, 26–9, 126, 184, 280–1
Doggerland 35
Domitian, Emperor 299
Donald, Clan 335
Dorset 99, 297, 306, 315
Dowth, Ireland: passage graves 179
Druids 266–7, 297
Dublin 66, 92, 152, 153, 157, 169, 182–4, 212–13, 271
Dugall, Clan 335
Dumnonii, the 297
Dun Carloway, Lewis 219
Dun Telve, Scotland 219
Dunbar, Scotland 35
Dundee, Scotland 205

Ealdgyth, Queen 272
Eanfrith 271
East Anglia 97, 99, 113, 287, 306, 307, 310–11, 317–18, 323–4, 325, 337
Eber 164
Edinburgh 75, 182, 205, 230, 241, 250
Edington Down, battle of (879) 311
Edmund, King of East Anglia 310
Edward the Confessor 313–14
Edward I 38–9, 40, 45, 51–2, 162, 239, 274, 275

Edward II 240, 274
Edward III 40
Edwin, Saxon king 271
eggs, human 127–8, 130–1
Eigg, Isle of 254
Eigr 49
Eleanor of Castile, Queen 38
Elizabeth I 54–5, 116, 156, 224
Elizabeth II 240
embryos: and chromosomes 130, 131
England 287–91
  Angles 86, 306
  British tribes 86, 148, 294–8, 299, 307–8, 328
  collecting DNA 316–23
  DNA analysis 301–2, 323–6
  Jutes 86, 306
  Norman Conquest 102, 287, 313–15, 321
  Picts 303, 304–5
  Roman occupation 160, 293–302, 303
  Saxons 84–5, 86, 303, 305–8
  Vikings and Danes 309–12, 315
  see also Cornwall; Yorkshire
enzymes, metabolic 132, 133
Eratosthenes 291
Eremon 164
Eric Bloodaxe 312
Eshu, clan of 151, 193, 233
Essex 306, 307, 312, 324–5
Euskara 220
Exeter 265, 297
eye colour: Beddoe's classification 89, 91, 99, 100, 101

farming/agriculture 26–7, 81, 175–8, 255, 330–1
  in England 290
  in Ireland 177, 208–9, 211
  in Scotland 208, 211
Fennius Farsa 164
Ferghus mac Roich 168
Ferriter's Cove, County Kerry 177
Fertile Crescent 175
Finn mac Cumhaill (Finn mac Cool) 196
Fir Bholg 166
Fisher, R. A. 112–13
Fleure, H. J. 278, 285
flint tools 29, 33, 35, 171, 290
Fomorians 166
Fosse Way 265, 297
Foxe, John 56
France 32, 33, 49, 54, 79–80, 81, 138, 156, 177, 178, 259, 308
  Lascaux Caves 240
  Vikings 312
  see also Gaul; Normans

Gaelic language 66–8, 72–3, 74, 198, 221, 248, 254, 269
Gaels 164, 222, 224, 253, 259, 269, 332
Galicians 199
Gaul/Gauls 53, 68, 69, 293, 294, 301, 308, 338
Genghis Khan 39, 258, 260–1
'Genghis Khan effect' 158–9, 160, 258, 260, 336
Geoffrey of Monmouth
The History of the Kings of Britain 40–55, 60, 62, 163, 307
Vita Merlini 50
George, St 65
Germans/Germany 53, 57–8, 60, 62–4, 69
Aryan myth 63–4
blood groups 114
Gildas: *The Ruin of Britain* 54, 55–6, 304–5, 308, 337
Glasgow 66, 74, 145, 146, 204–5, 250
Glastonbury: King Arthur's tomb 38–9, 40, 51, 162
Gloucester 266, 300
Godwine, Earl of Wessex 313–14
Goidel 164–5
Goodacre, Sara 142, 226
Gorlais, Earl of Cornwall 49
Grampian region, Scotland 244–6, 249, 251–3, 260, 262, 282, 285, 331, 335
Greece 42, 43, 69, 70, 80, 81, 138, 185–6
Gruffudd ap Llywelyn 272, 273
Guinevere, Queen 38, 50, 51
Gunn, Neil 74
Gurness, Orkney 220, 296, 333
Guthrum 311
Gwynedd, Wales 271, 272, 273–4

Hadrian's Wall 270, 299–300, 304
haemoglobin 122, 128
hair colour: Beddoe's classification 89, 90, 91, 97–9, 100, 102
Hallstadt culture 180, 332
Hampshire 297, 306
Harald III, of Norway (Hardraade) 314
Hare, John 58
Harold, King of Denmark (Bluetooth) 312
Harold I, of England (Harefoot) 313
Harold II, of England 272, 314–15

Harthnacnut, King 313
Hastings, battle of (1066) 272, 314–15
Hazara tribe 39
Hebrides 34, 72, 99, 203, 213, 223, 248, 250–2, 254–7
DNA analysis 250, 254, 255–7, 335
see also Skye
Hedges, Robert 24
Helena, clan of 135, 137, 138, 150, 282, 323–4
Helgason, Agnar 235–6
Hengist 46–8, 85, 305
Henry I 119, 224
Henry II 40, 51, 154–5, 157–8
Henry III 274
Henry VII 52, 53
Henry VIII 52, 53, 54, 55
Hercules 42–3, 44, 167
Herschfeld, Hanka 109–10, 111
Herschfeld, Ludwig 109–10, 111
Heyerdahl, Thor 25
Kon-Tiki expedition 25
Hickey, Eileen 142, 233, 319–20
Hill, Emmeline 197
Homo sapiens 29, 30, 172, 264
Howgego, Chris 147
Hrolfe of Norway *see* Rollo
Hue and Cry (periodical) 96
Human Genome Project 129
Hume, David 60
hunter-gatherers 21, 26–7, 174–5, 177–8, 189, 205–6, 211, 264, 289–90, 330
Huntly, Scotland 249

Iberia *see* Portugal; Spain
Ice Ages 31–3, 34–6, 153, 172, 173, 203, 205, 264, 288
Iceland 49, 54, 116, 162, 291
blood groups 116–18
DNA results 236–7
Viking settlements 118, 236–7
Iceman from the Alps 24
Iceni, the 267, 297–8
Inchtuthil, Scotland 299
Indo-European languages 63, 220
Iona, island of 161, 212, 248
Ireland (*and* Northern Ireland) 32, 33–4, 35, 152–3, 173–4, 176
Anglo-Norman invasion 116, 154–5, 162, 197–8, 201, 224
Arthur's invasion 49, 54
Beddoe's expeditions and observations 92–3, 97, 99, 100, 102
blood groups 115, 116, 117, 119
Britons from 68

Celts 65, 66, 67–8, 72, 74, 84–5, 102, 180–1, 192, 332–3
DNA 182–5; *see* maternal DNA; paternal DNA (*below*)
emigrants 74–6, 156–7
Gaelic 67, 68, 198
Gaels 164, 253
Great Famine 156–7
Leabhar Gabhála (*Book of Invasions*) 163–6
maternal (mitochondrial) DNA 160, 185–92, 198, 200, 237, 256
medieval kings 154–5, 157–9
Mesolithic settlements 171–2, 174; *see also* Mount Sandel
monks and monasteries 161–2, 163, 212, 236
myths and legends 163–9, 332
name changes 155
Neolithic era 178–80
paternal DNA (Y-chromosomes) 158–60, 192–201, 233, 259, 261, 285
political struggles 153–4, 155
and Romans 160
Scottish plantations 155–6
and Spain 156, 165, 199, 201, 239, 330, 332
surnames 197–8, 258–9
Vikings 212–13, 232, 309
and Wales 269–70, 282
Irish Free State 155
Irish Republican Army (IRA) 153–4
Irish Sea 34, 263
Isha, clan of 324
Islay, island of 34, 207, 222
Isle of Man 213, 222, 232, 262
Isle of Wight 297, 306
Italy 32, 105, 138, 256
Ith 165
Ivar the Boneless (Ivar Ragnusson) 310

James I, of England (VI of Scotland) 55, 58, 156, 224
James II, of England 155
James III, of Scotland 213
James, Simon: *The Atlantic Celts* . . . 70
Jarlshof, Shetland 214
Jarrow, Northumbria 212, 306
Jasmine, clan of 135, 137, 138, 139, 150, 189, 192, 244, 247, 255–6, 324, 330–1
Jefferson, Thomas 60
John, King 51, 57
Jordan 334
Jura, island of 207
Jutes 86, 306

Katrine, clan of 135, 137, 138, 150, 237, 257, 262
Kenneth MacAlpin 222–3, 239, 248, 273
Kent 37, 46, 295, 306, 307, 309–10, 338
Kintyre peninsula 202, 207, 221–2, 249
Kirkwall, Orkney 212, 227
Knights of the Round Table 40
Knowth, Ireland: passage graves 179
Knox, Robert: *The Races of Men* 61, 83–4, 85–7
Knoydart, Scotland 73–4
Kopec, Ada 115

Lampeter, Wales 284
Lancet: Herschfelds' article 110
Landsteiner, Karl 106
languages
  Aryan 63
  Breton 68
  Celtic 66–7, 68, 72–4, 308
  Cornish 68
  Euskara (Basque) 220
  Gaelic 66–8, 72–3, 74, 198, 221, 248, 254, 269
  Indo-European 63, 220
  Pict 220, 221
  Welsh 61, 62, 68, 119, 221, 269, 276, 308
Lascaux caves, Dordogne 240
La Tène culture 80, 180–1, 291, 332
Leabhar Gabhála (Book of Invasions) 163–6
Leinster 192, 197, 198
Lerwick, Shetland 227, 228
  Up Helly Aa 231–2, 238
Lewis, C. S. 70
Lewis, Isle of 81, 100, 145, 146, 257
  Callanish stone circle 209
  Dun Carloway 219
Lhuyd, Edward 67, 68, 69, 79
  Archaeologia Britannica 68
Lia Fail see Scone: 'Stone of Destiny'
Lincoln 265, 300, 305
Lincolnshire 46, 97, 99
Lindisfarne 161, 212, 213
Llywelyn ap Gruffydd, Prince of Wales 52, 274
Locrinus 45, 55
London 44–5, 250, 296, 298, 305, 333
Lud 45
Lugh 166, 167, 168
Luther, Martin 57
Luxeuil, France: monastery 162
Lyndhurst, John Copley, Lord 85

Macaulay, Vincent 189
McBeal, Ally 319–20
Macdonald Clan 336
McDonnell, Sir Ranald 73–4
McEvoy, Brian 258, 259
machair 204
Machynlleth, Wales 275
Maclean, Sorley 71
'The Cuillin' 71–2
Macleod Clan 336
MacMurrough, Dermot 154, 158
Maes Howe passage tomb, Orkney 210–11
Magna Carta 57
Marcher Lords 273–4
Mary I, Queen 116
maternal clans 140, 329–30
see 'clan mothers'
mDNA *see* mitochondrial DNA
Medb, Queen 167–9
Medical Research Council 115
megaliths 81, 178, 180, 209, 264, 290
Meigen, battle of 271
Mercia 270, 272, 306, 307, 308, 309, 310, 311, 325
Merlin 47, 48–9, 52, 55, 58
Mesolithic era 171–2, 174–5, 177, 180, 205, 207–8, 264, 288–9, 330, 331, 332–3, 335
microliths 171, 172, 206
middens 174, 175, 177, 178–80, 206–7
Middle East: DNA samples 190, 334
Middlesex 306, 307
Milesian Irish 164–5, 332
Mil/Milesius/Míle Easpain 164–5, 223, 239
mitochondria 126–7
mitochondrial DNA (mDNA) 126–7, 131–2, 133–9, 142–3, 148–51, 160, 184
see 'clan mothers'
Mons Badonicus, battle of (500) 307
Mons Graupius, battle of (83) 299, 302
Montesquieu, Charles de Secondat, Baron de 60
Montgomery, Treaty of (1267) 274
Mordred 50
Morgan La Fay 51
Morrigan, the 169
Mount Sandel, County Antrim 170–5, 176, 185, 289, 330
Mourant, Arthur 112–13, 114–15, 117, 118, 120, 121, 125
The Distribution of the Human Blood Groups 113–15, 117
Mousa, Shetland: broch 333

Mull, island of 34, 222
Müller, Max 63
Munster 192, 197, 285
Mynydd Carn, battle of (1081) 273

Nazis 64, 328
Neanderthals 24, 29, 185, 280–2
  Tregaron 279–80, 282
Neolithic era 176, 177–80, 189, 192, 264, 290, 330–1
Nero, Emperor 266, 298
New Zealand 25, 75
Newgrange, Ireland: passage graves 179–80, 210, 264
Nial 164
Niall of the Nine Hostages (Niall Noigiallach) 259, 269
Niav of the Golden Hair 196
Nicholson, Jayne 142, 226, 228, 233, 257
Norfolk 297, 305
  see also East Anglia
Norfolk, Thomas Howard, 3rd Duke of 53
Norman Conquest 56, 102, 272–3, 287, 313–15, 321
Normans 57, 58, 102, 312, 337
  see also Anglo-Normans; Norman Conquest
Norsemen *see* Vikings
North Sea 32, 33, 34–5, 173–4
Northern Ireland *see* Ireland
Northumbria 37, 161, 212, 306, 307, 308, 310–11, 314
Norway 35, 49, 54, 138, 212, 213, 227, 233–4
  blood groups 114, 117–18
  maternal clans 236–7, 324
  paternal clans 233–7
  Saami reindeer-herders 114, 138
  see also Vikings

O'Connor, Rory 154
Oetzi (Iceman from the Alps) 24
Offa, King 270, 309
Offa's Dyke 270
Oisin 196
  clan of 151, 193, 196–9, 233–5, 246, 285–6, 325–6, 334–5, 336, 337
Orange Club of Ireland 84
Order of the Garter 40
Ordovices, the 265, 267, 268
Orkney Islands 34, 81, 100, 199, 202, 204, 208, 222, 227, 264
  Bookan stone circle 210
  Gurness broch 220, 333
  Kirkwall Cathedral 212
  Maes Howe passage tomb 210–11

maternal clans 235–6
paternal clans 233–6
Pict symbol stones 218
place-names 214
Ring of Brodgar 210
Skara Brae 209–11
Stenness stone circle 210
Vikings 212–15, 232, 235, 248, 251, 261, 323, 333
Oronsay, island of 206–7, 211, 289
Osric 271
osteogenesis imperfecta 124, 310
Oswestry 224, 277
otoliths 207
Owain ap Gruffydd Glyn Dwr (Owen Glendower) 275
Oxford Ancestors 139, 144, 184, 187
Oxford Genetic Atlas Project 141, 148, 151, 229, 276, 279, 316, 319, 320, 321

Pakistan: Hazara tribe 39
Palaeolithic era 172, 185, 189, 264, 330
paternal clans 151
see Eshu; Oisin; Re; Sigurd; Wodan
Patrick, St 65, 161, 162, 173, 259
'patrilocality' 335–6
Paulinus, Gaius Suetonius 266–7, 296, 297–8
Paviland Cave, south Wales: skeleton *see* 'Red Lady of Paviland'
Pembroke, Richard de Clare, Earl of 154–5, 158, 224
Pembrokeshire 272, 273, 278, 283–4
Pennines, the 288
phrenology 92, 93
Picts 42, 49, 54, 101, 215, 217, 221, 222, 224–5, 241, 269
brochs 218–20, 333
derivation of name 217
DNA analysis 241–2, 244–7, 251–3, 332–3, 336
language 220, 221, 248
in Orkney and Shetland 218, 233–4, 237, 238, 252–3
and Romans 217–18, 296, 299, 300, 301, 303–5
symbol stones 218
Pike, Luke Owen 86–7
Pitlochry, Scotland 246
Plantagenets 40, 51
Plautius, Aulus 295, 296, 297
Pliny the Elder 291
Plynlimmon, Wales 278–9, 285
Polynesians 25–6, 39, 132, 238
Pontnewydd Cave, north Wales: tooth 29, 264

Portugal 81, 177, 178, 180, 330–1
Poseidon 42–3
Prasutagus 298
proteins 22, 122–3
Pytheas: *On the Ocean* 291–2

racial theories, 19th-century 60–4, 83–7
Raedwald, King 292, 307
Raftery, Barry 181
Re, clan of 151, 192, 233
'Red Lady of Paviland' 30, 32, 178, 264
Reformation, the 55
Renfrew, battle of (1164) 224, 257
Rhodri Mawr (Rhodri the Great) 271, 283
Rhuddlan, Statute of (1284) 274
Rhys ap Twdwr 273
Richard II 275
Richard III 52
Richard, Duke of Normandy 313
Richards, Martin 188–9, 192
Richborough, Kent 295, 297
ring-barking 175, 176, 290
Robbie the Pict (Brian Robertson) 217
Robert the Bruce 223
Robert II 223–4
Robertson, Brian *see* Robbie the Pict
Robertson, J. M. 62
Rognvald, Earl of Orkney 212
Rollo 312
Roman Catholic Church 53–7
Romans
  and Arthur 50
  genetic legacy 301–2, 337–8
  invasions of Britain 42, 45, 69, 265, 287, 293–6
  and Ireland 160
  occupation of England 293–302
  in Scotland 217, 220, 299
  slaves 300, 302, 303, 334
  in Wales 264, 265–9, 298
  withdrawal from England 45–6, 259, 301–2, 303–4
Rome 43, 50
Rona, Isle of 145–7
Roots, Anne 77
Rowena 46, 48
Royal Anthropological Institute 95
Royal College of Physicians 95
Royal Irish Academy, Dublin 182–3
Royal Society, London 95, 182, 183
Rum, Isle of 34, 208, 254
Runrig (band) 66

Saami, the 114, 138
Sabhal Mor Ostaig College, Skye 73
Saxons
  Beddoe's findings 101, 102
  genetic legacy 312, 337
  and invasion of Britain 42, 45–8, 49, 52–3, 54, 301, 303, 305–8
  19th-century views 61–2, 83–6
  and racial superiority 55–6, 57, 58–60, 85–6, 111
  and Vikings 309–12
  in Wales 270–1, 272, 276
Scafell Pike 288
Scone, Scotland: 'Stone of Destiny' (*Lia Fail*) 223, 239–41
Scota 223
Scotland 34, 35, 99, 202–5
  agriculture 208–9, 211
  Anglo-Normans 224–5
  blood groups 115, 117
  Britons 68
  Celts 71–3, 224–5, 247–8
  DNA collection 228, 241–3, 249–50
  emigrants 74–6, 77
  Gaelic 67, 68
  Highland Clearances 72, 73–5, 84, 254
  Highlands/Highlanders 35, 88, 99–100, 101, 115, 153, 203, 204, 251, 258
  and Ireland 155–6, 259, 261
  Mesolithic settlements 205–8, 211
  Palaeolithic settlements 205
  surnames 257–60
  see also Argyll; Grampian; Hebrides; Orkney; Picts; Shetland; Tayside; Western Isles
Scots (*Scotti*) 164, 223, 239
Scott, Sir Walter: *Waverley* 70–1
Scythia 164
'Seven Daughters of Eve' 136, 150, 335
Shakespeare, William: *King Lear* 45, 55
Shetland Islands 34, 100, 202, 208, 226–8, 291
  DNA collections 228–30, 232
  maternal clans 235–6
  paternal clans 233–6, 260, 325
  Picts 233–4, 238, 252–3
  place-names 214
  Science Festival 228–9
  and Scotland 214, 230
  Up Helly Aa 231–2, 238, 241
  Vikings 212–15, 227, 231–4, 235, 248, 251, 261, 323, 333

Shrewsbury, Earl of 273
Sigurd, clan of 151, 193, 233–5, 246–7, 283–4, 325
Sigurd Hlodvisson 231
Silures, the 265, 266, 267, 297
Skara Brae, Orkney 209–11, 264
skin colour 88, 97
Skye, Isle of 34, 71–3, 144–6, 249, 254
  DNA analysis 250, 251, 256–7
  and Highland Clearances 72, 73–4, 254
  Road Bridge 216–17
  Sabhal Mor Ostaig 73
Smalley, Kate 277
Snowdonia 101, 263, 265–6, 267
Somerled 213, 224, 257–8, 335
Somerset *see* Cheddar Men; Glastonbury
South Africa: Celts 75
Spain/Iberia 32, 81, 101, 102, 138, 177, 178, 180, 239, 256, 332–3, 334
  conquest of South America 85–6
  and Ireland 156, 165, 199, 201, 239, 330, 332
  last Neanderthal 281
Spenser, Edmund: *Faerie Queene* 54–5
sperm 127, 130, 131
Stamford Bridge, battle of (1066) 314
Starr Carr, Yorkshire 289, 290, 330
Stirling, Scotland 205
stone axes and tools 81, 171, 172, 176, 177, 208
Stonehenge 209, 264, 290
Stornoway, Isle of Lewis 100, 334
Strata Florida, Wales 279
Strathclyde, Scotland 225, 307, 331
Stuart dynasty 55, 224
Suffolk
  flint tools 29, 35
  Sutton Hoo burial 292, 308
  see also East Anglia
surnames 257–60, 320–2, 337
Sutton, County Dublin 177
Sutton Hoo: royal burial 292, 308
swabs, taking 228–30
Sweden 35, 118, 138, 227
Sweyn, King of Denmark 313
symbol stones, Pictish 218
Syria 138, 175, 334

Tabun skull 280–1
Tacitus 57, 60, 160, 161, 266–7, 298, 299, 300, 301, 304, 328

Taín Bó Cúalnge (*Cattle Raid of Cooley*) 167–8
Tara, Ireland 159, 164, 259
Tara, clan of 135, 136–7, 138, 140, 145, 150, 237, 244, 255, 256, 262, 330
Targett, Adrian 28–9
Tayside and Fife, Scotland 244–6, 260, 262, 282, 335
Teutonic superiority, myth of 56–7, 58, 59, 60, 61–4, 66
Thames, River 34, 44
Tiberius, Emperor 294
Times, The 61–2
Tintagel, Cornwall 49
Togodumnus 295, 296
tools
  flint 29, 33, 35, 171, 289–90
  stone 81, 171, 172, 208
Totnes, Devon 44, 48
trade, European 79–82, 291, 293–4
Tregaron, Wales: Neanderthals 279–80, 282
Trinovantes, the 294, 298
Troy and New Troy 43–5, 332
Tuatha Dé Danaan 164–6
Tuesley, Surrey 307

Ui Neill Clan 222, 248, 259–60, 269, 335, 336
Ulaid (Ulstermen) 167
Ulrike, clan of 150–1, 324–5
Ulster 152, 155–6, 192, 197, 253, 261
  Neolithic site 180
  war with Connacht 167, 168–9
Ulster Cycle 167, 169
United States of America 57, 75, 157
Ursula, clan of 135, 137, 138, 150, 185–8, 190–2, 199–200, 247
Usk 266
Uther Pendragon 48–9

Valentinian, Emperor 301
Vega, Emilce 319, 320
Velda, clan of 135, 137, 138, 150
Vergil, Polydore 53, 54, 62
  Anglica Historica 54
Verica, King of the Atrebates 295
Verstegen, Richard: *Restitution of Decayed Intelligence* 58
Vespasian, Emperor 297
Vikings
  Beddoe's findings 100, 101–2
  DNA results 232–8, 250, 323, 333
  in England 57, 212, 213, 309–12, 314

Vikings (*cont.*)
in France 312
in Iceland 118, 236
in Ireland 212–13
in Orkney and Shetland 212–15, 231–4, 238, 248, 261, 323, 333–4
in Scotland 223, 225, 242, 248, 250, 261
in Wales 119, 271–2, 276, 283–4
Vortigern 46–7, 48, 56, 305
Vortimer 46

Wales 88, 262, 263–5, 271–2, 273–5
and Act of Union (1563) 275
Anglo-Normans 272–4, 276
Beddoe's findings 88, 99
blood groups 115, 119, 271, 278
Britons 47–8, 52, 56, 307
Celts 37, 52, 72, 74, 265–7
collecting DNA 276–8, 322–3
DNA analyses 269, 282–6, 335
English domination 52–3, 274–5
and Ireland 269–70, 282
language *see* Welsh
Roman campaigns 265–9, 298
Saxons 47–8, 270, 271–2, 276
Tregaron Neanderthals 279–80, 282
Vikings 119, 271–2, 283–4
Walter, Archdeacon of Oxford 41, 53
Walter, High Steward of Scotland 223–4
Waltzer, Michael 78
Wanda, clan of 324, 325
Watkin, Morgan 119, 284
Wednesbury, Staffordshire 307
Wellcome Trust 139, 318
Welsh (language) 61, 62, 68, 119, 221, 269, 276
Welsh Marches 263
Welsh National Eisteddfod (1867) 95
Wessex 306, 307, 309, 311–12, 314
Western Isles 34, 100, 145, 162, 203, 213, 248–9, 250, 254, 256, 261, 332, 334
see also Lewis, Isle of
Wick, Scotland 89
Wiener, Alexander 112
Wilde, Sir William 92
Wilhelm I, Kaiser 64
William I ('the Conqueror') 273, 314–15
William of Orange 55, 155
Wilson, Jim 199

Wiltshire 99, 306
Wodan, clan of 151, 193, 233–5, 246–7, 284–5, 325–6, 335, 336–7
Wroxeter 267, 306

X-chromosomes 129–31
Xenia, clan of 135, 137, 138, 150, 324, 325

Y-chromosomes 128–31, 140, 148, 151, 184, 192–201, 224
and 'Genghis Khan' effect 158–60, 258, 336
see also paternal clans
York 300, 304, 305, 310, 314
Yorkshire 99, 101, 102, 289, 297, 311, 312, 322
Younger Dryas 173, 205, 288

Zeus 42–3

THE SEVEN DAUGHTERS OF EVE
by Bryan Sykes

In 1994 Professor Bryan Sykes, a leading world authority on DNA and human evolution, was called in to examine the frozen remains of a man trapped in glacial ice in northern Italy five thousand years ago. Remarkably, Professor Sykes was able to track down a living relative of the Ice Man in Britain.

How did he do this? *The Seven Daughters of Eve* is a first hand account of his research into an extraordinary gene which passes undiluted from generation to generation through the maternal line, allowing us to track our genetic ancestors through time and space. Professor Sykes has found that almost all Europeans can trace their ancestry back to one of seven women, whom he has named Ursula, Xenia, Helena, Velda, Tara, Katrine and Jasmine.

In this amazing scientific adventure story, we learn where our ancient genetic ancestors lived, what their lives were like and how every one of us is a testimony to the almost miraculous strength of our DNA. It is a book that not only re-examines the way we have evolved, but also addresses our sense of individuality and identity.

'A wonderful tale of archaeology and genetics that should be read by anyone concerned with what we are . . . a terrific book, written with humour and humanity'
Sunday Times

'An engrossing, bubbly read, a boy's own adventure in scientific story-telling that fairly bounces along . . . a thumping good read'
Observer

'Sykes's wonderfully clear book should be compulsory reading for politicians . . . an eye-opening guide to the new branch of science that is changing the human race's view of itself'
Literary Review

9780552148764

CORGI BOOKS

ADAM'S CURSE
A Future Without Men
by Bryan Sykes

Drawing on his own work at the forefront of modern genetics, Bryan Sykes takes us on a remarkable scientific exploration of the mysteries of the science of sex and gender – with some surprising and controversial results.

Genetically speaking, the only difference between men and woman is that where women have two X chromosomes, men have one X and one Y. This one chromosome difference, out of a total of forty-six, holds the key to understanding the huge difference between the sexes.

But a closer look at the all-important Y chromosome reveals some shocking news for men. It is getting smaller. As the generations pass the Y chromosome is being cannibalised by the female genome and worn away by its own inability to recombine. Women are winning the evolutionary battle of the sexes.

The conclusion: men are slowly, but surely, headed for extinction.

'Bryan Sykes is a specialist in deciphering the histories written in our genes'
Sunday Telegraph

9780552149891

CORGI BOOKS

THE HUMAN MIND
and how to make the most of it
by Robert Winston

It is the most complex and mysterious object in the universe. Covered by a dull grey membrane, it resembles a gigantic, convoluted fungus. Its inscrutability has captivated scientists, philosophers and artists for centuries. It is, of course, the human brain.

With the help of science we can now begin to understand the extraordinary complexity of the brain's circuits: we can see which nerve cells generate electricity as we fall in love, tell a lie or dream of a lottery win. And inside the 100 billion cells of its rubbery network is something remarkable: you.

In this entertaining and accessible book, Robert Winston takes us deep into the workings of the human mind and shows how our emotions and personality are the result of genes and environment. He explains how memories are formed and lost, how the ever-changing brain is responsible for toddler tantrums and teenage angst, and he reveals the truth behind extra-sensory perception, *déjà vu* and out-of-body experiences. He also tells us how to boost our intelligence, how to tap into creative powers we never knew we had, how to break old habits or keep our brain fit and active as we enter old age.

The human mind is all we have to help us to understand it. Paradoxically, it is possible that science may never quite explain everything about this extraordinary mechanism that makes each of us unique.

'Richly informative'
Independent

9780553816198

BANTAM BOOKS

HUMAN INSTINCT

How our primeval impulses shape our modern lives

by Robert Winston

From caveman to modern man . . .

Few people doubt that humans are descended from the apes; fewer still consider, let alone accept, the psychological implication. But in truth, man looks, moves and breathes like an ape, he also thinks like one.

Sexual drive, survival, competition, aggression – all of our impulses are driven by our human instincts. They explain why a happily married man will fantasize about the pretty, slim, young woman who is sitting across from him in the tube. Why thousands of people spend their week entirely focused on whether their team will win their next crucial match.

But how well do our instincts equip us for the twenty-first century? Do they help or hinder us as we deal with large anonymous cities, stressful careers, relationships and the battle of the sexes? In this fascinating book, Robert Winston takes us on a journey deep into the human mind. Along the way he takes a very personal look at the relationship between science and religion and explores those very instincts that make us human.

'Wide-ranging and thoroughly entertaining'
New Scientist

9780553814927

BANTAM BOOKS

THE COMMON THREAD
A story of science, politics, ethics and the Human Genome
by John Sulston & Georgina Ferry

'Unputdownable stuff . . . an insider's story of one of the century's greatest technopolitical ventures'
Steven Rose, *Guardian*

John Sulston led the British arm of the extraordinary collaboration of scientists that mapped the entire human DNA sequence, a success due in no small part to his own determination, passion and scientific excellence.

Taking us behind the scenes of one of the largest international scientific operations ever undertaken, he reveals the politics, personalities and controversy that shaped the seven years of research and frankly attacks the intervention of Craig Venter and Celera Genomics, who threatened to undermine the international community's attempts to make the sequence freely available to everyone. Sulston makes it clear that the quest for profit must not be allowed to restrict research or unreasonably limit access to treatment.

Compelling and impassioned, this is a story of our shared human heritage, offering hope for the future and a whole new way to understand ourselves through science.

'Our nation is much the richer for Sulston's existence'
Robin McKie, *Observer*

'John Sulston is more than anyone else the man who made the Human Genome Project happen. Without his determination and scientific talent we would not now have this extraordinary new form of self-knowledge – one of the great scientific achievements of all time'
Matt Ridley, author of *Genome*

'A compelling and frank account'
Mark Henderson, *The Times*

'Burns with a passion and a sense of injustice that I have never felt before in a book by a successful scientist . . . anyone who is fascinated by the politics and ethics of research should read it'
Clive Cookson, *Financial Times*

9780552999410

CORGI BOOKS